THE
KILLING
ROOM

BY PETER MAY

THE ENZO FILES

Extraordinary People
The Critic
Blacklight Blue
Freeze Frame
Blowback
Cast Iron

THE CHINA THRILLERS

The Firemaker
The Fourth Sacrifice
The Killing Room
Snakehead
The Runner
Chinese Whispers

THE LEWIS TRILOGY

The Blackhouse
The Lewis Man
The Chessmen

STANDALONE NOVELS

Entry Island
Runaway
Coffin Road
I'll Keep You Safe

NON-FICTION

Hebrides with David Wilson

PETER MAY

THE KILLING ROOM

New York • London

Quercus

New York • London

© 2001 by Peter May
First published in the United States by Quercus in 2018

ISBN 978-1-68144-083-5

Library of Congress Cataloging-in-Publication Data

Names: May, Peter, 1951– author.
Title: The killing room / Peter May.
Description: First edition. | New York : Quercus, 2018.
Identifiers: LCCN 2018014358 (print) | LCCN 2018015328 (ebook) |
    ISBN 9781681440828 (ebook) | ISBN 9781681440811 (library ebook) |
    ISBN 9781681440835 (softcover) | ISBN 9781681440828 (eISBN)
Subjects: LCSH: Campbell, Margaret (Fictitious character) – Fiction. |
    GSAFD: Mystery fiction.
Classification: LCC PR6063.A884 (ebook) | LCC PR6063.A884 K55 2018 (print)
    | DDC 823/.914 – dc23
LC record available at https://lccn.loc.gov/2018014358

Distributed in the United States and Canada by
Hachette Book Group
1290 Avenue of the Americas
New York, NY 10104

Manufactured in the United States

10 9 8 7 6 5 4 3 2 1

www.quercus.com

For Steve, Trenda and Danielle

PROLOGUE

The rain, like tears, streaks his view of the world from the back seat of his limousine. A blue-grey view smudged by this chilly sub-tropical November deluge. The American has come to celebrate a union spanning continents, a powerful conjoining of East and West. But all the money in the world cannot protect him from the horrors that are only minutes away.

Towers of steel and glass rise into the mist around him, insubstantial and wraith-like. They remind him of something strangely incongruous. A remote and rugged coastline on the north-west extremes of Europe. A trip made in search of his roots to a distant Scottish island, where fingers of stone reach for the sky in strange circular arrangements. Standing stones raised in worship to who knows what God.

Beyond the colossal pagoda-like Jin Mao Tower, its peak lost in cloud, more towers loom out of the misted distance, rising from the ashes of Mao's dream of a communist utopia. The once desolate marshlands of Pudong, fed by their privileged status of "special economic zone," now sprout tower blocks like weeds, watched in wonder by the Shanghainese across the river, a whole generation thinking, what next? The American looks up at these twenty-first century standing stones, and knows that the only God worshipped by those who raised them is Money. And he smiles. A sense of satisfaction in this. For he worships at the same altar.

They pass a high, sweeping wall painted salmon pink and topped by spiked black railings. His limo draws in behind others it has been following. Umbrellas, black and shiny, cluster immediately around his door. He steps out on to red carpet, and water pools around his feet as the weight of his steps squeezes rain from the pile.

Through open gates, the site unfolds before him, a forest of steel rods rising out of the concrete blocks already sunk there. On the far perimeter two tiers of workmen's huts rise from the mud. Pale oriental faces gather in the rain to watch with dull curiosity as the party makes its perilous way across the quagmire, red carpet submerged now in liquid mud that sloshes over black shiny leather, spattering the bottoms of freshly pressed trousers. The American feels cold water seeping between his toes and curses inwardly. But his outward smile remains, fixed and determined for his Chinese hosts. They are, after all, partners in the biggest Sino-American joint venture yet attempted, although it is hard for him to believe that this sodden site will support the massive construction of steel and glass that will become the New York-Shanghai Bank, the tallest building in Asia. But he is reassured by the knowledge that his position as its chief executive officer will make him one of the most powerful men on earth.

He climbs the stairs to the stage, protected from the rains by its huge canvas awning, and steps into the glare of the world's press, television lamps flooding this grey winter morning with a bright blue-white light, cameras flashing in the rain like fireflies. His PR people have done their job.

Strings of coloured bunting hang limp in the wet as his Chinese opposite number, smiling, approaches the microphone to begin the obligatory speeches. The American lets his mind and eyes wander. Above the temporary construction of the stage, a huge hopper leans over, its snout pointing downwards to the deep trench below. When he steps forward to release its lever, tons of concrete will pour from its mouth into the bowels of what will be his bank – a ceremonial foundation stone upon which he knows he will build a future of unparalleled success.

A sprinkling of applause, like water pouring from a jug, breaks into his thoughts. A hand on his elbow steers him towards the microphone. Fireflies flash. He hears his own voice, strange and metallic, through distant speakers, words he has learned by heart, and he cannot help but notice that the trench below him is rapidly filling with water, thick brown water like chocolate, boiling in the rain.

More applause, and he steps forward from the cover of the awning on to a small, square projecting platform, a Chinese at his right hand holding an umbrella above his head, beaded curtains of water tumbling around him. He takes the lever in his hand, and with a sense of absolute control of his own destiny, draws it down. All faces lift expectantly towards the hopper. For a moment, it seems, everyone is holding their breath. Only the tattoo of rain on canvas invades the sense of expectation.

The American feels something shift beneath his feet. There is a loud crack, then a strange groaning like the rattle of a dying man's last breath. The struts supporting the boards of his tiny platform give way as the walls of the trench below collapse inwards. He turns, clutching in fear at the sleeve of the arm holding the umbrella, but already he is pitching forward through the curtain of rain. The sensation of falling through space seems to last an eternity. His own scream sounds disconnected and distant. And then the shock of cold liquid mud takes his breath away. The whole world appears to be falling in around him as his flailing arms endeavour to prevent him from being sucked under. He sees an arm reaching out towards him and thinks, thank God! He clutches the hand and feels its flesh oozing between his fingers. But he has no time to consider this. He pulls hard to try to haul himself from the mud, but the outstretched arm offers no resistance, and as he falls back again he realises that it is not attached to anything. He lets *go immediately, repulsed and uncomprehending. He can hear voices shouting above him as he flips over in time to see a woman's breasts emerging from a wall of mud, followed by her shoulders and belly. But no arms, no legs, no head. His own arms windmilling in panic, he kicks away again, only to find himself staring into a face with black holes where the eyes should be, long dark hair smeared across decaying flesh. He feels bile rising in his throat with his scream, and as he looks upward in a desperate appeal for help, he sees again the standing stones rising over him in the mist. Only now he sees them quite differently, clustered together like headstones in a cemetery.*

CHAPTER ONE

I

The cold, dry earth rattled across the lid of the coffin as it left her mother's hand. Margaret, too, stooped to lift a handful and felt the frosted dirt stick to her skin. She let it fall from her fingers into her father's grave, and lifted her eyes to a pewtery sky. The first snow of winter fluttered on the edge of an icy wind that blew in across the distant lake and she shivered, pulling her coat tight around herself to contain her grief.

She turned away from the handful of mourners at the grave-side, a few relatives and friends, a representative from the university, some old students of her father. There was something primitive about the ritual of burial that seemed somehow absurd to Margaret. Placing a person in a wooden box in the ground and leaving them to rot. She had seen enough bodies in various states of decomposition to have decided long ago that when her turn came she would be cremated. It was simpler, cleaner. More final, somehow. She knew the stages of decay that the body they had buried would undergo, and she did not want to think of her father like that.

The wind rattled the branches of the empty trees, stark in their winter nakedness. The last leaves of fall lay rotting on the ground, silver edged by the previous night's frost. Somewhere, away to their left among the rows of tombstones, she knew, lay the graves of famous gangsters from the city's colourful past. Alphonse Capone, and his father and mother; the infamous John May and his wife Hattie; "Machine Gun" Jack McGurn; Antonio "The Scourge" Lombardo; and dozens more Italian immigrants and their descendants who had helped sow the seeds of America's organised crime in this windy place. Her father had kept better company in life.

But his family had all been buried here at Mount Carmel, to the west of Chicago, a ragtag bunch of undistinguished antecedents of Scots and Irish origin. Her mother's family were of German descent, and she supposed that's where she got her pale freckled skin and fair hair. Her father had had Celtic black hair in his youth, and incongruously blue eyes. It was a comfort to her that she had inherited at least some of his genes.

News of his death had reached her in Beijing in a short, cold phone call from her mother, and she had sat for a long time in the tiny apartment provided by the University of Public Security, aware of a peculiar sense of emptiness, disturbed by her lack of emotion. It was nearly two years since she had last seen him, and they had spoken a mere handful of times on the phone. It was only when she awoke to her own tears in the middle of the night that she discovered the grief she feared might not be there.

Now she was at a loss. The tragic circumstance of her father's death had finally forced her to break her ties with China, fragile ties held in place only by a man she thought she loved. And now that she was "home," she would have to make decisions she had been putting off for far too long. Decisions about where her future really lay. Decisions she did not want to face.

She had been back in Chicago for nearly three days, and not once had she ventured to the north side to check on her apartment in Lincoln Park. She had left neighbours collecting mail and watering house plants. But she had been gone for more than eighteen months, and she was afraid of what might greet her there. Afraid, too, of a past she did not wish to revisit, memories of a man she had lived with for seven years. The man she had married. Instead she had opted for the safety of her old bedroom in the redbrick house where she had grown up in the leafy suburbs of Oak Park. Everything there was familiar, comforting, filled with recollections of a time when she had no cares or responsibilities, and life had still held the promise of something magic. She was, she knew, just hiding.

"Margaret." Her mother's voice carried to her on the wind and had the same chill edge to it. Margaret stopped and waited for her to catch up. They had barely spoken in the last three days. They had embraced briefly, but without warmth. There had been the polite enquiries about their respective well-being, the mechanical exchanges of necessary information. It wasn't that they had ever really fallen out, their relationship had simply been sterile for as long as Margaret could remember. Loveless. A strange relationship for mother and daughter. "You'll help me serve up the food when we get back to the house?"

"Of course." Margaret didn't know why her mother was asking. They had been through all this earlier. Perhaps, she thought, it was just for the lack of something else to say.

They walked to the gate in silence then, side by side, a space between them that a husband and father might have filled. As they reached the cars her mother said with a tone, "So what now? Back to China?"

Margaret clenched her teeth. "I don't think this is the time
or place, Mom."

Her mother raised an eyebrow. "I take it that's Margaret
code for 'yes.'"

Margaret flashed her a look. "Well, if I do go back, it'll
probably just be to escape from you." She opened the rear
door of the hired limousine and slipped into the cold leather
of the back seat.

II

"Deputy Section Chief Li." The defence lawyer spoke slowly,
as if considering every syllable. "There is no doubt that if
one compares these shoe prints with the photographs of the
footprints taken at the scene of the murder, one would be
led to the conclusion that they were made by the same pair
of shoes." Photographs of the footprints and the correspond-
ing shoe prints were laid out on the table in front of him.

Li Yan nodded cautiously, uncertain as to where this was
leading, aware of the judge watching him closely from the
bench opposite, a wily, white-haired veteran languishing
thoughtfully in his winter blue uniform beneath the red, blue
and gold crest of the Ministry of Public Security. The scribble of
the clerk's pen was clearly audible in the silence of the packed
courtroom.

"Which would further lead one to the conclusion that
the owner of these shoes was, at the very least, present at the
crime scene – particularly in light of the prosecution's claim
that traces of the victim's blood were also found on the shoes."
The lawyer looked up from his table and fixed Li with a cold
stare. He was a young man, in his early thirties, about the same
age as Li, one of a new breed of lawyers feeding off the recent

raft of legislation regulating the burgeoning Chinese justice system. He was sleek, well groomed, prosperous. A dark Armani suit, a crisp, white, button-down designer shirt and silk tie. And he was brimming with a self-confidence that made Li uneasy. "Would you agree?"

Li nodded.

"I'm sorry, did you speak?"

"No, I nodded my agreement." Irritation in Li's voice.

"Then, please speak up, Deputy Section Chief, so that the clerk can note your comments for the record." The Armani suit's tone was condescending, providing the court with the erroneous impression that the police officer in the witness stand was a rank novice.

Li bristled. This was a cut-and-dried case. The defendant, a young thug up from the country who had claimed to be looking for work in Beijing, had broken into the victim's home in the north-east of the city. When the occupant, an elderly widow, had wakened and startled him in the act, he had stabbed her to death. There had been copious amounts of blood. The warden at a workers' hostel had called the local public security bureau to report that one of the residents had returned in the middle of the night covered in what looked like blood. By the time the police got there the defendant had somehow managed to dispose of his bloody clothes and showered away all traces of blood from his person. No murder weapon was recovered, but a pair of his shoes matched footprints left in blood at the scene, and there were still traces of the victim's blood in the treads. Li wondered what possible reason this supercilious defence lawyer could have for his apparent confidence. He didn't have to wait long to find out.

"You would further agree, then, that the owner of these shoes was most probably the perpetrator of the crime."

"I would." Li spoke clearly, so that there could be no ambiguity.

"So what leads you to believe that my client was the perpetrator?"

Li frowned. "They're his shoes."

"Are they?"

"They were found in his room at the hostel. Forensic examination found traces of the victim's blood in the treads, and footwear impressions taken from them provided an exact match with the footprints found at the scene."

"So where are they?" The lawyer's eyes held Li in their unwavering gaze.

For the first time Li's own confidence began to falter. "Where are what?"

"The shoes, of course." This delivered with an affected weariness. "You can't claim to have found a pair of shoes in my client's room, tying him to a crime scene, and then fail to produce them as evidence."

Li felt the blood pulsing at his temples, a hot flush rising on his cheeks. He glanced towards the procurator's table, but the prosecutor's eyes were firmly fixed on papers spread in front of him. "After forensics had finished with them they were logged and tagged and – "

"I ask again," the lawyer interrupted, raising his voice, a voice of reason asking a not unreasonable question. "Where are they?"

"They were sent down to the procurator's office as exhibits for the court."

"Then why are they not here for us all to see?"

Li glanced at the procurator again, only this time it was anger colouring his face. Clearly the prosecution's failure to produce the shoes had been well aired before Li had even been called to give evidence. He was being made to look like an idiot. "Why don't you ask the procurator?" he said grimly.

"I already did," said the Armani suit. "He says that his office never received them from your office."

A hubbub of excited speculation buzzed around the public benches. The clerk snapped a curt warning for members of the public to remain silent or be expelled from the court.

Li knew perfectly well that the shoes, along with all the other evidence, had been dispatched to the procurator's office. But he also knew that there was nothing he could say or do here in the witness box that could prove it. His eyes flickered towards the table next to the procurator, and met the hate-filled glare of the victim's son, and he knew that when the defence was done with him he would have to face the wrath that the victim's representative would be entitled to vent. He felt every eye in the court upon him as the defence lawyer said, "Surely, Deputy Section Chief, it must be obvious even to you, that without the shoes my client has no case to answer?"

Li closed his eyes and breathed deeply.

He pushed through glass doors, brushing past a row of potted plants that lined the top of the steps, and started angrily down towards the car park. The procurator chased after him, clutching a thick folder of documents. Above them rose the five storeys of Central Beijing Middle Court, topped by a huge radio mast. Off to their left, where armed officers guarded the vehicle entrance to the holding cells, the red Chinese flag hung limply in the winter sun over the Ministry of Public Security badge of justice. Justice! Li thought not. He pulled on a great-coat over his green uniform as he hurried down the stairs, and hauled a peaked cap down over his flat-top crew cut, his breath billowing before him like fire in the cold morning air.

"I'm telling you, we never got them," the procurator called after him. He was a short, spindly man with thinning hair and thick glasses that magnified his unusually round eyes. His uniform appeared too large for him.

Li wheeled around halfway down the steps and the procurator almost ran into him. "Bullshit!" Even although the procurator was on the step above, Li towered over him, and the smaller man positively recoiled from Li's aggression. "You would never have brought the case to court if we hadn't provided the evidence."

"Paper evidence. That's all you sent me," the procurator insisted. "I assumed the shoes had been lodged in the evidence depository."

"They were. Which makes them your responsibility, not ours." Li raised his arms with his voice, and people flooding out of the court behind them stopped to listen. "In the name of the sky, Zhang! My people work their butts off to bring criminals to justice . . ." He was distracted momentarily by the sight of the Armani suit and his exultant client passing them on the steps. He had a powerful urge to take his fist and smash their gloating faces to a pulp. But then, he knew, justice and the law were not always compatible. He turned instead to the procurator to vent his anger. "And you fucking people go losing the evidence, and killers walk free. You can expect an official complaint." He turned and headed off down the steps jamming a cigarette in his mouth as he went, leaving Procurator Zhang fuming and only too aware of the curious faces regarding him. Policemen did not speak to procurators like that, certainly not in public. It was a humiliating loss of *mianzi* – face.

Zhang shouted lamely at Li's back, "I'm the one who'll be making the complaint, Deputy Section Chief. To the

Commissioner. You needn't think you can live in the protective shadow of your uncle forever."

Li stopped dead and Zhang knew immediately he had gone too far. Li turned and fixed him with a silent stare filled with such intensity that Zhang could not maintain eye contact. He turned and ran up the steps, back into the safety of the courthouse.

Li stared after him for a few seconds, then hurried through the parked vehicles to the street, struggling to control his rage. The urge to hit someone, anyone, was extremely powerful. A group of people standing at the notice board where the week's trials were posted in advance looked at him curiously as he strode past. But he didn't notice them. Neither did he see the vendor at the corner of the street offering him fruit from under a green and yellow striped awning, nor smell the smoke rising from lamb skewers cooking on open coals in the narrow confines of Xidamochang Street. He turned instead towards the roar of traffic on East Qianmen Avenue, not even hearing the honk of a car's horn sounding behind him. Only when its engine revved and the horn sounded again did he half turn, and an unmarked Beijing Police Jeep drew up beside him. Detective Wu leaned over to push the passenger door open. Li was surprised to see him. "What d'you want, Wu?" he growled.

Wu raised his hands in mock defence against Li's aggression. "Hey, Boss, I've been waiting for you for over an hour."

Li slipped into the passenger seat. "What for?"

Wu grinned, jaws grinding as ever on a piece of leathery gum that had long since lost its flavour. He pushed his sunglasses up on his forehead. He was the bearer of interesting information, and he wanted to tease it out, make the most of the moment. "Remember that case during Spring Festival? The dismembered girl? We found her bits in a shallow grave out near the Summer Palace . . ."

"Yeah, I remember the case," Li interrupted impatiently. "We never got anyone for it." He paused. "What about it?"

"They found a whole bunch more just like her down in Shanghai. Some kind of mass grave. Maybe as many as twenty. Same MO."

"Twenty!" Li was shocked.

Wu shrugged. "They don't know how many exactly yet, but there are lots of bits." He relayed this with a relish Li found distasteful. "And they want you down there. Fast."

Li was taken aback. "Me? Why?"

Wu grinned. "'Cos you're such a fucking superstar, Boss." But his smile faded rapidly in the chill of Li's glare. "They think there could be a link to the murder here in Beijing," he said quickly. "And there's big pressure to get a result fast on this one."

"Why's that?" Li had forgotten his courtroom debacle already.

Wu lit a cigarette. "Seems there was this big ceremony down there this morning. Concrete getting poured into the foundations of some big joint venture bank they're building across the river in Pudong. Anyway, the CEO of this New York bank comes to do the ceremonial bit on the building site. All the top brass are there. Place is bristling with American Press and TV. Only it's pissing from the heavens. The building site turns into a swamp, and the platform they built for the VIPs tips this American exec right into the hole they're going to fill with concrete. And he finds himself floundering around in the mud with bits of bodies coming out of the walls, like they just dug up some old burial site. Only the bodies are not so old."

Li whistled softly. He could picture the scene. A media feed-ing frenzy. Not the Chinese press, they would only print what they were told. But there would be no restraining the Western media. "TV cameras?" he asked.

"Beaming right out of there, live on satellite," Wu con-firmed, enjoying himself. "Apparently the powers that be are in a real state. Bodies in the bank vault are not good for busi-ness, and apparently the Americans are talking about pulling out of the whole deal."

"I'm sure the victims will be sorry to hear that," Li said.

Wu smirked and reaching over to the rear seat heaved a fat folder into Li's lap. "That's the file on the girl we found in Beijing. You'll have time to refamiliarise yourself with it on the flight, which leaves . . ." he checked his watch, ". . . in a little over two hours." He grinned. "Just enough time for you to pack an overnight bag."

Li sat on the edge of the bed, watery sunlight slanting in from the street through the last dead leaves clinging to the trees that shaded Zhengyi Road in the summer. A kindly face smiled down at him from the wall, a tumble of curly black hair, streaked with silver, swept back from a remarkably unlined face – his Uncle Yifu, with whom he had lived for more than ten years on the second floor of this police apartment block in the Ministry com-pound. Li still missed him. Missed the mischief in his eyes as he endeavoured to trip Li up at every turn, imparting the experience of a lifetime, teaching him to think laterally. *While the devil might be in the detail, therein also lies the truth,* he used to say. Li still ached when he remembered the circumstances of the old man's death. Woke frequently in the night with the bloody image skewered into his consciousness. This had been Yifu's room, and now it was

Xinxin's. She often asked Li to tell her stories about the old man who smiled down at her from the wall. And he always made the time to tell her.

Now, reluctantly, he stood up and wandered back to his own room. He was destined, it seemed, to be forever haunted by Yifu. With every failure, his uncle was cast up to him as an example he should follow. While every success was attributed to the old man's influence. Those who were jealous of his status and achievements put them down to his uncle's connections. And those senior officers who had worked with his uncle made it clear that his footsteps were much too big for Li to walk in. And through every investigation he felt the old man's presence at his shoulder, his voice whispering softly in his ear. *No use, Li, in worrying over the might-have-beens. The answer's in the detail, Li, always in the detail. It is a good thing to have a broken mirror reshaped. Where the tiller is tireless, the earth is fertile.* He'd have given anything to hear that voice again for real.

Quickly he stripped out of his uniform and felt the freedom of release from its starched constraint. He pulled on a pair of jeans, a white tee-shirt and his favourite old brown leather jacket, and began packing some clothes into a holdall. One of Xinxin's books lying on the chest of drawers caused him to pause. He would need to arrange for Mei Yuan to look after the child while he was gone. And there was no Margaret to step into the breach.

He sat for a moment lost in thought, then reached over and lifted Margaret's hairbrush from the bedside table and teased out some of the hair trapped in its teeth. It was extra fine and golden in the pale sunlight. He put it to his nose and smelled her perfume, experiencing a moment of acute desire, and then emptiness. He ran his hand lightly across the unmade bed where they had so often made love, and realised that he missed her more than he knew.

III

Margaret had never quite understood the Irish concept of the wake – a celebration of the life, rather than a mourning of the death. How could you celebrate a life that was gone, something that once was vital and full of hope and warmth and giving, that now was cold and dead? Like the procession of bodies that had passed through her autopsy room, all animation extinct, just meat on a slab.

She could not bear to think of her father like that. She had not even had the courage to view his body, laid out in his coffin, colour carefully applied to his face by the mortician in an attempt to create the illusion of life. In any case, she knew, it was not her father who lay there. He had long vanished, existing now only in the memories of others, and in flickering, fading images on old home movies from the days before video tape. They had never bought a video camera.

There were always the family photo albums. But Margaret felt that these fixed, two-dimensional images rarely caught the person. They lacked the spirit that was life and character, a personality. They were just moments in time without any reference point.

She heard voices raised in laughter coming from the living room, the chink of glasses, and felt resentful that these people should come into her father's home on the day he was buried and take his passing so lightly. She slipped out of the kitchen and moved down the hall to the room at the back of the house which had been his den. She shut the door on the sounds of the wake and listened to the silence. The room was laden with it, what little light remained of the late afternoon soaked up by the heavy net curtains. If there was anything left of him, it was here in this room where he had spent so much time. She breathed in the smell of him in the dry, academic atmosphere of his own private space. Everything had been left as it was from the day he dropped dead in his lecture room at the university from a massive coronary thrombosis. Quick, painless, completely unexpected. The best way to go, Margaret thought, except for those who remained, devastated by the suddenness of it, left to cope with the huge hole it made in all their lives.

She wandered around touching things. His books, hundreds of them gathering dust on the shelves. All the great modern American writers. It had been his subject, his speciality. Steinbeck, Faulkner, Fitzgerald and, of course, Hemingway, who had grown up just a few streets away in this quiet upscale Chicago suburb. All thumbed and marked and annotated. She picked one out. *Winesburg, Ohio*, a collection of short stories by Sherwood Anderson. The pages were yellowing now around the edges, the paper dry, almost brittle. It fell open at a story called *Hands*. She remembered it. A sad story about a simple man whose love of children led to a tragic misunderstanding. There were copious notes down the margins in her father's tight distinctive handwriting, the hallmark of a generation.

She moved to his desk. A piece of English reproduction furniture. Mahogany, with red leather inlay. It was chipped and scarred from years of use. Papers and books were piled untidily around his iMac desktop computer. A half-smoked pipe lay in an ashtray, the pale scrapings of his teeth around the mouthpiece of the black stem. As a child she had loved the sweet smell of his tobacco. She ran her fingers lovingly round the smoothly polished cherrywood bowl. He had no doubt intended to relight it. Now he never would.

In a frame to the left of the computer, partially obscured by a pile of unmarked exam papers, was a photograph of Margaret in her graduation gown. She moved the papers to get a better sight of it, and felt a strange ache as she saw the young face below the mortar board gazing back at her out of the picture, full of hope and youthful idealism. She wondered how often her father had looked at it in idle moments. Wondered what he had thought of her. Had he been proud or disappointed? As a little girl she had adored him. And he had given her so much of his time, so much of his love. But since her teens they had not been particularly close, and now she regretted it. It had been her fault. She had been too busy making a life for herself that had nothing to do with her parents. A life that had turned to failure and disappointment. And now there was no going back. No way to say, Sorry, Dad, I loved you really. She quickly turned the frame face down on the desk and turned on the computer, just for something to do. It whirred and hummed as it booted up its operating system, before presenting her with its desktop screen. From here she could access all his files. Mainly they were word-processing documents. Lectures, notes for students, a critical analysis of some new American classic. There were letters, too. Hundreds of them. But she had no interest in violating his privacy.

He had only recently gone on-line, discovering that he could stay easily in touch by e-mail with his daughter in China. All it took was a click of the mouse. But, then, beyond his initial enthusiasm for the Internet, he had not had much to say to her, and his e-mails had tailed off. She wondered what use he had made of the Net, and booted up his browser, a piece of software that connected him to the worldwide web, allowing him

to visit any one of millions of Internet sites around the globe.
The default page that it took her to was the home page of his
Department at the University of Illinois in Chicago. Down the
left side of the screen were four tabs, like name tabs on folders
in a filing cabinet, which is what they were – or, at least, their
electronic equivalent. While she waited for the UIC home page
to load, she pointed the on-screen arrow to the HISTORY tab
and a file opened up as if she had drawn it out of a cabinet.
This showed the last five hundred Internet sites her father had
visited. She went to the top of the list, the last site he had gone
to on the day before he died. It was something called *Aphrodite
Home Page*. She clicked on the Internet Explorer icon beside it
and within seconds the screen was wiped black, and photographs of naked women began downloading under headings
like *SAMANTHA – Click me to watch live*, and *JULI – I like women*.

Margaret's face flushed red. A mixture of shock, embarrassment, revulsion. She went back to HISTORY and downloaded
the next address on the list. More pornography. *ASIAN BABES DO
IT FOR YOU*. Skinny Asian women with silicon-boosted breasts
revealed parts of their anatomy that Margaret had only ever
seen on the autopsy table. She felt sick. Her dad was accessing
pornography on the Internet. Her *dad*! She could not reconcile
this with the sweet, gentle man she knew as her father, the
most scrupulously fair and honest man she had ever known.
But, then, she thought, had she ever really known him at
all? Why would he want to look at filth like this? Men, she
knew, had needs that women simply didn't understand. But
her *dad*?

She didn't hear the door of the den opening and was startled
by the sound of her mother's voice. "What are you doing, Margaret? Everyone's asking where you are."

Margaret was flustered, as if caught in some illicit act. She quickly moved the arrow to shut down the computer before her mother could see what was on the screen. "Nothing," she said guiltily. "Just going through some of dad's stuff."

"Well, there'll be plenty of time for that," her mother said. "You have guests to see to."

Margaret bridled. "They're not *my* guests," she said. "You invited them. And, anyway, they seem to be having a pretty good time through there, drinking dad's Scotch. They won't want me spoiling their fun."

Her mother sighed theatrically. "I don't know why you bother affecting the grieving daughter. You had no time for him when he was alive. Why start pretending now?"

Margaret was stung, both by the unfairness and by the truth of her mother's words. "I'm not pretending," she said, fighting back the tears. She hated her mother to see any sign of weakness in her. "I loved my dad." She hadn't realised just how much until she had received the phone call in Beijing. "But don't worry. I won't cause any posthumous embarrassment at your funeral by pretending I ever felt anything about you."

She saw the colour rise on her mother's cheeks and experienced an immediate stab of regret at her cruelty. Her mother had always had the knack of bringing out the worst in her. "In that case," her mother said coldly, "perhaps you'd be better not going." She turned back to the door.

"You never loved me, did you?" The words were out before Margaret could stop them, and they halted her mother in her tracks. "That day my brother drowned. You wished it had been me and not him." Her mother turned and flashed her a look. Things that had never been said, feelings long suppressed, were bubbling to the surface. "You spent your life wishing failure on me because I could never live up to the expectations you had of him. Your boy. Your darling."

Her mother's jaw was trembling. Her eyes filling. But like her daughter, she would show no sign of weakness. "I didn't have to wish failure on you, Margaret. You brought all the failure you could ever need on yourself. A failed marriage, a failed career. And now an affair with some . . . Chinaman." She said the word as if it left a bad taste in her mouth. "And don't talk to me about love. You don't know the meaning of the word. You were always so self-contained. So cold. All those people you cut open. Just so much dead flesh to you. You never needed anything from anyone, did you? And never gave a thing of yourself."

Margaret's eyes were burning. Her throat felt swollen. She wished she had never come home. Was it true? Was she really so cold, so ungiving? Her mother had always been squeamish about her decision to become a pathologist, but she had never realised just how much it disgusted her. The words hurt. She wanted to hurt back. "Maybe," she said, "that's because I took after you. You were always the Queen of Frost." She paused. "And maybe that's why dad had to go looking for his sexual pleasures on the Internet." As soon as the words were out she regretted saying them. But there was no way to take them back, and she remembered the lines from one of her father's favourite poems – *The Moving Finger writes; and, having writ, | Moves on: nor all thy Piety nor Wit | Shall lure it back to cancel half a Line, | Nor all thy Tears wash out a Word of it.*

All the colour that their argument had raised on her mother's face drained out of it. The carefully controlled façade slipped, and she looked suddenly haggard and old. "What do you mean?" she asked quietly.

Margaret found she couldn't meet her eye. "Nothing, Mom. We're just being stupid here. Trying to hurt one another, 'cos dad's gone and left us and who else are we going to take it out on?"

Her mother nodded towards the computer. Her voice had become very small. "He spent hours in here on that damned thing." She looked at Margaret. "Your father and I hadn't made love for years." She became hesitant. "But I had no idea . . ."

Margaret closed her eyes. There were things about your parents you'd rather you never knew.

"I'm not interrupting anything, am I?"

Margaret opened her eyes and saw a young man standing in the doorway. For a moment, in the semi-dark, she had no idea who he was. It was his voice which sparked off the memories of those pre-graduation years. "David?"

"That's me," he grinned. "Thought I'd show my face. You know, for old time's sake. But, hey, you know, if this is a bad moment . . ."

"Of course not, David." Margaret's mother had immediately recovered herself, slipping back into the role of the bravely grieving widow. "But if you'll excuse me, I really should be seeing to my guests. I'll leave you two to get reacquainted. It must be quite some time."

David nodded. "Almost ten years."

"I'll speak to you later, then." The widow smiled and was gone, leaving Margaret and this ghost from her past standing in the silence of her dead father's den.

"Ten years?" Margaret said, for something to say. "You sound like you've been counting."

"Maybe I have." He stepped into the room and she saw him a little more clearly. Sandy hair, thinning now, a lean good-looking face, strong jaw, well-defined lips. David Webber was tall and powerfully built. She remembered those arms holding her, his lips on her neck. And unaccountably she burst into tears. "Hey," he said, and immediately he was there, those same arms drawing her to him, and she surrendered to the comfort of his warmth and strength and made no effort to stop the sobs that broke in her chest.

For a long time he just held her and said nothing, until gradually the sobs began to subside. Then he drew the hair back from the streaky wetness of her face and smiled gently down at her. "What you need is to get out of here," he said. "I'm going to take you to dinner tonight. And if I don't have you laughing by the end of the evening, I'll pick up the tab."

Which made her smile, in spite of everything. She remembered how she had always insisted they went Dutch, and how he had always made her laugh.

IV

Her life flashed before her eyes, like that moment people experience just before they believe they are going to die. All the familiar places she had haunted as a student, and then later during her residency at UIC Medical Centre. She had been more of a hermit during her time at the Cook County Medical Examiner's office.

The cab took them along Armitage, lights blazing in the early evening dark. On Halsted they had passed familiar-looking restaurants, a bar where she had once spent an hour drinking with a boyfriend, waiting for a table in a nearby eatery. By the time it was ready they were too drunk to eat.

Now she saw the used CD store where she used to browse when she was low on funds, only in those days they still sold vinyl, too. And the little speciality tea and coffee shop where she had got her favourite blend of roasted beans and Earl Grey tea by the pound. And all the chichi shops and boutiques where she would happily spend hours picking out what she would buy if only she could afford it.

They passed under the El, and Margaret suddenly began to get a bad feeling. "Where are we eating?" she asked.

David smiled knowingly. "I don't think you'll be disappointed."

But when the cab took a right into Sheffield and drew up outside Sai Café, she was. "*Sushi!* Jesus, David," she said, trying to make light of it, "I just spent the last eighteen months eating Asian, I was kind of hoping you might take me somewhere different. Somewhere *American*, you know, even a burger joint."

"Oh." He looked crestfallen. "You always liked *sushi*. I just thought . . ." His voice trailed off. He shrugged. "But, hey, doesn't matter. We can always go somewhere else."

His disappointment was palpable. Margaret relented. "But you made a reservation, right?" It helped to make a reservation for Sai Café if you wanted to be sure of getting in.

"Sure. But somebody else'll be happy to get our table."

"No, it's okay, let's eat here." She started to get out of the cab. She knew he wanted to bring her here because it was where they had eaten together as students, when they could afford it. Only, David could always afford it. It was Margaret who had trouble scraping her share together. She watched him pay the cab driver. No tip. Nothing had changed. "Listen," she said when the cab pulled away, "don't mind me. It's just today, you know? I'm a bit cranky."

David guffawed. "Hey, Mags, you always were."

She felt a little chill run through her. *Mags* is what Michael had called her. That was something David had obviously forgotten about Sai Café.

The place was packed. People stood around the bar and sat drinking at tables in the window waiting for seats in the restaurant proper. Ahead and to the right, in the main eating area, customers perched on low stools along the *sushi* bar, chatting to Japanese chefs as they wielded sharp blades to carve up delicate pieces of raw fish. The girl at the lectern checked their reservation, and they followed her between crowded tables to one at the far wall. Candles flickered in the smoky atmosphere, and Margaret remembered that David, like Li, was a smoker. After all these months in China it didn't bother her as much as it used to.

Steaming hot towels were brought to the table, and they ordered *miso* soup and *moriawase* – mixed *sashimi* platters. David lit up as soon as they had placed their order. "So," he said, "how long are you planning on staying?"

"Don't," Margaret said. "You sound like my mother."

"Jesus, I hope not." David laughed and gazed at her fondly. "You two never did get along, did you?"

"Nope."

"I always reckoned you were more like your dad."

And Margaret remembered how David had never really known her. He had been attracted to her, physically, and that had been more important to him than anything else. She had thought he was good-looking, and the physical side of their relationship had always been rewarding – until she got pregnant. And then there had only been one course of action as far as he was concerned, and she had allowed herself to be talked into it. She had never forgiven herself. Or him. "You still in medicine?" He had made the youngest ever cardiac consultant at Chicago Hope.

"Sure." He laughed, although a little uneasily, she thought. "Still single, too."

Margaret hoped he had developed more subtlety in telling patients they were terminally ill. "I'm sure you had lots of girls after we split up."

"Lots." He drew on his cigarette and blew a jet of smoke over her head. "But, then, you were a hard act to follow."

She grinned. "Oh, come on, David, it's me you're talking to. I never did fall for your bullshit."

He returned the grin ruefully. "No, and neither has anyone else." He patted the top of his head. "And now I'm losing my hair I'm not such a catch any more. Women just pull out the hook and throw me back."

"Oh, sure. Like there aren't a million women out there who wouldn't die for a good-looking thirty-something cardiac consultant."

"Maybe I've just set myself too high standards. That's what my mother thinks."

"She never thought too much of me."

"Yeah, but she never knew you like I did."

"Thank God." She grinned and he grinned back. And then there was an awkward silence that neither of them knew how to fill.

But they were rescued from their embarrassment by the arrival of the soup. The taste of it was familiar and comforting, pieces of *wakame* and *tofu* cubes in hot *dashi* stock thickened by red *miso*. They slurped in silence for minute or two.

Then, "Good food, weird people," David said.

Margaret looked confused. "What?"

"The Japanese." He grinned stupidly. "Don't think I'd much like to be practising over there. Neither would you."

"Why not?"

"You know, they got this weird religion in Japan. *Shinto*. It's peculiarly Japanese, but it's kind of soaked up bits of Buddhism and other stuff as well. They've got a pretty strange view of the sanctity of the dead body. And, you know, they only got around to defining brain death as a legal condition a few years back." He laughed. "Last time a doctor over there performed a heart transplant was in nineteen sixty-eight, and he got charged with murder."

Margaret said, "I can think of a few doctors who should be charged with that." And she remembered her fear in the moments before she lost consciousness in the operating theatre, and then coming to and knowing that they had killed her child. She looked at David and wondered if he even remembered.

"I read all about you when that business was in the news about the rice," he said suddenly. "Jesus, Margaret, that was scary stuff."

She just nodded.

"Nearly put me off *sushi* for life."

She managed a pale smile.

He tried again. "You want to tell me about it?"

She shook her head. "Nope."

"Okay." He raised his hand. "Margaret says subject off limits." He hesitated, then, "So what *have* you been doing in China all this time?"

"Lecturing mostly. At the University of Public Security. It's where they train their cops. Kind of like the Chinese equivalent of West Point."

"Does it pay well?"

"Nope. The money's lousy. But they give me an apartment I can just about swing a cat in, and as much rice as I can eat. So you can see why I was tempted to stay on."

He chuckled. "So why do you?"

She shrugged. "I've got my reasons."

"Which you don't want to share with me."

"Not particularly."

"Jeez, Mags," he leaned across the table and put his hand over hers, "what the hell are you thinking? You had a great job here. You could have ended up Medical Examiner in a few years."

She said very quietly, "Don't do that, David."

He withdrew his hand like he'd had an electric shock. "I'm sorry."

She shook her head. "I mean, don't call me *Mags*. It's what Michael called me."

"Oh, shit, I'm sorry, Margaret. I never thought . . ."

"Doesn't matter." She wasn't going to remind him that this is where she'd met Michael, that it was David who'd introduced them. A fact that had clearly not loomed large in his recollection, along with the termination of her pregnancy.

"But, hey, you know, the question's still relevant. I mean, why China? It's a communist state for Christ's sake."

"Oh, right." Margaret felt her hackles rise. "And you want to turn it overnight into a democracy? Like Russia?"

"Hey, come on, Margaret, I'm just saying . . ."

"Saying what? That you want to see people dying in the streets of cold and hunger, watch organised crime take the money out of honest people's pockets, see a breakdown of government, a descent into civil war?"

"Of course not!" David was annoyed now. "I wouldn't wish Russia on anyone, even the Russians. It's *this* country, the USA, that sets the standard. People here have got rights."

"Yeah, the right to get shot because their democratically elected government isn't strong enough to stand up to the vested interests of the gun lobby. The right to justice if they can afford to pay for a sharp lawyer."

David looked at her, uncomprehending. "Jeez, Margaret. What have they done to you over there?"

"Nothing, David. Not a thing. I've just got a perspective now on the world that I never had before. I mean, what do you *know* about China? Have you ever been there?"

"No, but — "

"No, but what? That doesn't make any difference? Is that what you were going to say?"

"I was going to say," David said levelly, "that I read the papers and I watch the news. I know all about their record on human rights, what they do to dissidents. Like the clampdown on that religious sect . . . what is it? . . . *Falun Gong.*"

"Oh, right," Margaret said. "*Falun Gong.* They're the ones whose leader claims to be an alien . . . someone from outer space. That sounds like someone worth following."

"That's not the point. The point is that people should be allowed to follow whatever religion they want."

"Like here."

"Like here." He nodded, satisfied that he'd finally made his point.

"Like the Branch Davidians?"

"Oh, for Christ's sake, Margaret!"

But she wasn't going to be deflected. "You remember the Branch Davidians, don't you? They're the ones the FBI massacred down at Waco. Women and children burned alive. I mean, I should know, I assisted on a fair number of the autopsies."

David breathed his irritation. "That's not a fair comparison."

"That's just the trouble." Margaret slapped the table, and heads turned in their direction. "Comparisons never are. The Chinese have no history of democracy in five thousand years of civilisation. So how can you compare it to the United States?

And whatever hell that society's been through in the last hundred years, it is changing, David. Slowly but surely. And regardless of what people here might like to think, the man in the street doesn't harbour dreams of democracy. He doesn't even think about politics. He thinks about how much he earns, about putting a roof over his head, about feeding his family, educating his kids. And you know what? Right now he's better off than he's ever been at any time in history."

David looked at her in astonishment for several moments. Eventually he said, "I suppose there are lots of ways you can be brainwashed without even knowing it."

"What are you talking about?"

"I'm talking about your . . . *Chinaman*."

It wasn't just the word, or even the fact that he had used it at all, but the way he said it, that started alarm bells ringing in her head. It was a very accurate parody of her mother's use of the derogatory term. "What do you know about my 'Chinaman'?"

But it wasn't a question he was going to answer. He was intent on pressing home what he saw as his advantage. "That's the real reason you never came back, isn't it? The same reason you can sit there and bad-mouth your own country."

"I love my country," Margaret said fiercely. "Whatever I think or feel about China won't ever change that." She paused to control herself. "But you didn't answer my question."

"What question?" He had realised his gaffe now and was being evasive.

"She told you, didn't she?"

"Who?"

"My mother. That's why you were at the house this afternoon. I bet you'd made reservations for this place long before you even asked me to dinner." He blushed and she knew she'd hit the mark. "So what did she want you to do? Try and persuade me to stay? I mean, why would she even care?"

"This has got nothing to do with your mother, Margaret. *I* care. I always have. You know that. You were the one. You were *always* the one."

Margaret shook her head in disbelief. "David . . ." She let out a sigh of exasperation. "You and I never had a future. Not then, not now." She drew a deep breath. "I won't be a pawn in my mother's little game of matchmaking. And in case you didn't know, it's not you she's impressed by, it's your family's money." She remembered how impressed her mother had been by David. He'd gone to the University of Chicago because his parents could afford it. Margaret had only been there because she'd won a scholarship. After a moment she added, "And if you want to know the truth about my 'Chinaman' . . . I'm head over heels in love with him."

The waitress brought two wooden platters of neatly sliced pieces of raw bream, bass, salmon and tuna beautifully displayed with squid rolls, thread-cut *daikon* radish and a single quail's egg. The *sushi* rice came in separate bowls. Margaret and David sat in silence surveying the food for half a minute, maybe more, before Margaret stood up and lifted her purse. "I think I should go," she said. "You can pick up the check if you like."

He smiled sadly. "I didn't even make you laugh."

"I think maybe I've forgotten how."

And she turned and pushed off through the tables.

V

The airplane turned low beneath the clouds, wheeling over the slow-moving flow of the Yangtse River delta, dragon-tongues of water that had travelled four thousand miles from the high mountains of Tibet, snaking out into the slow grey swell of the East China Sea. Li turned from the window and closed his eyes as the plane began its descent into Hongqiao Airport. But the same images remained, projected on to the back of his retina by his mind's eye. Dreadful images of a poor dead girl, clinically dissected and then brutally butchered.

He had re-read her file during the flight, the autopsy report, the forensic evidence, the dozens of leads that had taken them nowhere. The only real clue to her identity had been distinctive gold foil dental restorations, expensive and unusual in China. But none of the Beijing clinics capable of such work had had any record of her. Found buried in a shallow grave on waste ground on a bleak February morning during Spring Festival, they knew no more about her now than they did then.

A heavy jolt and the squeal of tyres brought him back to the present. He glanced out across wet tarmac to the low, old-fashioned terminal building. Twenty bodies in a single grave! It seemed inconceivable to him. The spectre of some grim room with decomposing bodies laid out side by side rose up before him, and he wondered what it was that had ever drawn him to join the police. And then Yifu was there again at his shoulder, and he had no need to answer his own question.

The Arrivals concourse was crowded with travellers, mostly from internal destinations now that Hongqiao had become eclipsed by the new international airport at Pudong. Expectant faces were turned towards the exit gate as the passengers from Beijing flooded out. Some cards were raised with names scrawled in untidy characters. Li saw his name held above the head of an attractive young woman with long hair divided in a centre parting and tumbling over narrow shoulders. She was scanning the faces in the crowd and appeared to recognise him immediately. She smiled, a broad, open smile that dimpled her cheeks. And Li saw that she had very dark eyes, almost black, and that one of them turned in very slightly. But it didn't spoil her looks so much as lend her a sense of quirky individuality. She was wearing jeans and a denim jacket over a white sweatshirt, and a pair of scruffy blue and white trainers.

"Deputy Section Chief Li?"

Li nodded. "That's me." Physically he towered over her, but she had a presence, an innate sense of self-confidence that lent her stature, and she didn't seem so small.

"Hi." She held out her hand.

He shook it and was surprised by the firmness of her grip. He said, "I was told I would be met by my opposite number here, Deputy Section Chief Nien."

She cocked an eyebrow at him. "Were you?" And she reached out to take his holdall. "I'll take your bag."

Her move caught him by surprise. "That's okay," he said. But she had already snatched it and turned towards the sliding glass doors, swinging it up and over her shoulder.

"I've got a car waiting outside," she said.

Li hurried after her. "So what happened to Nien?"

The girl never broke her stride. "The Deputy Section Chief's got better things to do than provide a taxi service for some hotshot from Beijing." A dark blue Volkswagen Santana saloon sat idling at the kerb. The girl lifted the trunk and dropped Li's bag in.

Li felt his hackles rise. This was not the courtesy or respect an officer of his rank was entitled to expect. *Hotshot!* And he remembered Wu's sarcasm in Beijing. *You're such a fucking superstar, boss.* Is that how people saw him, just because of the publicity a couple of high profile cases had brought? "What's your rank, officer?" he said sharply.

She shrugged. "I'm just the driver. Do you want to get in or do you want to walk?"

There was a long moment of stand-off before Li finally decided this was not the place to deal with her. Silently fuming he walked around the car and climbed in the passenger side. The rain battered down on glistening asphalt, red and white flags hung limply in a row, a ghostly mist, like gauze, almost obscured the car park and the pink multi-storey buildings beyond.

The girl slipped into the driver's seat and set the wipers going to clear the windscreen. "Your name," Li said through clenched teeth.

She looked at him, affecting confusion. "I'm sorry?"

"I'd like to know your name, so that I can take the appropriate action when we get to headquarters."

"803."

He glared at her. "What?"

"That's what it's called – the headquarters of the Criminal Investigation Department. 803. A cop show here on Shanghai TV called us that because of our address – 803 Zhongshan Beiyi Road. It stuck." Suddenly her face split into a grin and she started laughing, an odd braying laugh that was strangely beguiling.

Li found a puzzled smile sneaking up on him, in spite of himself. "What? What's so funny?"

She held out her hand. "Maybe we should start again, Deputy Section Chief. I'm Nien Mei-Ling."

He frowned. "Nien . . . Deputy Section Chief Nien?"

She laughed again. "Is it really so hard to believe that a mere woman could achieve the same rank as the great Li Yan? Or is it only in Shanghai that women hold up half the sky?"

Li shook the outstretched hand, startled and bemused. "I'm sorry, I thought – "

"Yeah, I know . . . that I was just some junior officer sent to pick you up. Couldn't possibly be Deputy Section Chief Nien." But there was no rancour in this, no chip on the shoulder. Just a wicked sense of mischief. And Li found her smile irresistible, and held on to her hand perhaps a little longer than necessary.

The expressway from the airport became Yan'an Viaduct Road, a six-lane highway raised on concrete pillars that ran through the heart of Shanghai, bisecting it from west to east. Li gazed out through the rain in amazement as all around tower blocks rose up in white and pink stone, a monolith made entirely, it seemed, out of green glass, rows of incongruous villas that owed more to the architecture of ancient Greece than ancient China, whole blocks of square three-storey buildings in cream stucco and red brick, strange silver cylindrical towers that disappeared into the cloud. Gigantic neon signs on every other rooftop advertised everything from Pepsi-Cola to Fujifilm. It was nearly fifteen years since he had last been in Shanghai, and it had changed beyond recognition. There were still the single-storey blocks of traditional Chinese shops and apartments crammed into crowded narrow lanes, still the bizarre pockets of European colonial architecture left by the British and the French from the days of the International Settlement. But from the seeds planted by Deng's concept of a socialist market economy, a whole new city had grown up around them, a city filled with contradictions around every corner, bicycles and BMWs, a city of extremes and excesses, a future vision of China.

Mei-Ling glanced at him. "Changed a bit since you were last here?"

Li nodded. "You could say that."

She smiled. "Wait till you scratch beneath the surface. It's changed more than you think."

"What do you mean?"

"Sex shops and massage parlours. All-night clubs and discos – hell, we even own a few."

"We?"

"Public Security." She took in Li's astonishment. "People's Liberation Army, too. Disco till dawn with the PLA." A small bell hanging from her rear-view mirror chinged as she swerved around a slow lorry and switched lanes. "And then there's the dogs."

"Dogs?" Li was puzzled.

"Seems they're off the menu and on to the accessory list. These days you're no one if you don't own a dog. The European purebreds are particularly popular. The Russian mafia's making a fortune doping them up on vodka and smuggling them down on the Trans-Siberian express. We've got pet parlours and veterinarian surgeries springing up all over the city." She paused. "And, of course, there's the Taiwanese Mafia. They're moving in big-time, running protection rackets and prostitution. There's only one China as far as they're concerned. We've got a population of fourteen million in this city, a hundred and seventy-five thousand taxis, the highest rate of economic growth in China, the fastest growing crime rate and eighteen bodies in a building site in Pudong. Welcome to Shanghai, Mr. Li."

"Eighteen? I thought it was twenty."

"Well, on a head count, literally, we've got sixteen. But there are eighteen torsos, and we're still finding bits."

They swooped past the granite-blocks, colonnaded columns and spectacular golden spire of the Shanghai Exhibition

Centre, built in the fifties by the Russians in the excessive Stalinesque style of the time.

"So," she said, "do you want to tell me about the body you found in Beijing?"

Li dragged himself away from the sights and sounds and revelations of Shanghai and focused his thoughts on the file he had read on the plane on the way down. "A young girl, we think early twenties. She was found by public utility workers on a piece of waste ground in Haidian district near the Summer Palace last February, during the New Year holiday. There had been heavy rain, and they were drawn to the spot by what looked like blood pooling in the mud. They started digging. She was just a couple of feet down in two black plastic bags. The pathologist reckoned she'd only been there about a week."

"Cause of death?"

"Uncertain. Her heart stopped. That's the only thing we know for sure. She'd been opened up by someone with pretty sophisticated surgical skills. Heart, liver, pancreas and one kidney had all been removed."

"Organ theft?"

Li shook his head. "No. The organs were all still there in one of the plastic bags."

"And the rest of her?"

"In the other one. Hacked to bits by someone with a butcher's saw by the look of it."

"Anything else of significance?"

Li shrugged. "It's difficult to know what's significant. She had the most common blood group – O. But she'd had some pretty expensive dental work, though not done by anyone in Beijing. It's possible she'd had treatment in the West."

"Any clothes?"

"Not a stitch. And no jewellery. No distinguishing marks. And the AFIS came up with zip on her fingerprints."

Mei-Ling looked thoughtful. "And motive? Would you hazard a guess?"

"Couldn't even begin," Li said. "Not sexual, at least not in any conventional way. There was no sign of violation, no mutilation of the sexual organs or the breasts." He was aware of feeling slightly uncomfortable discussing these details with a woman. He shrugged. "We hit a brick wall."

They passed under a sweeping junction of crisscrossing flyovers, and through a maze of buildings to their left Li caught sight of the remodelled People's Square with its circular museum and glass theatre and vast white municipal monolith. Ahead through a forest of skyscrapers he spotted a strange green spire punctuated twice in its upward sweep by red and silver globes, all supported on four gigantic splayed legs. It looked for all the world like a Martian rocket ship. "What the hell's that?" he asked.

She followed his eyeline and grinned. "Oh, that? That's the Pearl TV Tower, across the river in Pudong." She glanced at him. "You know that before the Second World War Shanghai was known in the West as the Paris of the East? Now the good citizens of the city like to think they have their very own Eiffel Tower."

"It's certainly as ugly," Li said. But the tower sank out of sight as the road dipped down and ran underground to the tunnel that would take them under the Huangpu River. He said, "What about the bodies you found this morning? Anything I described sound familiar?"

She nodded. "Very. But I'll let you see for yourself first, then you'd better go meet my boss."

"What about the American? The guy who fell into the pit. They never told me what happened to him."

"Oh," she said casually, "they got him out alive okay. Then he just went to pieces."

She flicked him a glance, and there was a moment of uncertainty between them before air escaped from her lips in a series of small explosions and she burst out laughing, her strange, infectious braying laugh, and he found himself laughing, too. Humour, no matter how black, was the only defence they ever had against the sick world they moved in.

Their Santana glided through the wide empty streets of Pudong's Lujiazui financial district. Street lights reflected on wet sidewalks in the gloom of the late afternoon. All around them thirty-storey buildings soared into the darkening sky, but lights shone in only a few solitary windows. Investment in construction had so far outstripped demand. Across the river, traffic had come to a standstill along the Bund, a broad, waterfront boulevard characterised by its sweep of grand, stone-built European-style buildings with domes and spires and clock towers. At a glance they might have been in Paris or London. From the river itself came the mournful call of vessels sounding foghorns in the haze.

On their right, through open gates in salmon-coloured walls, floodlights raised on tall stands shone behind sheets of clear plastic that gave the appearance of breathing in time with the cold wind that blew in off the water. Beneath them, blurry figures in white moved about like ghosts, working in the freezing cold liquid mud in a painstaking search for more body bits. Armed guards stood by the gates, and more than two dozen police and forensic vehicles were drawn up haphazardly in the street outside.

"That's the building site," Mei-Ling said. "We commandeered the basement car park of the office block over there." She nodded towards a tall dark tower block across the street. "It's empty. The pathologists are laying the bodies out there until we're sure we've found all the pieces." She turned left, through a break in the central reservation, crossed the opposite carriageway, and drove down a ramp into a subterranean car park where she drew in behind a phalanx of other vehicles. Li recognised the distinctive *hu* character, signifying Shanghai, followed by the letter "O," that preceded the registrations on all unmarked police cars.

Mei-Ling flashed her maroon Public Security ID at the uniformed officer who challenged them, and Li followed her between pillars into an area brightly lit by improvised lamps. The intensity of the light created a sense of unreality about the scene that greeted them. More than twenty trestle tables covered in white paper ranged against a bleak grey concrete wall, lined up side by side and with just a couple of feet separating them. On some, bits of body lay wrapped in the plastic bags they had been brought down in. Others had been removed and arranged in bizarre parodies of the human bodies they had once been, legs and arms laid next to torsos and heads, a gruesome jigsaw of human pieces. Most of the bits were still unrecognisable, except where assistants in white plastic suits were gently hosing them down to reveal the decaying dimpled flesh of hands and feet, knees and elbows, breasts and bellies. Only the smell brought home the reality. The sweet, heavy smell of decomposing human flesh that filled this underground chamber of horrors and almost made Li gag. He made a determined effort to breathe through his mouth. He glanced at Mei-Ling, but she did not appear to be affected.

On the wall, behind each table, crude paper charts had been pasted up itemising the parts laid out on each, and listing the bits still missing. There were roughly drawn diagrams of each of the bodies.

"Ah, Miss Nien. At last you honour us with your presence." A tall man in his late fifties, thin black hair scraped back across his scalp, crossed the concrete floor to greet them, his breath billowing before him in the cold air. His eyes were little more than bloodshot slits through which he peered myopically. His skin was mottled and brown, and his teeth stained from years of smoking. He was smoking now, a cigarette between his lips, dropping ash down his stained white coat. The illusion of myopia, Li decided, was created by his need to screw up his eyes against the smoke that seemed to seep from his face as if from cracks in a flue.

Mei-Ling said, "Dr. Lan, this is Deputy Section Chief Li from Beijing."

Dr. Lan scrutinised Li carefully, then permitted himself a small smile. He held out his hand. "Of course. It is an honour to meet you, Mr. Li."

"Dr. Lan is our senior pathologist," Mei-Ling said. And she turned to him. "Any initial thoughts, Doctor."

"Very preliminary." He walked them past the bodies, lighting another cigarette from the remains of the previous one. "Of course, I received my training in the army, so I have seen much worse. What's disturbing about this is that all the victims are women."

Li was taken aback. "All of them?"

"Every last one, Deputy Section Chief. Ranging in ages, I'd say, from late teens to early thirties."

Mei-Ling glanced at Li. "A sexual motive?"

"Too early to say, Miss Nien. We're still trying to figure out which bits go with which." He stopped at one of the tables and waved his cigarette towards a partially decomposed head, black holes where the eyes should have been. Li noticed that a "Y" incision had been made in the torso beneath it, and ribs cut open to expose the chest cavity. "As you can see, decomposition is well under way," Lan said. "Only somebody very close to this young lady might be able to make a visual identification. It's also making visual matching of the pieces virtually impossible. We're comparing the bone ends where the limbs have been hacked off – we x-rayed all the pieces as they came down in the bags. But the best bet is DNA comparison. I've had small sections of skeletal muscle cut away from each of the body parts and sent on ice to the lab. Once we've found and matched all the bits, I'll have the assembled parts of each body sent over to the mortuary and put in separate drawers in the chiller."

"Can you say how long they'd been buried?" Li asked.

"Not with any degree of accuracy. But if you want to put your hand inside one of the body cavities, Detective, you'll find that it's pretty cold in there."

"I'll take your word for it," Li said. "What's the significance?"

Lan grinned. "I'd say they'd been frozen. If you examine the bits closely you'll find signs of freezer burn on the flesh. They were probably buried straight from the freezer. The most dense pieces, the torsos, are almost, but not quite, fully defrosted. Given that they were only two to three feet down, they were probably buried about four or five days ago."

"So it's going to be impossible to determine time of death."

Lan laughed. "I see you've inherited your uncle's penchant for stating the obvious, Mr. Li."

Li stiffened. "You knew him?"

"Of course."

"My uncle used to say, Doctor, that it is the obvious which is most often overlooked. It's one of the things that made him such a good cop."

The pathologist guffawed and began choking on the smoke from his cigarette. Noisily he hawked the loose phlegm from his lungs and spat it out on the floor. When he recovered his breath he looked at Li, dark eyes twinkling behind the slits. "I see you've inherited more than just his pedantry."

"So you'll understand if I continue with the pedantic theme of time of death."

But Lan was intent on taking his time. He lit another cigarette and threw away the old one before he said, "They could have been in the freezer for weeks, or months, Deputy Section Chief. In all likelihood they were killed at different times and put into cold storage. There's no way to determine when any of them died."

Mei-Ling said, "But you will be able to determine cause of death?"

"Most likely, Miss Nien, once we've done the autopsies." He took a long pull on his cigarette and peeled it away from his lips. "The only trouble is, someone's been there before us."

"What do you mean?" Li asked.

Lan clamped his cigarette between his lips again. "Just what I say, Detective. At least partial autopsies were carried out on every one of these poor ladies before they were put in the freezer."

Outside, night had fallen, and the bleak, dark concrete landscape of Lujiazui had been transformed into a multi-coloured light show. The Pearl TV Tower and a vast globe at its base were floodlit green. Those forlorn and empty office blocks Li had seen an hour before, now soared proudly into the night sky, glowing orange, yellow, green and blue. Upriver to the south, a permanently anchored cruise ship which was now a bar and night club, burned fluorescent turquoise, painted against the blackness of the night as if by a Disney animator. Across the river the Bund blazed in luminous splendour, architectural details picked out by carefully contrived lighting. And along the curve of the north bank, where cruise ships docked at the international passenger terminal, glass buildings fired up the night, competing with gigantic neon hoardings that burned ads for beer and cars and TVs into the sky. On the river, the lights of cruisers, ferries and barges cast broken reflections on choppy waters, while above them a brightly lit dirigible advertising cigarettes plied up and down between the coloured beams of powerful searchlights that raked randomly across the sky.

Li gaped at it in wonder. It did not seem quite real. Beijing had blazed with lights on the fiftieth anniversary of the People's Republic, but it had been nothing like this. Mei-Ling smiled at him, as though he were some bumpkin up from the country. And in some ways he was. Beijing was the capital, the centre of art and culture in the north. But it was staid and conservative compared with the commercial excesses of the south. "It's like this every night?" he asked, wondering what the cost of it all must be.

She nodded. "Until ten. Then it's lights out and the city comes to life in another way altogether." Which sounded ominous to Li, and for a moment he felt a fleeting insecurity. He missed the safe, comforting familiarity of Beijing. Shanghai was as alien to him as Hong Kong or Chicago had been.

Mei-Ling drove them back through the tunnel and up on to the Yan'an Viaduct, and they swept west through the city, turning then on to Nanbei Gaojia Road, another multi-lane viaduct that cut north to the long arc of the northern ring road. Li sat in silence, barely taking in the city lights or the long lines of commuter traffic. He thought of the eighteen women sliced up and laid out on trestle tables in the concrete tomb of an underground car park. Someone had murdered them, coldly and clinically, and then performed autopsies on the bodies before crudely dismembering them and freezing the parts. Then sometime within the past week, the frozen remains had been buried in a shallow grave on a building site where tons of concrete should have entombed them for eternity. There were similarities with the body they'd found in Beijing, although Li was not convinced yet that they had died by the same hand. But what he knew with absolute certainty was that when he went to bed tonight and closed his eyes, each and every one of them would be there, seared into his memory, sightless eyes appealing for him to find their killer. And the smell of their poor decaying bodies would be with him for days.

He had a thought and turned to Mei-Ling. "Whoever dumped the bodies knew that the site was about to be buried in concrete. That must narrow the numbers."

She said, "The joint venture was big news here. Press and TV had been covering the story for days. Discounting children and old folk, that would narrow it down to about ten million people."

The bell that dangled from the rear-view mirror chimed as Mei-Ling turned the Santana off the Zhongshan Beiyi expressway and then doubled back beneath the overhead road to turn right into the headquarters of the Criminal Investigation Department. They stopped at a white-marble gatehouse opposite the large gold numerals, 803, mounted on an angled wall, and suspicious eyes peered out at them from behind brightly lit windows. Then a wave of recognition as Mei-Ling smiled out of the driver's side, and the gate concertina-ed. open to let them through stone columns into a paved courtyard bounded by well-kept flower beds and neatly trimmed trees. Raised on a plinth was an ebony bust of a famous Shanghai detective, Duanmu Hongyu, now deceased. Multi-storeyed pink-tiled buildings rose up on three sides.

Mei-Ling glanced hesitantly at Li, then said, "Don't expect a very warm welcome in here."

Li was not entirely surprised. "Is there a problem?" he asked.

"Not exactly." She seemed a little embarrassed. "Just that some people figure we don't need help from Beijing to solve crimes in Shanghai."

"And your boss?"

She shrugged. "Don't take it personally. He's a little distracted these days."

She pulled up outside a covered entrance opposite a wall on which large gold characters urged officers to extremes of courage and dedication in their pursuit of justice. They took the lift up to the third floor where pale-faced detectives wilted under fluorescent lights in the pursuit of the killer or killers of eighteen women.

The detectives' room was crowded, a buzz of telephones and conversations, the clack of keyboards, the hum of computer terminals. Officers looked up curiously from their desks as Mei-Ling led Li through to the office of the Section Chief. The door stood ajar. She knocked and Li followed her in. The room was in darkness except for the bright ring of light cast on the desk by an Anglepoise lamp. A man of medium height and stocky build stood by the desk speaking on the telephone.

The reflected light from the desk cast a slightly sinister uplight on his shadowed face. He flicked nervous watery eyes towards Li and Mei-Ling as they entered.

"So what's the prognosis?" he asked his caller, turning his back on the two deputy section chiefs. "Well, when will you know?" The response clearly did not please him and he said curtly, "Well, call me when you've talked to him." He hung up abruptly and turned back to Li and Mei-Ling, and Li saw that he was a good-looking man of about forty-five, with thick hair swept back from a square face. But he looked drawn and tired.

"How is she?" Mei-Ling asked softly.

He shook his head. "Not good."

Mei-Ling nodded and said, "Tsuo, this is Deputy Section Chief Li from Beijing. Mr. Li, this is my boss, Huang Tsuo, Chief of Section Two." As the two men shook hands she added, "We're roughly the equivalent of your Section One, investigating serious crime, murder and robbery."

Huang's handshake was cold and cursory. He barely met Li's eyes before he turned to his deputy. "Mei-Ling, I want a full briefing meeting when Mr. Li and I get back." He lifted a briefcase from his desk and took his coat from a stand by the door.

Mei-Ling was caught off-balance. "Get back? Where are you going?"

"We have an appointment with the Mayor's policy adviser." And he ushered Li out of the door.

People's Square, which once formed part of the old Shanghai racecourse, was ablaze with lights reflecting from every wet surface, as if it had just been freshly painted. The drum-shaped museum on the south side glowed orange. Directly opposite, and dominating the square, was the huge floodlit home of the

Shanghai Municipal Government, a monumental white building studded by row upon rising row of featureless windows. It was flanked on each side by bizarrely shaped glass buildings lit from within and capped by fantastical sweeping roofs. Vast skyscrapers, washed in coloured light, crowded all around the square. Li and Huang stepped out of their car at the foot of steps leading up to the marbled entrance of the government building, and Li was immediately assaulted by a cacophony of sound: the roar of traffic and honking of horns; pop music blasting out of shops along the east side; the soundtrack of a movie playing on a giant TV screen that filled the whole of one side of an office block on the south-east corner; a foxtrot playing from a ghetto-blaster on the steps of the museum, a gathering of elderly couples dancing incongruously across the concourse below it. They didn't appear to mind the rain which wept still out of the night sky. The metallic voice of a conductress rang out from the loudspeaker of a passing bus. A taxi pulled up across the road, and as the driver reset his flag a soft electronic female voice said in English, *Dear passenger, thank you for using our taxi. Please come again.*

It was all in stark contrast to the tense silence that had filled the car on the twenty-minute drive from 803. Li had made several attempts to engage Huang in conversation only to be rewarded with grudging, monosyllabic responses and the odd grunt. He was no nearer now to discovering why the Mayor's policy adviser wanted to see them than when they had left.

He followed Huang up the steps, past armed guards and through glass doors into an expansive lobby. A group of around a dozen men in suits and wearing heavy dark coats was advancing towards them. At the head of the group was a man Li recognised. He had seen him on television and in newspaper photographs, a short, bull-headed man with close-cropped steel grey hair. There was a sense of power and energy in every confident step he took. A taller, slightly older man in the uniform of a Procurator General, was stooping to speak quietly in his ear as they approached. Neither missed a stride, and as the group reached Li and Huang the short man said, "You're late, Huang."

"My apologies, Director Hu. We were held up in traffic." Li had to admire the way Huang could lie to one of the most powerful men in Shanghai without batting an eyelid.

"Well, I can't wait. I have another engagement. You'll have to come with us." And he sailed past them and out on to the steps. The Procurator General flicked his head to indicate Li and Huang should follow, and they fell in with the rest of the entourage.

As they descended the steps, a line of official cars drew in at the sidewalk, headed by a black stretch limo flanked by two police cars. And as Director Hu slipped into the limo, the rest of the group divided as if in well-rehearsed syncopation and jumped into the other vehicles. Li and Huang found themselves ushered into the Director's car by the Procurator General, who got in after them. The line of cars pulled away accompanied by the sound of police sirens, muffled by the soundproofing in the limo. Li barely had time to draw breath, and realise that he was sitting facing Director Hu, before the chief adviser to the head of the Shanghai government reached out his hand. "Deputy Section Chief Li Yan," he said, "it is a privilege to meet you." Li shook his hand and reminded himself that this man was the confidant and adviser to a possible future leader of China. The immediate predecessors of his boss as Mayor of Shanghai were now the country's President and Premier respectively.

"I am honoured that you should even know who I am, Director Hu," Li said, and he remembered the Chinese proverb, *the nail that sticks up gets hammered down.*

"You cast a large shadow, Detective Li. Big enough, perhaps, to eclipse that of your uncle."

"I have always lived in my uncle's shadow, Director Hu. I expect always to do so."

The adviser nodded, satisfied. Modesty was a virtue. He waved a hand in the direction of the taller man beside him. "This is Procurator General Yue." The Procurator General inclined his head in a curt, cold nod. "You have visited the site where the bodies were found?"

"I have seen the bodies, or the bits of them that have been recovered."

"And what are your thoughts?"

Li hesitated. He felt as if he were being tested somehow. "It is too early to reach any conclusions, Director Hu."

The adviser nodded again, apparently satisfied by this response. "A single word is worth a thousand pieces of gold," he said. He glanced momentarily at Huang who sat mute diagonally opposite, a black hole of disapproval in the corner of the car. "This . . . incident . . ." the adviser was picking his words very carefully, "is not only a severe embarrassment to our country, Li, captured as it was on live television across the world, but it could also seriously damage Shanghai's inward investment – the lifeblood of this city." Li wondered if anyone cared about the serious damage done to the health of the victims, but he knew better than to ask as much. The adviser continued, "What we have here is a high profile crime of appalling magnitude, uncovered in the full glare of world publicity. What the Mayor wants is a high profile solution in the shortest possible time, and in the full glare of the same publicity." He drew in a short breath. "Which is why he wants you to take charge of the investigation."

And Li understood immediately why Huang was so resentful of his presence, and why Procurator General Yue was being equally cool.

"Of course, Director Hu," he said cautiously, "I would be only too happy to assist in the investigation. But, naturally, I will have to seek permission from my superiors in Beijing."

The Director waved his hand dismissively. "It's already done, Li," he said. "The Commissioner of Police in Beijing is happy to lend you to us for the duration of the investigation." He leaned forward. "But we don't want you assisting. The Mayor wants you to lead the inquiry. Which means he will hold you personally responsible for any failure to bring it to a satisfactory conclusion."

Li knew now that he *was* that nail that sticks up, and it felt like a very lonely thing to be. He said, "In that case, I have one request, Director Hu."

"Speak," the Director said.

"I have had only the briefest opportunity to make an assessment of this case, but it seems to me that because of its nature, the pathology will be of paramount importance. I would therefore ask that I am allowed to employ the services of the American pathologist, Margaret Campbell."

Huang immediately started to voice his protest, becoming animated for the first time, but the Director raised a hand to silence him. "Why?" he asked Li.

Li said, "While I have every confidence in Dr. Lan, Miss Campbell is infinitely more experienced. The Americans, after all, are more practised in the art of murder." Which raised a smile from the Director for the first time. Li pressed on, "She has worked in China, so she knows how we operate." He paused. "And if you want a high-profile solution, then a high-profile collaboration between the Chinese and the Americans would be good public relations."

The Director sat back and smiled. "I'm glad to see we're on the same wavelength, Li. Huang and Yue will facilitate all your requirements."

Huang and Yue looked as if they would like to facilitate Li's speedy demise.

The Director pressed a button and told his driver to pull over. The driver informed the police escort by radio, then pulled the car in at the side of the road. The entourage followed suit. "Good luck," the Director said to Li as the door sprang open, and Li realised he was expected to get out.

He stepped out into the rain, followed by Huang. The pavement was crowded with curious on-lookers, the deafening blare of police sirens filling the night air. Director Hu's entourage of cars moved off again and Li looked at Huang. "What now?"

"We get a taxi back to my car," Huang said through clenched teeth, and he pulled up his collar against the rain. "And I don't give a shit what Director Hu says. You report to me. Understood?"

CHAPTER TWO

I

The briefing meeting lasted less than half an hour. Before it, Li had had a fifteen minute meeting with Huang and the Shanghai Deputy Commissioner of Police, finalising details of Margaret's inclusion in the investigating team. He had then requested the use of a computer with Internet access and filed a lengthy e-mail to an aol.com address.

There were nearly twenty detectives in the meeting room, ranged around a group of tables pushed together to make a large rectangle. Most of the officers were smoking, and their smoke filled the room like fog. Mei-Ling glanced curiously at Li and Huang as they made their entrance. She had not been made privy to their discussions with the Deputy Commissioner. But she showed no surprise when Huang announced that he was putting Li in charge of the investigation, in collaboration with his deputy. All eyes around the table flickered towards Li, eyes that harboured both interest and hostility. There was no love lost between Shanghai and Beijing.

The briefing consisted of an update on what little they already knew. Statements were quickly accumulating, taken from everybody who had been at the ceremony at Lujiazui that morning. One of the detectives had discovered that there was a night watchman at the site. They had made every attempt to locate him during the day, without success, but he was due back on-site at seven. A number of detectives consulted their watches and realised it was already past that. Mei-Ling brought the meeting up to date on the body count, and Dr. Lan's initial thoughts. The fact that partial autopsies had already been carried out on the victims created quite a stir around the table. But there were no constructive suggestions.

Li then took control. He looked at the rows of guarded eyes looking back at him. He fumbled in his pockets. "Anyone got a cigarette? I seem to have run out." Several of the officers nearest him immediately held out packs. "Okay," he said. "So now we know who the brown-noses are." There was a big laugh around the table, except from those holding out the packs. Li grinned. "Only kidding, guys." And he took a cigarette from the nearest pack, and everyone was aware of an immediate easing of the tension in the room. He lit up and leaned forward on his elbows. "If I was a betting man," he said, "which of course I'm not, because it's illegal . . ." which got another laugh, "I'd put my money on finding most of our victims in the missing persons files. So it would probably be a good start if we got hold of those files and extracted details on all women between the ages of, say, fifteen and forty. We're not going to know who killed them, or why, until we know who they are. So our priority should be trying to identify them as quickly as possible. And here's a thought . . ." You could have heard a pin drop in the silence. "We found eighteen bodies in a mass grave today. But there could be other graves, other bodies. And there might be other women going about their everyday lives as we sit here, who're going to end up in one of those graves. So we owe it as much to the living, as to the dead, to get this guy as quickly as we can."

When the meeting broke up, Huang hurried out without even looking at Li. Mei-Ling approached him. "Well done," she said. "That could have been nasty." He grinned and took out a pack of cigarettes, and lit one. She smiled. "I thought you'd run out."

"They were in an inside pocket." As an afterthought he held out the pack towards her. "I'm sorry, do you smoke?"

She shook her head. "I've seen first hand what it does to the lungs." She paused. "So what now?"

"I'd like to go back to the site. See if that night watchman's shown up yet."

When they arrived back at Lujiazui, the officer on duty at the gate told them that the night watchman had turned up about half an hour earlier and was ensconced in his hut on the far side of the site.

Pathologists and forensics experts still sweated in white plastic suits beneath the floodlights and the polythene sheeting in their gruesome search for any remaining body parts. Digging in the wet, nearly liquid, mud was close to impossible. For several minutes Li stopped and watched their thankless labours, aware of the presence of Mei-Ling's burning, unasked questions at his side. In the car, she had resisted the temptation to ask about the meeting with Director Hu, and afterwards with the Deputy Commissioner. But now she was barely able to contain her curiosity. He turned and caught her watching him. Rain glistened on her face in the light of the flood lamps and he thought how attractive she was. "I guess it wasn't Huang's idea to put you in charge of the investigation," she said. It didn't sound like a question to Li.

"I think Huang would have been happier to bury me in the mud with the CEO of the New York bank," he said.

Mei-Ling shrugged. "Like I said, don't take it personally. Huang has problems right now."

"Yeah, like an extreme loss of face." Li was treading carefully. He had no idea how loyal, or otherwise, Mei-Ling might be to her boss. "It must be pretty humiliating to have the Mayor's policy adviser appoint a junior officer over your head."

Mei-Ling chewed her lower lip thoughtfully. "But I doubt if losing face means much next to losing the person you love," she said.

Li frowned. "What do you mean?"

"I mean that his wife's terminally ill. And from the sound of it, I don't think she has long to live. So don't flatter yourself, you probably don't come very high on his list of priorities at the moment."

Li lit a cigarette and drew on it thoughtfully. It certainly explained, if not exactly justifying, the man's lack of courtesy. "Let's go talk to the night watchman," he said.

They picked their way through the mud and puddles to a small blue-painted wooden hut at the rear of the site. A light blazed at the window, and through it they could see a young man leaning back in an old wooden armchair, feet up on the table, nursing a jar of cold green tea and watching a small portable television. He stood up as soon as they came in, apparently excited by their visit. He drew up two stools for them to sit on, but Li declined the offer. "I don't mind answering anything you want to ask," the watchman said. "I told the cops I spoke to when I arrived everything I know, but I want to help any way I can. You want some tea?"

Li shook his head and drew on his cigarette. "You worked here long?"

"Only for a couple of months, since they started delivering materials to the site." The young man waved a finger at Li's cigarette. "Those things'll kill you, you know. You ever seen the inside of a smoker's lungs?"

Li glanced at Mei-Ling, the echo of her earlier words resonating silently between them. Then he took a good look at the night watchman. He figured the boy was no more than twenty-one or twenty-two. He wore jeans and good boots, and a warm winter coat over a heavy jumper. A pair of thermal gloves lay on the table beside a pile of magazines. There was no heating in the hut.

"And you have seen the inside of a smoker's lungs?" Mei-Ling asked.

"Sure," the young man said. "They're all black and full of holes and kind of slimy and pickled-looking. Put me off smoking for life."

"And how would *you* get to look at the inside of someone's lungs?" Li said.

"Easy. You always section the lungs when you do an autopsy." He grinned at their consternation. "Hey," he said, "night watchman on a building site is not my idea of a career plan."

Li said, "And what is your career plan?"

"Surgery. Or pathology. I haven't quite decided yet. But probably pathology. That way I get trained in forensics, too, and get to work with you guys on cases like this. Spooky stuff, huh?"

Li and Mei-Ling exchanged glances. "Are you saying you're a doctor?" Li asked.

"Medical student," the young man said. "At Shanghai Medical University, out in Xuhui District." He put out his hand to shake theirs. "Jiang Baofu," he said. "I heard what had happened earlier today. The university was buzzing with it. I couldn't wait to get back here tonight. But they won't let me see anything." He seemed disappointed. "You know, I nearly stayed on this morning to watch the ceremony. But we had practical surgery today, and I never miss that."

"So this is just part-time?" Li said.

"Sure," said Jiang. "I'm not like some of those rich kids at the university. My parents died when I was just young. I live with my grandparents back home, and no way can they afford to put me through med school. I work nights and holidays, anything I can get. Usually at one of the hospitals, but this paid better." He waved his hand vaguely at the window. "Not that anyone's going to steal anything here. But the Americans are fussy about security. That's why the money's so good."

Mei-Ling said, "Clearly, then, they didn't get their money's worth when the night watchman didn't even notice someone digging a hole big enough to dump eighteen bodies in."

The medical student looked hurt. "Hey, how am I supposed to keep an eye on the whole place? It's pitch black out there after ten at night. They don't even give me a flashlight."

"But whoever buried those bodies must have had light to work by. You'd have seen that surely?" Mei-Ling's directness impressed Li.

"Not if I was sleeping." Jiang was getting defensive now.

"But weren't you supposed to be on watch?" Mei-Ling wasn't going to let him off the hook. "I mean, isn't that what a night watchman's supposed to do? Watch?"

"Maybe he was too busy watching TV," Li said. He glanced at the set, which was tuned in to the Hong Kong music channel, "V." "How come they don't give you a flashlight but they provide you with a television set?"

Jiang laughed. "They didn't provide the TV! That's mine."

"So you watch TV all night?" Mei-Ling said.

"Until about twelve. Then, usually, I sleep for a few hours."
He glanced from one to the other, absorbing their disapproval.
"Hey, I said they paid better than the hospital, but not enough
to stay awake all night. I've got to work all day, too, you know."

"So you didn't notice anything unusual in the last week?"

"No, I didn't. And if I had, I'd have told your people when
I got here. Look . . ." he was anxious to justify himself, "usually I get here about seven, do a tour of the site, then lock the
gate. I do another check around before the lights go off at ten.
Then the only light out there is from the streetlights way over
on the far side – and most of that's still in shadow because
of the wall."

"What about the workers' huts over there?" Li asked.

"What about them?"

"That's their accommodation during construction, isn't it?"

"Yeah, but there's nobody living there yet. Won't be until
they start the construction proper and take on crew. Then there
won't be any need for me."

Mei-Ling perched on the edge of the table and looked at
the magazines Jiang had been reading. "*Human Pathology*," she
read out in English and looked at the student. "Where did you
get these?"

"Subscription," he said. "It's an American journal. They
send it every month." And then, again, defensively, "I'm interested. It's my subject."

Li said, "Interested enough to go abducting young women
and practising your technique on them?"

Jiang grinned. "Hey, now you're joking, right?" But Li
didn't smile and Jiang's grin faded. "I didn't kill anybody. The
only people I've ever cut up were on the practice slab at the

university." He paused and leaned forward confidentially. "One of your guys told me they'd been hacked to pieces – the bodies out there. Is that right?"

Li thought the boy's relish was unhealthy. "You shouldn't go listening to gossip," he said. "Or repeating it."

Mei-Ling took out a business card, scored her name off it and wrote in another. She handed it to Jiang. "Go to 803 Zhong-shan Beiyi Road first thing tomorrow morning and ask for Detective Dai. He'll take your statement."

"I've got classes tomorrow," the student protested.

"Be there," Mei-Ling said, and she stood up to open the door.

Li said, "One last thing. Where do you live, Jiang?"

"I got a place up near Jiangwan Stadium."

"No, I mean where's your home? Where do you come from?"

"Yanqing, in Hebei Province."

"That's just north of Beijing, isn't it?"

The boy nodded, and as they turned to go, added, "Listen, if your people need any help, the pathologists or anyone . . . If they're looking for assistants or anything, you know, I'm happy to volunteer my services. It'd be good experience."

"We'll keep that in mind," Li said.

As they crossed the site towards the main gate, Mei-Ling said, "That boy's really creepy!" But Li was lost in thought. She glanced at him. "You all right?"

He said, "This kid lives with his grandparents, who can't afford to send him to university. So he has to take on all these part-time jobs and work the holidays. But he can afford a colour TV set. And that was good quality gear he was wearing. Expensive gloves lying on the table. And it must be pretty costly to subscribe to an American medical journal and have it sent to China every month."

"What are you saying?" Mei-Ling asked.

"I'm saying here's a kid who has the requisite skills to do what was done to those women. He had the opportunity to dispose of their bodies right here on the site where he's working as night watchman. And he seems very affluent for a student who's having to work his way through medical school."

"You don't think *he* did it, do you?" Mei-Ling was shocked. "I mean, I know he's weird, but usually I have an instinct about these things, and right now it isn't telling me this is our killer."

"Neither is mine," Li confessed, and he knew it would have been just too easy. "But if someone broke into the site, dug a hole and buried eighteen bodies in it, why didn't he see them? Why didn't he hear them? And why would someone dump the bodies some place there was a night watchman?" He lit a cigarette. "I know it's early in the investigation, but I think our medical student's got to be the first name on the suspect list."

"Maybe," Mei-Ling said. "Anyway, we'll have a better idea just what we're looking for once we've got the autopsy reports."

"That might be a few days," Li said.

Mei-Ling was surprised. "Why? Dr. Lan can start tomorrow."

Li said, "I'm bringing in another pathologist to do the autopsies."

She was taken aback, and stopped suddenly, feet squelching in the mud. "Does Dr. Lan know?"

Li shook his head. "No. And he probably won't be very pleased."

"No, he won't," Mei-Ling said. "Talk about losing face . . ." She paused. "Who is it? Someone from Beijing?"

"An American," Li said. He took in her expression. "Oh, I know. I got the same speech from Huang. How the Chinese don't need the Americans to show them how to do anything."

Mei-Ling shrugged. "Jiang Zemin said we must learn from foreign experts."

Li looked to see if she was sending him up, but she appeared perfectly serious. "I've worked with her before," he said, "and she's *very* experienced."

Mei-Ling started for the gates again and said, a little too casually, "She?"

"Margaret Campbell," Li said. "She's been lecturing at the Public Security University in Beijing."

Mei-Ling nodded but said nothing, and they continued picking their way through the mud.

They passed the lights, and the polythene flapping in the wind. Li caught sight of the face of one of the forensics people working in the mud. A young man, his face almost blue with the cold, pinched and distressed. He would never have envisaged this when making his career choice. And Li had a sudden sense of the futility of all their jobs, working as they did on the edge of sanity, picking their way through the dark side of the human psyche, and all the horrors that lay therein.

Mei-Ling suddenly lost her footing in the quagmire and, with a cry, almost fell. Li caught her arm and held her firmly until she regained her balance. She laughed, embarrassed, clutching his jacket, and he felt the swelling of her breast against the back of his hand.

"Careful," Li said, suddenly self-conscious. "You almost dropped your half of the sky. Just as well there was a man around to catch you."

"Oh, you men are so versatile," Mei-Ling said, smiling. "You can hold up your half of the sky and pick up women at the same time." She steadied herself and checked her watch. "Nearly eight. You won't have eaten."

"Not since this morning."

"Me neither. If you're hungry, I know a place that serves till late."

"I'm starving," Li said.

She smiled, her dark eyes gleaming. "Good. Let's go."

II

Margaret had heard the news the previous night about the discovery of a mass grave on a building site in Shanghai. She had seen the pictures on CNN, and watched with interest and a slightly remote sense of horror. She did not make any connection with Li, there was no reason why she should. But it had aroused her professional interest. Since the first pictures had come through, the Chinese authorities had imposed a media black-out, much to the annoyance of the news networks. But this morning, statements issued by the New York bank involved were generating plenty of copy, and one of the associates had got an exclusive interview with the CEO who had taken the mud bath with the bodies. There was no accurate information about how many corpses had been recovered from the site, but the CEO's description of his experience had been fairly lurid – arms, legs, torsos, heads. Margaret felt a pang of regret that she was not involved.

She lay in bed watching the re-runs of the story on breakfast news. Whatever her mother might think, it was her job, and she missed doing it. She missed China. She missed Li. And still she had not summoned the courage to go to her apartment in Lincoln Park. It was symbolic, somehow, of another life, another Margaret Campbell, someone else whom she used to be and didn't wish to revisit. But she couldn't just leave the place to gather dust, junk mail accumulating with the neighbours, pot plants dead in the kitchen sink. If her encounter with David the other night had taught her anything, it was that there was no refuge in the past. Whatever direction she chose to take, she had to move on.

She found herself looking at a photograph on screen of a young woman with short-cut fair hair. For a disconcerting moment, the face seemed uncannily familiar, before she realised with a start that she was looking at herself. She sat bolt upright, heart pounding. It was her all right. A few years younger, though. A stock photograph taken at the time she assisted on the autopsies at Waco. The TV announcer was saying, "... *American pathologist, Margaret Campbell. The authorities in Shanghai have, this morning, taken the unusual step of issuing a Press Release announcing the invitation. Dr. Campbell, who has worked previously with police in the Chinese capital of Beijing, grabbed headlines worldwide eighteen months ago when she issued a warning on the Internet about genetically contaminated rice. Latest reports from Shanghai, where it is now nine in the evening, suggest that the body count has risen to eighteen.*" The report switched from news to weather, and Margaret sat very still on the bed, her heart pounding. She was confused, disorientated. From somewhere in the house came the distant ringing of a telephone. Why would the authorities in Shanghai ask for her help? She didn't know anyone there.

Then she was struck by a thought. E-mail. In the last few months, she had introduced Li to the delights of e-mail as a fast and direct means of communication. He had written to her almost every day since she left to go to her father's funeral. She leapt out of bed and quickly crossed the room to the dresser where she had set up her iBook laptop computer. She wakened it out of sleep mode and went on-line. Her e-mail software scanned her electronic mailbox before downloading "one of one," and a soft female voice told her she had mail. She double-clicked on an e-mail titled *Autopsies*. It was from Li.

There was a knock at her bedroom door and her mother entered in her housecoat. "Margaret, did you know you're on television? Diane just phoned to say she'd seen your picture."

Margaret was scanning Li's e-mail with increasing excitement and waved her mother to be quiet. But her mother was not to be put off. She advanced into the room.

"For God's sake what are you doing, Margaret? Why are they running your picture on television?" Margaret wheeled around and her mother frowned at her. "For Heaven's sake cover yourself up."

Margaret realised she was stark naked, and was immediately embarrassed in front of her mother. She snatched her robe and pulled it on. "I'm going back to China," she said.

"Did I ever think you were going to do anything else?"

"Frankly, Mom, I don't care what you thought. I hadn't made any decisions about my future. Until now. They want me to do the autopsies on those bodies they found in Shanghai."

Her mother's mouth curled in distaste. "I'll never understand you, Margaret. I never have."

"And you never will." Margaret paused. "Mom . . . I don't want to fight with you."

"Oh, don't worry," her mother said coldly. "I wouldn't give you the pleasure." She turned to go, but stopped at the door. "And when is it you intend leaving? Just so I can be sure the maid has your laundry ready."

"This afternoon," Margaret said, and she thought she detected a reaction, like a stoic response to a slap when you don't want to show how much it has hurt. And she wondered what her mother had expected, why she had talked David into trying to persuade her to stay. Surely she hadn't thought some kind of reconciliation was possible after all these years of dislocation? And yet, she saw the hurt in her mother's eyes, and for a moment had an urge to cross the bedroom and throw her arms around her and just hold her, as if that could somehow wipe away all the cruel words, the barbs and the battles. But she didn't do anything, and her mother turned and walked out of the room, pulling the door shut behind her.

Margaret turned back to the computer and re-read Li's e-mail, more slowly this time. He signed off, as he always did, with three simple words. *I love you.*

III

Mei-Ling steered Li through the crowds that thronged the narrow streets leading to the heart of the Chinese old town, streets that were alive with traders selling all manner of cooked and cold foods from barrows and braziers, street vendors trading in everything from chopsticks to walking sticks, silks to silverware. Shiny wet cobbled streets ran off to left and right, lit by neon strips and long slabs of bright yellow light flooding out from dozens of shop fronts. Banners and lanterns waved in the breeze. They passed a window where two women in white coats and chef's hats were making dumplings, folding tasty nuts of spiced minced meat into rolled-out circles of dough for steaming. A crowd was gathered to watch them, hungry eyes following every move.

"This was all slum land until just a few years ago," Mei-Ling said. "They've spent a fortune restoring it." A narrow tunnel ran off an alleyway, and beyond it Li saw the lights of a Buddhist temple, incense burning at the altar, saffron-robed monks moving about in the dull light of an interior room.

The street opened out into a packed square, the four-storeyed Green Wave restaurant dominating the far side and looming over the five-sided Huxinting teahouse which sat in the middle of a rectangular lake, bounded on one side by the walls of the ancient Yu gardens. Every sweep of curling eave was outlined in yellow neon against a black night sky. The teahouse was packed, hundreds of faces crammed together in lit windows, sipping tea and smoking and watching the crowds outside. A zigzagging bridge crossed the water to its main entrance. "The bridge of nine turnings," Mei-Ling said. "To keep out the evil spirits. Apparently they can't turn corners." She laughed, and Li was affected by her enthusiasm.

"Shanghai your home town?" he asked.

"Is it that obvious?" Her eyes sparkled in the flickering neon light.

"There's a pride you only ever take in showing off the place you come from."

"Actually my family come from Hangzhou, which is a couple of hours away. We have a saying, maybe you know it. Above there is Heaven, and on earth there is Hangzhou and Suzhou. But I was born right here in Shanghai and it's my idea of heaven. I wouldn't ever want to leave it." She smiled. "Come on." And she slipped her arm through his to lead him across the square. It was a completely natural and unselfconscious act, far too intimate for two people who had just met. She realised it almost immediately and withdrew her arm quickly, blushing and trying to pretend it had never happened. "I thought we'd eat at the Green Wave," she said hurriedly to mask her discomfort. "If we can get a window seat on the third floor we'll get a view out over the tearoom and the lake."

For Li, it had all happened so fast it was over almost before he realised, and he knew at once that it was an act of intimacy she was accustomed to indulging in with someone else, someone who, in a dangerous moment, she had mixed up with Li.

What was more disconcerting to him, was the tiny frisson of pleasure it had given him.

The third-floor salon was still busy, waitresses in traditional full-length *qipao* dresses flitting between pillars and among tables, feeding dish after dish on to Lazy Susans on banqueting tables, delivering plates of food and glasses of beer to more intimate tables of fours and twos. Mei-Ling acquired them a table by an open window with the view over the tearoom she had hoped for. Above the chattering at the tables, and the crowd out in the streets, the sound of running water filled the air from a fountain on the lake. Mei-Ling ordered for both of them, half a dozen dishes and half litres of Tsing Tao beer.

"So what's the story with your American pathologist?" she asked out of the blue.

Li felt himself blushing. "What do you mean?"

"You said you'd worked with her before."

"That's right." He wondered why he was being evasive.

"Well, is it just a professional relationship . . . or is there something personal as well?"

Li chose his words carefully. "I make a point of never letting my personal life intrude on my job."

She laughed. "Which doesn't really answer my question."

He grinned. "So what would you say if I told you it was none of your business?"

"I'd say you were trying to pull the wool over my eyes and failing miserably."

He accepted defeat then, nodding reluctantly. "Okay, so we have a relationship that isn't exactly professional. But that had absolutely no bearing on my asking to have her brought into the investigation."

She leaned her elbows on the table and rested her chin in her cupped palms, smiling at him. "Pity."

"What is?"

"The most attractive men are always taken." But she didn't give him time to dwell on this. "Is she pretty?"

He shrugged. "I guess."

"I bet she's got blonde hair and blue eyes."

"Why would you think that?"

"Because if a Chinese man is going to have a relationship with an American woman, he's not going to pick one with black hair and brown eyes. China's full of them already."

Li cocked an eyebrow. "You disapprove?"

But she wouldn't commit herself. "Each to his own," she said, and turned to gaze out of the window. "I suppose men don't have the same choice these days, with so many fewer women to choose from in China." Li was not sure if there was a barb in this. It was true that with the One Child Policy, and so many women aborting baby girls when ultrasound tests revealed the sex of the foetus, the male population was rising in direct relation to the fall in the numbers of females. He decided to switch the focus of their conversation.

"That would work to your advantage then."

She looked at him.

"How's that?"

"Puts women in demand. Particularly if they're attractive, and intelligent as well."

She lowered her head and looked up at him with a demure smile. "You're not very subtle, Mr. Li."

He shook his head. "No, it's not something I've been accused of very often." And she laughed, and he found himself laughing with her. When the laughter died there was a moment, a temporary lull between them, and he said, "So . . . who's the lucky guy?"

Her face clouded immediately and she gave a noncommittal shrug. "There isn't one." And he knew that there was pain here, a raw nerve that he had touched, and that he should proceed with care.

"You live alone, then?"

"No." She shook her head. "I live with my family." He looked at her again, and tried to gauge her age. At least thirty, perhaps even thirty-five. She caught his look and smiled wryly. "Thirty-seven," she said, as if she had read his mind. "And, no, I've never married. Never wanted to."

"Never wanted a kid?"

"Sure. But I always thought I'd wait. Career first, then settle down and start a family." She gazed off ruefully into the middle distance. "But, then, you turn around and you're thirty. You turn around again and you're thirty-five. Suddenly you see forty on the horizon, and you begin to think you've missed your chance."

"Thirty-seven isn't so old," Li said. "It's never too late."

Her eyes flickered back to meet his. "Maybe not," she said.

The food arrived then. A plate of fried dumplings, brown and crispy with a soy and chilli dip. Spring rolls. A dish of chicken pieces in a very hot Sichuan sauce. Deep fried tofu in hot and sour sauce. Butterflied shrimp in batter. A bowl of noodles. They ate for a time in silence, chopsticks clicking. "This is great food," Li said.

"It is," she said. "But next time I'll take you somewhere better. Somewhere special. I just need more notice."

"Where's that?"

"Home." He paused with a shrimp caught in his chopsticks, midway between his plate and his mouth, which was open to receive it. She laughed, that strange braying laugh again that made him smile, too. "My father and my aunt own a restaurant," she said. "Nothing much to look at. A small family place tucked up a back alley near the Hilton. We may not be very grand, but we've got posh neighbours, and the food's fantastic."

Li popped the prawn in his mouth. "I'll look forward to it." He chewed thoughtfully for a moment. "Your father and your aunt?"

"My mother's dead. Has been for years. My dad's sister never married." She chuckled. "Maybe I take after her. Anyway, she's a sort of surrogate mom. My dad's brother's boy is the chef, and a couple of local girls come in to chop the veg. It's . . ." she searched for the right word to describe it, "cosy."

"I'll look forward to it," Li said.

They finished their beer and ordered more, and Mei-Ling said, "You never married either?"

He shook his head. "I'm like you. The job always came first."

"But you're younger than me."

"A little," he conceded.

"So did you never want a kid?"

For a moment or two he avoided her eye. Then he said, "In a way I've got one."

She was taken aback. "What do you mean?"

"My sister's kid, Xinxin. She's only six. But when her mom got pregnant again, then found it was a boy, she left Xinxin on my doorstep – almost literally. And she went off into hiding somewhere to have the boy she'd always dreamed of." He looked grim. "Sometimes I wonder if the One Child Policy doesn't create as many problems as it solves. All those unwanted little girls. All those kids growing up without brothers or sisters. A whole generation with no aunts or uncles."

"What about Xinxin's dad?"

"He didn't want to know. He'd wanted my sister to have an abortion, and when she ran off he just washed his hands of her and the kid."

"So you're bringing up the kid on your own?" Mei-Ling was incredulous.

He shrugged his frustration. "She stays in my apartment, but I have to make arrangements for someone to take her when I'm working, which can be all hours of the day or night."

"Who's looking after her now?"

Li said, "A friend. But it looks like I could be here for a while. So I'm going to have to try and make arrangements to bring her to Shanghai."

"Anything I can do to help . . ." She looked at him earnestly across the table, her sympathy written clearly on her face. "I mean it. I can get the department to fix things." She put her hand over his, and he smiled.

"Thanks." And he gave her hand a small squeeze of gratitude. It felt small and warm and smooth, and he was aware suddenly of how dry his mouth was.

Mei-Ling turned the Santana off the Bund into Yan'an Dong Road. The light show was over for the night, and the city looked very ordinary and dull under its pale yellow wash of sodium street lights. The river was extraordinarily black, a train of barges toiling upstream, its reflected lights scattering across the broken water. Mei-Ling drove west in the shadow of the viaduct road overhead before cutting left across the flow of traffic to pull up outside number 343, the Da Hu Hotel, yellow paint peeling off seven floors of anonymous concrete.

Above them, traffic roared past on the viaduct no more than six feet from the windows of the hotel's second floor. She smiled apologetically at Li in the passenger seat. "Cheap and cheerful," she said. "The best the department has to offer visiting cops. I'm sorry."

Li shrugged. "It's somewhere to lay my head."

There was an awkward moment between them then, when neither of them knew how to say goodnight. Finally she said, "I'll pick you up in the morning."

He said, "Thanks for tonight."

She said, "Shanghai hospitality. If I was to wait for a Beijinger to put his hand in his pocket I could grow old in the process." She reached across, and for a moment he thought she was going to kiss him. He moved quickly to avoid her, a knee-jerk reaction.

She laughed and said, "Hey, what are you so jumpy about?" And she unlocked the door to swing it open. "I don't usually attack men the day I meet them. Normally I wait till day two."

Li grinned stupidly, feeling very foolish. "I'd better wear my protective gear tomorrow, then."

She said, "You'd better believe it. Seven a.m. Sharp."

He slammed the door shut when he got out and went round to retrieve his bag from the trunk. She peeped the horn and pulled away with a squeal of tyres. He watched the car go for a minute, then walked under the overhang of the building to the hotel entrance, a revolving door of shiny chrome and glass. Inside, a girl in black at reception sat beneath a row of clocks showing the time around the world and watched unsmiling as he filled in his registration card.

His room was on the third floor, looking directly on to the traffic on the viaduct. He almost felt he could reach out and touch it. The room was basic but clean. A net curtain hung in the window. He pulled it aside and slid the window open and let in the cold night air and the growling of the traffic. The circular tower of the Agricultural Bank of China, still lit, punctured the sky. Out there, in this city of fourteen million, people made love and slept and ate and worked and died. He wondered how many felt as lonely and confused as he felt right now. He thought of Margaret arriving tomorrow, of those poor women in their collective grave, of Xinxin, and of the dangerous feelings that Mei-Ling had aroused. And he felt a wave of fatigue wash over him.

He slid the window closed, undressed and slipped between the cool starched sheets and drifted quickly away into a dark, dreamless sleep, the only escape he ever had from life.

CHAPTER THREE

I

Margaret was too tired to be excited. She had already crossed at least two timezones and an international dateline, and was not sure if she was arriving tomorrow or yesterday.

She looked out of the window at the featureless mud flats below as her plane circled in from the ocean and descended rapidly to the new international airport at the south-west extreme of Pudong New Area. From the air, the curved roofs of the terminal building looked like the outstretched wings of some giant bird in flight.

Inside the cavernous terminal, a high ceiling studded with lights reflected off a polished marble floor into an unfocused distance. Solitary travellers were dotted about among vacant rows of white seats, while cream columns soared up from an endless line of airline desks. The passengers from Margaret's flight, which had felt very crowded, were quickly dispersed and swallowed up in its vastness.

Margaret passed expeditiously through immigration. Her two heavy suitcases were already circling on the carousel when she reached it, and there was not a soul on duty at customs. On the sparsely populated concourse she looked around for signs in English, or a familiar face. She found neither. Only a group of elderly wide-eyed men and women in blue Mao suits, being shepherded around by a patient tour-guide wearing jeans and a tee-shirt emblazoned with the letters NYPD. Piped muzak somewhere in the background was playing "My Way."

"You know, you can always spot an American. They never travel light." The American accent drawling at her right ear made Margaret spin around, and she found herself looking into the smiling face of a man of around forty, boyish good looks below an untidy mop of hair that was quickly going grey. He nodded towards the travel-scarred cases on her trolley. "Bet they weigh a ton, too. You need a hand?"

"No, thank you," Margaret said curtly.

"Well, that's a relief," he said and held out his hand. "I'm Jack Geller." Very reluctantly she shook it. "Pleased to meet you, Miss Campbell."

Margaret was taken aback She couldn't believe that Li had sent this man to pick her up. He certainly didn't look like he had anything to do with the Chinese police. He wore baggy brown corduroys, a shapeless green jacket that had seen better days and a grey, open-necked shirt. "How do you know my name?" she said.

He grinned and pulled a rolled up newspaper from his jacket pocket and held it up so that it unravelled to reveal the front page. It was all in Chinese. But there, in the top right corner, was a large photograph of Margaret with short hair, the same one they had used on the TV news. "See, you're famous here already."

She regarded him suspiciously. "You weren't sent here to pick me up."

"No, that was my idea. But if you're expecting someone else, you know, you could be in for a long wait. Traffic in town just grinds to a halt sometimes, and we're a long way out. I, on the other hand, have a taxi waiting and would be happy to give you a ride."

"I don't think so," Margaret said. She paused. "Who exactly are you, Mr. Geller?"

He fished in an inside pocket and produced a dog-eared business card and presented it to Margaret in the Chinese fashion, holding the top two corners between thumb and forefinger and offering it with both hands so that it can be read by the recipient. Only it was in Chinese. Margaret flipped it over. On the other side it read: *JACK GELLER Freelance Journalist*, and listed his address, and home and mobile numbers. She sighed and handed it back. But he held up a hand, refusing to take it. "No, keep it. You never know when you might want to give me a call."

"I can't imagine a single circumstance," Margaret said with irritation, slipping it into her purse.

"That's a pity," he said. "I was hoping you might give me an interview, ahead of the pack."

"I won't be giving any interviews to anyone," Margaret said, and started pushing her trolley away from him.

"The taxi rank's the other way," he said.

Gathering as much dignity as she could, Margaret turned her trolley around and headed past him in the other direction. He tagged along beside her. "The foreign press here are going to be on your tail for as long as this investigation's on-going. You can make it easy on yourself, or hard." When she didn't respond, he said, "A contact here at the airport checked the manifests for me. So I knew what flight you were coming in on. I always figured initiative deserved reward."

"And I always thought," she said, "that the individual had a right to privacy."

"Hey, you're in China now," he said. "No such thing as the individual. And anyhow, in a kind of a way you're representing your country here. Freedom of information and all that."

"Like you said, Mr. Geller, we're in China now."

Glass doors slid open at their approach and Margaret pushed her trolley through them out on to a huge covered concourse, an empty four-lane highway running beyond it. Everywhere appeared deserted, apart from a short line of taxis at the far end. The lead driver looked hopefully in her direction, but she shook her head firmly.

"Well," Geller said, "I'd have thought if they were picking you up they'd have been here by now."

"They'll be here," Margaret said.

He shrugged. "I'll catch up with you later, then. At the Peace Hotel."

"Where?"

"The Peace Hotel. That's where you're staying, isn't it?"

"I have no idea."

"Well, take my word for it." He raised two fingers to his temple in a small salute, gave a slight nod and moved off towards the taxi rank.

Margaret stood for a quarter of an hour watching the rain fall on the empty road, growing colder and more irritable with every passing minute. She raised her eyes hopefully each time she heard the sound of a car, but usually it was just another taxi dropping someone off and then joining the line. After twenty minutes she felt she knew every cold concrete surface in this bleak approach to International Arrivals and was contemplating going upstairs and getting the first flight back out. She had expected to see Li. It was what had sustained her across all the hours of the flight. And now she felt dashed, hurt mixed with anger. How her mother would have enjoyed the moment.

Then a car drew up in front of her and her heart immediately lifted. She stepped forward to see Jack Geller leaning across the rear seat to open the door and her heart sank again. "You might as well get in," he said through the open window. "Unless your Chinese is pretty good, you're going to have a lot of trouble trying to tell a taxi-driver you want him to take you to the headquarters of the criminal investigation department." He paused. "How *is* your Chinese by the way?"

"If it was good enough to tell you to go forth and multiply, I would." She sighed, acquiescing reluctantly. "But since it's not, I guess I'd better just accept your offer gracefully."

He grinned and rattled off something in Chinese to the driver, who hurried out of the car to take Margaret's cases and put them in the trunk. A small, wiry man of indeterminate age, he heaved and strained to lift them.

An almost empty six-lane highway sped them north and east through the mist and rain of a flat, featureless landscape reclaimed from ancient mud flats. Huge billboards raised on polished chrome stalks flashed by on each side of the road, like enormous weeds. On one of them, what looked like four giant glasses of carrot juice prompted the slogan, in English, PROTECT THE VIRESCENCE, CHERISH THE LIFE. Another depicted a group of prosperous-looking children running across a green meadow towards a cluster of red-roofed villas, school satchels slung across their shoulders. It was an ad for the Shanghai Commercial Bank, a depiction of the new Chinese dream. Yet another, beneath a portrait of Deng Xiaoping, proclaimed, DEVELOPMENT IS TRUTH.

Geller laughed. "The Chinese authorities still haven't got over their need to sloganise. It's just the messages that are different, and a little more confused. Mind if I smoke?"

Margaret shrugged. "It's your cab. And your life."

He lit up, then rolled down the window a little to blow out the smoke. "I was at a racetrack down in Canton recently. Horse-racing's really catching on again in China. You've never seen anything like it. The car park was filled with expensive imported cars, punters were queuing up to place bets at computerised betting windows. Wealthy businessmen were crowded into private rooms in the stand, cheering on horses with names like 'Millionaire' and 'GetRichQuick.' But, anyway, right above them all, draped from the roof, was a giant red banner proclaiming, 'Resolutely Implement the Central Government's Order on Forbidding Gambling.'" He laughed uproariously.

In spite of her mood, Margaret's face cracked in a smile. Although she would have been loath to admit it, there was something quite likeable about this wry and slightly tousled reporter who smelled faintly of alcohol.

"See what I mean about confused?" he said. They passed another billboard, a photograph of the Great Wall with the slogan, LOVE OUR SHANGHAI, LOVE OUR COUNTRY. "Of course, Shanghai and Beijing hate each other's guts," Geller said. "Beijing's got all the power, and Shanghai's got all the money, and each one envies the other. But for me, Shanghai wins hands down. It's quite a place. You been here before, Miss Campbell?"

Margaret shook her head. "No."

"The Whore of the Orient."

"I beg your pardon."

"Some people called it the Paris of the East, but I like the Whore of the Orient. I think it probably characterises best what it was like here between the wars. You know the place was virtually run by the British and the Americans? And the French. Oh, and the Japs."

"No, I didn't." Margaret was curious for the first time. She really knew nothing about Shanghai. "How did that happen?"

"Oh, the Chinese were forced to grant various trading concessions to foreign powers in cities up and down the coast after the Opium Wars," he said. "But Shanghai's where it really took off. The place became the commercial gateway to China." He drew on his cigarette and focused somewhere away in the middle distance. "We got together with the Brits to create what they called the International Settlement. The Frogs, as always, did their own thing in the French Concession. The 'foreign devils' ran everything here. Police, sanitation, building regulations. They were completely self-governing, dominated by the most powerful business interests. The Chinese got squeezed into the slums of the old town and never got a look in. It's hardly any wonder this is where the Chinese Communist Party started up." He sat back with a kind of dreamy smile on his face and took another long pull on his cigarette. "Shanghai was the most cosmopolitan city in the world. There were people here drawn from across the widest spectrum of East and West, from Nazi spies and Filipino band leaders to Arab gendarmes and Indian princesses." He turned and grinned at her, "I'd have loved to have been around in those days. The place was teeming with gangsters and adventurers. A twentieth-century Sodom and Gomorrah." He put on an English accent. "Spiced up by Lea and Perrin's sauce and played out to the accompaniment of Gilbert and Sullivan."

"Not very Chinese," Margaret said.

"Not at all," Geller conceded. "But then large parts of Shanghai aren't. You'll see for yourself in time. Even the hotel you're staying in is very British old colonial."

After Beijing, this was not what Margaret had been expecting. Another billboard flashed past advertising Haier electrical goods under the slogan, HAIER AND HIGHER. Off to their right a collection of Greek classical villas with white pillars, balustraded balconies and red roofs, just like those in the ad, stood behind gated security walls in a compound called LONG DONG GARDEN. Geller grinned at Margaret. "Always makes me smile. Juvenile, isn't it?"

Now Margaret saw the skyscrapers of the Lujiazui financial district emerging from the mist, the Pearl TV tower and the river beyond, and almost before she knew it, they were sweeping over the Nanpu Bridge and cruising north along the waterside expressway, the Bund appearing out of the rains like a mirage, wholly incongruous, like water in a desert. For a fleeting moment, Margaret experienced the illusion of being transported back to sometime in the late 1930s, drifting past grand European edifices, banks built by the French, consulates established by the British and Russians, cathedrals of commerce where one paid homage to the great business empire of Jardine, Matheson and Company.

"That's your hotel," Geller said, pointing out of the window and breaking the spell. It was on the corner of Nanjing Road, a huge stone structure on fourteen floors with a steeply sloped green copper roof. "Used to be the Cathay Hotel, the most luxurious hotel in the east. Pure Art Deco. It's still pretty stunning." And a couple of buildings further on, he pointed up towards a line of statues, mythical heroes holding up a crenellated roof. "The Communists covered them up when they came to power. A symbol of the oppressed worker or something. They revealed them again in all their glory on the fiftieth anniversary of the Republic. I suppose now they are seen to symbolise strength and power."

On the river side of the Bund, a wide promenade was jammed with Chinese tourists in from the country, all jostling to have their photographs taken with the Oriental Pearl TV tower in the background.

Their taxi swung across the Waibaidu Bridge over Suzhou Creek, in the shadow of the impressive Shanghai Mansions and the old Stock Exchange building, now converted to cheap hotel rooms and apartment rentals. They headed north then, through burgeoning high-rise suburbs, afternoon traffic choking narrow streets, to join up with the northern ring road. By the time the car pulled up outside the gates of 803, Margaret was completely disorientated.

"This is you," Geller said.

"This is me where?" Margaret asked peering through the rain at the white gatehouse and the pink-tiled buildings beyond.

"The headquarters of criminal investigation." He spoke to the driver who retrieved her cases from the trunk. "Sure you don't want a hand with those?" he said as he pushed open the door for her.

"I can manage fine, thank you," she said.

"You won't mind if I don't get out, then. It's kind of wet out there." He grinned. The driver got back in and Geller pulled the door shut. He rolled down the window. "I'll see you at the press conference."

"What press conference?" Margaret asked, confused. Geller appeared to know so much more about her movements than she did. But the car was already pulling away. She realised she was getting soaked, and pulled up the collar of her cotton jacket. She was not dressed for rain.

A uniformed guard watched implacably as she dragged her cases over to the window of the gatehouse, to discover that nobody there spoke English. It was another fifteen minutes, after much to-ing and fro-ing and phoning back and forth, that a young uniformed policewoman who spoke English after a fashion said, "You follow me," and led her into the main building where they took the lift up to the eighth floor. No one had offered to give her a hand with her cases. Her wet hair was smeared over her face, and her temper, short at the best of times, was strained to breaking point. At the end of a long corridor, they stopped at the open door of the detectives' room. "You wait," the policewoman said.

Margaret stood, silently fuming, and watched as the young woman crossed the busy office, and then for the first time she saw Li at a window on the far side of the room. He was deep in earnest conversation with an attractive Chinese woman who appeared to be hanging on his every word. He said something that made her laugh, a strange braying laugh that Margaret could hear above the noise of the office, and she saw the woman touch the back of his hand. Just lightly, with the tips of her fingers. But there was something oddly intimate in it, and Margaret felt a sudden surge of fear and insecurity, swiftly followed by anger. She had not travelled six thousand miles across the world to watch her lover sharing an intimate moment with another woman.

The uniformed policewoman spoke to Li and he glanced quickly across the room to see Margaret in the doorway. His face lit up in a smile and he hurried across towards her. And for a moment Margaret's anger and insecurity melted away and all she wanted was for Li to take her in his arms and hold her. But, of course, he couldn't. And she saw that the woman who had touched his hand had followed immediately behind him.

"Margaret," he said, strangely formal. "I thought you'd be here earlier."

"I would have been, if I hadn't had to find my own way from the airport." Her voice could have frosted the windows on the other side of the room.

Li frowned. "But I sent a car out to meet you." He turned to the Chinese woman. "You put in a request for one, didn't you, Mei-Ling?"

"Yes," she said, looking very puzzled. "I do not understand what could have happened. I will make enquiries about it." She spoke in very good, clear English, with a slightly English accent. And Margaret knew immediately that Mei-Ling had somehow contrived to sabotage the pick-up. There was something in the smile she flashed at Margaret. Something slightly knowing, slightly superior. And all of Margaret's instincts told her that this woman was after her man.

Li seemed oblivious. "I am really sorry, Margaret. I would have come for you myself, but I have been up to the eyes." He paused. "This is Nien Mei-Ling. She is my opposite number here in Shanghai. We are working together on the case."

Mei-Ling gave her a winning smile and shook her hand. "Hi," she said. "Li Yan has told me so much about you."

"Has he?" Margaret shook her hand a little more firmly than required. You did not cut through human ribs with heavy shears without developing greater than average hand strength. She saw Mei-Ling's smile become a little more fixed.

Barely a dozen words had passed between the two women, but there had been an unspoken declaration of war, clear and unequivocal, with Li as the disputed territory.

Li had heard only the dozen words and had no reason to take them at anything other than face value. He glanced at his watch. "We had better move. The press conference is in half an hour."

Margaret forced her thoughts away from Mei-Ling. "Press conference?" So Jack Geller really did know his stuff, she thought.

II

The press conference was held in the Peace Palace Hotel, directly across Nanjing Road from the Peace Hotel where Margaret was able to book in quickly and have her cases taken to her room. Geller had been right again. She barely had time to take in the marbled splendour of the place with its tall arched windows of polished mahogany, its stained-glass galleries with wrought-iron lamp holders and pink glass uplighters, before Li hurried her back out into the rain. They had not even had an opportunity to discuss the case.

They joined Mei-Ling under the protection of two large black umbrellas, and dodged the traffic in the fading light to cross to the old Palace Hotel, recently acquired by its more affluent neighbour across the way. Inside the cream and redbrick building it was very dull, the light absorbed by darkwood panelling from floor to ceiling. A broad, dark staircase took them to an upper landing where armed uniformed guards ushered them into a large function room packed with the world's press. TV lights created an overlit sense of unreality. Cameras were ranged right along the back of the room. The Chinese media had pride of place at the front. This was an unusual experience for them. The authorities were not in the habit of holding press conferences to discuss the investigation of crimes.

On a raised dais, a table and half a dozen chairs faced the room. Microphones bunched together, one taped to the other, sprouted like strange metallic flowers on the table top, cables spewing over the edge and on to the floor. Li, Margaret and Mei-Ling, aware of curious eyes upon them, were shepherded quickly into a side room where hasty introductions were made to what Margaret gathered, in the confusion, were the Commissioner of Police, two deputies, Section Chief Huang Tsuo — Mei-Ling's boss at Section Two — and an interpreter. There was very little time to log exactly who was who. Section Chief Huang was steering the Commissioner away across the room, speaking quickly and quietly into his ear. Another man, with neatly clipped hair, hurried in and introduced himself as the head of public relations. He interrupted Huang and spoke quickly to the Commissioner, and Margaret surmised that the conference was about to begin. The tension was palpable as they entered the main suite and stepped up to the platform. If the press was unused to attending press conferences, then the Commissioner of Police was equally unused to holding them. He was clearly nervous.

On the platform the TV lights were blinding, and Margaret had to squint beyond the glare to see the rows of faces looking up at them expectantly. She saw Geller about five rows back. He was sitting with a notebook on his knee, a pair of silver-rimmed half-moon spectacles perched on his nose. He peered at her over the top of them and winked. Margaret looked away self-consciously, and began to wonder what the hell she was doing here. This was all happening so fast, and she was still quite disorientated. She glanced at Li who was, apparently, listening intently to the Commissioner as he droned on in a high-pitched staccato voice. Margaret let her mind wander, barely listening to the interpreter as he conveyed the Commissioner's long preamble in English. She looked appraisingly, instead, at Mei-Ling. Grudgingly, Margaret had to concede that she was very attractive. Older than she appeared at first sight, but poised and confident and very petite, like a bird. She could speak Li's language, she shared his culture. Beside her, Margaret felt big and clumsy, and crumpled after all the hours of flying and then being caught in the rain. Her make-up, she knew, was faded and smudged, her hair a tangle. She couldn't speak Chinese, she had little or no empathy with the culture. How could she even begin to compete with someone like Mei-Ling? And she felt a cloud of depression settle over her, ready almost to concede the fight even before it had begun.

Then suddenly her attention was brought sharply back into focus by the interpreter. She heard him saying, "Initial fears that these were victims of a mass killer have proved unfounded. Preliminary examination by our pathologists at 803 have concluded that the most likely explanation is that these women died of natural causes . . ." He broke off as a buzz of speculation rose among the reporters. "We believe that their bodies may have been subject to illegal medical experimentation or, even more prosaically, for illicit practice by medical students."

Margaret flashed an angry look at Li who met her eye and gave an imperceptible shake of his head.

The Commissioner spoke again, turning and smiling towards Margaret. Clearly he was pleased with the way things were going. The interpreter said, "Our main task will be to identify the bodies. And, to that end, we are fortunate to have acquired the services of leading American pathologist, Margaret Campbell, who has worked before with the Chinese police." Margaret felt all eyes turning towards her.

"Jesus!" Margaret said. "I can't believe you got me all the way over here for this." She strode across the lobby of the Peace Palace Hotel after the press conference. Li hurried after her. "A bunch of bodies that have been hacked up by medical students!"

"That is only a theory, an initial thought," Li said.

"Then why are you telling the press? You're only going to look fucking stupid if it turns out not to be true." She pushed through the revolving door and out into the street. The pavements were choked with affluent shoppers and people hurrying home from work, umbrellas fighting for ascendancy in the airspace above their heads. Someone got into a taxi at the kerbside, and an electronic voice said, *Dear passenger, you are welcome in our taxi.*

"That was not my idea," Li said. "The Commissioner thought it would take the heat out of the situation."

"Which shows how many press conferences *he*'s taken." Margaret was scathing. "First rule of public relations: you never tell the press anything you don't know for certain. Let them do the speculating, not you."

Mei-Ling appeared on the steps above them. "Is there a problem?"

Margaret said, "If your people have already started carrying out autopsies, then I'm wasting my time."

"Well, why do we not go and look at the bodies right now, and you can make that judgement for yourself." Mei-Ling was the voice of perfect reason.

Margaret glared at her and turned her anger on Li. "I busted my butt to get here. The least you could have done was wait."

The city mortuary was out in the north-west of Shanghai, beyond Fudan University, in a quiet street off the residential

Zhengli Road. They turned in a gate and passed the administration building, a cream-painted house with a steeply pitched
red-tile roof that looked like a Swiss guest house. There was an
area of green lawn dominated by a large conifer tree. Flower
beds bloomed with red and yellow roses, even in November.
There was a large parking area, at the far end of which stood
the mortuary itself, an elegant two-storey building in the
same style of cream and red-tile. Shrubs and small trees had
been planted around it. Nothing about the place would have
indicated its purpose.

There were several cars parked out front. Mei-Ling drew
the Santana in beside them and led Li and Margaret inside,
turning right out of a small entrance hall into a long cold
room. One wall was lined with two tiers of metal doors opening on to refrigerators where the bodies were kept on roll-out
shelves. Each door had a gold number on it. There were forty
doors.

"There are two roll-out shelves in each," Mei-Ling said. "We
have a capacity for storing eighty bodies in total here."

There were two autopsy rooms off, one table in the first,
two in the other. Everything was clinically clean, white-tiled
floors and walls, scrubbed stainless steel autopsy tables with
proper drainers, water fed from below and controlled by levers
and buttons at knee height. Margaret noticed closed-circuit TV
cameras mounted high on the walls. A stainless-steel work top
ran the length of one wall in each room, and above, taped to
the tiles, were the charts originally assembled in the underground car park as the bodies were brought in. These included
lists of the body parts, photographs of each piece as it had
been found, envelopes containing all the initial x-rays and the
crudely drawn diagrams of each body, indicating which bits
were present and which were missing.

Margaret walked along the wall in the second room, looking at the charts. Dr. Lan entered quietly behind them. He was wearing a dark blue jacket over light-coloured pants and a blue, grey and white striped roll-neck. He stood in the doorway watching Margaret in silence for a few moments before clearing his throat. The others turned, startled, and after a moment of hiatus Li made the introductions in Chinese and English. Lan bowed slightly, a tiny smile playing around his mouth that did not reach his eyes, as he shook Margaret's hand. "I speak a little English," he said, in what sounded to Margaret like very good English. He waved his hand around the room. "You like our facility here?"

Margaret nodded solemnly, aware of how Lan's position had been undermined by her arrival. But he was, at least on the surface, coping well with the loss of face. "It's excellent, Doctor," she said. "As good as I've seen anywhere."

His smile widened a little, but still did not make it past his upper lip. He ran a hand down the side of the door and looked at his fingers. "Cleaner than most hospitals," he said. "We have fifteen pathologists here, Dr. Campbell, and among us we perform a thousand autopsies each year. We are equally qualified in forensic science, and have, in addition, seven lab technicians at our disposal. We matched all the body bits by DNA comparison."

Margaret thought that Dr. Lan had more than a little English. And she understood that he was using it to lay out his credentials in case she thought she was dealing with someone of inferior qualification or experience. She looked at the diagrams on the walls. "How many of these women have you already autopsied?"

"Two. Although I have made a preliminary examination of them all."

"Did you establish cause of death?"

"Not yet, no."

"But on the basis of what you've seen, you have concluded that these women were simply corpses used for practice by medical students, or for some kind of medical research?"

"It is not a conclusion, Doctor. Just an early thought."

"May I see one of the other bodies?"

Lan nodded, and they followed him through to the refrigeration room. He opened one of the lower doors and rolled out the upper shelf. He made a small movement of his hand towards the far end of the room, and two white-coated assistants wearing thick rubber gloves stepped forward and unzipped the white body bag that lay on the shelf. Inside were the roughly assembled pieces of a young woman. The smell of decaying flesh was powerful, even in the refrigerator. Arms, legs and one hand were severed, as was her head. Cold, dried mud still clung to the bleached yellow flesh. A "Y"-shaped incision that cut in from each shoulder to the breast bone, and then down to the pubis, had opened up the torso, revealing a chest cavity which had been stripped of its organs and then sewn up with rough twine. Margaret looked quickly at Lan. "I wanted to see one that you hadn't autopsied."

Lan said, "She is as we found her."

Margaret frowned, and bent down to examine the cut more closely. "May I have some gloves and a piece of cotton?" she said. Lan spoke to one of the assistants, who hurried off. Margaret asked, "Have all the bodies been cleaned off to this extent."

"They were very carefully washed down," Lan said. "By pathologists. There is no loss of evidence."

Margaret said nothing. When the gloves came she pulled them on and then took the cotton and rubbed very gently along

one edge of the incision. She peered at it very closely for a
long time. Finally, she straightened up and peeled off the
gloves. "Well," she said, "this one certainly wasn't a corpse
used for practice."

Lan stiffened, colour rising high on his pallid cheeks. He
frowned, and glanced down at the contents of the bag. "How
can you know that?"

"I'm not prepared to commit myself, Doctor, until I've done
the autopsy."

"Which will be when?" Lan asked.

"When I've had some sleep," she said. "In the meantime, I
don't want any more autopsies carried out."

Lan said stiffly, "I am instructed to proceed as quickly as
possible."

Margaret turned to Li. "Who is the lead pathologist on
this case?" He had called her in, he was going to have to take
responsibility. If he didn't back her now, she was out of there.

Li glanced uneasily at Lan. Then, "You are," he told Margaret.

"Good, then we'll start the autopsies in the morning." She
nodded to Lan, handed the gloves and the cotton to the assistant, and headed out into the hallway. Li followed her, leaving
Mei-Ling to deal with Lan's loss of *mianzi*.

Li lowered his voice almost to a whisper. "Was that really
necessary?"

"What?"

"Putting me on the spot like that?"

This was not how Margaret wanted it to be. She had taken
a momentous decision, travelled a long way to be with Li, and
already they were at one another's throats. But there were
principles at stake. "I'm the one who's on the spot here,"
she said, struggling to keep her voice down. "You've brought

me in on an investigation that some people would clearly like to see just disappear."

"What do you mean?"

"That press conference," she said, "was a joke. The Commissioner of Police is telling the press that these women weren't murdered, even before the investigation's got properly under way. And Dr. Lan might be a very good pathologist, but I think he's just fulfilling some wishful thinking on behalf of his bosses."

"Are you saying he's concealing the findings of his autopsies?"

"Not necessarily," Margaret said. "But maybe he's just not looking very hard." She sighed. "You're a good cop, Li Yan, but when it comes to politics you can be pretty naïve."

Li frowned. "You think someone is actually trying to subvert the investigation?"

She shrugged. "Well, it's all pretty embarrassing, isn't it? For the authorities."

Li said, "It was the Mayor's policy adviser who put me in charge. It was he who gave me permission to bring you in."

"Then maybe there are others who don't like decisions like that being taken over their heads."

Li thought about it. His meeting with Huang and the Deputy Commissioner had been pretty frosty, and the Commissioner himself had been briefed by Huang. But he found it hard to believe that any one of them would contrive to hide the truth. Why would they?

Margaret said, "The point is, I have my integrity and a professional reputation to protect. Either I get full access and complete co-operation or I'm on the first plane home."

For a moment, Li wondered where she meant by "home." The United States? He was confused. She had stayed on in China to be with him and had only returned to the States to attend her father's funeral. He dragged his thoughts back to the case. He said, "You have my guarantee on that."

She nodded. "Then that's good enough for me." And suddenly she wilted, fatigue etching itself on her face. She wanted to touch him, feel his skin under her fingers, his soft warm lips on her neck. "Let's go back to the hotel. I need a shower, then we can get something to eat, and . . ." Li looked uncomfortable. "What?"

"We must attend a banquet tonight."

She felt all the strength drain out of her. All the Chinese ever seemed to do was hold banquets. "Aw, Jesus, Li, not tonight. Please."

He shrugged helplessly. "I have got no choice. It is being hosted by the Mayor's policy adviser, and you and I are the guests of honour. I think he wants to show us off."

Mei-Ling came out from the refrigeration room and cast Margaret a chilly look. She said to Li, "I will give you a lift back to your hotel after we have dropped off Miss Campbell."

Margaret frowned and said to Li, "Aren't you staying at the Peace Hotel?"

Mei-Ling answered for him. "I am afraid the budget does not run to two rooms at the Peace Hotel, Miss Campbell. We Chinese have to content ourselves with something a little more austere."

For the first time, Li became aware of the friction between the two, and was puzzled by it. After all, they had only just met.

Mei-Ling said, "But do not worry, we will come back and pick you up on the way to the banquet tonight."

Margaret bristled. "We? Do I take it that you are also going to the banquet?"

Mei-Ling smiled. "Of course."

III

Margaret's shower had lifted her appearance, but not her spirits. Her hair fell in freshly laundered golden waves across her shoulders. She had put on an elegant but conservative sleeveless black dress for the banquet. But her eyes were stinging from lack of sleep, she felt tired and depressed and in need of alcohol. She wandered in search of the bar along endless marbled corridors dominated by gold and pink squared ceilings and elaborate Art Deco uplighters. But there were no signs in English that she could see. In a lounge opposite the reception lobby, people sat drinking coffee and beer at tables, but it was not exactly what Margaret had in mind.

"S'cuse me. You Miss Maggot Cambo?"

Margaret turned to find a smiling young Chinese man standing timidly in front of her.

He held out his hand. "Ah . . . My name . . . Jiang Baofu." His English was hesitant, but he was determined to persevere. "Medical student . . . Read about you in paper, Miss Cambo."

Reluctantly she shook his hand.

"How do you do?"

"Ah . . . very well, thank you." He bowed slightly. "You . . . mmmm . . . very farmers, Miss Cambo."

She frowned. "Farmers?"

He nodded enthusiastically. "*Very* farmers." And she realised suddenly that he meant "famous."

"I don't think so," she said.

"Oh, yes. I . . . mmm . . . wanna be pathologist like you." He smiled, still nodding enthusiastically. "I . . . mmm . . . night watchman, where they find bodies."

And Margaret was immediately on her guard. She had thought, initially, that the young man was harmless enough, but now she had major misgivings. "In that case," she said, "you are a material witness and we shouldn't be talking."

She strode off across the lobby, but he hurried after her. "I like to help," he said. "I like to help investigation. I like to help you."

She spun around. "Just how did you know where to find me?" she asked.

"Oh . . ." he said. "I give statement at 803. Aaa-ll day. I . . . mmm . . . follow you to hotel."

Margaret was distinctly unhappy now. She looked at him again. She saw that despite the almost cringing obsequious-ness of his demeanour, he was a powerfully built young man. He had a strong physical presence, and his lack of confidence was only in his English. "I think you should go," she said, and turned away. But he caught her arm, and she felt the strength of his fingers as they bit into her bare flesh.

"No, no . . . I only wanna help," he said.

She pulled her arm free. "Don't ever touch me again," she said dangerously, and with more confidence than she felt.

"Lady in need of assistance?" She turned at the sound of the voice on her right hand and felt a huge wave of relief to see the familiar smiling face of Jack Geller.

"Yes," she said, trying to remain composed. "I was looking for the bar."

"Then you found the right man to take you there," he said. He glanced at Jiang Baofu, then steered her away past the cur-rency exchange to a narrow wooden staircase leading up to a small mezzanine bookshop. "What was all that about?" he asked.

She shrugged it off. "Nothing."

"Didn't look like nothing to me."

"Believe me, women alone in hotels are always getting pestered." She looked around at the rows of books and racks of magazines. "Actually, when I said 'bar' I was thinking more of something that sold booze, not books."

He grinned. "Keep walking." They passed along a narrow corridor where tall, elaborate glass and wrought-iron lamp-stands stood sentinel. On one side there were large semi-circular stained-glass windows from floor to ceiling, on the other a marble balustrade protecting a view down into the well of the reception lobby below. The bar opened out before them. Big, comfortable armchairs and sofas gathered around low coffee tables, windows along one side looked down on to the lounge.

They sat on stools at a long, polished bar. An old-fashioned golfer in plus-fours and cloth cap peered at them through round spectacles with real lenses. He was all of three feet high, brightly coloured paint on glazed china. Margaret could imagine executives of Jardine, Matheson gathering here at the day's end seventy years before to quaff their gins and tonic and discuss the day's dealings. Although the bar was empty, their ghosts still haunted it. A young waitress in a *qipao* took their order.

Margaret had a long draught of her vodka tonic and felt the alcohol hit her bloodstream almost immediately. She closed her eyes and let the feeling relax her. Geller watched her with interest over the rim of his beer glass. He said, "Dead fodder for medical students. That's all they were, huh?"

She opened her eyes slowly and looked at him. "You expect me to comment on that?"

"You don't have to. It's all bullshit."

"Why do you say that?"

"Aw, come on. Eighteen young women, most of them under thirty . . . ? I don't think so. Life expectancy here is seventy plus, and there's a hell of a lot more men than women. If they'd all died of natural causes, the law of averages would make most of them over fifty, and a majority of them male."

Margaret made no comment. But she couldn't argue with the logic. "And if someone had been conducting research on, say, declining fertility in young women across a twenty-year age range . . . ?"

"Were they?"

"I have no idea. I'm just making an argument."

"It would still be bullshit."

"Why?"

"Because eighteen young women, all dead from natural causes and conveniently available for illicit medical research, still goes against the law of averages." He took another sip of his beer. "By the way, has anyone told you you're very attractive for someone who cuts up people for a living."

"Oh yes," she said, "I've often been told how attractive I am by men who want to get into my pants. But a blow-by-blow account of how I dissect the male organ during autopsy is usually enough to put them off."

Geller grinned, "I love it when a woman talks surgery."

And, to her surprise, she found herself laughing. She looked at him a little more appraisingly and noticed there was no ring on the left hand. "Did anyone ever tell you you're not bad-looking for someone who hacks people to pieces in print?"

"Once," he said. "My editor. Sadly he was a guy. My kind of luck."

"You never married, then?"

"Thought about it once. For a whole five seconds." He rubbed his chin thoughtfully. "Or was it as long as that?" He finished his beer. "You want another of those?"

She nodded. He ordered another round and she said, "So who do you work for out here?"

He smiled. "Remember I told you about the Whore of the Orient? Well, I am that whore. I'll do it for anyone who pays me."

"And who pays you?"

"*Newsweek*, sometimes. *Time*, A couple of wire services, some of the big papers back home when their regular correspondents go off on a rest cure to a massage parlour in Thailand." He shrugged. "It's a living."

"How long have you been in Shanghai?"

"Too long."

She shook her head. "You're a fund of information, aren't you?"

"I try not to be. Listen, I'm the hack here, I thought I was the one supposed to be asking the questions."

Their drinks arrived and Margaret lifted her glass. "The best way to avoid answering questions is to ask them." She took a long draught, then checked her watch. "Oh, my God! Is that the time? They'll be waiting for me in the lobby." She took another hurried drink and put her glass back on the bar. "I'm sorry, Mr. Geller, I'm going to have to love you and leave you."

He shrugged ruefully. "I'll settle for that – with or without the leaving bit." She grinned and slipped off the stool. "So where are you off to?" he asked.

"A banquet. Hosted by some policy adviser to the Mayor."

If she thought he'd be impressed she was wrong. "Ahh," he said seriously. "Director Hu. The Director is not a very nice man."

IV

Mei-Ling eased the Santana through the crowds of people, cars and bicycles that choked Yunnan Nan Road. Two elderly women in the light blue uniform of traffic wardens were waving their arms at the junction, and blowing their whistles like demented birds. The Santana passed under a traditional Chinese gate and into a neon wonderland. Red lanterns and yellow banners were strung overhead. Every shop front and restaurant was lit in this narrow street, each fleck of coloured light coruscating in the rain. Steam rose from open windows where great racks of dumplings cooked over boiling water, smoke issuing from open barbecues, spicy skewers of lamb and chicken hissing and spitting their fat on the coals. A group of drunken young women with painted faces, staggering precariously on very high heels, banged on the hood of the car and leered in the window at Li. Margaret sat in the back, feeling remote and isolated from Li who sat up front next to Mei-Ling. There had been very little said since they left the hotel.

When Mei-Ling drew the Volkswagen into a tiny car park next to the twelve-storey Xiaoshaoxing Hotel, they made a dash through the rain to the front entrance. The elevator to the eighth floor slid silently up one of two glass tubes built on to the side of the building. From here they had an ascending view of the chaotic jumbled sprawl of rooftops and balconies below, washing hanging out across the street on long poles, wetter than when it had been put out.

They followed a waitress along quiet, panelled corridors, turning left and then right, past several private banqueting rooms. Director Hu and his guests awaited them in a large room at the end. They were standing in groups around a very large circular table, smoking and chatting animatedly, classical Chinese music playing quietly from large speakers in each corner. Li introduced Margaret to the Director. His eyes were on a level with hers and they ran up and down her appraisingly. His handshake, she thought, was limp and slightly damp. He had a wide smile, revealing unusually even and white teeth. He wore an immaculately cut designer suit, and she caught the briefest whiff of Paco Rabanne. She looked at his smooth, round face and thought that the aftershave was more for effect than any practical purpose. She resisted a sudden absurd urge to run her hands over his head to see if his closely cropped grey hair was as velvety to the touch as it looked:

"Dr. Campbell," he said, "I have heard very much about you. It is an honour to meet you." He turned and introduced her to his other guests – the Commissioner of Police and Section Chief Huang whom she had already met; the Procurator General, still in his uniform; another of the Mayor's advisers, a square-set and unsmiling man; a personal friend, Mr. Cui Feng, and his wife; and a couple of aides, younger men who nodded and smiled and ushered everyone to their seats. Li was placed on one side of the Director, Margaret on the other.

Tall waitresses in elegant pink *qipaos* filled their small toasting glasses with red wine. Nearly everyone was drinking beer, except for the Director who sipped at a glass of bright red watermelon juice. The ritual of toasting began with the Director, and was followed around the table by his guests. Each time a toast was drunk, there was a chorus of *"gan bei,"* and the toasting glasses were emptied and then immediately refilled. Plate after plate of food arrived and was placed on the revolving Lazy Susan in order to allow everyone to help themselves.

The Commissioner of Police sat on Margaret's right. "You like Hormez?" he asked.

Margaret replayed the question in her head, but could make no sense of it. "I beg your pardon?" she said, pronouncing her words very carefully. The wine, after the vodka, was beginning to have an effect. And now she took a long pull at her beer.

The Procurator General, round spectacles perched on an unusually long nose, leaned over. "We have great love of detective fiction in China," he said. "Many police officers write detective stories."

Director Hu laughed. He said, "I believe in Beijing they have courses at the Public Security University in the History of Western Detective Fiction."

Margaret had not heard this before. "Really?" It was one of those strange Chinese curiosities she continually stumbled across.

"Many police officers take this course," the Commissioner said. "They are very inspired by Hormez."

Margaret glanced towards Li for help, but he was engaged in polite conversation with Mrs. Cui. She became aware of Mei-Ling smiling at her discomfort from across the table. "And who exactly is this . . . Hormez?"

The Commissioner looked at her in astonishment. "You don't know Hormez? Ohhh . . . he ve-very farmers in China. Sherlock Hormez."

And suddenly it dawned on her. "Holmes! You mean Sherlock Holmes!"

"Yes," said the Commissioner. "Hormez. You know Hormez?"

Margaret had to confess that she had not actually read any of the Conan Doyle books. But when she was younger, she said, she had seen a number of the old black and white movies with Basil Rathbone. Everyone else looked puzzled.

Someone was turning the Lazy Susan, and a plate piled high with prawn crackers stopped in front of her. Margaret looked in horror at the small black scorpions crawling over the crackers before she realised that they weren't actually moving.

"Deep fried whole scorpion," Mei-Ling said from across the table, and Margaret saw that it was Mei-Ling who had stopped the dish in front of her. "They are a great delicacy."

Other conversations around the table tailed off, and smiling faces turned in Margaret's direction. Western sensitivity to Chinese "delicacies" was well known, and everyone was anxious to see Margaret's reaction. The Commissioner took one in his chopsticks and popped it into his mouth, crunching enthusiastically. "Scorpion valued for medical reason," he said. "You try one."

Margaret's jaw set. The Chinese could be so goddamned superior at times like this, and she felt as if she were representing the whole of Western culture here. She forced herself to smile, lifted one of the brittle black insects with her chopsticks and with a great effort of will put it in her mouth. As she crunched on its bitterness it was all she could do to stop herself from gagging.

"Bravo," Director Hu said and clapped his hands. "I can never bring myself to eat the bloody things. They are disgu-usting."

Margaret took a long draught of beer to try to wash the taste away, and a waitress immediately refilled her glass. To her relief, the focus shifted away from her again as conversations restarted around the table. The alcohol and the fatigue were beginning to make her feel quite heady. After all, she had barely slept in more than twenty hours. She had noticed earlier that Mei-Ling's boss, Section Chief Huang, was distracted and dour, and she saw now that he only picked at his food,

troubled somehow, and taking no part in the social inter-
course. She watched him for a moment or two. He was a good-
looking man, but careworn somehow, as if carrying a heavy
burden through life. She could not recall having seen him
smile once.

She was wondering why he was here at all when a waitress
came in and whispered something in his ear. He paled slightly
and stood up immediately. He spoke rapidly to Director Hu
in Chinese. The Director nodded gravely and said something
back, and Huang turned with a curt nod and hurried out. The
Commissioner whispered to Margaret, "I am afraid the wife of
the Section Chief is very unwell."

"I wonder, what is your view on our one-child policy,
Doctor?" Margaret realised the question was being addressed
to her, and turned to find Cui Feng, the Director's personal
friend, smiling at her across the table.

"I think it is draconian and barbaric," she said bluntly.

Mr. Cui was unruffled. He nodded. "I agree. But a necessary
evil."

"I'm not sure that evil is ever necessary."

"Sometimes," Mr. Cui said, "evil is the only option, and it is
necessary to choose whichever is the least unpalatable. Without a policy to reduce the birth rate we would be unable to
feed our population and many millions of people would die."
He ran a hand thoughtfully over his smooth chin. He was
taller than his friend, the Director, with a head of thick, black
hair and a very gentle demeanour, like a doctor with a kindly
bedside manner. "You know, in Shandong Province alone,
the population would now have reached nearly one hundred
and fifty million. But because of our birth control policy, the
population is only ninety million. We have cut the birthrate
by more than half since nineteen seventy, and cut the rate of

infant mortality to thirty-four per thousand – which is far less than the world average of fifty."

The Procurator General said with a mischief-making smile, "Mr. Cui has a vested interest here, Doctor. Five years ago he opened a number of joint-venture clinics in Shanghai and persuaded the government to give him the contract to carry out all the abortions in the city."

And Margaret thought how being a personal friend of the Mayor's policy adviser would not have hindered that process, though she didn't say so.

"Three hundred thousand of them a year," the Director said. "Which was placing a heavy demand on limited government resources."

"Three hundred thousand *abortions*!" Margaret said, incredulously. "A *year*?"

"In Shanghai alone," Mr. Cui said.

"Then your policy is failing," Margaret retorted. She felt an anger building in her, and ignored the warning looks from Li.

"How so?" asked Director Hu coldly.

"It is one thing to *persuade* people to have only one child. It is another to *force* them to have abortions." She recalled with horror and regret the emotional blackmail that had forced her to abort her own unborn child. *It'll ruin both our lives*, David had said, and she had lived with the pain and the guilt ever since. She said, "You are simply substituting the death of people by starvation with the murder of children in the womb. I can accept abortion when the life of the mother is in danger, but not as a matter of convenience."

"It is not convenience," Mei-Ling said. Her tone was as aggressive as Margaret's. "These women have *had* babies. They made a mistake getting pregnant again, or were greedy, and it is their duty to have the children aborted."

Margaret glanced at Li, but his face was impassive.

Mr. Cui said, more softly, "Family planning in China has not only reduced the birth rate, Doctor, it has increased living standards, and life expectancy is now more than seventy years."

"Well, of course, as someone who's profiting from other people's misery, you would say that, wouldn't you?" It was out before Margaret could stop herself. She felt her face flush red as she realised the bluntness of what she had said.

There was a moment's shocked silence around the table. Only Mr. Cui remained, apparently, unperturbed. He retained his soft bedside manner. "Of course we are in business to make money," he said. "As are doctors and hospitals in the United States. But we also offer advice and counselling. These women would have had their abortions in state hospitals where the procedure would have been performed on a production line basis. We, at least, try to make the process more human."

Margaret confined herself to a quick nod, not trusting herself to open her mouth again.

But if Mr. Cui had remained understanding, Director Hu was not so forgiving. He said pointedly, "It seems, Dr. Campbell, that developments regarding the bodies at Pudong are unlikely now to require your extended attention."

"And why is that?" she asked levelly.

"You were at the press conference, I believe," said the Director.

"In my experience," Margaret said, "there is often a big gap between the truth and what the press is told."

The Director leaned forward and placed his chin very carefully on his interlocked fists. "Meaning?"

"The body I examined tonight, albeit briefly, was not that of a corpse subjected to student practice or medical research."

Director Hu tensed visibly. Much as he would doubtless have liked to put Margaret on the first plane back to the States, he was a prisoner of his own high-profile decision to bring her in. "Then how did she die?" he asked.

"I should be able to tell you that after the autopsy." She was aware of the looks that flashed quickly between the Director, the Commissioner and the Procurator General. If they had harboured hopes of this thing going away quickly and easily, this ill-mannered American was clearly intent on dashing them. What had started out, perhaps, as a celebration banquet, had very quickly turned sour. And it did not last much longer.

Half-hearted toasts were drunk, glasses raised in thanks to the host, and then Director Hu stood up, signalling that the meal was over. His guests immediately stood also, and began making their farewells. Margaret stood isolated near the door and watched as the Director took Li to one side. Mei-Ling approached her, a smile playing mischievously about her lips. "Well done," she said in a stage whisper. "You have just made an enemy of the second most powerful man in Shanghai."

Li was cursing himself for having trusted Margaret in this situation. He had smelled the vodka on her breath when they picked her up at the hotel. He had watched her empty all the toasting glasses, and consume several beers. Alcohol always lowered her already limited levels of self-restraint.

He felt the grip of the Director's short, thick fingers on his arm as he steered him away from the table. "That *Meiguoren* . . ." he almost spat out the Chinese word for American, "had better not embarrass us, Li."

Li said, "You told me you wanted the truth, Director Hu. I believe she will give us that."

Director Hu glared at Li, no doubt regretting the haste in appointing him and his agreeing to the involvement of the American. "A word of advice, Deputy Section Chief. Marry a dog, stay with a dog; marry a rooster, stay with a rooster. You should choose your friends carefully."

As their taxi drew away from the kerb, Margaret caught a fleeting glimpse, like a smear on the window, of Mei-Ling's unhappiness. Li had turned down her offer of a lift back to the hotel and told her he and Margaret would take a taxi. And so Mei-Ling had been left standing on the sidewalk in the rain with the Procurator General and the Commissioner of Police. The Director's entourage had already departed. But it was of small comfort to Margaret. She could almost reach out and touch Li's anger. It seemed that working together always brought them into conflict.

As soon as they were on their own in the back of the taxi, Li said, "What the hell were you playing at?"

Margaret immediately felt her hackles rise. "I was expressing my mind. Where I come from that's not a crime."

"Well, where I come from, it is extremely bad manners to show disrespect to your host and his guests by being rude to them. But then, I should have known – Americans are not renowned for their sensitivity."

"And the Chinese are famous for their intolerance towards other people's ideas. But I suppose that's what comes of running a one-party state. The powers that be aren't used to being questioned. And they don't like it when they are." The irony of their fight was not lost on Margaret. Thirty-six hours earlier she had been defending China to David in Chicago.

Li held up his hand and through gritted teeth said, "Do not start, Margaret. Please do not start."

She sat back and folded her arms across her chest, clenching her jaws to fight back the impulse to give voice to all the thoughts going through her head. They sat in silence for several minutes as their car left behind the lights of Yunnan Nan Road, and headed east towards the river.

Finally Li said, "And your performance at the mortuary this afternoon is going to make things very difficult as far as working with Dr. Lan is concerned. You know how important *mianzi* is to the Chinese. Mei-Ling says he was acutely embarrassed."

"Oh, does she? And what else does Mei-Ling say?"

"She thinks maybe you are not the right person to work on such a highly sensitive case."

"Oh, and what about *your* loss of face? After all, you're the one who brought me in."

"You are the one who is causing me to lose face," Li said angrily.

"And that's what all this is about, isn't it?" Margaret snapped back. "Face! Everybody's face, or the loss of it. It's all you goddamn people seem to care about." And she wondered what on earth had possessed her to come back. "And, of course, you and Mei-Ling will have discussed all this during your intimate little rides to and from your hotel this evening. Did she come in and hold your hand while you changed?"

Li sighed theatrically and turned to stare out of the window. "Do not be so ridiculous!"

"Oh, so I'm ridiculous now. Not only am I an embarrassment who causes you to lose face, but I'm ridiculous as well. And I suppose it would be equally ridiculous of me to imagine that there might be anything going on between you and Mei-Ling."

"What?" Li looked at her incredulously. "That is not even worthy of a response." And part of him was gripped by an acute sense of guilt at the feelings that Mei-Ling had aroused in him the night before. He looked quickly away again.

"You mean you're not even going to deny it? Two attractive people thrown together on a stressful job in a strange city? It wouldn't be the first time it had happened."

"You are being unreasonable and paranoid," he said.

"So the count's up to four, now. Not only am I embarrassing and ridiculous, but I'm also unreasonable and paranoid. I don't know why the hell you ever wanted me to work on this case."

He turned angrily on her, "Neither do I."

It was like a slap full in the face. Margaret felt it stinging. Li knew he had gone too far, but it was too late to take anything back. Light from a shop front caught her hair as they passed it, and he wanted to reach out and touch it. He remembered how they had been together, remembered the first time they had made love in a cold railway carriage in the north. Her arrogance had always infuriated him, and her vulnerability always drawn him. Each emotion fought with the other in him now as he sat there in the taxi beside her. But he could not bring himself to bridge the gap of their argument, to hold out the olive branch that would lead to reconciliation and the feel of her skin on his in a warm bed in the Peace Hotel.

Margaret had gone cold inside. She was determined not to cry, determined not to show him how much he had hurt her. All she had wanted from the moment she arrived was to hold him, and have him hold her. To make love and lie in his arms and forget, at least for a time, all the things that stood in the way of their relationship.

The taxi pulled up outside the Peace Hotel, and a bellboy in red uniform and carrying a black umbrella, stepped out of the shelter of the canopy to open her door. She swung her legs out, then turned back towards Li. She said quietly, "I wish I'd never come back."

And she hurried through revolving doors to ride in solitude to her room on the sixth floor and cry herself to sleep on a big, cold empty bed.

CHAPTER FOUR

The body is apparently that of an adult Asian woman that has been mutilated. The head and extremities have been amputated and the body has been incised along its chest and abdomen.

Margaret spoke clearly for the microphone. Experience had taught her that the Chinese who transliterated the tape would be easily confused by any lapse by her into slang or dialect. The vocabulary was arcane and difficult enough.

The body lay on the cold stainless steel of the autopsy table, its amputated pieces assembled in a grotesque parody of the complete human form they had once comprised. The head lay at an odd angle, black holes where the eyes should have been gazing into nothing. One foot was missing. Deterioration was more advanced in some pieces than in others. Parts of the dismembered limbs had become purple-black and slimy, and blisters filled with decompositional juices were forming on the skin. The sweet smell of rotting human flesh filled the room, like luncheon meat that has been left in the refrigerator and discovered two weeks too late.

The body is nude, unembalmed, and is cold to the touch. Rigor mortis is not appreciated. The body is in an early to moderate stage of decomposition characterised by areas of red and green-black discoloration of the abdomen and legs, drying of the face and digits, and patchy drying of the body surfaces. There are also discernible areas of adipocere.

"What is that?" Li asked, and Margaret glanced up at him through the plastic of her goggles.

She enjoyed the anonymity of the pathologist during autopsy. She could hide beneath the shower cap, behind the goggles and surgeon's mask. She could conceal her vulnerability under the surgeon's pyjamas, plastic apron and long-sleeved gown. Barely any part of her was exposed to scrutiny. Gloves, steel mesh, latex and waterproof sleeves cloaked every inch of exposed flesh. Even her shoes were shrouded in plastic.

Today she felt particularly exposed to scrutiny. She knew that Li was watching her closely wondering if, perhaps, their relationship had reached its end. Mei-Ling, too, was carefully examining her every move. Perhaps she was also wondering about the state of Margaret's relations with Li, and what might have passed between them last night. And, of course, Dr. Lan was waiting for the first slip, the first wrong move, the first ambiguity, to justify his previous findings. The autopsy assistants were courteous and professional, but they were Lan's men and made that clear to Margaret by their exaggerated deference to her Chinese counterpart. At the back of the room a green-uniformed forensics expert stood watching with interest. He was a young man, with round, gold-rimmed spectacles. Unusually for a Chinese there was stubble on his jaw. He could have done with a shave. Margaret felt the heat building beneath all her layers, and glanced up at the closed-circuit TV camera on the wall. Somewhere, she knew, in another room, other eyes were also watching.

"Adipocere . . ." she said, but paused and glanced at Dr. Lan. "Perhaps you would like to explain to the Deputy Section Chief,

Doctor." She could not tell what his expression was beneath his mask. He nodded curtly.

"Adipocere," he said, "is a white-tan waxy deposit, especially over the face, breasts and buttocks. It is formed by conversion of the oily fats in the body fat to solid fats during slow decomposition, suggesting that a body has been dead for at least three months. In addition, in this case, there are patchy white dry spots which would suggest direct exposure to cold air, probably in a freezer."

Margaret nodded, raising an eyebrow in approval, and then turned her attentions to an examination of the head.

The head has been separated from the neck at the third cervical vertebra. It is normocephalic. The hair is partially sloughing, but the remaining hair is coarse, straight, black, and measures fourteen inches on the top of the head. The skin is dry and there is adipocere over the face. The eyes are not identified, and there is brown, waxy and pasty material in the orbits.

She worked the mouth open with her fingers.

The lips are dry, darkened, but apparently free of trauma. The oral mucous membranes are sloughing, but also free of trauma. The teeth are natural and in fair repair, except for the identification of shallow grooves on the occlusal surfaces of the incisors.

Margaret examined the neck and moved down to the chest where an entry wound extending in a "Y" shape from each shoulder, meeting at the breastbone and carrying straight down to the pubic bone, had been roughly sutured with a coarse, black, braided, waxed twine.

Dr. Lan said, "The same twine appears to have been used to suture the wounds in all the victims." Margaret nodded.

There is mottled drying of the skin of the chest and abdomen, patchy areas of mould, freezer burn and adipocere.

She leaned over to examine the wound more closely.

There is also a faint yellow-brown discoloration of the skin of the chest and abdomen.

The colour rose high on Dr. Lan's face, and he also leaned over to make a closer examination of the wound. Margaret said, "Were you aware of this during the other two autopsies?"

Lan shook his head. "The bodies were still quite muddy. It is possible I overlooked it."

"Is it significant?" Li asked.

"We'll discuss that later," Margaret said coldly, and returned her attentions to the torso. She was afraid to speak directly to Li in case the emotion was apparent in her voice. She had slept for only a couple of hours before her body clock had wakened her, and she had lain for the rest of the night thinking about Mei-Ling, and about Li, and about their argument. Was it really just her paranoia and insecurity that made her distrust Mei-Ling? She had determined that today she was going to be only what she was good at – a professional pathologist.

The breasts are those of an adult female and are free of masses or trauma. The abdomen likewise bears the sutured incision but is otherwise free of trauma.

She pressed the flat of her hands on the soft, giving abdomen and then felt around with her fingers.

The abdomen is flat and on palpation appears to be missing organs. The external genitalia are those of an adult female and are free of trauma. The anus is patulous and atraumatic.

She moved on to the severed limbs, examining them for signs of trauma, other than amputation. But when she couldn't find any, she turned the body to examine the buttocks and the spine, and then moved back to where the head had been severed, for further external examination of the wound.

The amputation edge of the head is sharp, bloodless, and passes through the third cervical vertebra. The bone bears several deep sharp

tool marks, with the appearance of having been chopped. There is a
small amount of clotted blood adherent to the surface, but the tissues
are otherwise pale and bloodless. The amputation wounds of the upper
extremities are similar to the head amputation wound. They are cleanly
cut, bloodless and pale. There are no saw marks and they, likewise, have
the appearance of having been chopped at the level of the upper third
of the humerus. The leg amputation edges at mid-femur have the same
appearance.

"Is that important?" Li asked. "The lack of blood at the
amputation edges?"

Mei-Ling said, "All it means is that they were not hacked to
death. They were chopped up afterwards."

Margaret glanced at her and wondered why she was surprised. After all, Mei-Ling must have attended many autopsies.
Why shouldn't she understand the significance of the bloodless wounds? Mei-Ling shifted self-consciously under her piercing gaze and said, "We had a murderer here in the nineties
who liked to hack up his victims."

Margaret nodded, and then said, "Before going internal,
perhaps we should take her fingerprints. It's unlikely that any
of these women have criminal records, but it is a possibility.
And since identification is paramount here . . ."

Lan looked at her, surprised. "But that is not possible."

"Why?"

Lan lifted the fingers of the right hand. "The degree of decay,
Dr. Campbell. It would be impossible to take clean prints."

Carefully, Margaret took the hand from him and examined
it minutely, noting for the record an area of callus between the
top knuckle and the tip of the third finger. Then she started
easing the wrinkled skin away from the rotting flesh of the
fingers. "The process of degloving has already begun," she said.
"All we have to do is help it on its way." And slowly, delicately,

she eased the skin of the whole hand free from the decaying muscle and tissue inside. The fingernails came away also, so that she was left holding what looked much like a very thin, discoloured latex glove with neatly trimmed fingernails. It hung limp in her hand. Everyone around the table watched with fascinated horror a technique which was new to them. "If someone would bring an inkpad and card . . ." Margaret left the request hanging.

Lan nodded towards the uniformed forensics man, who hurried out and returned a few moments later with an ink-pad and several fingerprint cards. The young man looked perplexed when Margaret handed him a pair of latex gloves and asked him to put them on. Again he looked to Dr. Lan for guidance and again was given the nod. He pulled on the gloves and Margaret said, "Now slip your right hand inside the degloved skin."

There was something close to panic in his eyes now, and Margaret saw perspiration beading across his forehead. He hesitated, but a sharp word in Chinese from Lan prompted him to do as he was told, and he carefully slipped on the skin of the dead woman's hand like another layer of glove. "Now," Margaret said, "take a set of fingerprints as if they were your own."

The tension in the young man was apparent as one by one he rolled the "gloved" fingers of his right hand across the ink-pad, and then repeated the process on the white card, creating a perfect set of the dead woman's prints.

Apart from a faint humming of the lights, there was complete silence in the room and Margaret said, "After we have finished here, and before we carry out any further autopsies, we should examine the hands of all the victims for signs of trauma or other evidence, and then repeat this process. It will speed up any possible identification."

Lan looked at her, and she saw in his eyes for the first time, a glimmer of respect. He nodded his solemn agreement. "I agree, Doctor," he said.

Margaret's standing in the room had suddenly risen, and she returned to the body of the poor woman on the table to begin the internal examination.

There is a twenty-three inch "Y"-shaped sutured incision of midline anterior torso, running from each shoulder to the breastbone and down to the symphysis pubis.

She turned to Lan. "In my experience, Doctor, Chinese pathologists normally employ a single post-mortem incision running in a straight line from the laryngeal cartilage to the pubic bone. Similar to the practice of pathologists in Europe."

Lan nodded. "That is correct."

"The 'Y' incision is peculiarly American. The cut that I would make during autopsy."

Lan nodded again, but added, "I have made a 'Y' cut myself on occasion. But I agree, in China it is the exception rather than the rule."

Margaret carefully began unpicking the suture to ease open the chest cavity.

Upon removal of the suture, the edges of the incision are seen to be oily with decompositional change, but are otherwise erythematous, and there are multiple areas of clotted blood on the incision's edges.

She glanced up at Lan, and again the colour rose on his face. The exchange of looks was brief and wordless, but Li did not miss it. He decided to save any questions for later.

There are several areas of black gritty material in areas of haemorrhage of the incision edges of the abdominal wall. The sternum has been cut vertically and bears no sternotomy wires. The heart, lungs, kidneys, liver and pancreas are absent.

"What are sternotomy wires?" Li asked.

Again, before Margaret could answer, Mei-Ling said, "They are loops of wire that are used to close the sternum after open chest surgery."

Margaret inclined her head slightly. "You know your surgery, Miss Nien." And Mei-Ling blushed.

Margaret returned to a systematic examination of the internal organ systems, working her way through the remains of the pericardial sac and the various arteries and pulmonary vessels left by the removal of the heart. Suddenly she stopped as she uncovered the ends of what looked like two very small sutures of blue-coloured thread. She examined them for a moment, a frown of puzzlement on her face, and glanced at Dr. Lan. His dark eyes gave no clue as to his thoughts.

The major pulmonary vessels each bear a knot of suture, appearing to be a monofilament polypropylene, approximately half an inch in length.

She detailed the missing lungs and sectioned the neck before moving down to the stomach and intestine, noting the absence of the liver, gallbladder and pancreas, finding nothing abnormal until she began pawing her way through the retroperitoneal fat to make sure that the kidneys really were absent. There she found further suture knots on the renal arteries, and for a moment lost her scalpel as it slipped through fingers made greasy by the fat.

The spleen is normal size, shape and position . . . She stopped and thought about that for a moment. *The capsule is grey-purple and wrinkled. Sectioning reveals an oozing red-purple, autolytic cut surface with no recognisable follicular pattern.*

She moved, then, down to the pubic area and said, "Virgin territory. No one's been down here before us. At least, not with a scalpel." With the bladder exposed, she stuck a needle into it to try to draw out some fluid. None was forthcoming, and she made a small incision with her scalpel so that she could look inside. Satisfied that there was, indeed, a small amount of fluid there, she twisted the needle off the syringe and drew out about 10 cc of cloudy amber urine with the syringe alone, and handed it to an assistant for dispatch to the lab.

Now she cut out the bladder to expose the uterus which was pink-tan in colour, and shaped like an upside-down, flattened pear. At its lower end it opened into the cervix, a small tough ring which was pale tan in colour and shaped like the lips of a carp. "Looks like someone's lost their mom," Margaret said grimly.

"How can you tell?" Li asked, peering more closely.

"The cervix is normally round in nulliparous women – that is, a woman who hasn't had kids. When a woman has had children, the cervix is stretched and takes on the shape of a fish mouth. Like a carp. See it?"

Li nodded. This woman had probably delivered a child who would never see her again, who might not even know what had become of his or her mother. It was too easy to forget that these slabs of rotting meat on a table had once been living human beings just like them.

Margaret pulled the body of the uterus up, away from the vagina, felt for the cervix and cut across the vagina just below, leaving a small cuff of vagina around it. The fallopian tubes with their attached ovaries were connected to the uterus at the opposite top corners. She smiled to herself and said, "I always see this picture of a kind of homely, faceless bald kid. See . . . ? His ears would be the tubes and ovaries, and the cervix would be where his neck is."

If any of the others saw what she saw, they did not find it amusing, and there was an embarrassed silence. Margaret shrugged and sighed. People never recognised the need for some kind of relief from this constant exposure to death and decomposition, the ceaseless reminder of your own mortality. No matter how absurd, humour was at least some kind of escape. She caught Lan's eye and for a moment there was a twinkle in it. "I took up smoking," he said. And only Margaret understood the allusion.

She turned back to the womb, removing the tubes and ovaries and serially sectioning each to ensure that they were normal. Then she took a long set of forceps and tried to slide them up through the cervix into the body of the womb. It was a trick she often employed, using the forceps as a guide for her knife so that she could draw it up through the womb and cut it neatly in half. But in this case, she was unable to slide the forceps in. She tutted with irritation, and when she had finally bivalved the uterus, saw that adhesions on the inside wall had scarred it closed.

The uterus is grossly unremarkable, with the exception of a two by one centimetre area of scarring of the endometrium.

"What caused the scarring?" Mei-Ling asked.

Margaret looked up briefly. "Who knows? Probably some complication during childbirth. It is not uncommon. Certainly not as the result of sexual abuse, if that's what you're thinking. There is no indication that this woman has been sexually abused in any way."

One of the assistants held the head in place while the other cut through the top of the skull with an oscillating saw, allowing Margaret to ease out the brain.

The scalp, skull and dura are intact and free of trauma. The dura is thin and translucent. The brain is apparently symmetric, but softened and pale green with decompositional change. The convolutional pattern

cannot be evaluated due to decomposition. Serial sectioning and pal-
pation of the brain, brainstem and cerebellar material shows no gross
evidence of haemorrhage or mass lesion.

"So nobody smacked her over the head," Margaret said.

When she had completed her examination of the mus-
culoskeletal system, and examined the x-rays, she moved
away from the table, perspiration gathering in her eyes, and
removed her mask and goggles with a sense of relief. Off came
the gloves and the steel mesh that protected her non-cutting
hand, and as she removed her shower cap, her hair, damp with
sweat, fell free over her shoulders. Only then did her sense of
vulnerability return, and she steeled herself to mask it.

"Well . . . ?" Li asked impatiently.

But she ignored him and turned to Dr. Lan. "A few questions, Doctor, about your other autopsies." He nodded acquiescence. "Have you had the results of the urine tests back from
toxicology yet?"

"They came in this morning."

"Did the lab do a gas chromatography urine acidic drug
screen?"

"They did."

"And did they by any chance detect traces of succinic acid?"

Lan stared at her for a moment, a frown of confusion or
perhaps disbelief was etched on his brow. "How did you know
that?" he asked.

"And a benzodiazepine?"

Lan was astonished now. "Well . . . yes."

"In both victims?"

"But, Doctor, how can you — ?"

She raised a hand to cut him off. "Bear with me, I'm indulging in some intelligent guesswork here," she said. "It could save
us some time." She thought for a moment. "I would suggest a

search for succinylcholine in the brain tissue, and that we get the lab to do a mass spectrograph of the urine to confirm the possible presence of midazolam." She stripped off her apron and gown and crossed to the sink to wash her hands.

"Well?" Li asked.

"Well what?"

"What do you think?"

Margaret looked at Lan. "I think we should re-autopsy the first two victims, don't you, Doctor?" And she added quickly, before he was forced to lose face, "We very often see what we expect to see, and when the bodies have been in the ground and decomposed to this degree . . . well, I think comparisons would be invaluable." He nodded, aware of her consideration, and grateful for it.

"Do you wish to conduct all the autopsies?" he asked.

"No." She shook her head. "It would be far too much for one person." She flicked her head towards the camera on the wall. "I presume we had an audience. Your people?" He acknowledged with an almost indiscernible nod. "Then they'll know what to look for. Pick your best pathologists and we'll share the load. If you'll permit me to supervise, we could have them all done by tomorrow night." She dried her hands on a towel. "Now, I could do with a coffee."

They sat in a room at the end of an upstairs corridor. White leather settees on a polished wooden floor, brown curtains drawn on large windows. Two monitors set on tables pushed against a half-panelled wall showed camera-eye views of the autopsy rooms downstairs. The viewing room was still filled with the cigarette smoke of the pathologists who had watched Margaret at work. She sipped on a mug of hot green tea as the leaves rehydrated and sank to the bottom. She had forgotten that the Chinese rarely, if ever, drank coffee, and she could have done with a caffeine hit right now.

Li and Mei-Ling, and Lan and the forensics officer, sat sipping tea also, and watching her expectantly.

"Okay," Margaret said. "What do we know?" She drew a deep breath. "We know that she was an Asian woman, probably in her early thirties. We know that she was probably the mother of one or more children." She tilted her head slightly towards Mei-Ling. "Although with the enforcement of the One Child Policy, no doubt just the one." Mei-Ling did not react, fixing Margaret instead with a long, cold stare. Margaret continued, unaffected, "I would hazard a guess that she might have been a seamstress or a tailor's assistant." And she took pleasure in seeing a frown furl Mei-Ling's brow.

"How do you know that?" Li asked, astonished.

"There were tiny grooves on the occlusal surfaces of her front teeth. The kind of grooves that might be worn over many years of holding pins between them, as a seamstress does when she's pinning a pattern or fitting pieces on a tailor's dummy. I've often seen grooves like them, only bigger, in the teeth of joiners, where they hold nails between the incisors."

There was a small gasp from Dr. Lan. "Of course," he said. "The callus above the knuckle at the top of the middle finger. It would be caused by a sewing ring."

"A sewing ring?" Margaret asked. "You mean a thimble?"

"Not a thimble. In China a seamstress wears a ring at the top of her third finger to protect it as she pushes the needle through the material. It often leaves a callus, like a normal ring does at the root of the finger."

"Which makes it just about conclusive, then," Margaret said. "This woman almost certainly worked in the rag trade." She paused and chose her next words with care. "What I cannot say with any certainty is whether or not the poor woman had been experimented on by medical students or researchers . . ." This to let Lan off the hook. "But I can say with absolute certainty that she was not the subject of a post-mortem."

Li frowned and glanced at Dr. Lan. "But I understood Dr. Lan to have concluded that all these women had had autopsies performed on them."

Margaret said, "Dr. Lan was not entirely incorrect in that conclusion, Deputy Section Chief. The difference is that the woman I examined this morning had had an *ante-*, as opposed to a *post-*, mortem performed on her. In other words, she was very much alive when they cut her open." She looked at Lan. "Am I right, Doctor?"

He nodded gravely.

"How do you know?" Mei-Ling asked.

"The yellow-brown colour of the skin around the long central wound. Caused probably by betadine, an iodine tincture used to disinfect the skin before making an incision. You don't need to disinfect the skin of a dead person."

"And that is conclusive?" asked Li.

"No. But there were plenty of other clues. There was blood clotting around the chest and abdominal wounds. Doesn't happen if the person's dead. Also, the black gritty material I described along the incision edges was caused by an electrocautery device used to heat-seal small bleeders that aren't big enough to suture. Miss Nien made the point herself when she described to you why the wounds were bloodless where the limbs and head had been severed. The woman was certainly dead when they hacked her up." She took a sip of her tea. "And then there were those sutures inside, tying off bleeding arteries where organs had been removed. Like I said, dead people don't bleed."

Mei-Ling flicked her hair back from her face and said, "You mentioned something about succinic acid and midazolam found in the urine."

Margaret nodded. "I'm pretty sure the lab will find succinylcholine in the brain tissue. I would suspect that it was used, in conjunction with the midazolam, to keep the victims compliant. The midazolam sedates. It is often used in the induction phase of anaesthesia. It would need to be injected in small doses every few minutes to keep the victim riding on the edge of unconsciousness. The succinylcholine is a neuromuscular blocker. It would have paralysed the victims so that an ambu bag would have been required to force air into the lungs and keep the blood oxygenated. It sounds complicated, but it's quicker and easier to apply than full anaesthesia."

There was a long silence as everyone in the room took in the implications of Margaret's findings. Eventually Li said, "It looks like I am going to have to revise my initial thoughts on organ theft."

Margaret frowned. "What were those?"

Li said, "The reason I was brought in on this case is because of a body we found in Beijing last winter. A young woman, cut open and then dismembered. Identical in almost every detail to the Shanghai victims. I dismissed the thought that she might have been murdered for her organs because, although they had been removed, they were found with the body in a separate bag."

Margaret shook her head. "I don't think you can look for a motive in organ theft."

"Why not?"

"Well, for a start the lady I examined today appeared to me to have had a partial autopsy performed on her, albeit a 'live' one. And, as you know, the organs are always removed during autopsy to be sectioned."

"Why would anyone want to perform a 'live' autopsy?" Mei-Ling asked.

"I have no idea. But it certainly helps to establish cause of death. After all, if you remove someone's heart it is going to kill them. So the victim would die halfway through the procedure. Perhaps that's why the ante-mortem was not completed, why the spleen and the lower organs were left intact. Who knows?" She looked around the faces watching her, hanging on her every word, her every thought. "But more compelling still," she said, "there would be no need to keep someone alive in order to remove their organs for transplant. You would simply kill them and remove the organs afterwards. Cleaner, quicker, easier. I cannot think of a single reason why you would want to keep the person alive." She took another gulp of her tea. "The facts are these. Our seamstress was murdered by sterile surgical procedure. Her legs, arms and head were then crudely hacked off with some kind of heavy chopping instrument. The pieces were stored in a freezer for at least three months, and then dumped across the river anything up to a week ago, the process of thawing having increased the rate of decomposition. These are the facts. And other than indulging in wild speculation about it being the work of some kind of psycho surgeon, I'm afraid I can't offer you a single clue as to why."

CHAPTER FIVE

I

And still the rain fell. Li and Margaret stood on the step outside the mortuary door, under the cover of a red-tile canopy. She wanted air. He wanted a cigarette and the chance to talk to her. But for several minutes he said nothing, and she did not seem inclined to conversation. He sneaked a glance at her and saw that her pale skin was pink, the freckles dotted across her nose more pronounced, somehow, than usual. Her eyes appeared bluer than he remembered them, startling, like chips of ice set in rose gold. She caught him looking at her, and he glanced away guiltily. Finally he turned to look at her again and said, "Margaret, I am sorry about last night. I said things that – "

"Don't," she said. "It was my fault. I was tired and drunk, and stupid and thoughtless, as usual." She paused. "I hardly slept."

"Me neither."

She wanted to reach up and touch his face, and kiss his lips, and tell him she loved him. "Li Yan, I . . ."

But from somewhere Mei-Ling's voice came to them. The tail end of a conversation with Dr. Lan. She laughed at something he said, that long, braying laugh that Li found so endearing. And Margaret thought how it sounded just like a donkey in heat. She knew it was a laugh which, if she heard it often enough, could tip her over the edge. Like chalk on a blackboard, it made her flesh crawl. She gritted her teeth, and Mei-Ling came smiling out on to the step to join them.

"Hey," she said to Li. "We had better go. Detective meeting at 803 in fifteen minutes." And she headed for the car.

Li turned to Margaret, reluctant to go. "See you later."

"Sure," Margaret said, made sour again by Mei-Ling's interruption, and as he hurried through the rain to the passenger door, she called after him, "Just tell your detectives to keep that creepy medical student away from me in future."

Li froze, his fingers on the handle of the door. He half turned. "What medical student?" Mei-Ling started the car and peeped the horn and he lifted his hand from the door to silence her.

"I can't remember his name," Margaret said, raising her voice above the roar of the engine. "He's the night watchman at the place you found the bodies."

Mei-Ling cut the motor and opened the door.

"Jiang Baofu?" Li said as she got out of the car.

"Yeah, that sounds like it," Margaret said.

Mei-Ling looked from one to the other. "The medical student?"

Li ignored her. "When did you see him?"

"He approached me at the Peace Hotel yesterday evening, not long before you came to pick me up."

Li's jaw slackened in amazement, and he exchanged looks with Mei-Ling. "And he knew who you were?" Mei-Ling asked, quickly picking up the conversation.

"Sure. He said he'd seen my picture in the papers and wanted to help in the investigation."

Li was very still, like an animal that smells danger and is waiting to see the direction from which it is coming. "What did you say?"

"He freaked me," Margaret said. "Told me he'd followed me to the hotel from 803. I told him he shouldn't be talking to me and I didn't want him coming near me again."

"Why in the name of the sky did you not tell me this last night, Margaret?"

"I'd forgotten about him," Margaret said, irritation in her voice now. "And, anyway, last night didn't seem like an appropriate time to bring it up." Li stopped himself from saying that she had managed to raise much more inappropriate subjects. Margaret asked, "Should I be worried?"

"Jiang Baofu," Mei-Ling said, "currently tops a suspect list of one."

And Margaret remembered his grip on her arm, and a tiny shiver of fear ran through her.

"I want to know everything about him," Li said. "Everything. Where he lives, who his friends are, where he's worked. I want to know about his family, his girlfriends, his taste in clothes. I even want to know how often he takes a dump. And I want to know how a student struggling through medical school can afford to buy his own colour TV set."

Several of the detectives around the table scribbled notes. There was a tension in the air today, most of it emanating from the cold, still presence of Section Chief Huang sitting in silence in the chair nearest the window. Most of the section were aware that at the previous day's press briefing the media had been told that the eighteen bodies recovered from the site in Pudong were not murder victims. They also knew that their boss had briefed the Commissioner of Police prior to the press conference. And today they were being told by this Beijing cop, appointed by Director Hu, that the American pathologist he had brought in believed exactly the opposite.

No one had dared to look at Huang as Li briefed them on that morning's autopsy, on the pathologist's verdict that the victim had been drugged, and then been the subject of a "live" autopsy, or ante-mortem, and that the most likely cause of death was surgical removal of the heart. It was a bizarre conclusion, and neither Li nor his pathologist had been able to suggest a motive.

One detective had come up with Li's idea of organ theft, and Mei-Ling had repeated Margaret's assertion that if the victims had been murdered for their organs there would have been no need to keep them alive for the procedure. She also pointed out that the Beijing victim had been found with her organs in a bag beside the body.

"So we are sure, then, that this murder in Beijing is tied in with the bodies here in Shanghai?" the detective had persisted.

"No, Detective Dai," Mei-Ling had told him. "We don't know for sure. Not yet."

And Li said, "The body in Beijing has been kept in the freezer. I asked two days ago for it to be taken out and defrosted. In another couple of days it should be sufficiently thawed to allow for it to be re-autopsied. By then we will have sufficient evidence from Shanghai to make a definitive comparison. In the meantime I suggest we keep an open mind."

That had been half an hour earlier, since when there had been a long and animated discussion about the facts of the case, what they knew, what they didn't know, what they thought, what they thought they ought to do. It was the classic collective Chinese detective meeting, where everyone had a voice, an opinion, and the right to express it. But as yet it had borne no fruit. There had been an argument about how far back they should go in extracting records of women from the missing persons file. Li had decided on twelve months, which had brought a groan from around the table. It meant there could be hundreds of files to process. With the growth of the floating population, which now ran to several millions in Shanghai, people were always being reported missing. Very often it transpired they were not missing at all but had gone off in search of work, or run away to be married, or simply dropped out. There was a high, and growing, drop-out rate among the younger generation. Many teenage girls were drawn to the bright lights of Canton and Shenzhen where they often fell prey to drugs and prostitution, both of which were on the increase. And sometimes women who got pregnant, when they had already had a child, simply "disappeared" to have the baby somewhere else, away from the prying eyes of the local authorities.

When Li steered the meeting on to the subject of Jiang Baofu, and the revelation that he had followed Margaret back to her hotel, it had created a considerable stir in the room.

"You took his statement yesterday, Dai," Mei-Ling said. "What did you make of him?"

Dai leaned back and chewed his pencil thoughtfully. He was a young man very conscious of his image, from his immaculate white roll-neck sweater and powder blue Italian jacket, to his beautifully cut dark pants with a crease he could almost sharpen his pencil on. His hair was short, but expensively styled, and swept back from his face with gel. He tucked the thumb of his free hand into the shiny silver belt buckle at his waist. "He gave me the creeps," Dai said, and Li remembered Mei-Ling's words after they had talked to him at the site. *That boy's really creepy.* Margaret had called him a *creepy medical student*, and there had been something else she'd said . . . He thought for a moment, then remembered. *He freaked me*, she'd told them.

"I couldn't get him to shut up," Dai was saying. "Hell, usually it's the other way around with these people, like pulling teeth. But this guy had verbal diarrhoea. At a guess I'd say he was enjoying the whole process. He was asking more questions than I was. Unhealthy, you know. Morbid. Too helpful. In the end it was all I could do to get rid of him."

Another detective said, "But if this guy's involved, isn't he making himself a bit conspicuous? I mean, it's like he's deliberately trying to draw attention to himself."

"Perhaps," Mei-Ling said, "that's exactly what he wants us to think. Maybe he believes that by making himself high-profile, we'll dismiss him as being too obvious. And, well, being the night watchman at the site does make it all seem too easy. But, remember, if he did bury those bodies there, he never expected them to be found. He thought they'd be safely buried under tons of concrete by now, and he'd be home free."

Li said, "And the other thing to consider is that maybe he's just crazy." He remembered Margaret's half-joking, half-serious allusion to a *psycho surgeon*. "I mean, performing live autopsies on eighteen women – and probably more that we don't even know about yet – is not exactly the action of a sane person."

Dai said, "But he couldn't have been acting alone, could he? Someone else would have had to be administering the midazolam and pumping the ambu bag."

Li paused. He had not considered this. Of course the killer could not have been acting alone. It had to have been a collaborative effort, in which case it could not have been the action of a solitary madman. Could there be two, or more, of them. How did people like that find each other? Was it possible for insane people to work efficiently in a team? "That's a good point, Detective Dai," he said at length. "But we shouldn't let speculation on this deflect us from our first priority – to identify these victims as quickly as we can."

The scraping of a chair being pushed back abruptly turned all their heads towards the window, where Huang now stood silhouetted against the light behind him. Beyond the Section Chief, and beyond the east wing of the department, Li could see the traffic streaming by on the overhead road. But Huang said nothing. He simply turned towards the door and made his exit in silence. None of them knew whether it was a comment on Li's handling of the case, or whether he simply had another appointment. But it left a tension in the room that did not dissipate until Li called the meeting to an uneasy close.

II

Margaret was exhausted. Her eyes were stinging. Every muscle in her body gave the impression of having seized up. Her limbs had, apparently, doubled in weight, and lifting her legs or arms in the simple act of walking or raising a drink to her lips was a colossal effort. She felt battered and bruised, and all she wanted to do was lie down. Jetlag and the emotions of the last few days had finally caught up with her.

The hands of all the remaining bodies had been examined and fingerprinted. Then together with Dr. Lan, she had carried out repeat autopsies on the first two bodies and found the same betadine colouring around the entry wounds after cleaning away the dirt that still clung to the decaying flesh. They had also found several small sutures, tying off arteries where organs had been removed. Dr. Lan made no comment on the fact that these had not appeared on his initial reports. It was clear to Margaret that the autopsies had been cursory and careless, and yet Dr. Lan did not strike her as a careless man. His professional and personal embarrassment was patent. His integrity had been compromised, and Margaret suspected that he had been a reluctant instrument of political convenience. No doubt he had not envisaged having his work scrutinised by another professional. In order to keep him on side, she decided not to say or do anything that would draw attention to the obvious shortcomings of the initial autopsies.

She had concentrated, instead, on going over all the toxicology reports, with Dr. Lan translating, and together they had discussed another possible cause of death. She had then studied all the x-rays taken of the body pieces as they had been found, and then the whole-body x-rays.

Although she had not felt like it, she had agreed to Lan's suggestion that they begin three fresh autopsies, Dr. Lan and one of his team working in the twin-tabled room, Margaret in here on her own. The Chinese pathologists had made a point of asking her through to consult on every new or unusual finding, wishing to have her corroborate an opinion or make an alternative suggestion. Her concentration was now wavering.

She had almost completed her autopsy, having dealt fully with the torso and limbs and moving now to the head. Because the head had been severed so far down the neck, she had decided to leave the dissection of the neck until she dealt with the head. The larynx, trachea and mainstem bronchi were normally the most boring and routine of the autopsy procedures, only occasionally enlivened if the victim had been unfortunate enough to have choked to death on a piece of food that was still lodged in the throat. She had already noted that the distal portions of the trachea and the oesophagus were absent because of the removal of the lungs. Now, working on that portion of the neck still attached to the head, she lifted the skin of the front of the neck, using her fingers to bluntly dissect it from the underlying tissue, while pulling it up towards the chin. Then she freed the remaining trachea and oesophagus together from the surrounding muscles and blood vessels, running her scalpel along each side and pulling. At this stage, they would only come partially free, because they were still attached by the tongue at the top end.

Carefully, so as not to break through the skin of the neck from the inside, she took a long blade like a six-inch fillet knife and cut the tongue free from the jawbone by blindly drawing the blade gingerly along the inside of it. She then stuffed the tip of the tongue backwards, as if down the throat, and pulled it free, in the same movement completely removing the neck organs – tongue, portions of oesophagus and trachea, larynx and thyroid gland.

Flipping them over, she then took a pair of scissors and cut open the oesophagus, like opening up a soft hose, which she then cut free from the trachea. Now that the trachea, held open by incomplete rings of cartilage, was revealed, she was able to run the scissors up the back of it, taking advantage of the break in the cartilage. She checked the laryngeal cartilage, or Adam's apple, for fractures, then finding none pried it apart to reveal the smooth pink-grey mucosa of the vocal folds. Immediately she spotted the whiter patches of several polypoid nodules.

"How is it going?"

She looked up, her concentration broken for the moment, to see Li standing in the doorway. He looked tired, too, but she immediately felt her own fatigue lifting. "Hi," she said. And then almost straight away her lassitude returned as she saw

Mei-Ling appearing behind him. Apparently it was impossible for Li to go anywhere without her.

He walked in and glanced at the woman on the table. She looked unreal somehow, waxen yellow and lifeless, like pieces of a wax corpse used for instruction in a professor's teaching lab. There was something about the expression fixed on her face, barely discernible now because of decomposition, that was odd. As if it had been frozen in a moment of pain or fear or both. Her hair was smeared across it, and there was something terribly sad conveyed by her expression, an insight into the last moments of her life, made almost eerie by the absence of her eyes.

"Were the eyes gouged out in some kind of attempt to disguise the face, do you think?" he asked.

"They weren't gouged, they were surgically removed," Margaret said, and Li had an immediate picture in his mind of a large glass jar filled with eyes staring out at him.

"Why would someone want to do that?" Mei-Ling asked.

"Why would someone want to do any of this?" Margaret said.

Li was looking at the dead woman's face again. "Was she in pain, do you think, when she died?"

Margaret looked at her expression. "Trying to reach a high note, maybe." She smiled wanly and Li frowned.

"What do you mean?"

She indicated the neck she had just sectioned, running a finger down each of the pink-grey folds she had uncovered. "The vocal cords," she said. "If you look closely you'll see small patches of white, and if you look more closely still, you'll see that they are caused by tiny reactive pedunculated polyps. Effectively small, non-cancerous tumours, known in the trade as 'singer's nodules.'"

"You mean this woman was a singer?" Mei-Ling asked.

"Can't say for sure," Margaret said. "But she was someone who used her voice a lot. And if you look at her teeth you'll see she was a heavy smoker. Which always makes the condition worse. Now, maybe she was one of those conductresses you hear screaming through the loudspeaker system at passengers on passing buses, but if you look at her fingernails you'll see she'd had a manicure not long before her death. I know you don't like to talk about 'class' in China, but I don't think your average bus conductress gets her nails manicured. Wrong class. So my guess would be that this lady was a classical singer of some sort. Aged maybe around thirty."

Li nodded appreciatively. "Well, that at least gives us something to go on."

"And something else," Margaret said. She crossed to the long, polished stainless steel worktop and shuffled through the envelopes of x-rays lying there until she found what she was looking for. She removed two x-rays from one of the envelopes and laid one on a lightbox and switched it on. Immediately they saw that it was the x-ray of a foot. "This is one of the ladies being autopsied next door right now." She lifted the sheet off and replaced it with the other. "This one shows it better." She leaned over it, and with her finger traced the line of the second and third metatarsals. "These bones that run between the toes and the rest of the structure that makes up the ankle and the heel . . ."

"Metatarsals," Mei-Ling said.

Margaret flicked her a thoughtful glance. "That's right." She turned back to the x-ray. "You can see scarring there on these middle two. Small calluses where stress fractures have failed to heal. Difficult to tell from these whether they are incomplete fissures or actual breaks."

"What does that tell us?" Li asked.

"Regardless of what caused the fractures, continued and unprotected weight bearing has almost certainly caused them to heal poorly. And if you want to take a look at the girl on the table next door, you'll see how well developed the muscles are in her legs, and in her shoulders and arms and neck. My guess is that she was an athlete of some sort, possibly a gymnast."

Li looked at Margaret afresh, with the admiration and respect he always had for her when she was doing her job. Her observation of detail, her insightful interpretation, the breadth and range of her knowledge and experience. He had never worked with anyone quite like her. It reminded him of why he felt about her the way he did, when by any other measure she was a very difficult person to love. That, and the acute vulnerability that lay beneath her well-polished veneer of cynicism and acid wit.

Mei-Ling was also clearly impressed, although endeavouring not to show it. "Could be worse," she said. "Three possible clues to identity out of . . . how many autopsies?"

"Six," Margaret said. "And you're right. It could be worse. You could still be labouring under the illusion that the victims had all died a natural death." She switched off the lightbox and slipped the x-rays back in the envelope. "In fact, we are now looking at yet another possible cause of death."

"Oh?" Mei-Ling was still stinging from the force of Margaret's rebuke. She glanced at Li, but he appeared to be oblivious.

"What is that?" he asked.

"The midazolam," Margaret said. "It's quite commonly used in minor surgical procedures as a sedative to produce amnesia of the procedure . . . if you were having a tooth pulled, or a burn scrubbed out, a scope put down your throat, or even . . ." she glanced at Mei-Ling, ". . . if you were having an abortion."

She paused for a moment, but Mei-Ling was not rising to the bait. "Like I said, it would be used in small, frequent doses. In a high dose, though, it can cause cardiac arrest. So that might well have been a quick and easy way of finishing the victims off at some point during the procedure."

"But since we don't have the hearts to hand, you can't say for sure," Mei-Ling said.

"Having the heart available wouldn't help," Margaret corrected her. "It would take about twelve hours for the heart tissue to show a visible reaction – and none of these women lived that long. It's the tox that's important here."

She returned to the table to complete the final elements of the autopsy. "With four of us taking three autopsies each, we should be through the rest of them by tomorrow night. Although it will be a day or two before all the results are back from toxicology." She peeled the woman's scalp back from the skull. "By the way, I've got dinner reservations for us tonight at the Dragon and Phoenix restaurant on the eighth floor of the Peace Hotel. Apparently it has wonderful views of the Bund." She glanced up at Li and said, pointedly, "A table for two, that is. We haven't had a chance to talk since I got back from the States."

Li glanced at Mei-Ling uncomfortably. But she smiled sweetly. "Yes," she said to Margaret, "it is a wonderful view. You should make the best of the limited time you have. After all, you will be leaving for Beijing the day after tomorrow."

"Will I?" Margaret looked at Li.

"Had you not told her?" Mei-Ling said.

Li said quickly, "I need you to look at the body we found in Beijing, Margaret. I have asked them to translate the original autopsy report, and the body has been out of the freezer for two days now. So another couple of days and it will be thawed."

"I see." Margaret turned back to the severed head. She could not meet Mei-Ling's eyes. Although Margaret knew Mei-Ling could not have arranged it this way, it still felt like she had somehow won a battle of wills.

Li said, "And I need to ask you a favour." When Margaret did not look up he elucidated. "I would like you to collect Xinxin and bring her back down with you."

Margaret's face immediately lit up at the prospect, and she looked at Li with shining eyes. "Of course," she said. "Is she with Mei Yuan?"

He nodded. "You will need to pick her up at nursery school. One of the kindergartens here in Shanghai has agreed to take her temporarily. My hotel has been able to give her an adjoining room, and I am paying a babysitter to look after her in the evenings, and weekends if I am working."

"That's great," Margaret said. "We'll be able to spend some time with her."

"Yes," Li said enthusiastically. "Mei-Ling managed to fix everything up for me here in Shanghai. She loves kids, too. So Xinxin won't be short of people to play with her."

And Margaret's face clouded again. It felt like Mei-Ling was invading every part of her space. "That'll be nice," she said with a tone, and switched on the oscillating saw to cut through the skull.

III

The room was small and square with plain, white-painted walls. The paint had come away in patches where papers or posters taped to the walls had been removed, leaving their outlines clearly visible, like ghosts. There was one square window on the back wall, giving out on to seedy-looking police apartment blocks, lights shining from hundreds of windows in the dark, wet night. There was a desk charred with cigarette burns, an uncomfortable-looking chair, and a single strip light hanging from the ceiling and casting a harsh glow around the room. This was to be Li's home for the duration of the investigation. Like Section Chief Huang, it did not exactly feel welcoming. Next door was the audio-video room, and the sound of tapes being run and re-run boomed through the wall. The detectives' room was at the far end of the corridor, and Mei-Ling's office was beyond that.

"It's not much," she said. "But someone loved it. He didn't want to leave it."

"Should I know who it was?" Li asked.

She shook her head. "Better not."

There was a sharp rap on the open door, and they turned to find Detective Dai standing there clutching an armful of files. "There's a call for you, boss," he said to Mei-Ling.

She nodded and said to Li, "Talk to you later."

When she was gone, Dai put the files on to Li's desk where there were already several dozen piling up. He glanced at Li, somewhat uncertainly. "I read up about those serial killings you solved in Beijing," he said, and Li realised that Dai was a little in awe of him. "Pretty smart bit of detective work."

"I got lucky," Li said. "And even luckier still to be alive."

Dai nodded. "I knew Duanmu Hongyu," he said. Li frowned, trying to remember where he'd seen the name. Then it came back to him. The ebony bust in the courtyard. Duanmu Hongyu had been a famous Shanghai detective working out of 803. Dai was trying to impress him. "He kind of took a fatherly interest in me, you know. A kind of mentor. He was a great guy."

Li nodded and rounded his desk to pull up his chair and sit down. He fumbled in his pockets for his cigarettes, but

Dai had a pack out before he could find them. Li took one and Dai lit it. As Dai lit his own, Li asked him, "What age are you, detective?"

"Twenty-eight, Chief," Dai said.

"I'm not a chief," Li told him. "Just a deputy."

Dai nodded. "So, have they got many women in the department in Beijing?" he asked.

"Sure."

"I mean, high-ranking. You know, like Deputy Section Chief Nien."

"Not right now," Li said.

Dai nodded sagely and drew on his cigarette. "Women are okay, I guess. They can hold up as much sky as they want, but they're a bastard to work for."

"Oh?" Li was not going to comment, but he was interested to hear what Dai wanted to say.

Dai rested one butt cheek on the edge of Li's desk. "Yeah, you know, sex always comes into it. You can't get away from it. I mean, Mei-Ling, she's all right. But she's got this thing for senior officers. You know, like rank or something turns her on. Like she looks down on the rest of us, 'cos we're not good enough for her."

Li had heard enough. "It's Deputy Section Chief Nien to you, Dai," he said. "And I don't approve of detectives referring to senior ranking officers in that way."

"Oh." Dai seemed surprised, but not unduly put out. He shrugged. "Sorry, Chief." He stood up. "Oh, by the way, top of that pile there's a file on a lady called Fu Yawen. Comes from Luwan District in the old French Town."

"What about her?"

"She and her old man worked in a small tailor's shop on Songshan Road. She went missing about five months ago."

When Dai had gone, Li pulled the file on Fu Yawen in front of him, but he couldn't concentrate on it. He wondered what Dai had meant when he said Mei-Ling had a "thing" for senior officers. What senior officers had he been talking about? Or was it just jealousy and gossip? He was aware that Mei-Ling was attracted to him. It was clear in her eyes, in the way she would touch him from time to time, in brief unguarded moments of intimacy. And yet, he had always had the strangest sensation that this familiarity she had displayed towards him, almost from the moment they met, was habitual, a transfer of feelings from another relationship.

He was reluctant to admit to himself that he found her attractive, too, that he enjoyed those fleeting moments of unguarded intimacy, the touch of her fingers on the back of his hand setting butterflies fluttering in his belly and a strange, distant stirring in his loins. For if he were to allow himself to acknowledge these emotions, they would surely be accompanied by a haunting sense of guilt, and raise questions he did not want to face right now about his feelings for Margaret.

And then he thought about Margaret, and her odd, paranoid behaviour, her antipathy towards Mei-Ling, the directness of her question about what was going on between them. *Two attractive people thrown together on a stressful job in a strange city — it wouldn't be the first time it had happened*, she had said. And he remembered his guilt. Why had he felt guilty? And what instinct was it that had led Margaret, within hours of arriving in Shanghai, to suspect the existence of feelings he had not even admitted to himself? The instant hostility between Margaret and Mei-Ling had been immediately apparent to him, but still remained a mystery. Not for the first time in his life, he found himself being confounded by his own emotions, and thrashing his way clumsily through the uncharted waters of an uncertain relationship. He checked the time. He was due to meet Margaret for dinner in two hours, and somewhere deep inside he found himself dreading it.

He forced himself to focus on the file in front of him. Here, he thought, he would find himself on safer, more familiar ground.

IV

Margaret found the note from Geller pushed under her door. *I'm in the bar if you feel like a drink.* She felt very much like a drink. But first she needed to shower, to wash away the olfactory residue of the autopsy room, to change her clothes and become that other person she was when she wasn't being Margaret Campbell the pathologist. That other Margaret Campbell who always let her down, always said the wrong thing, always fell in love with the wrong people.

By the time she found her way to the bar she had relaxed a little. The hot water of the shower had taken some of the tension out of her muscles, and an overwhelming sense of fatigue had caused her to lower her customary defences. She didn't really want to think too much about anything, just let a little alcohol course through her veins and forget for the moment all life's little unhappinesses.

Geller was sitting on his own at the bar nursing what Margaret guessed was not his first beer. He glanced at her as she hoisted herself on to the stool next to him. "Vodka tonic?"

"You learn quickly."

"I come from a long line of circus animals. We're easily trained." He waved his hand at a girl who was hiding behind the coffee maker and she was forced to come out into the open. He ordered a vodka and another beer. "Good day?" he asked Margaret.

"As days go."

"You want to tell me about it?"

"No."

He shrugged. "Well, that's pretty unequivocal."

She grinned. "That's what they call me. Unequivocal Campbell."

"Hey, sounds like the title of a movie from the nineteen fifties." He paused for a moment. "Jeez, was that really last century? Makes me feel so old."

The drinks came, and Margaret took a long, appreciative pull at hers. The alcohol immediately relaxed her even further. She looked at Geller, then glanced around the empty bar. "Not exactly busy, is it?"

"That's because the prices are so outrageous," he said. "Of course, you wouldn't know, since you always leave me to pick up the tab."

She laughed. "Well, why don't we just put this one on my room?"

"Naw," he said. "I can claim it on expenses."

"Of course," she said. "I keep forgetting. I'm just work to you."

"Pretty goddamned hard work, too," he drawled, and then grinned.

"I'm surprised to find you on your own," Margaret said. "Didn't you tell me that the press pack would be pursuing me relentlessly while I was here?"

"Yep."

"So where are they?"

"Probably camped out at the Westin Tai Pin Yang Hotel on the road out to Hongqiao Airport."

Margaret was taken aback. "What are they doing out there?"

"Could be that's where they think you're staying." He took a long draught of beer.

She looked at him with amusement. "And where would they get an idea like that, Mr. Geller?"

He shrugged very casually. "Beats me. And, hey, it's Jack. Okay? Nobody calls me *Mister* Geller except my landlord when the rent's a week overdue."

"That's very polite of him."

"You should hear what he calls me after a month."

"You don't make a very good living, then?"

He rubbed thoughtfully at a jawline that needed a shave. "Sometimes yes, sometimes no. Depends on whether the news is good or bad. If it's good I can go hungry. See, Margaret . . . you don't mind if I call you Margaret?"

"It's a lot nicer than what a lot of people call me."

He chuckled, and she knew from the warmth in his eyes that he liked her. It was good to have someone liking her for a change. Too often it was hostility she saw in people's eyes. "See, trying to sell a story idea to a paper or a newsmag is a lot like being pregnant – a heavy burden and lots of labour. Cynic that I am, I can also tell you that you are more likely to get screwed at the end of the project rather than the beginning."

Margaret laughed. She liked Geller, too. He was easy company. Spoke the same language, shared a sense of humour. Nuance was no problem.

"So I guess you're still not going to tell me anything about progress on the inquiry?" he said.

"I'd say that was a pretty fair guess."

Then he threw one out of left field and caught her completely off-guard. "So are you and Deputy Section Chief Li still an item then?"

For a moment she didn't know what to say. There didn't seem any point in denying it. He had obviously done his research. So she said, "For the moment."

Something in her tone caused him to look at her more closely. "Trouble in paradise?"

She shrugged, trying not to show concern. "Oh, you know how it is: American girl meets Chinese guy, falls in love. Chinese guy meets Chinese girl, American girl can't compete."

"Why?"

"Language, culture, politics, you name it. How do you bridge a culture gap that's five thousand years wide? She's a fish out of water here, he's a fish out of water there. What other pool can they swim in?"

"Hey, Margaret," he said, returning to his beer, "if I knew the answer to that one I wouldn't be spending so much of my life picking up a bar-room tan." And Margaret knew immediately that this was more than just a smart line. There was a depth of feeling somewhere in there that hinted at an unhappy experience, perhaps not dissimilar to her own.

Li hurried through revolving doors from the street. The lights of arcade shops to the left and right reflected brilliantly off a polished marble floor. He hurried past the foreign exchange counter and into the sprawling lounge area opposite reception. The sound of a live jazz band drifted out from the entrance to a bar in the far corner. He walked briskly across the lobby to where a young Chinese attendant stood guarding double doors leading to the sound of Dixieland beyond. She wanted him to pay an entrance fee. He glanced into the room behind her and saw that the bar was huge, with long lines of neatly ordered and empty tables. The music was deafening. Margaret had said she would meet him in the bar, but this surely couldn't be it. "Is there another bar?" he asked.

The attendant clearly thought he was some kind of Chinese cheapskate and pointed condescendingly up the stairs.

The Art Deco bar on the first-floor mezzanine was empty also. He saw a waitress hovering behind the coffee maker hoping he wouldn't notice her. He went back downstairs to the reception desk and asked what room Miss Margaret Campbell was in, then rode the elevator up to the sixth floor and wandered down a long, thickly carpeted corridor until he found room 605. There was a bell push on the wall beside the door. He pressed it and heard a doorbell chime distantly in the room. He waited, but there was no response. He rang again and when there was still no response, knocked on the door and called, "Margaret?" Quietly at first, and then louder. A door opened further down the hall and an elderly Japanese gentleman glared at him.

He went back down to reception and asked them to call the room. The receptionist waited patiently as the phone rang out. Li asked if Margaret's key had been returned. The receptionist checked and said no, the key was still out. Li was initially perplexed, and then annoyed, and somewhere in the background a little relieved. He waited around in the lobby for another fifteen minutes before writing a quick note which he left with the receptionist. And then he headed with righteous indignation back to the Da Hu Hotel to lie on his bed listening to the traffic rumble past his window on Yan'an Viaduct Road, and to try to make sense of the confusion of conflicting emotions in his head.

V

At first she had no idea what had wakened her. Some sound or smell or movement had entered her consciousness. Her eyelids were so heavy she could barely force them apart. She saw a thin line of light coming under the door from the corridor, and smelled the faintly pungent odour of some distantly familiar oriental perfume. Then she heard the slightest swish of silk on silk, like a whisper, and turned over on to her back to see a figure standing over her, dressed in a long, hand-embroidered gown. At first she could not see the face, but knew it was a woman from the small, slender build. She was standing motionless, just looking down at Margaret in the dark. Quickly, Margaret fumbled for the light switch, and blinking in the sudden glare of electric light, she saw that it was Mei-Ling, dark eyes burning like coals. Suddenly Mei-Ling's clasped hands shot above her head and Margaret saw the glint of light on a long, slender blade as it came arcing down towards her.

She screamed and sat up suddenly in the dark, the sound of blood pulsing through her head, the echo of her own voice still reverberating around the room. She was alone in the room, fully dressed, sitting up on top of a bed that had not been slept in. The red numerals of the digital clock at the bedside glowed in the dark. They showed 3:12. Margaret blinked in confusion. She was disorientated. Had she been dreaming, or was this the dream? Where was she? A hotel room. She saw light flooding out from the open door of the bathroom. China. Shanghai. And, suddenly, she remembered her dinner with Li. She looked again at the clock and at first could make no sense of the time it was showing. Twelve minutes past three? How was that possible? Was it morning or afternoon. And, then, with a sickening sense of realisation she knew what had happened.

She had spent an hour in the bar with Jack, talking, and then she had told him she was meeting someone for dinner and was going to her room to freshen up. She had lain down on the bed for a moment, just so that she could close her eyes and stop the room spinning. She had only had one drink, but the effects of the alcohol combined with a serious shortage of sleep had been fatal. She must have slept for more than eight hours. She still found it hard to believe that it was the middle of the night, that she had missed her dinner with Li by seven hours. Seven hours! It did not seem possible.

She went into the bathroom to repair the make-up smudged around her eyes, and took the lift down to the ground floor. The girl at reception remembered Li quite clearly. He had gone up to Margaret's room, she said, and when he couldn't get a reply had come down and asked them to phone from there. He appeared sort of angry, she said.

"Did he leave a note?" Margaret asked.

"One moment." The receptionist searched beneath the counter for a few seconds and then handed Margaret an envelope. She tore it open and found a folded sheet of hotel letter headed paper. Li had scrawled a telephone number and his room number, and a terse "Call me" on it.

"Can I use the phone?" Margaret asked.

The receptionist gave her an odd look. "Now?"

"Yes, of course, now," Margaret snapped.

The receptionist lifted a phone on to the counter and Margaret quickly dialled the number Li had left. Someone answered in Chinese, and Margaret, frustrated, could not get her to speak English. She thrust the phone at the receptionist. "Ask them to get me room 223," she said.

The receptionist spoke into the receiver, and after a lengthy conversation handed it back. It was ringing. After an eternity, Margaret heard a sleepy male voice saying. "*Wei?*"

"Li Yan?"

A moment's silence, then, "Margaret?"

"Li Yan, I'm so sorry," she blurted.

"Do you know what time it is?" He must have checked his bedside clock and was clearly aggravated.

"I fell asleep," she said lamely. "I just lay down for a minute and . . . I don't know, the next thing it's three in the morning. I was just so tired."

"Yeah, well, right now I'm pretty tired, too," he said, barely able to keep the irritation out of his voice. "We can talk about this tomorrow." And he hung up.

Margaret was taken aback by his abruptness. She replaced the receiver in the cradle and hurried away before the receptionist saw her hurt and embarrassment. She went back up to her room, but she was wide awake now and she knew there was no point in even getting into bed. She turned on the television and tried to watch a film on HBO Asia, but it was halfway through, and she couldn't concentrate for a thousand thoughts crowding her mind. She got up and went to the window, drawing the curtain half open so that she could peer down into the deserted Nanjing Road. It had stopped raining, for the first time, she thought, since she had arrived. And suddenly she had an overwhelming desire to breathe fresh, cold air, to feel the breeze on her face, to stretch her legs along the deserted waterfront of the Bund. She found a jacket and tied a scarf at her neck. In the corridor, an attendant in a white jacket lay asleep stretched across two chairs in the open doorway of a service cupboard. She guessed he must have been there when she went down to reception. But she hadn't noticed. Now she tiptoed past him to the lift.

The Bund was deserted, and without its light show as dull as any city street anywhere in the world, all colour bled out of it by the pervasive yellow of the sodium street lights. Gone were the green, yellow and blue floodlights, the giant neon ads that just a few hours ago had shone brilliantly against the night sky. *Maxell, L'Oréal Paris, Sharp, Nescafé.* Gone were the teeming crowds of tourists and Shanghainese that constantly ebbed and flowed along the length of the promenade. Across the river, only the red winking navigation lights on the tops of buildings betrayed the existence of the financial miracle that was Pudong. The six lanes of the Bund were eerily empty. The clock face on the tower halfway along glowed like a pale moon rising over the deserted city. It was nearly a quarter to four.

An occasional cyclist drifted past, heading perhaps for an early shift at some factory. The odd taxi cruised by, slowing down as it passed Margaret on the sidewalk, its driver leaning over expecting her to signal that she wanted a lift. It was inconceivable that some *yangguizi* would wander the empty streets at four in the morning without requiring a taxi. She waved them all on.

Half a dozen cabs were pulled into the kerb opposite the end of Nanjing Road, on the river side of the Bund. A woman in a white jacket and round white hat squatted on a stool by a brazier. A large pot of soup bubbled and steamed on top of the coals, and she filled mugs from it with a ladle for the drivers who stood around talking and smoking and stamping their feet in the early morning chill.

The drivers watched curiously as Margaret looked both ways along the Bund before running across the six lanes, pausing only briefly at the central reservation. There was no traffic, only the distant lights of a truck approaching from the direction of the Nanpu Bridge. All conversation around the brazier had come to a halt. For a moment, perhaps, they thought she was going to ask for some soup. But she hurried past, running quickly up the steps to the long, deserted promenade. It was darker here, away from the street lights. Umbrellas still stood open at stands where earlier vendors had sold drinks and snacks and Fuji film. Now there was not a soul in sight. An elaborate fountain, usually illuminated by green lights, had been switched off. She crossed to lean on the wall and look out over the black waters of the river. A heavily laden barge chugged by, so low in the water it was hard to believe it would not sink. There was one small lamp burning in the pilot's cabin, but no navigation lights. From somewhere a long way upriver came the blast of a ship's foghorn.

She breathed deeply and was sure she could smell the sea, which was not so far away in the Yangtse River estuary. She walked slowly north along the promenade, arms crossed, hugging herself to keep warm. A deep depression had settled on her. Li was the only reason she had ever stayed in China. The only reason she had come back. Without him there was no reason to be here. Ever. She didn't even want to contemplate the possibility of what she would do if she lost him. "Home" had seemed so alien to her during the few days she had been back there. And yet she could not bring herself to think of China as home. She felt displaced and, although her mother was still alive, orphaned by the death of her father, as if her anchor chains had been severed and she had been cast adrift on an uncharted sea. God knew what shore she would wash up on. All she could do, she thought, was go with the flow, let the currents take her where they would. There was no point in fighting against them. It was futile and exhausting. She would complete her work on the Shanghai murders, re-autopsy the body in Beijing, bring Xinxin back south and then see what happened. If Li was really drawn to Mei-Ling, then she knew she couldn't compete. As she had told Jack, they both swam in very different pools.

She reached the gates of Huangpu Park. They were locked. And beyond them, in the dark, she could just see the Shanghai People's Hero Memorial Pagoda in the reflected light of the streetlamps. There were trees and shrubs here that screened the promenade from the road. The occasional passing vehicle seemed very distant. And on the other side of the wall, the river slapped dully, erratically, against the stone. The sound of movement in the darkness of the bushes startled Margaret. She stood stock still. Had it been an animal? But she wasn't going to stay to find out. She turned and started walking quickly, back the way she had come. The moonface on the clock tower was a very long way away. She had come further than she thought. She didn't look back for a long time, concentrating on control-ling an urge to run. It had probably been a dog, or maybe even a rat. She glanced over her shoulder for reassurance, and saw, about a hundred metres back, the shadowy figure of a man hur-rying in her wake. She almost screamed, and now had no diffi-culty giving in to her impulse to run. She ran until she reached the dry bed of the fountain and looked back again. But there was no one there. No sound or sign of movement. She stopped to regain her breath, momentarily relieved. Had she just imag-ined it? She decided to get down on to the sidewalk and the lit, wide open space of the road. In the distance she could see, still gathered around the soup pot, about half a dozen drivers. They were almost within shouting distance. She ran down a flight of steps, passing the entrance to an underpass, walls lined with illuminated posters that threw out a strong, bright light. A movement in her peripheral vision caused her to turn, catching her breath, and for a moment she saw a man's face, caught full in the light of the underpass. He was short and thick-set, with long, straggling hair and a broad, flat, Mongolian face. His eyes were like black slits. She could see no light in them, and the upper half of his mouth was stretched over brown, protruding teeth, turned up and horribly distorted by the ugly scarring of a hare-lip. He froze, like a rabbit caught in headlights. She would have screamed, but she couldn't seem to find a breath. For what felt like an incredibly long moment, their eyes met. She could almost have reached out and touched him. And then she turned and ran down the rest of the steps to the sidewalk and sprinted towards the little gathering of taxi drivers drinking soup.

By the time she reached them they had all turned and were staring at her in astonishment. She slowed to a stop, gasping, her lungs burning. She turned around and the street behind her was empty. Not a soul nor a vehicle in sight. She turned back to meet the curious faces of the drivers and the soup lady who gaped in wonder at this blonde-haired blue-eyed woman out running in the middle of the night. For an absurd moment she wondered if they had thought she was jogging. It was clear from their expressions they thought she was insane. She glanced back, but there was still no sign of the man with the hare-lip. She fought to bring her breathing back under control and tried a half smile that she knew was probably more like a grimace. Still they stared at her in mute amazement, some of them holding mugs in suspended animation, halfway to their mouths. She felt compelled to say something and muttered, absurdly, "*Ni hau.*"

Compelled, out of habit, to respond to a foreigner saying *hello* in Chinese, they mumbled *ni hau* in return. She looked either way along the road, and then forced herself to walk calmly across it. She could almost feel their eyes on her back.

She passed the lights of a twenty-four-hour Citibank, with a row of glowing ATMs behind sliding glass doors. Inside, a night watchman was reading a book and playing loud music. She turned up Nanjing Road and took one final look back. There was no one there except for the taxi drivers and the soup lady. She pushed, relieved, through the revolving doors of the Peace Hotel and realised that in all the months she had spent in China, this was the first time she had felt any sense of threat in the streets.

CHAPTER SIX

I

Li sat lost in his own thoughts as Mei-Ling steered them west through the traffic on Huaihai Road. The rain had stayed off and the streets were almost dry. This had once been the heart of the old French Town, the former Avenue Joffre, as smart a shopping street as any to be found in Paris. But there was very little evidence left of the French settlement, only perhaps the art nouveau Printemps department store further west. They passed a bar called The Jurassic Pub, with a sign reading *This Way to Dinosaurs*, and Li wondered briefly what was happening to five thousand years of Chinese culture in this town. They turned south then into Songshan Road, and Mei-Ling pulled into the kerb. "We're more likely to find it on foot from here," she said.

They got out of the car and Li looked down the length of the street. It was lined with trees on either side, leaves only now beginning to yellow. Cramped, narrow shop fronts fought for space along the edge of the sidewalk, beneath two storeys of crumbling apartments, rotting wooden balconies groaning with the detritus of overspill from tiny rooms. Vendors' goods spilled out on to the pavements, bales of cloth and baskets filled with household goods, boxes of fruit and electrical equipment. Every few metres, narrow alleyways opened off left and right, whitewashed brick, poles slung overhead, bowed with the weight of fresh, wet washing.

"How was the Dragon and Phoenix?" Mei-Ling asked.

He frowned his confusion. They had barely spoken since they left 803. "Last night . . . the restaurant at the Peace Hotel?"

He looked away, embarrassed to meet her eye. "Margaret never showed up," he said. "She fell asleep, apparently."

"Oh, that's a shame," Mei-Ling said, and Li glanced at her sharply to see if she was being sarcastic. But she seemed genuine enough. "The food's not brilliant there, but the view is great." They walked in silence for a moment, checking the numbers above the shop fronts. "Listen," she said eventually, "why don't you both come and eat at my family's restaurant tonight. My father and my aunt would be happy to meet you. The view's nothing special, but I can promise you the food is wonderful."

Li's spirits lifted momentarily. "I'd like that," he said. And then he wondered how Margaret would react. But he decided that he was not going to spend his life worrying about what Margaret was going to think or say or do next. She lived, he felt, in a very different world from him, even when they were sharing the same space at the time. If she was unhappy eating with Mei-Ling's family, then she could eat on her own.

They crossed the street and found the tailor's shop about halfway down. It was really just an opening in the wall. A tiny room, hung on all sides with finished clothes and lengths of material. In the back a young girl in a red jacket with a black-and-white checked collar worked a hot iron over yellow silk under the glare of a single fluorescent strip. On her left was a small table with an ancient hand-cranked sewing machine, a small striplight fixed to the wall above it. At the front, behind a short glass counter, an old woman in a beige jacket was sewing the seam of a black *xiangyun* silk suit on an equally ancient machine. Both women wore pink plastic sleeves to protect their jackets, and Li noticed that they both had sewing rings on their right hands.

Incongruously, a tall white mannequin, with blue eyes and short blonde hair, stood at the open entrance to the shop, modestly draped from the neck in patterned blue cotton. It was missing an arm. And next to it, the lower half of another dummy stood on one leg, a brown skirt hanging loosely from the waist. A bizarre coincidence, Li thought, that the woman they believed might have worked here had been found in pieces, and was also missing a foot.

The woman in the beige jacket turned and looked at them expectantly, and Li saw that she was about seventy, maybe older. But her hair was still black with just a few seams of silver, and it was drawn back in a loose bun. She ran her eyes over Li from top to bottom, perhaps mentally measuring him up for a suit. He showed her his maroon Public Security ID and she was immediately on her guard. "I don't know what you want here," she said. "We're honest people just trying to make a living. I've been in this city more than fifty years and I've never had trouble."

Mei-Ling said, "Is this the place Fu Yawen used to work?"

"Ye-es." She was even more guarded now. "Why? Have you found her? Has she shown up finally?"

"Any idea where she went?" Li asked her, ignoring her questions.

"How would I know? She only worked here. You should ask her husband. I bet he'd like to know where she went. Off with some fancy man probably." The woman had lost her reserve and was warming to her subject.

"How long had she worked here?" Li said.

"About three years. Mind you, I'd no complaint about her work. She was a good worker, knew what she was doing. Her own father trained her from when she was just a girl. Just like my father trained me." The woman shook a stray strand of her hair back from her face. "But she had an eye for the men, that one. Couldn't keep her hands to herself."

"And you have no idea what happened to her?" Li asked again. He glanced towards the girl in the red jacket who was trying to keep her eyes on her work, but who was clearly listening with interest.

The woman followed his eyes, and cast half a glance at the girl in red. "Get on with your work," she snapped. "This is none of your business." And to Li and Mei-Ling, "She'll be no help to you. She never knew Fu Yawen. I brought her in as a replacement. She'll be hoping that you haven't found her. At least, not alive." She sighed exaggeratedly. "They have no idea, these young ones. They never saw the war, like I did." She puffed herself up proudly and spat beyond them on to the sidewalk. "In the forties I made the *qipaos* for all the young ladies who went to the bars and the balls. The young ones think they're daring now, but the dresses were slit just as high in those days."

"You didn't answer the question," Mei-Ling said impatiently.

"How can I reply to a question when I don't know the answer?" the old woman said boldly. She had lost all her fear now, and Li thought this was not a person he would like to work for.

"You can reply here, or at headquarters," he said, but the threat only served to harden her defiance.

"And the answer would still be the same. You can't frighten an old woman like me. And, anyway, I told you. Ask her husband."

"And where would we find him?" Mei-Ling asked.

The woman flicked her head. "Down there," she said, indicating an alleyway running off from the side of the shop. "At the table on the corner."

"They both work for you?" Li asked, surprised.

"Only one of them works for me now," she replied. "And I wouldn't have the other one back if she came to me on bended knee."

The girl in red never lifted her eyes from the ironing board. But Li sensed her relief.

Fu Yawen's husband sat on a stool working an electric sewing machine at a small table pressed against the wall under a corrugated plastic awning. A striplight hung at an angle from a makeshift hanger, throwing a cold light across a trestle table covered with white cloth and strewn with tools. At another table, beyond racks of threads and buttons, a woman was repairing shoes. Wet clothes dripped overhead. It must be cold, Li thought, working out here in the depths of winter.

He was a good-looking young man, his hair cut short and neat. He wore a warm woollen jacket and an apron the colour of dried blood. Li saw in his eyes that he knew why they had come the moment he showed him his ID.

"Is she dead?" he asked quietly, rising to his feet.

"We don't know yet," Mei-Ling said. "We have a body. We are trying to make an identification."

"Tell me about her," Li said. "Did she leave you? Is that why she disappeared?" And he thought how bald, almost cruel, his question was.

The young man sat again, slowly, his eyes clouded by unhappy memories. "I don't know. We have a five-year-old son. Each morning we took it in turns to take him to the kindergarten before coming to work . . ." Some memory bubbled to the surface and he had to stop, to hold back involuntary tears. He took a moment or two to collect himself. "It was my turn that day. She left before me to come to the shop. I took our son to the nursery school, but when I got here there was no sign of her. She just never turned up. And I have not seen her since."

"You hadn't had a fight, or . . . ?" Mei-Ling started to say, but he cut her off.

"We never fought," he said fiercely. And he glanced angrily up the alley towards the street. "Whatever that woman might have told you, we loved one another, me and Yawen. We loved our child. Sure, she was a good-looking woman. There were always men sniffing around after her. They would come to the shop to get something made, just so she would have to measure them and put her hands on them when they had the fitting. But it never turned her head. Not once. That ugly old cow was just jealous." He put a shaking hand on the table to steady himself. "Our little boy cannot understand where she has gone. He still asks every day when she is coming home. And sometimes he wakes crying for her in the night." He shook his head. "He was his Mommy's boy. I am no substitute."

For a moment neither Li nor Mei-Ling knew what to say. Then Mei-Ling asked softly, "Did Yawen have any distinguishing marks or features that might help us identify her?" He shook his head blankly.

"Doesn't matter how small," Li said. "The smallest, most insignificant thing could help us to rule her in or out. An accident, maybe. Something that left a scar . . ."

The young man slumped on to his stool and sat trying to wade his way through a morass of painful memories, searching to pick out something that might help. Then, suddenly, he remembered, "She broke a finger once, a couple of years ago. Her right index finger. She caught it in a door, and she wasn't able to work the needle for several weeks." He looked up, his face eager and anxious. It was his dead wife he was trying to help them identify, and Li felt overwhelmingly sorry for him.

Li and Mei-Ling walked back to the car in silence. When they got there, they slipped into the front seats and Mei-Ling said, "There's never an easy way, is there?"

Li shook his head. *Someone's lost their mom*, Margaret had said, and she had known because she was cutting up the mother's womb on an autopsy table. And he knew that if the x-rays showed a break in the right index finger, the young man who spent his days huddled over a sewing machine in a draughty alleyway, and his nights trying to reassure a young boy who'd lost his mother, would have to try to identify her remains. And Li would not have wished that upon his worst enemy.

Mei-Ling's mobile started ringing, and she fumbled in her purse to find it. Li didn't pay much attention as she answered the call and talked for about a minute. He couldn't rid himself of the image of a small boy constantly asking about his mother, and a young man with no answers who could provide no comfort. And he couldn't help making the comparison with Xinxin, those emotional months after her mother had abandoned her and her father had refused to take her back. What a big change in a small life, what huge adjustments she had had to make. And how inadequate to the task of helping her through it he had been. Living with an unmarried uncle, constantly in the care of a string of babysitters . . . it was no life for a little girl. She needed a family, some stability.

"I think we might have found our singer." Mei-Ling's words crashed into his consciousness. She was putting the phone back in her bag.

"What?"

"Dai found a girl in the missing persons file. A twenty-eight-year-old teacher and singer at the Shanghai School of Music and Opera." She consulted a note she had hastily scribbled. "Xiao Fengzhen. She went missing just under a year ago."

II

The Yi Fu Theatre sat in the corner of Fuzhou Road and Yunnan Road, a stone's throw from People's Square. It was a white stone building with a semi-circular façade decorated by dozens of small coloured flags and a giant representation of a Peking Opera mask in vivid red, pink, yellow and black. Staff were just raising shutters and opening glass doors to the entrance lobby and booking office when Li and Mei-Ling arrived. A sour-faced woman behind the illuminated window of the booking office glowered at them. "We're not open yet. Another half-hour."

Mei-Ling flashed her ID, and the woman looked as if an electric current had just passed through her seat and up her rectum. "We're looking for somebody from the music school," Mei-Ling said. "We understand the students are putting on a performance here sometime today."

"This afternoon," the woman said, suddenly anxious to help. "An extract from one of the Peking Operas – *Romance of the Western Chamber*. They are just beginning the dress rehearsal. You can go around the back to the stage door."

In the entrance to the stage door in Shantou Road, an attendant sat on a stool smoking and sipping from a glass jar of tepid green tea. A pile of cigarette ends was gathered on the floor around him, and he watched as labourers heaved great wicker baskets filled with the elaborate costumes of the Peking

Opera from a large blue truck. A cage elevator slid slowly up the side of the building, carrying the hampers to an opening in the wall which led to the wardrobe department. Hundreds of bicycles lined a wall bordering waste ground on the other side of the street. The attendant hawked a gob of phlegm from his throat and spat it out on to the pavement as Li and Mei-Ling approached. Li reached for his ID, but the man just pointed up above his head. "Second floor," he said. "They phoned through from the front."

A maze of corridors on the second floor led to several dressing rooms and the make-up and wardrobe departments. From the auditorium, they could hear the ten-piece orchestra and some of the singers rehearsing. It was a bizarre cacophony, even to Chinese ears, which were becoming increasingly attuned to the sounds of Western music. The screeching falsetto of the female vocalists, the loud clacking of the clappers, the strident shriek of the *hu-gin* violin and the seemingly random clatter of drums and cymbals. Li's Uncle Yifu had taken him once to the Peking Opera in the Stalinesque Beijing Exhibition Centre which contained a vast theatre built by the Russians in the middle of the last century. Hard wooden seats rose in curved tiers. They were not designed for comfort, and the audience had fidgeted all the way through the performance, eating noisily from picnic hampers, drinking and smoking, taking and making calls on mobile telephones. The music and the story were almost less important than the spectacle – extravagant costumes and startling masks placed against a sweep of bold sets on a vast, imaginatively lit stage. The costumes, his uncle had told him, were such a garish collection of contrasting colours because the stages upon which the original operas were performed had been lit only by oil lamps.

Li opened a door, and a young woman, who was bent over a costume hamper, turned guiltily. Vividly coloured costumes were draped over chairs and desks, rows of them hanging from rails along one wall. Empty hampers were piled up in one corner, another was appearing in the elevator as it drew level with the hole in the wall. Beyond the waste ground opposite, a cream and brown building had a huge neon billboard mounted on its roof advertising Mitsubishi. Where the Japanese had failed to hold on to Shanghai by force, they were conquering it now with commerce. "In the name of heaven," the girl said, "you gave me a fright! I thought you were the director for a minute."

"We're looking for somebody who knew Xiao Fengzhen," Mei-Ling said.

"I really don't have the time just now," the girl said. "I'm way behind schedule here, and if I don't have all the singers dressed by noon, the director's going to kick my ass all the way across People's Square." Li showed her his Ministry ID and she went very still for a moment. "What about her?" she said.

"Did you know her?"

"Sure. Everyone knew her. She was the star pupil at the school. She was only teaching till she could go professional. What a voice that girl had." She paused. "Whatever happened to her?"

"That's what we're trying to find out," Mei-Ling said.

The girl frowned. "But she disappeared – what, about a year ago?"

"We have a body," Li said. And all the colour drained out of the wardrobe mistress's face. "We're trying to identify it."

"Oh, no . . ." The girl appeared genuinely distressed. She pulled up a stool and sat down. "Not Fengzhen. She was such a lovely girl. Everyone thought maybe she'd just gone off to Beijing or something. I figured she'd be a star by now."

"So you weren't surprised when she just disappeared?" Li said.

"Oh, yes," said the girl. "It wasn't like her, you know, not to say anything. She just didn't show up for a couple of days, and we thought maybe it was her throat again. She had a lot of trouble with her voice if she was singing too much. But, then, I remember her mother came to the school wondering where she was. That was the first time any of us knew she was missing. I never did hear what happened after that."

"Did she live with her mother?" Mei-Ling asked.

"Oh, sure. She had a kid, but no husband. Her mother looked after the kid. 'Cos, you know, we keep pretty strange hours in this business. And then we can be away touring."

Li said, "Who was the father?"

The girl shrugged. "No idea. She was pretty tight, you know. Kept herself very much to herself. Left her personal life at the door when she came in. Maybe that's one of the reasons she was so popular. She never got close enough to anyone to fall out with them." She stopped and thought for a moment, and her clear, bright face clouded. "Was she . . . you know . . . murdered?"

"We don't know," Mei-Ling said. "Do you know where her mother lives?"

The girl shook her head. "Like I said, Fengzhen kept her private life to herself. But I do remember where her mom worked." She chuckled. "It's not the sort of thing you forget."

"Where?" Li asked.

The girl smiled, her face colouring a little from embarrassment. "The sex museum."

The door burst open behind them, and a red-faced man with only a few grey strands of hair scraped back across a bald pate shouted at the girl, "Cheng, where the fuck are those costumes!"

The entrance to the Museum of Ancient Chinese Sex Culture was tucked away in an alley between the Sofitel Hotel and an upmarket department store off a pedestrianised stretch of Nanjing Road. It was only ten minutes' walk from the theatre.

Mei-Ling laughed when Li had expressed incredulity at the existence of a museum of sex in Shanghai. "You're all so stuffy and stiff-lipped about sex in Beijing." She laughed again. "Come to think of it, that's about all that would be stiff in Beijing. You're just like the British. Sex is all right behind closed doors, just let's pretend in public that it doesn't really exist. We're a little more sophisticated than that in Shanghai. We can acknowledge the existence of sex without sniggering behind our hands like schoolboys – or schoolgirls."

Li found her superiority mildly irritating. "And just what sort of *sophisticated* exhibits are there in this museum?" They climbed a couple of steps to the entrance hall and took the elevator to the eighth floor.

"Oh . . ." Mei-Ling said vaguely, "I don't know, dirty pictures, jade dildos, that sort of thing."

"What?"

She laughed again, that braying laugh. "How would I know? I've never been."

"So much for sophistication," Li said.

The lift doors opened and a woman's recorded voice said, with an exaggerated English accent, "Eighth floah." They turned left, through glass doors, into a large and airy entrance lobby. A girl sitting in a booth told them that tickets were fifty yuan each.

Mei-Ling told her who they were and who they were looking for. The girl was flustered. "Ma Hanzhi is not here right now. She has gone to collect her granddaughter. The heating has broken down at the school and they have closed it for the day."

"Will she be long?" Li asked.

The girl checked her watch and shook her head. "Not long. Ten minutes, maybe."

"We'll wait," Mei-Ling said, and then under her breath to Li, "It'll give us a chance to see the exhibition."

Li was not sure that he wanted to see the exhibition. Across the lobby two women in white coats stood behind a counter selling all manner of seductive underwear and sexual apparatus, from transparent negligées and peek-a-boo bras to blow-up sex dolls with absurdly gaping mouths. He felt his face colouring, and he let Mei-Ling steer him away into the exhibition itself. Three bronze statues stood in the entrance, each with its own proclamation: It was the Source of Life; Welcome Guests from Afar; and No Shame for Nature.

The museum was centred around three main rooms with low, black-painted ceilings and concealed lighting. A video of the history of sex was running continuously, with a monotonous commentary in English. A plaque on the wall proclaimed, There are two instincts and basic needs of human life, one is food, and the other is sex. The exhibition proceeded to demonstrate this point in row upon row of glass display cases filled with sexual paraphernalia from across the centuries, mostly artificial penises in stone, or porcelain, and even iron. Mei-Ling could not contain her mirth when they actually came across a double-headed jade dildo used, apparently, by lesbians in the tenth to thirteenth centuries. There were photographs of copulating

Japanese racehorses, a statistical chart of eighteenth-century prostitutes from Han Kou, an ivory horn carved into a series of figures engaged in every sexual act imaginable, from oral to rear entry. Li was shocked, and found himself blushing to the roots of his hair. To his intense private embarrassment he found that he was becoming sexually aroused, although that had more to do with the proximity of Mei-Ling than any graphic depiction of sex acts in erotic paintings from the Ming Dynasty. She was very close to him, and he could feel her heat through his clothes. When her hand touched his it was like receiving an electric shock. He was both confused and disturbed by his reaction.

She was laughing again and pointing to a stone carving of a reclining man with a huge penis. "Now, that's what I call sophisticated!" she said.

"You were looking for me?" a voice said, and they turned to find a small woman, perhaps fifty or fifty-five, standing holding the hand of a young girl who could have been no more than six or seven years old. The girl was gazing at them with great curiosity, and the woman had a frown of deep concern etched on her face. Li felt guilty and embarrassed, as if he had been caught looking at dirty pictures. And he was appalled that a child had been brought into this place.

"We'll talk outside," he said quickly. "Is there somewhere you can leave the child?"

"We can talk in the office," the woman said. "The girls will look after Lijia."

One of the women selling sex goods took Lijia by the hand and led her behind the counter. Li and Mei-Ling followed Xiao Fengzhen's mother into an office through the back.

"I don't think you should be bringing a child into a place like this," Li said immediately she had shut the door.

The woman shrugged. "You tell me what else I can do with her. I have to work." Then she paused, hardly daring to ask. "You have news of Fengzhen?"

Li took a deep breath. "We have uncovered a number of bodies. We are trying to identify them. We do not know for sure if your daughter is among them. I am sorry to have to upset you like this."

"What makes you think Fengzhen might be one of them?" she asked in a small voice.

Mei-Ling said softly, "We believe that one of the women we found was a singer."

The woman let out a low, animal-like moan and closed her eyes. Li felt her pain almost physically. He took her hand and led her to a seat. He drew up a chair and sat beside her, holding her hand between both of his. It felt very small and cold. "Can you tell us," he said gently, "anything at all about the circumstances of Fengzhen's disappearance?" He could feel her trembling. But she made a great effort at composure.

"She went to try and patch it up with him," she said.

"Who?" Mei-Ling asked. But Fengzhen's mother wasn't really listening.

"He used to beat her up. He was a monster. I told her he was no good, even if he was the father of her child. I don't know why, but she seemed to love him. I just couldn't understand it."

"She had a meeting with him?" Li asked.

"She went to his apartment. For the weekend, she said. Told me she'd be back Sunday night. When she never showed up I guessed maybe there had been a reconciliation. But by Tuesday I was getting worried, so I went to the music school, and she hadn't been there either." She turned and looked at Li with big, moist, dark eyes. "I always thought he had something to do with it. She threw her life away for that bastard!" There was real venom in her voice now.

"What did he have to say about it?" Li asked.

"Hah! He told the police she never came to his apartment. Told them he thought she'd just changed her mind. But he knew her better than that. He knew he had her in the palm of his hand. She was such a lovely, lovely girl." Her face betrayed the range of emotions that were going through her head, from love to anger to tears. Then she turned to Li, a bitterness in her voice now. "And what's worse . . . every time I look at the child, it's him I see, not her." Her mouth set in a line that conveyed something close to hatred. "It's a curse!"

"Do you know where we can find this boyfriend?" Mei-Ling asked.

"An Wenjiang works on the boats. Or, at least, he did the last time I heard. Huangpu River cruises for tourists." She gazed off into space, an angry thought clearly forming. "He's never once been to see his daughter. I pray at night that he will fall overboard and drown. With luck, perhaps, he already has."

Outside, life ebbed and flowed along the length of Nanjing Road, people going about their lives, oblivious to the tragedies of others being played out all around them. But then, Li supposed, everyone had their own personal tragedies. Why should they be concerned about those of other people.

"I hate this," he said to Mei-Ling. They were only stirring it all up again for these poor people. The memories, the hopes, the fears. And offering them nothing in return. Not hope, not even an end to it. Just more uncertainty.

She gave his arm a small squeeze. "Me, too." They walked back in silence to where they had parked the car, and Mei-Ling revved the engine and they dodged the bicycles in Guangdong Road to set a course for the river.

The booking office for the Huangpu River cruises was in a triangular granite edifice at the ferry terminal at the south end of the Bund. Mei-Ling parked the car in the street opposite, and they negotiated a complex network of pedestrian overpasses that led them, eventually, down to the quay. The first cruise of the day left at ten forty-five and it was almost that now. The waiting room was deserted, apart from a bored-looking girl standing at a drinks counter and a couple of uniformed women behind the sales desk. Clocks on the wall behind them gave the time in New York, London, Beijing, Tokyo and Sydney. Li wondered, distractedly, why anyone embarking on a two-hour river cruise in Shanghai would want to know the time in London.

Mei-Ling asked one of the women at the sales desk where they could find An Wenjiang. "He drives the boat," she said, pointing through glass doors towards the quay. "But they are just leaving."

Neither Li nor Mei-Ling wanted to hang around for two hours waiting for him to come back. "Come on," Li said, and they sprinted for the door.

"You haven't bought your tickets!" the woman called after them.

A sodden red carpet ran out across the landing stage beneath an arch of woven bamboo. The cruisers were berthed three-deep. The boat about to leave was on the outside. They could hear its engines gunning. Mei-Ling followed Li as he jumped aboard the first boat, ran across the bow and leapt on to the middle boat. He shouted to a couple of deckhands on the outside boat who were in the process of casting off. The cruiser was just beginning to ease away from its neighbour. "Open the gate!" Li called, and he waved his Public Security ID at them. They opened the gate in the safety rail and he jumped across the two-foot gap without looking down, then turned to hold out a hand for Mei-Ling. The gap was widening all the time. She hesitated. He shouted at her to jump. She took a deep breath and leapt across. Several pairs of hands grabbed her and held her safely.

The elder of the deckhands slammed the gate shut and turned on Li. "I don't care who the fuck you are," he said, "don't you ever do that again. I'm responsible for the safety of people on this boat. It's my neck as well as yours."

Li held up his hands. "Sorry, friend," he said. "Urgent police business. We need to talk to An Wenjiang."

The deckhand frowned. "Why, what's he done?"

"None of your business," Mei-Ling said. "Where is he?"

The old man raised his eyes and flicked his head upwards. "On the upper deck, in the wheelhouse." And he gave them both a surly look.

There was no one at the bar in the downstairs cabin as they passed through to the stairs at the stern. All the tourists were packed on to the open upper deck as the cruiser nosed its way out into midstream and the broad sweep of slow-moving grey water. This was not a day to see Shanghai at its best. Although it was not raining, the cloud was low over the city and the air was heavy with humidity. The Bund stood on one side, representing the old world. Pudong, facing it directly, represented the new. Both had faded in the mist, losing substance and colour, dominated by the breadth and depth and timelessness of the river that separated them.

There was no wheel in the wheelhouse. The cruiser was guided by a joystick which apparently controlled both the rudder and the engine speed. The man with his hand on the joystick turned as Li opened the door. He looked to Li as if they were about the same age. But beneath his baseball cap his hair was long and greasy. He wore jeans and a denim jacket, his hands were black, engrained with oil, his fingernails broken and filthy. There was a cigarette burning in an overfull ashtray, and a jar of green tea slopped about on the dash. "What the fuck do you think you're doing! You're not allowed in here!" His voice was coarse, and there was a sneer on his lips. Li thought of the opera singer and wondered what she could possibly have seen in this man, what they could possibly have had in common.

"Watch your language," Li said, and he showed him his ID. "There's a lady present."

An Wenjiang looked at Mei-Ling as if the last thing he believed her to be was a lady. "She a cop, too?" he asked.

"Do you have a problem with that?" Mei-Ling said.

"I have a problem with cops." He glared at Li. "What do you want?"

"I want you to keep your eyes on the river and to answer a few questions."

Reluctantly An Wenjiang dragged his eyes away from Li and back to the river. He steered them around a line of barges heading upriver and set a course towards the Pudong side. "Questions about what?" he said.

"Xiao Fengzhen," Mei-Ling said, and his eyes immediately flicked back towards them.

"What about her?"

Li said, "I want you to tell us about her."

"Why?" He squinted at them suspiciously.

"Do you know what happened to her?" Mei-Ling asked.

"How would I know that? The cow ran off and left me."

"You weren't living together," Li said.

"That was only because of her mother. We were going to patch it all up and she and the kid were going to move back in with me."

"So what happened that weekend she was going to stay over and you were going to sort things out?"

"She never showed up. I told you people at the time. I think her mother thought I killed her or something."

Mei-Ling said, "You used to beat her up."

"Once!" he almost spat at her. "And she was asking for it. Wanted to get pregnant again without telling me. Stopped taking precautions. A little girl wasn't good enough for her. Oh, no. She wanted a little boy. And what kind of shit would we have been in then? Huge fines from the family planning people. I soon knocked that idea out of her." He glared out across the water. "You want to know what I think? I think she ran off, and I think her mother put her up to it. She didn't think I was good enough for her precious daughter. And, hey, you know, Fengzhen didn't either. Never took me to any of her fancy dos at the opera with all her hoity-toity pals. Didn't want them asking her why she was fucking some lowlife like me."

"And why was she?" Mei-Ling asked, and it was clear from her tone that it was beyond her comprehension, too.

An Wenjiang turned and leered at her, a sick grin on his face. "Because she liked a bit of rough trade, darling. And I knew how to pull her trigger." Mei-Ling shuddered visibly, which appeared to please him. His grin widened to reveal nicotine-stained teeth. "And all that stuff about wanting kids . . . it was just about sex. I mean, at the end of the day she ran off and left the kid the same as she left me. She didn't give a shit about the kid."

"Oh, and you do," Li said. "How many times have you been to see her?"

"Never." An Wenjiang wore his indifference like a badge. "I never wanted a kid in the first place. That was her idea. I don't like kids. Never have. That's not a crime, is it?"

"No," Mei-Ling said. "But murder is."

An Wenjiang's reaction was strangely mute. He stared dead ahead for some moments before he said quietly, "You telling me she's dead?"

"We're trying to identify a body," Li said.

An Wenjiang looked at him sharply. "She one of those bodies they pulled out of the mud over there in Pudong the other day?"

Mei-Ling said, "What do you know about that?"

"Only what I read in the papers. I thought they'd been cut up by medical students or something."

Li said, "Did you ever have any medical training? Work in a hospital, someplace like that?"

Now An Wenjiang just laughed. "Me? Are you serious?" Then his smile faded. "You want me to identify her? Is that what you're asking? Because if it is, I'll do it." He saw that his cigarette had burned away and he lit another with trembling fingers. "Was she murdered?" It was what the girl at the theatre had asked.

Li nodded, and to his surprise saw what looked like tears gathering in the other man's eyes. An Wenjiang looked away quickly. "Fuck," he said. "You find out who did it, you let me know." And Li realised that whatever they thought of him, An Wenjiang had felt something for his opera singer that went deeper than just the sex that he boasted about.

They left him then and went out on to the top deck and felt the breeze whip cold, damp air into their faces. They had navigated the bend in the river, past the international passenger terminal. On their left the city disappeared into a haze of factories and apartment blocks, and on their right they cruised past the Shanghai No. 10 Cotton Textile Mill and the Li Hua papermill. The great rusting hulks of what had once been ocean-going liners were berthed forlornly at the Shanghai Shipyard among cranes that rose above them like dinosaurs picking over dead meat.

"What do you think?" Mei-Ling asked.

Li shook his head. "I think," he said, "that I will never understand what makes people tick."

They sat and watched the river pass by. They still had more than an hour to kill before the cruiser would return them to the terminal. Li looked back and saw the city crowding either bank, a city of irreconcilable contradictions, of past, present and future, of enormous wealth and terrible poverty. A long barge passed them, its hold laden with bricks, water slapping dangerously at its sides. In a cabin at the rear, a man sat barefoot in the open doorway wearing only a singlet and a pair of dark-blue cotton trousers. He was bent over a bowl of water, washing his hair. Behind him a small boy peered out at the tourist cruiser and waved. The barge was probably their home, Li realised. It was possible that such people never set foot on dry land.

They passed row upon row of similar barges, each tied to the other, berthed along the south bank. Lines extended front to rear, clothes put optimistically out to dry in the cold and humid air. Fishing boats and cargo tramps hung anchor chains from huge rusting buoys in the middle of the river, rising and falling gently in the slow swell that rolled up from the estuary.

Mei-Ling shivered and moved closer to him, hugging her arms around herself. "It's cold," she said. "I'm not dressed for this." He put an arm around her so that she could share his warmth, and she looked at him, surprise in her expression, and he immediately felt self-conscious. He took his arm away.

"Sorry," he said.

"No it's all right. It helps." She moved a little closer, and he put his arm tentatively around her again. "What sign are you?" she asked.

He frowned, not understanding. "Sign?"

"Birth sign."

He smiled. "Oh. That. I was born in the year of the horse."

She did a quick mental calculation. "So you're *two* years younger than me."

He acknowledged with a tilt of his head. Now it was his turn to do the calculation. "You're a tiger," he said.

She grinned mischievously, "Men are always telling me that."

"So there have been a lot of men in your life," he said.

Her grin turned rueful. "I wish."

Li shrugged. "A good-looking woman like you . . . there must have been someone special, at some time."

She clouded. "Not really." And he knew she was keeping something from him.

"You never get involved with another cop?" He tried to make it sound innocent, but she looked at him sharply and moved away, breaking free of his arm around her shoulders.

"You've been listening to departmental gossip," she said coldly.

"I never listen to gossip," Li said. "But sometimes I can't help hearing it."

"I swear to my ancestors, they're nothing but a lot of old women in that detectives' office." Mei-Ling seemed unaccountably agitated. "They think they're a bunch of hard men, but they're worse than schoolgirls. Men!" She glared at Li. "You're all the same. Only ever think of one thing, and think that women do, too. Well, they don't!" The tiger was showing her claws.

"Hey," Li said defensively, "don't lump me in with all the rest. I don't think anything. I was just asking, that's all. You asked about me and Margaret. I told you."

There was a moment of tension between them, then Mei-Ling dropped her shoulders and relented. "I'm sorry," she said. "It's not just about being the only woman in an office full of men. It's also about being their boss. It doesn't matter how hard you try, there's always a sexual tension there. There's always guys who think they can make you. And when they can't, they make things up about you."

The sky above them suddenly opened up, and there was an unexpected wash of sunshine across the water. And there, lit against the black sky beyond it, was the impressive span of the Yangpu Suspension Bridge. The cruiser started to make its turn, and Li saw An Wenjiang watching them from the window of the wheelhouse.

"Forget I asked," he said. "It's not important."

III

Margaret sat in the viewing room with Dr. Lan and the other pathologists on the team. They were drinking mugs of hot green tea in silence when Li and Mei-Ling walked in. Margaret glanced up wearily at Li. She had been wide awake at four in the morning, now she was barely able to keep her eyes open. And she had no desire to have to fend off recriminations about last night. It had been a very long day.

"Finished the autopsies?" Li asked.

She nodded.

"And?"

"I can confirm," Margaret said, "that they are all quite dead." When this was met with a cold silence, she added, "We had one other positive ID. From fingerprints."

"We know about that," Mei-Ling said. "There is someone working on it already."

Margaret shrugged. "But there's nothing much else to go on. The MO's the same in every case. While it wouldn't stand up in court, I'd pretty much stake my reputation that all the operations were carried out by the same surgeon."

"Operations?" Li asked. It seemed like an odd way to describe what had been done to these women.

But Margaret was in no mood for semantics. "Operations, procedures, whatever you want to call them. The victims were all alive at the beginning and they were all dead at the end."

Dr. Lan intervened. "I think what Margaret is trying to say is that they were all killed at the hand of a skilled surgeon." Li noticed that Lan referred to Margaret by her first name. There had obviously been some sort of reconciliation, even bonding, during the course of the day. And he remembered Margaret once telling him that to share the experience of an autopsy was to share in a heightened sense of mortality. Margaret and Lan had worked together on eighteen bodies. That was a lot of sharing, a lot of mortality.

"Are we any nearer to determining why they were killed?" Mei-Ling asked impatiently.

Margaret shook her head. "Dr. Lan and I have discussed this at length. In other circumstances I think we would probably have reached the conclusion that this was some kind of organ harvesting on the grand scale."

"All the transplantable material has been removed from the bodies," Dr. Lan said. "Heart, lungs, liver, kidneys, pancreas..."

"Even the eyes," Margaret said.

"Eyes?" Li frowned. "You cannot transplant eyes, can you?"

"Corneal tissue can be used in eye surgery," Mei-Ling said.

"But they did not take the spleen," said Lan, "which is not transplantable."

"Or anything else," Margaret said. "In fact, nothing else was even touched – apart from the subsequent hacking up of the bodies."

Li accepted a mug of green tea from a white-coated assistant and sat down. Mei-Ling waved the assistant aside and remained standing. Li said, "Would the returns really be worth the risk? I mean, who is going to buy an organ? How much could it possibly be worth?"

Margaret leaned forward. "In the United States alone there are more than sixty thousand people waiting for life-saving organ transplants. I read somewhere that about twelve Americans die every day waiting for one, and that about every fifteen minutes another name is added to the waiting list."

"So what you have worldwide," said Lan, "is a huge demand."

"And a very limited supply," Margaret said.

"Ah, yes," said Li. "Supply and demand. The life-blood of capitalism. The American Way."

"A simple fact of life," Margaret said. "And people with money will pay anything to buy themselves a few more years. I've heard that the going rate for a single kidney transplant is more than a hundred thousand dollars. There are clinics in India making millions from the procedure. Of course, there the donors are alive and willing to give a kidney or an eye in return for what they see as a passport out of poverty."

Li was astonished. He had heard rumours of organ theft, but had never actually encountered it, or ever really considered the economics. "But how would it work? I mean, you could not keep the organs fresh for very long, could you?"

Dr. Lan shrugged. "The heart, no. Four hours, maybe. The recipient would need to be on hand."

Margaret said, "I'd have to check, but most of the other organs could probably be kept fresh for anything up to two or three days, the liver certainly for up to thirty-six hours. They would just flush the organs through with iced water, or with a solution of high-molecular-weight sugars, plop them in a cold box on wet ice, and they could be flown out to almost anywhere in the world as hand luggage."

Mei-Ling was looking at her sceptically. "But you do not believe that is what is happening here?"

"It would certainly be the easy answer," Margaret said.

"So why is it not?" Li asked.

"Well, for a start," Margaret said, "while there have been plenty of rumours of children being killed for their organs in the streets of South America, or orphanages in Egypt being turned into organ farms, there is not, to my knowledge, a single certified case of someone being murdered for their organs. I mean, think about it. You'd need trained medical staff, sterile operating conditions, proper medical aftercare. These are not the kinds of things that criminals have easy access to."

"And heaven forbid there should be any crooked doctors in the world," Mei-Ling said. Which did not go down well in a roomful of pathologists. She shifted uncomfortably in the silence that followed. Then she said, "So there is a first time for everything. Why else do you not believe it?"

"The victims are all female," said Lan. "Why only choose females? In China it is men who are in more plentiful supply. It does not make sense."

Margaret added, "Then there's your body in Beijing. The organs were removed, certainly, but not taken. And, of course, the most compelling reason of all that we discussed yesterday. There is no medical or any other reason for keeping the victims alive during the procedure. You'd have to be insane to even contemplate it."

"Which brings us back to your psycho surgeon," Li said, "and a point raised at the detectives' meeting last night."

"Oh, yes?" As Margaret's energy was fading, so was her interest.

"Your surgeon, or whatever he is, could not have been acting alone, could he? There must have been at least one, possibly two others, assisting in the procedure."

Margaret nodded, and Mei-Ling said, "So immediately we have the scenario you have just been discounting – a team of medically trained people collaborating in a crime."

Margaret shrugged and got to her feet. "I never said doctors were saints." She looked at Li. "Did you manage to identify any of our victims today?"

Li said, "The boyfriend of an opera singer who went missing about a year ago is coming in to look at your girl with the singer's nodules."

"And we need you to look at an x-ray," said Mei-Ling. And Margaret thought how like a team they were already. "The seamstress. The husband of the woman who we think she might be says she broke her right index finger a couple of years ago. You can tell that from the x-rays, right?"

"Right," Margaret said.

They went downstairs, leaving Dr. Lan and the others to finish their tea, and found the x-ray of the seamstress's right hand. Margaret put it on the light box and traced the luminous image of the dead woman's index finger with her own.

"There it is," she said. She lightly tapped the callus formed on the bone by the healed fracture. "I guess that seals it."

Li turned to Mei-Ling. "We had better get the husband in for a visual identification."

She nodded grimly. "I will go and fix it."

Li and Margaret found themselves alone for the first time since she had failed to meet him for dinner the previous night. They stood in an awkward silence, Margaret not sure how to apologise, Li again guiltily aware of the feelings that Mei-Ling had aroused in him just a few hours earlier.

Margaret scuffed her foot at a cracked tile on the floor. "I'm sorry," she said in a small voice. "About last night. I guess I was just out of it." And she thought how often it was she seemed to be apologising for the night before. Perhaps tonight she could make up for it.

To Li she looked suddenly very small and tired and vulnerable, and he was immediately overcome by familiar feelings of love and affection, and a desire to comfort her. He took her in his arms and drew her close, and she yielded so completely that her legs nearly buckled under her. They stood for several moments, just holding on.

"It won't happen again," she said. "I promise. Tonight we'll forget about dinner and go straight to my room. Then if I fall asleep you can think of interesting ways to wake me up." Almost before the words had left her mouth she felt him tense, and she drew back to look at him. "What's wrong?"

"I told Mei-Ling we would have dinner with her tonight at her family restaurant."

Her expression hardened, and she felt her weariness giving way to anger. "Li Yan, we've hardly had five minutes alone together since I got here."

"That's hardly my fault." He felt his hackles rising.

She said, "Well, maybe you'd better just go on your own. It's you she wants to have for dinner anyway, not me."

Li sighed. "Actually, she made a point of asking you. It is only a small restaurant. It is going to be a family meal with her father and her aunt . . . I think she was very generous to ask you at all, considering how you have been treating her."

"Why?" said Margaret. "Is the contempt showing?"

Li threw his hands up in despair. "Oh, well, maybe you should not come, then. Because if this is how you are going to be, you will only spoil it."

"And we wouldn't want to do that, would we? Seeing as how *generous* sweet little Mei-Ling's being." They stood glaring at each other before finally she said, "You'd better pick me up at the hotel. I'll make a determined effort not to fall asleep this time."

"You sure you want to bother?" Li said. By now he was almost hoping she wouldn't.

"Oh, yes," Margaret said. She wasn't going to let Mei-Ling get him that easily. "If her family's gone to the trouble of preparing a meal for us, then we really shouldn't let them down, should we?" She paused. "Six o'clock?" He nodded and she hurried out.

When she'd gone he stood for a moment, a cocktail of conflicting emotions stirring inside him. Then he looked up and saw the video camera on the wall and realised that the whole scene had been played out for the watching pathologists upstairs. If the sound was up they'd have caught the whole gory episode. He felt sick. They would never have witnessed anything quite like it in an autopsy room before, like some cheap TV hospital drama, and in his head he could hear their laughter echoing around the mortuary.

IV

They had acquired a desk lamp for him, and he was able to sit in the darkened office with only a pool of light focusing his attention on the files that littered his desk. If he swivelled in his chair he could look out at the rising columns of lit windows in the police apartments opposite, wives preparing meals for husbands coming in from work, or sending them out on the night shift. Children watching television or surfing the Internet or doing homework from school. Li wondered what it must be like to have a family, an ordered life, someone waiting to welcome you home. Things he had never really known. A mother killed in the Cultural Revolution, a father who had never been the same after repeated beatings at the hands of the Red Guards who were his keepers. A sister who had run off and left him with her child, an uncle who had taught him everything and then been murdered in his own apartment.

And now he sat here on his own, with only the ghosts of eighteen murdered women for company, each one appealing to him to find their killer, requiring him to return order to a disordered world.

He thought of the viewing room at the mortuary where he had sat with the lights low watching the husband of the murdered seamstress identify her remains. A white body bag wheeled in on a gurney. The sound of the zip as it was opened to reveal the pitiful collection of body pieces that represented the remnants of the woman he had loved. His cry,

as if struck by a blow. The sobs that came slowly at first as
he stuffed a fist in his mouth to try to contain them, before he
backed up against the wall and slid slowly to the floor, pulling
his arms around his shins and rocking back and forth in his
abject misery, weeping openly. For as long as there had been
no word of her, there had always been hope. And now there
was none.

Li thought of how much this contrasted with the boyfriend
of the opera singer. His casual stroll into the autopsy room,
hands in pockets. His complete lack of reaction when the body
bag was unzipped, simply a curt nod of the head. No tears,
no visible emotion. But Li suspected that somewhere, later,
on his own, in the dark, An Wenjiang would be confronted
by his grief.

On the desk in front of him was the file on the girl they had
identified with fingerprints. Just twenty years old, a petty thief
convicted of shop-lifting. Her baby girl, a little under two years
old, had been placed in the custody of her grandparents while
her mother served time. Reform through labour. But no one
would ever know now whether she had reformed or not. Her
parents had told the detectives who interviewed them that they
thought she had gone to Canton or Hong Kong with one of the
boys she hung around with. They had never reported her missing. Her little girl would never know her. But at least her parents would be spared the need to identify the remains. The
body pieces had been DNA-matched, and the fingerprints were
conclusive proof of identity.

Murder by surgical procedure. That was how Margaret had
described what had happened to these women. But for no
apparent reason, and with no apparent logic.

Why *these* women? Was there a pattern? Was there something they all had in common that Li and everyone else was

failing to see? *The answer always lies in the detail*, he could hear his uncle whisper in his ear. A petty thief, an opera singer, a seamstress. What was it that connected them, apart from the manner in which they died? It was something, he knew, they would probably not be able even to guess at until they had identified them all.

There was a knock at the door and detective Dai entered without waiting to be asked. "Hey, Chief," he said, and dropped a file on Li's desk. Li had given up correcting him. "That's all the stuff we could dig up on that medical student who was doing the night watch at the building site. Jiang Baofu." Dai was silhouetted against the light of the corridor behind him, and Li didn't see the second folder until it dropped on top of the first. "And another possible ID."

Li turned the top file towards him and opened it to see a photograph of a young woman, cut out from a group, attached to a missing person's form that someone had filled out several months previously. Her hair was tied up in bunches, like a small girl, and she was wearing a tight-fitting, spangled costume of some sort. But Li could not determine what it was, because the photograph was cut off just below the collar bone. Someone had only been interested in her face. He glanced at the form. Name, age, occupation . . . Wu Liyao, aged thirty . . . He looked up at Dai, frowning. "An acrobat?"

"A member of the Shanghai Acrobatic Theatre. Missing for three months."

"What makes you think she's one of our girls?"

Dai pulled a face. "Don't know for sure, Chief. A long shot, really. But your pathologist said one of the women had stress fractures in her feet? Suggested she might be an athlete, or a gymnast?" He shrugged. "I figured an acrobat would fit under that heading, too."

Li nodded. "Yeah, that's a good thought, Dai. Well done," he said. "It's worth following up." He couldn't really see Dai's face, but he could hear his grin. Dai turned to go. Li said, "Detective . . ." Dai stopped in the open door.

"Yeah, Chief?"

"The other night . . ." he hesitated, "you seemed to be suggesting that Deputy Section Chief Nien was having a relationship with a senior officer in the department."

"Was I?" Dai asked innocently.

"Weren't you?"

Dai shrugged. "Sorry, Chief, but I was told by a senior officer that I wasn't to discuss that sort of thing." He closed the door behind him, and Li felt like his knuckles had just been rapped. He deserved it, he supposed.

He sat for a long time in the darkness wondering why he had even asked. Did it matter to him? Was he really interested in the possibility of entering into a relationship with her? And, if so, where did that leave his feelings for Margaret? He knew what he felt about Margaret. At least, he thought he did. He loved her. But, somehow, it had never been quite enough. There was something missing, but he wasn't quite sure what. Was it cultural, linguistic? He had always felt he could not make his home in the United States, and yet he had expected Margaret to make her home here. There was an unhappiness in her that was like a barrier between them, and he had no idea how to break it down.

He forced himself to refocus his thoughts on more important things. Eighteen women whose murderer or murderers were still at large, possibly adding more victims to a list that might already include others they did not know about. He opened the file on Jiang Baofu. He was twenty-three years old, born in the town of Yanqing in Hebei Province near Beijing.

His grandfather had been a farm labourer, his grandmother a teacher at the local kindergarten. He had an older sister who was married to an office worker in the capital. They lived near the university, in Haidian Road.

Jiang was in his final year at Shanghai Medical University. He was specialising in surgery, and had expressed an interest in going on to study forensic pathology. He rented an apartment in a tower block in Ming-Xin Village, a new suburb on the opposite side of the city. He had moved out of student accommodation the previous year.

Li paused and thought about this. It was yet another anomaly. How could a student from a poor family afford to move out of student accommodation to rent his own apartment? A student who, apparently, had had to take all kinds of vacation work to pay his way through medical school. He checked through the list of jobs Jiang had taken over the past five years. He had worked as an orderly and as a porter at various Shanghai hospitals and private clinics. He had spent one summer break manning a market stall at the old Chinatown bird market. He had taken a number of term jobs working nights: as a hotel porter in a seedy joint near the river; as a labourer on a building site; as a night watchman in various places – presumably so he could earn some cash and still snatch a few hours' sleep.

Li lit a cigarette and blew smoke thoughtfully into the light of his desk lamp, watching it billow and eddy before dispersing and rising into the darkness. There was another knock at the door, and this time it was Mei-Ling who entered.

"Wow, it's dark in here," she said.

"I like to think in the dark."

She closed the door and drew up a seat and sat opposite him, leaning back so that he could see her face in the reflected light from the desktop. "I prefer to think in the light," she said, "and save the dark for making love."

Li felt something flip over in his stomach, and for a fleeting moment he saw a picture of himself making love to her, her slender frame arched beneath him, small hard breasts pressed into his chest, fingers digging into his back, her breath hot on his face. He quickly banished the vision, alarmed by an apparently increasing loss of control. "Have you seen the file on Jiang Baofu?" he asked.

She nodded. "I think we've got to bring him in."

Li said, "I'd like to talk to his tutors at med school first, see what kind of light they can throw on him. And take a look around his apartment, too, when he's not there. Can we get a warrant?"

"Sure. I'll fix it. We can go out to the Medical University first thing tomorrow. I know some people there."

"Good." He paused. "And what about the acrobat?"

"They knocked the old Shanghai Acrobatic Theatre down. The troupe are based in a theatre out at the Shanghai Centre now. We should go and see them tomorrow also. Apparently she was married to one of the other acrobats." She glanced at her watch. "I'm going to head off now. We'll see you about seven?"

"That's fine."

"And Margaret?"

"I'm picking her up at her hotel."

She smiled. "Better take a sledgehammer then. In case you have to break down her door."

CHAPTER SEVEN

I

The underside of the Yan'an Viaduct Road glowed an incongruous fluorescent blue, lit by concealed striplights. Their taxi headed west, under the viaduct, their driver a surly, older man with thinning hair whose ambition in life appeared to be a desire to get in front of every other car on the road. He drifted from one lane to the other at high speed, punctuating his progress with a series of short, sharp blasts on the horn. Other drivers apparently appreciated that there was a lunatic in their midst and gave him a wide berth. Li leaned forward, tapping the driver on the shoulder through the cage. "Take it easy, pal," he said. The driver nodded and paid no attention.

Margaret wondered if being ignored by a taxi-driver amounted to a significant loss of face. If so, Li wasn't showing it, and Margaret wasn't about to ask. They had barely spoken since they left the Peace Hotel.

They turned south into Huashan Road and saw, ahead of them, the towering presence of the Hilton Hotel. On their right was the Hotel Equatorial, on the left a row of Spanish-styled two-storey brick apartment buildings, profiles traced in neon against the night sky. The driver made a suicidal U-turn in the face of on-coming traffic, to the accompaniment of a symphony of horns, and drew up outside a cheap-looking coffee shop which appeared to be empty behind thin veils of net curtain.

Margaret peered out of the window, unimpressed, as Li paid the driver. "Is this it?"

Li got out and held the door open for her. "In the alley, the driver says."

Margaret saw, beyond the coffee shop, a narrow opening between two lines of apartment buildings. Overflowing bins and empty crates were stacked up against one wall. The alleyway looked dark and uninviting. "Jeez," she said. "It's worse than I thought." This was the old French quarter, and behind the veneer of affluence which lined the main streets, lay a maze of seedy back streets and narrow alleyways where people scraped through life in less than salubrious conditions.

Li took her arm and led her into the alley. Further along its length, men were working by floodlight under a temporary tarpaulin covering. Through an open door, an old man stood staring off into space in the dim light of a yellow lamp by a table in a hallway. He held one hand in front him, clawlike and brown-spotted with age. It was trembling like a leaf trapped in a current of air.

Immediately on their right, the bright fluorescent lights of Mei-Ling's family restaurant spilled out into the alley. Pots and pans were piled up on a metal rack, and two young girls in spotless white jackets stood washing vegetables at a big porcelain sink under a blue awning outside the door. Through a window immediately above the sink, a tall young man wearing a white chef's hat was moving swiftly back and forth within the cramped confines of a tiny kitchen. One of the girls at the sink took a large cleaver and began finely chopping cabbage on a wooden board. She turned and smiled at Li and Margaret as they went in. "*Ni hau*," she said, reserving a wide-eyed stare of wonder for the blonde-haired, blue-eyed Western lady. It was distinctly possible, Margaret thought, that no Westerner had ever set foot in this restaurant.

They went down a couple of steps into a very small, brightly lit white-tiled room which made Margaret think of some places she had performed autopsies. There was one large round white plastic table, and another two smaller ones pushed against the far wall. Mei-Ling, her brother, father and aunt were seated at the large table, and they all rose expectantly as their guests arrived. Margaret knew that she was an object of attention for curious eyes. In China it was hard to escape that sense of being out of place, extrinsic. But Margaret could not remember ever having felt so completely alien. And with a sudden dawning, she realised why Mei-Ling had wanted her here. For that very reason. To make her feel like an outsider. To demonstrate, by contrast, all those racial, cultural and linguistic things that Mei-Ling and Li had in common that Margaret could never share. And, presumably, to make Li aware of them, too. But Margaret stopped herself from taking this conjecture any further. Perhaps, she thought, she was simply investing her insecurity in a huge dose of paranoia, as Li had so indelicately suggested two nights earlier. She composed a smile for her hosts.

Mei-Ling introduced Li first, providing Margaret with an opportunity to see how the land lay. Small bows and hand-shakes accompanied all the greetings, in Mandarin since Li could not speak the Shanghai dialect. What struck Margaret most forcibly was how small Mei-Ling's family all were. Her father and aunt were like tiny, if perfectly proportioned, human beings. They made Margaret feel tall, and Li positively towered over them. Mei-Ling's brother was the tallest of them, although he still looked a good five inches shorter than Li.

Margaret put him at around forty. The father and aunt looked to be in their sixties, although it was always difficult to tell with the Chinese, for they did not seem to age in the same way as people in the West. Their skin retained a clarity and freshness, often unlined until well into the seventies or even eighties. And, while there were exceptions, they appeared to keep the colour of their hair for longer, and the men were less inclined to baldness.

Mei-Ling turned to Margaret with a sparkling smile and introduced her family. All three shook her hand warmly, and greeted her with open, friendly grins, tempered a touch by timidity. They had little experience of foreigners, or *lao wei* as Margaret knew they called them when being polite; or *yangguizi*, foreign devils, when not. To Margaret's surprise, she discovered that Mei-Ling's brother, Jingjun, spoke English fluently, and that her Aunt Teng had a smattering. "I live in Hong Kong for little while," she said. "Everyone there speak English." Mei-Ling's father held Margaret's hand in both of his and spoke to her very earnestly. He held her eyes in a steady unblinking gaze. Margaret was both embarrassed and charmed.

When he had finished, and let go her hand, Jingjun said, "My father says it is an honour to welcome you in his house and his restaurant." For the first time Margaret realised that the family also lived here.

"It is my pleasure to be here," she said. And she began to relax. These seemed like nice people. Perhaps she had been a little hasty in jumping to her conclusions about Mei-Ling's motives.

"Please, sit," said Aunt Teng, indicating a chair at the table. They all sat then, and Margaret noticed for the first time that the table was strewn with strange charts covered with diagrams and copious scribblings in Chinese characters. A large teapot sat in the centre of the table and there were fine china cups at each place. One of the white-jacketed girls from outside materialised at the table to pour from the pot and fill the cups with the pale, steaming fragrance of jasmine tea.

Mei-Ling's father spoke again to Margaret, and Jingjun translated. "Mei-Ling has suggested that we should read the traditional Chinese horoscopes of our honoured guests. Aunt Teng has learned this art in Hong Kong." He paused. "My father asks if this would please you?"

Margaret glanced uncertainly at Li. "Well . . . yes, of course," she said. "I would be interested to see the process." She saw that Mei-Ling was watching her closely, the smile still fixed on her face like a diamond caught in the light. And she noticed that the slight cast in Mei-Ling's right eye gave the appearance of being more pronounced than usual. She caught Li looking at Mei-Ling, and there was something in his eyes that suddenly brought all Margaret's insecurity flooding back.

They began with Li, and for Margaret's benefit conducted the proceedings in English. Jingjun translated for his father.

After a brief consultation with Jingjun to get the English right, Aunt Teng said, "First we find your sexagenary number." She turned to Margaret. "In China we measure time based on lunar calendar and movement of sun. We have three hundred, sixty-five and one quarter days in each year. Everything come in cycle of sixty. Sixty day, sixty month, sixty year. Each year is six period of sixty day, plus five day. When your birthday, Li Yan?" she asked.

"December twentieth, nineteen sixty-six," he said.

"Okay." She drew a blank sheet of paper in front of her and lifted a pen to begin her calculations. "Nineteen sixty-six. We take away three. We have nineteen sixty-three. We divide by sixty." She made the calculation with extraordinary speed. "Is thirty-two point seven-one. We round down to thirty-two and multiply by sixty. Then we have nineteen twenty. We subtract from your birth year minus three and we have forty-three. This is sexagenary number." She looked up triumphantly, and Margaret wondered what on earth the point of it all was. "Okay," Aunt Teng continued. "We keep subtracting ten until we have remainder. And this is . . ." she scribbled furiously, and then looked up, her eyes alight with pleasure, "three. Oh, Li Yan, your Heavenly Stem is three. This is most lucky number you can have."

Margaret didn't like to ask what a Heavenly Stem was. Aunt Teng turned to her. "You know Yin and Yang?"

"Not personally," Margaret said, and when no one laughed she tried to cover her embarrassment. "Yeah, I guess . . ." she muttered. "Yang is male, Yin is female."

Aunt Teng nodded. "Number three is good mix of Yin and Yang, but is more for Yang Prosperity. You understand Yang Prosperity?"

Margaret looked helplessly towards Jingjun. He smiled. "In Chinese, 'prosperity-assistance' is the compound word meaning lucky. This is ve-ery good. Ve-ery auspicious. Also Yang equates with masculinity and positive energy."

"Which means," said Mei-Ling, "that good fortune and prosperity will accompany Li Yan all his life."

"I'm glad to hear it," Li said in Mandarin. "When will it start?" Everyone around the table laughed and Margaret looked at them uncertainly. Jingjun explained, and Margaret smiled politely, wondering why Li had got a laugh when she hadn't.

Aunt Teng pulled one of her charts towards her. It bore a diagram like an eight-sided compass, with south at the top and north at the bottom, east to the left, west to the right.

Each of the eight segments had its own colour and was divided into three strips. In an inner circle were eight groups of three strips, some broken, some unbroken. And at the very centre was the ancient symbol of Yin and Yang, like intertwined teardrops, one black, one white. "The eight ancient trigrams," Aunt Teng said.

Jingjun explained, "It is said that the sage Fu Hsi invented the trigrams more than four thousand years ago. Each represents a direction, a colour and an element, and each is given a name according to the strength of its Yin or its Yang. The broken strips represent the Yin, the unbroken the Yang. Too much of either one is bad."

Aunt Teng said, "Li Yan's Heavenly Stem of three also represent the Heavenly Element of fire. So his trigram is very wonderful. He faces south, which is most auspicious, and his trigram is called *Li*, which is his name. And the fire, it mean he is strong, dependable. It mean he is beautiful, like the sun. And best season for Li Yan is the summer."

Li was blushing now. Mei-Ling said, "Which makes you a very good catch for some lucky girl."

"Ah, but only if their animal signs are compatible," Jingjun said, grinning. "If you believe in that sort of thing." He turned to Li. "What are you, Li Yan?"

"Year of the horse," Li said.

Mei-Ling clapped her hands in delight. "And I'm the tiger," she said. Li flicked her a look. Now he knew the purpose of her "innocent" question earlier in the day.

"And no doubt horses and tigers are just made for each other," Margaret said with a tone.

Aunt Teng said, "There are twelve animal, in four group of three. The three animal in each group get on ve-ery well." She beamed at Li and Mei-Ling. "Tiger and horse in same group."

"Well, there's a surprise." Margaret couldn't help herself, although the irony of her tone was lost on everyone except Li and Mei-Ling. Li glared at her. "So," Margaret said, "where does that leave monkeys and horses?"

"You are a monkey?" Jingjun asked.

"People have been calling me that most of my life," Margaret said. "But I was born in sixty-eight, and I'm told that was a monkey year."

Jingjun grinned, but Aunt Teng shook her head. "No good," she said. "Monkey and horse in different group. No compatible."

"And monkeys and tigers?" Margaret asked, looking very directly at Mei-Ling.

Aunt Teng consulted a chart and cackled. "Hah!" she said. "Afraid Miss Margaret and Mei-Ling no get on. Tiger and monkey directly opposite. They clash. They deadly enemy."

Margaret smiled at Mei-Ling. "Maybe there's something to this after all."

Aunt Teng then worked out that Margaret's sexagenary number was forty-five, and that her Heavenly Stem was five. "Five in middle," she said. "No lucky, but no unlucky."

"Yes, not a very interesting number, really," Mei-Ling said.

"Heavenly element is earth," said Aunt Teng, "and trigram called *K'un*." She looked up suddenly. "You want more tea?" And she waved one of the girls to refill their cups. When the tea had been poured, Aunt Teng continued, "Characteristic of earth element mean you are docile, yielding lady, ve-ery motherly. It stand for mother earth, cloth, the belly and the colour black."

"Doesn't sound much like me," Margaret said. "Docile? Yielding?" She flicked a glance at Mei-Ling and forced a smile. "I wouldn't count on it." And she was aware of Li giving her another look, but avoided meeting his eye. "What about Mei-Ling?" she asked. "What's *her* Heavenly Stem?"

Aunt Teng shook her head. "Oh, we do this before. Mei-Ling have ve-ery bad number. Nine. Unlucky. And Heavenly Element, water. No good. Too much Yin make her Yang orphan."

Jingjun said, "A Yang orphan is like a child left alone in the world who must extend their self-reliance in a very Yang way. As it happens, just as Mei-Ling has done. She has become a boss lady in a man's world. But 'orphan-emptiness' is the Chinese compound word meaning unlucky. Which is not good."

"Water ve-ery bad, too," said Aunt Teng. "It mean danger, hidden thing, anxiety. And trigram, *K'an*, is colour of blood."

The reminder of her own inauspicious signs seemed to take the shine off Mei-Ling's discovery that she and Li were compatible while he and Margaret were not. There was a momentary flicker of darkness about her, like a premonition, a shadow falling across her face. Then she recovered. "Of course," she said, "if I were lucky enough to find a man like Li Yan, then he would bring balance and harmony to my life. His Yang would balance my Yin. His good luck would balance my bad."

"But you'd need the luck first," Margaret said. "And it doesn't appear to be in your stars."

Mei-Ling's father spoke then, and Jingjun said, "My father says we should eat."

He and Mei-Ling quickly cleared away all of Aunt Teng's papers and charts, and the girls in the white jackets set out plates and glasses and chopsticks and began charging the table with the first dishes. Steam rose from the table into the cold white of the tiled room, and strange, exotic smells rose with it. "We thought you might like to try some traditional Shanghai dishes," Mei-Ling said, "and some Chinese delicacies. The chef is very good. I told him you were particularly fond of deep fried scorpion." She paused. "But unfortunately he was not able to get them in time."

"What a pity," Margaret said.

"But we do have some other delicacies that I am sure you will enjoy just as much."

"You shouldn't have gone to the bother."

Mei-Ling smiled. "It is my pleasure."

Beer was poured into tall glasses from large pitchers, and their toasting glasses were filled with the evil-tasting and highly potent Chinese toasting liquor, *mao tai*. Margaret had several unpleasant memories of it. Mei-Ling's father proposed a toast to their guests, and Li and Margaret proposed return toasts in thanks for their hospitality. Mercifully everyone sipped the liquor, and no one called for a *gan bei* which would have required an emptying of glasses in a single draught.

As the Lazy Susan turned, and each dish arrived before Margaret, Aunt Teng explained what it was. A plate piled with slivers of what looked like meat or fish in a sauce sprinkled with spring onion, she explained, was called Dragon's Duel Tiger. "This Chaozhou cuisine," she said. "From south of China. Is wild cat and snake meat." Margaret blanched. Another plate was piled with brown-coloured eggs. Aunt Teng provided further illumination. "We call one thousand year eggs," she said. "But they not really a thousand year old. They soaked in horse urine for effect."

Margaret caught Mei-Ling watching her, delighting in her discomfort. But she was damned if she was going to give her the pleasure of seeing her succumb to the growing sense of nausea that was developing from the knot in her stomach. Li was studiously avoiding her eye. It must have been obvious to him, too, what Mei-Ling was attempting to do. Gamely Margaret picked her way through a succession of bizarre and unappetising dishes: butterflied prawn in batter covered with deep fried ants, stewed chicken's feet, snake, dried squid – washing everything down with copious amounts of beer. Each time she emptied her glass one of the white-jacketed girls would refill it. The beer seemed to wash away the nausea, replacing it with an increasing sense of lightheaded euphoria.

The waitresses brought a plate piled high with steamed whole crab to the table, and put a bowl of dark brown dipping sauce at each place. The crabs had white bellies and black backs covered with a fine golden hair. "Shanghai hairy crab," Jingjun said. "Seasonal speciality of Shanghai. They are *Da Zha Xie*, Chinese Mitten Crabs, taken from Yang Cheng Lake, to the north-west of the city." A crab was placed in front of each person at the table, and Jingjun showed Margaret how to eat it, pulling free a thumbnail-sized piece of shell from the underside, and using it to scoop out the yellow flesh beneath it, dipping it first in the sweet soy and vinegar mixture before eating. He watched Margaret as she ate, and then asked, "It is good?"

"Hmmm," Margaret said. "Excellent."

"Yes," Jingjun said, nodding, "the sexual organs are the best part." And Margaret immediately felt her enthusiasm waning.

Everyone then broke open the claws to suck out the more conventional crabmeat and, finally, the focus switched away from Margaret. Conversations started up around the table, and through a faintly alcoholic haze Margaret noticed tiny brown splashes appearing on Aunt Teng's cream-coloured blouse. Aunt Teng was engaged in conversation with her brother and was oblivious. Margaret looked up at the ceiling, but could not detect where the splashes were coming from. She began to wonder if the accumulation of alcohol and fatigue were making her see things. No one else, apparently, was aware of it. Li was talking animatedly to Mei-Ling and Jingjun. Eventually, Margaret tapped Aunt Teng on the arm and pointed to the spots on her blouse. "Something's splashing you," she said, and thought how foolish it sounded.

Aunt Teng looked at her blouse and exclaimed in annoyance. She took a paper napkin and brushed at the brown spots, managing only to smear them across the silk and make them worse. And even as she examined them, several more spots appeared, as if from nowhere. Margaret was perplexed. "Where are they coming from?"

Aunt Teng glared at a dish which one of the girls had placed on the table a few minutes earlier. "Drunken shrimp," she said.

Margaret looked at the dish and saw that the dozen or so shrimps lying in the brown-coloured liquid would occasionally jerk or twitch, sending tiny droplets splashing across the table and on to Aunt Teng's blouse. "They're still alive?" she asked, horrified.

"Not for long," Aunt Teng said. "They marinated live in soy and alcohol. Soon they drown, then we eat. Ve-ery good."

Everyone, now, was looking at the drunken shrimps. And as soon as they stopped twitching, Mei-Ling said, "You must try one, Miss Campbell. Like my aunt said, they are very good."

Margaret hesitated. "Perhaps someone had better show me how," she said, postponing the evil moment.

"Of course. Allow me." It was Jingjun. He turned the Lazy Susan around so that the plate was in front of him, and lifted out a shrimp with his chopsticks. He bit off the head and spat it on to the table, then popped the remainder into his mouth, complete with shell. For several moments he worked it around with his teeth, and then he spat out the shell, having somehow managed to suck out the flesh. He turned the dish back around to Margaret. She smiled and lifted a shrimp from the plate and copied Jingjun exactly. To her surprise she was able to free the flesh from the shell quite easily, and to her further surprise found that the shrimp tasted remarkably good. To Mei-Ling's clear disappointment, she licked her lips and said, "Delicious. May I have another?"

When she had taken a second shrimp, the plate went around the table and everyone else helped themselves. Margaret lifted her toasting glass and raised it towards Mei-Ling. "I'd like to propose a toast," she said, "to Mei-Ling, for her generosity and thoughtfulness in introducing me to the delights of southern Chinese cuisine." Mei-Ling reluctantly lifted her glass. "*Gan bei,*" Margaret said, and she tipped her head back and poured the foul-tasting *mao tai* down her throat in a single movement, banging her glass on the table.

Mei-Ling had no option but to follow suit. Margaret saw immediately by her poorly concealed expression how much Mei-Ling disliked the toasting liquor. She had barely taken any alcohol all evening, sipping instead at her jasmine tea. Margaret guessed that Mei-Ling never drank much, if at all, and probably had little tolerance for alcohol. Now she caught Li throwing her a warning look, and she returned it with a sweet smile. One of the white-jacketed girls refilled the toasting glasses. Margaret immediately raised her glass again. "And I'd like to propose another toast to Mei-Ling, for welcoming me so warmly to Shanghai and making me feel so much at home here. *Gan bei.*" And she tipped the contents of the glass down her throat.

Mei-Ling grimaced and, following Margaret's lead, downed her replenished glass. Her fixed smile had a little less sparkle, and her eyes were already developing that glassy look as the alcohol went straight to her head. Mei-Ling's father and brother looked at her with some concern, but Aunt Teng, more than a little inebriated herself, clapped her hands and shouted, "Bravo!"

One of the waitresses dipped her head to speak to Aunt Teng, and the old lady quickly nodded and moved her chair closer to Margaret, creating a space which the waitress immediately filled with another chair.

"Is someone joining us?" Margaret asked. Aunt Teng looked perplexed. Margaret pointed to the empty chair. "Someone else coming to eat?"

Aunt Teng looked at the chair and shook her head solemnly. "No, no," she said, but made no further attempt to explain, turning instead to her nephew and firing off some rapid observations in Shanghainese.

Margaret decided that another toast was in order, and immediately raised her glass again to Mei-Ling, offering meaningless thanks for some unintended hospitality. "*Gan bei*," she said and emptied her glass. This time a silence descended around the table.

To Margaret's annoyance, Li put his hand over Mei-Ling's and said, "You don't have to." But Mei-Ling shook it away and lifted her glass. "*Gan bei*," she said, responding to Margaret's toast. And she, too, emptied her glass.

Margaret saw hurt and accusing glances flicked in her direction from Jingjun and Mei-Ling's father. They did not understand. But Margaret had drunk so much now that she did not care.

A middle-aged man wearing a suit and thick glasses appeared from a room at the back and sat down at the table in the empty chair. Margaret glanced at him curiously, but no one else paid him any attention. A tense conversation had started up in Chinese. One of the waitresses placed a plate of what looked like white fish in front of the newcomer. Carefully, he lifted a piece with chopsticks which had been laid out for him, and put it in his mouth. He chewed slowly, thoughtfully, for nearly half a minute, before he nodded his satisfaction and swallowed the fish over. Then he stood up, making a small bow, and left the room. Still the others were in deep conversation. It was not until there was a momentary lull that Margaret was able to ask Aunt Teng who the man had been. At first she seemed confused. "What man?" she asked.

"The one who sat beside you and ate the fish," Margaret said.

"He is a taster," Jingjun said. "This fish . . ." he spun the Lazy Susan around to Margaret, "if it is not prepared correctly, is highly poisonous." All his earlier warmth towards Margaret had gone. "It is his job to taste the fish before we eat it."

Margaret was horrified. "And what if it wasn't prepared correctly?"

"He will die, and we will not eat the fish," Jingjun said matter-of-factly. "Please try some."

They were all looking at her now. She looked at the fish. It appeared innocuous enough, and the taster had walked out in one piece. "How long before the poison acts?" Margaret asked.

"Oh, about fifteen minutes," Mei-Ling said quickly, and Margaret saw that she was holding on to the edge of the table. Margaret also realised that the taster had been gone for less than five minutes. Was this Mei-Ling's revenge?

"Go ahead," Jingjun said. "It is very good."

There was absolute silence around the table as, reluctantly, Margaret lifted a piece of the fish with her chopsticks. With a picture indelibly forming in her mind of the taster lying writhing in agony behind the door to the back room, locked in his death-throes, she forced herself to put it into her mouth. To

her surprise it was soft and full of flavour and slightly aro-
matic. She smiled and nodded. "It *is* good."

Again she was in time to catch Mei-Ling's disappointment.
And this time Margaret lifted her beer glass. Mei-Ling's was
full and untouched. Margaret said, "I drink a toast to Mei-Ling
for being so thoughtful in letting me taste this wonderful delicacy." She heard her own words slurring slightly. "*Gan bei.*" She
raised her glass to her lips and slowly poured the remains of
her glass down her throat. She felt the alcohol "hit" that the
beer carried in its bubbles, and that sense of euphoria returned.

Mei-Ling sat staring at her for a long time. She could not
refuse the toast without suffering extreme loss of face. Everyone knew now what the game was here. She lifted the beer and
started to drink in a series of small gulps. She managed about
half the glass before she gagged. Once, then again. And then
suddenly she put a hand to her mouth and fled from the table
to a toilet somewhere through the back. In the silence they
could all hear her retching. The sound of it almost made Margaret gag, too. But she remained brittlely in control, sitting
very upright, enjoying a brief moment of victory and trying to
stop the room from spinning.

II

He did not want to fight in the taxi. There was no point in creating a spectacle for some curious taxi-driver. So he sat in
silence, nursing his wrath to keep it warm. Margaret, apparently, was oblivious. She was sitting staring straight ahead,
her hand clutching the grip on the door. Drunk, and trying
very hard not to show it.

Mei-Ling had not reappeared, and Li's embarrassment had
been acute as he expressed his gratitude to the stony-faced

Jingjun and his father when he and Margaret left. Aunt Teng
had either not noticed the *gan bei* episode or been too drunk
to care. She had wished them both fond farewells, remind-
ing Li again how luck and good fortune would be with him
all his life.

He reflected now on how both appeared to have deserted
him tonight.

When they reached the Peace Hotel, Li followed Margaret
through the revolving doors and along the hall to the elevators.
She was walking quickly, but carefully, and with a sense that if
she relaxed for a moment she might fall over. As they stepped
into the elevator she seemed surprised to see him. "Aren't
you going back to your hotel?" she said, over-enunciating her
words.

"Later," he said. "Right now we need to talk."

She fumbled with the key at her door before he took it
from her and opened it, slipping the key into its wall-holder to
activate the lights. Only one bedside lamp was switched on. As
he closed the door she turned to face him, steeling herself. He
turned from the door, and she swung her clenched fist through
the air and caught him high on the face, just below his left eye.
"You bastard!" she hissed.

He staggered back, more in surprise than from the blow.
"What the hell . . ."

She was shaking her hand, clenching and unclenching her
fist. "Jesus, that hurt!" Then she glared at him. "The only thing
that bitch was trying to do was humiliate me, and you were
just going to let her do it."

Li rubbed at his cheekbone and felt it swelling already.
He would be sporting a bruise there tomorrow. "She didn't
have to humiliate you," he said levelly. "You did a perfectly
good job of that yourself."

"Is that so?" She put a hand on the wall to steady herself. "Crabs' private parts. Wild cats. Eggs in horse's piss. Deep fried ants. Live shrimp. Poison fish . . . You trying to tell me she didn't know what any of these would mean to a Western palate?"

Li glared at her. He knew perfectly well what Mei-Ling had been doing. He did not understand what had prompted the instant loathing between her and Margaret, nor did he approve. But whatever Mei-Ling had started, Margaret had taken too far. "It was just a bit of fun," he said, and knew how lame that sounded.

"Yeah, like you saw me laughing," Margaret slurred.

Li shook his head. "Your trouble is you just don't know when to stop. It wasn't Mei-Ling you hurt, it was her family."

"Her family!" Margaret's voice rose in righteous indignation. "She was the one who was *using* her family to get at me. Sure, I feel sorry for them. They were nice people. But the meal was her idea. And all that horoscope shit. All that stuff about you and me being incompatible, and you and she being made for each other. She had all that planned. She was trying to make me feel like I didn't belong. Like you and I had no future." Her lip began to tremble. "And you know what, Li Yan? She damn well succeeded!"

She turned away to hide her emotion, to conceal her weakness, and she stumbled and almost fell, clutching at thin air for something to hold her up. He grabbed her quickly to stop her falling, and she turned on him, fists balled up and pummelling his chest and his face.

"I only ever stayed in China because of you." Only now did she weep. "I only came back because of you." Although there was no force in the blows, he still struggled to grasp her wrists and stop her. She turned her tear-stained face up to him. "I love you, Li Yan, and you've only got eyes for Mei-Ling. Touching her, looking at her, laughing with her. You couldn't even pick me up at the airport. If I had the faintest idea where home was I'd go running back there right now. But you've taken that from me, too."

All his guilt came flooding back. "Margaret, it is not like that. We are working together, that is all."

"If you believe that," Margaret sobbed, "if you think she's not after you, then you're even more naïve than I thought."

He looked into her blue, tear-blurred eyes, and saw the red blotches around them on her pale cheeks. He felt her body pressed hard against his where he had pulled her against himself to restrain her. And he felt himself growing hard against her as all the passion and anger and guilt found focus in the lust she had always provoked in him. He lowered his face to hers and kissed her. At first she tried to fight it, struggling to free herself from his grasp, but her resistance was short-lived, and he felt her yielding, growing limp, a sudden hunger in her mouth as she opened it to his. Her arms wound around his neck as he lifted her and carried her to the bed, still devouring her with his mouth. And then their passion simply took them both, fingers finding buttons and clasps, clothes flung to the floor. He felt the heat of her flesh against his, the hardness of her nipples as he took them in his mouth, each in turn. Then their lips were together again, and he felt her guiding him into her, and then thrusting against him, wanting to consume him, to hold him to her and not let go for fear of losing him. He gave in totally, then, to his lust, realising how much he had missed this, how much he loved making love to this woman. All the anger and frustrations of their relationship found resolve in this simple act. He felt her teeth sharp on his chest, her fingers digging into his back, her legs locked around his hips, urging him ever deeper, ever faster until, finally, spent, they lay panting side by side. He turned and saw the sweat glistening on her face, and rolled her into the crook of his arm, so that her head rested on his chest, her hair fanned out across him. He closed his eyes and realised that nothing had been resolved at all, except for their animal passion. It felt good and right to hold her like this, to feel her breath on his skin. But it didn't change anything. It didn't make their relationship any easier, or banish the feelings that Mei-Ling had aroused in him. He wanted to tell her he loved her, but he no longer knew if it was true. Then he became aware of her slow, shallow breathing and realised that she was asleep, and that he was spared from having to say anything.

CHAPTER EIGHT

I

The campus of the Shanghai Medical University sat behind high grey walls to the left and right of Dong'an Road, a jumble of mostly two-storey buildings linked by tree-lined private roads. Here students walked and cycled free of the traffic that choked the city streets outside, and a blink of late autumn sunshine lifted spirits otherwise destined for winter decline.

Li and Mei-Ling had driven here in silence. She had greeted him brightly enough at his hotel, putting a brave face on a disastrous night. No reference was made to Margaret, or the drink, or the food – or the bruise on Li's cheek. But Mei-Ling was pale and fragile. She had, she said, arranged for them to meet Jiang Baofu's course professor at the medical university. And little else had passed between them since.

Professor Lu was a broad man with a wide, flat face and narrow slanted eyes. His thick accent betrayed origins in northwest China. He wore a white coat open over a dusty cardigan and baggy pants, and on the rare occasions when he removed the cigarette from between his lips, he waved it around with nicotine-stained fingers. "Jiang Baofu?" He breathed smoke at Li and Mei-Ling. "A brilliant student." He shuffled papers absently on the desk in his small office. Sun slanted in between the slats of Venetian blinds and lit his smoke in blue wedges. "In all the years I have been teaching, I cannot recall a student with more natural ability. He handles a scalpel as if he was born with one in his hand. If he chose to he could become one of the top surgeons in the country." He paused and raised his eyes from his papers. "I hope he doesn't."

Li frowned. "Why?"

"Because that young man is more concerned with the dead than with the living."

"How do you mean?"

"I mean that he has an unhealthy obsession with death. Here, we try to instil in our students a sense of caring, a sense of obligation to the well-being of the patient." He flicked a cold glance at Mei-Ling. "Even if we do not always succeed."

Li glanced at Mei-Ling, confused now by a subtext he did not understand. There had been a certain familiarity in the greeting between Mei-Ling and Professor Lu which, Li assumed, had been established in a telephone call to arrange the meeting. Now, it was clear, there was more to it. But Mei-Ling remained impassive.

"In the case of Jiang Baofu," Professor Lu continued, "he has no interest whatsoever in the patient, only in the mechanics of the body and the techniques of surgery. He spends hours in pathology, cutting up bodies donated to research. We have tried to persuade him that his talents might best be suited to the field of forensic pathology." He gave Li a look that suggested little sympathy, and said with a tone, "I'm sure he would be an asset to you people." He lit another cigarette from the remains of his old one. "However, sadly he still remains undecided."

"Surely," Li said, "if he is so talented, his skills would be best used in the service of the living?"

The professor squinted at him through his smoke. "Tell me, Detective, would you rather have a doctor whose technique was impeccable, or one who actually cared about whether you lived or died?" But he did not wait for Li's response. "I know which I would choose."

"You don't like him much, then?" Mei-Ling said in a tone laced with sarcasm.

"Actually, I can't stand to be near the boy," the professor said bluntly. "He is . . ." and he thought about it for a moment, "uniquely and unremittingly unlikeable. I cannot think of anyone who likes him, staff or students. You never see him in the company of others. In the canteen he always sits alone." He shrugged. "What more can I tell you? I would describe him as abnormally brilliant, but I think abnormal would suffice." He pulled apart the Venetian blinds to let the sunlight fall upon his face. For a moment he closed his eyes, as if basking in its warmth. Then abruptly he let the blinds snap shut. "But don't take my word for it. Ask his professor of pathology. Dr. Mac-Gowan is a visiting lecturer from the United States. Jiang idolises him. But I think the good American doctor could quite happily strangle him." Professor Lu grinned as some private thought flashed through his mind.

"May we speak to Dr. MacGowan?" Li asked.

"Of course. If you can speak English."

"I could see that goddamn kid far enough, you know what I mean?" MacGowan dragged his attention away from the corpse that lay cut open on the table in front of him and looked up at Li and Mei-Ling. "This doesn't bother you, does it? I mean, I guess you people have seen plenty of stuff like this. I'm sorry if this one's a bit ripe."

"Sure," Li said. "It is not a problem" But you never got used to the perfume of rotting human flesh. He glanced at Mei-Ling and saw that, if anything, she was paler than when she'd arrived at the hotel. You needed a strong stomach for this sort of thing at the best of times. And for Mei-Ling, this was not the best of times.

She caught Li's look. "I am fine," she said.

There were five other bodies laid out on tables in this large, overlit room, each in various stages of decay and dissection. The doctor's students, first-year novices, were due in five minutes to pick up from an earlier session.

"Every time I turn around, there he is," MacGowan said. "Sitting at the back of a first-year lecture, hovering around pathology, hoping to pick up a spare corpse if one of the students doesn't turn up. Jesus, I even saw him in the street once outside my apartment. The kid must have followed me home. Pretty goddamn creepy, if you ask me."

There it was again, Li thought. *Creepy.* How many people had described him that way? *He gave me the creeps*, Dai had said, and *really creepy*, Mei-Ling had called him. A *creepy medical student*, were the words Margaret had used.

MacGowan was about forty-five, and losing his hair. He was lean, and very white – perhaps a consequence, Li thought, of all the hours spent under artificial light in rooms like this. Both Li and Mei-Ling found their eyes drawn to the black hair that grew thickly on his forearms. MacGowan seemed to notice and he became suddenly self-conscious. "So what more can I tell you?" he asked, moving away to a stainless steel sink to peel off his gloves and wash his hands.

"When you have finished with the bodies in here, what do you do with them?" Li asked, and he wondered if it was possible that the women they had found in the mud in Pudong had been hacked up in this very room.

"We burn 'em," MacGowan said. "But only after we get our money's worth out of them." He grinned.

But Li did not share his amusement. "Do you sew the bodies closed at the end of the process?"

"Sure. We dump all the crap back inside and then stitch them up, though not with the kind of embroidery they get taught to use on live patients." He grinned again.

"What kind of thread do you use?"

MacGowan appeared surprised by the question. He shrugged. "Oh, just some rough twine." He looked along the cluttered worktop beside the sink and grabbed a ball of coarse black twine. He tossed it to Li. "Stuff like that."

Li examined it. It looked very much like the twine that had been used to suture the women whose mutilated bodies filled nearly half the cooler space at the mortuary. "You always use *this* twine?"

Again MacGowan shrugged. "I guess. It's just standard supply. You'll probably find the same stuff used in all the hospitals and mortuaries."

"May I take a piece?"

"Sure." MacGowan lifted a pair of scissors and handed them to Li so that he could cut off a six-inch length. Li then dropped the twine into a plastic evidence bag and slipped it back in his pocket. "So, has this got anything to do with those bodies they found across the river?" MacGowan asked.

"What do you know about that?" Li asked.

"Only what they're saying on CNN." He paused. "They're reporting that you've got some American pathologist from Chicago working on it with you. That right?"

Li nodded. "That is correct." He was not going to elucidate. He glanced at Mei-Ling. But she did not appear to be listening. "One other thing, Doctor," he said. "When you are instructing your students on the entry cut to make during autopsy, what do you teach them?"

MacGowan frowned. "What do you mean?"

"I mean, do you teach them to make a straight incision or a 'Y' cut?"

"Oh, I see what you're getting at." He smiled. "I know it's normal practice to make a straight entry cut in China, but I prefer to make the 'Y.' I figure it gives you better access, so that's what I teach my students." He waved a hand towards the nearest table. "Take a look." And they crossed to the gaping corpse of a middle-aged man, cut open from shoulders to pubis in a neat Y. The rancid smell of the sewer rose from the body. "Aw, Jesus," MacGowan said. "Some kid's made a real mess of opening the intestine. Shit everywhere."

"Oh, my God!" Mei-Ling's involuntary exclamation startled them. Her hand flew to her mouth, and she ran from the room.

MacGowan smiled at Li apologetically. "Sorry about that. I didn't figure that she of all people would be affected that way."

Li was confused. "She's . . . not very well," he said.

"That explains it, then." MacGowan nodded. "Usually by your fourth year in med school you're over all that kind of stuff."

Li frowned, perplexed now. "What?"

"Or maybe it was fifth year." MacGowan raised his eyebrows to crinkle his receding forehead. "Pity. When the professor said you were coming today, he told me she'd been a really promising student. But, then, you know, sometimes people just ain't cut out for it. So to speak."

Mei-Ling glanced accusingly at Li in the passenger seat. "There are lots of things about me you don't know," she said. They were heading west on Zhaojiabang Road, a six-lane arterial route clogged with traffic. "I mean, it's not a secret. Everyone in the department knows I flunked out of medical school." She was clearly touchy about it, and now Li felt guilty for having made her confront again some failure from her past.

"I'm sorry," he said. "I'm not prying. Just interested. But if you don't want to talk about it . . ." He was learning that Mei-Ling was sensitive about more than one area of her life. It was making him a little wary around her now.

She sighed, her eyes fixed on the traffic ahead. "It's no big deal. I wanted to be a doctor since I was a little girl and watched my grandmother dying of cancer. It was during the Cultural Revolution. Medical resources were scarce, and there was nothing our doctor could do for her. I just felt so useless, watching her waste away, unable to do anything to stop the pain or ease the suffering. I used to sit in her room holding her hand. You could smell death coming. It was just a breath away, and yet you knew there was nothing you could do to stop it." Mei-Ling paused for a long time, lost in some distant childhood memory. "She was so brave, my grandmother. Never complained, never wanted to put us out. But there was one time, I remember, near the end. She was little more than a shadow. She sat up, suddenly, in the bed, her eyes wide. They were so big in her shrunken face. She let out a little groan, and the tears fell from her cheeks. It was the first time I had seen her crying, and I didn't know what to do. It only lasted a moment, then she wiped the tears away with the back of her hand and forced herself to smile and said, 'I'm sorry, Mei-Ling.' And she lay back down." Li saw that Mei-Ling's eyes had moistened at the memory. "It was as if a crack had somehow opened up in that brave front she put on, and she'd seen death peeking through at her, and for a moment she'd lost all her resolve, all her courage." Mei-Ling wiped her eyes with the back of her hand, a mirrored moment from a long time ago. "And all she could think to do was apologise to me." She took a deep breath. "So I was always going to be a doctor."

"Why did you drop out?" Li was genuinely curious.

She flashed him a sad smile. "Because doctors can't beat death any more than the rest of us, Li Yan, and I've never been good at handling failure. I was in my fourth year when my mother died of breast cancer, and I couldn't do a single thing to stop it. I felt just the same then as I had when my grandmother died, and I thought, what's the point? So I quit."

"And joined the police?"

She grinned. "I know. It doesn't seem like the obvious leap. And it didn't happen straight away. But that's a whole other story."

And Li wondered if that was another area of her life through which he would have to tread carefully in the future. There was a complexity about Mei-Ling that had not been immediately apparent. She leaned over and flipped open the glove box. "You'll find a search warrant in there," she said. "For Jiang Baofu's place. It'll take us about twenty minutes to get there."

II

Ming-Xin village was a development built at the end of the twentieth century in the far north-west suburbs of Shanghai, near Giangwan Stadium. It comprised low and high rise apartment blocks in pale pink, green and cream, set among landscaped gardens with roads and pathways threaded through them like a maze of crazy stitching. Ornamental evergreen trees marked the boundaries of tiny gardens, large grassy areas were bounded by lush green sub-tropical shrubbery and fleshy leafed trees. Li had seen nothing like it in Beijing. Mei-Ling parked in Nuan-Jiang Road, outside building No. 39, opposite a white three-storey block with terraces and arched windows.

The path to the main door was choked with parked bicycles and motor-scooters. Inside a dark entrance hall, post boxes lined one wall facing the windows of the caretaker's office. The caretaker was a sparrow-like middle-aged woman wearing a yellow cardigan over a black tee-shirt. She had a mean, thin face below a thatch of short-cropped hair. On the wall behind her was a clock, a calendar and a large coloured map of China. On her desk was a pile of cheap magazines. She was warming her hands on a jar of green tea and looked at Li and Mei-Ling suspiciously with darting dark eyes. "Can I help you?" she asked. Li showed her his ID and handed her the search warrant to scrutinise. Which she did, taking time and great care to read every character. She was not going to be intimidated by authority. Finally she handed the warrant back through the sliding glass window. "What's he done?"

"We don't know. Maybe nothing," Mei-Ling said. "Do you know him?"

The caretaker shrugged and pulled a face. "He's a weirdo. Comes and goes at all hours. Sometimes he'll talk to you, sometimes he just looks right through you."

"Does he have many visitors?" Li asked.

"In the year since he moved in I don't know of one," she said. "Of course, you'll have to ask my relief, but she's never mentioned any."

"And she would?"

"Well, not normally. But we have discussed the fact that no one ever comes to see him. So if she'd seen someone, I think she'd have mentioned it." She took a sip of her tea. "He's a medical student, isn't he?"

"*He* told you that?" Mei-Ling asked.

"On one of the rare occasions he opened his mouth. Of course, that was early on. I can't remember the last time he even acknowledged my existence. But you can smell it off him, you know?"

Li said, "Smell what?"

"You know . . ." Her face curled up in disgust. "Medical things. Dead people. They cut them up for practice down in that place, don't they? There's a smell. Like sickness, or hospitals. I don't know how to describe it. But it gives me the shivers."

She rode up in the elevator with them to the ninth floor and along a narrow corridor with windows down one side. On the other side, metal grilles and iron gates covered windows and doors to apartments. Sunshine slanted in through the outside windows, illuminating the passage, and Li saw in its light that the cream and green paintwork on the walls was immaculate. This was no cheap housing thrown up quickly to accommodate the masses. "Who lives in these apartments?" Li asked.

The caretaker said, "Mostly company people, a lot of retired folk, a few private individuals."

"Who does Jiang rent from?"

She shrugged. "I've no idea. Since the housing market went private it's impossible to keep track of who owns what." She stopped outside number 2001 and began to unlock the iron gate that guarded the door to Jiang's apartment.

"You wouldn't know how much he pays, then?"

"A lot, I can tell you that. None of these places are cheap." She swung the gate out into the corridor and unlocked the door, pushing it open into a small entrance lobby leading to a kitchen. "You see what I mean about the smell?" she said, and she wrinkled her nose. "The whole place stinks of it."

Li was immediately aware of a high-pitched antiseptic odour that suffused the atmosphere of the apartment. It made him think of hospitals and mortuaries, disinfectant and form-aldehyde. He stepped in front of the caretaker to stop her from entering. "Thank you," he said. "We'll let you know when we're leaving so that you can lock up."

She was clearly disappointed not to be allowed in, peer-ing past Li as he spoke, trying to catch a glimpse of what lay beyond. "So am I supposed not to tell him you were here?" she said, a distinct pique in her voice.

"I think we might be speaking to him before you do," Li said.

"So you know where he's gone, then?"

Li and Mei-Ling exchanged glances. "Gone?" Li said. "What do you mean?" Jiang Baofu had not been at the Medical Univer-sity when they had. Professor Lu had consulted his timetables and told them the student had no lectures until the afternoon. Li had half-expected to find him at home.

"He's gone away for a few days." There was a hint of triumph now in the caretaker's tone. She knew something they did not. "He told my relief he was going to visit a cousin somewhere."

"Where?"

"I don't know. You're the police. You should know that sort of thing."

"Did he say when he'd be back?"

"The weekend, I think. But I couldn't swear to it. You'll have to ask her."

"We will. Thank you," Li said, and he pulled the iron gate closed, and then shut the door on her. They heard her annoy-ance in the sharp click, click of her heels as she hurried off down the corridor. Li looked grimly at Mei-Ling. "You read his file?" She nodded. "He doesn't have a cousin, does he?"

She shook her head. "And Dai's pretty thorough," she said. "But we'll need to check."

The apartment was small and compact, just two rooms with a tiny kitchen and dining area. But by Chinese standards it was huge for a single occupancy. Li looked around with a sense of awe. The place was spotless, freshly painted walls of cream and pale lime, polished wooden floors gleaming in the sunlight that flooded in through large windows in the living room and bedroom. There was a spartan quality to the apartment. Everything, apparently, had a place and was in it. Cooking implements hung shining side by side from hooks on the wall. Jars stood in ordered rows on open shelves. Worktops on either side of the cooker were immaculate, food containers and an electric blender arranged carefully along the wall behind them. A microwave oven sat on top of a tall green refrigerator. Li looked inside the fridge. It was as ordered as the kitchen, and all but empty. Crockery was neatly stacked in a glass-doored cabinet, and Li recognised the portable television from the night watchman's hut at Pudong sitting on top of it. A small, square table with a single chair was covered in a lilac-patterned plastic cloth.

Net curtains hung from the window in the small living room. There was an uncomfortable two-seater settee, a desk below the window with a wooden stool pulled up to it. A bookcase next to it was crammed with volumes on medicine and surgery. In the opposite corner another television with a VCR on top of it sat on a stereo cabinet with a CD player and a rack of CDs. Two speaker cabinets, standing nearly three feet high, stood at either end of the wall. The walls themselves were neatly pinned with charts and diagrams: a representation of the human skeleton with all of its two hundred and six bones labelled; a large photograph of the underside of the brain and brainstem, with labels on each of the twelve pairs of cranial nerves; a poster-sized diagram of the blood vessels of the chest and abdomen with all of the arteries showing in red, the veins in blue, and the organs depicted as see-through shadows; a representation of the eye with its muscles and nerves attached, half of it cut through longitudinally to show its layers and chambers, including the retina, lens, cornea and sclera.

The bedroom walls were naked. Perhaps, Li thought, Jiang was afraid that body parts pasted on the walls here might invade his dreams. There was very little in the bedroom apart from a small wardrobe, a double bed, a chest of drawers with a television on top of it, a single bedside cabinet and one chair.

Li and Mei-Ling had not spoken as they wandered slowly through the apartment drinking in its ordered sterility. Now they stood in the living room looking around at all the hard, cold surfaces unbroken by a plant or an ornament, or anything personal. "This guy is very weird," Li said eventually, and the echo of his voice sounded odd in the chill silence of the place. "There is nothing of him here, not a single clue to his personality. Except for the place itself."

Mei-Ling nodded. "Filled with order, but no warmth." She let her eyes wander around the room. "How does he spend his time, do you think?"

"Watching television, apparently," Li said. "When he's not reading his medical books or examining his medical posters." He shook his head. "I have never seen so many televisions in one house. And did you notice the microwave, and the refrigerator, the blender, the stereo . . . ? How can this guy afford these things?"

"And where does he get the money to pay for the apartment?" Mei-Ling said. She stooped to open the glass door of the stereo cabinet and switched on the CD. There was a disk in it, and she hit the play button. The room was immediately filled with the cold string sounds of German chamber music. They listened to the strange, alien scrape of it for nearly a minute while Mei-Ling examined the other CDs in the collection. Bach and Beethoven, some traditional Chinese stringed music. She switched the chamber music off, and in the silence that followed turned her attention to a shelf of videos. She took one out at random, slipped it into the VCR and turned on the television. It was a recording, made live, during a heart-transplant operation. The surgical team were speaking in English and sounded American. As it played, Mei-Ling worked her way through the other tapes. "They're all the same," she said, examining the labels. "Edited recordings of operations, commercially produced for instruction in US medical schools." They watched, fascinated for a moment, as the bloody hands of the lead surgeon gently massaged the pumping muscle of a new heart.

Li said, "He's obsessed." He let his eyes drift again around the posters on the wall — see-through organs, cranial nerves, corneal sections. "I think we should get forensics to go through this place with a fine-toothed comb." But he wasn't sure that they would find anything. It was as if the place had been sterilised. It was not the environment of a normal human being. "And we need to find Jiang Baofu as soon as possible and bring him in for questioning." He wasn't quite sure why, but he felt a sudden sense of urgency, as if perhaps he sensed that further lives were now at risk.

III

Margaret felt the chill edge of the wind cut through her as she hurried from the new Arrivals terminal at Beijing Capital Airport to the taxi rank. After the mist and rain of Shanghai, the capital was bright and crisp and clear. The sky was cloudless. The late autumn sunshine, set lower now in the sky, cut deep shadows against the sunlit surfaces of the proud new buildings that lined the expressway into the city. Everything here seemed more ordered. From the compass-oriented grid system of roads and buildings, and broad bicycle lanes lined with trees, to the taxi queues and the white-gloved traffic cops pirouetting on circular podiums at road junctions. It was all in stark contrast to the jumble of buildings and streets, and the confusion of traffic and cyclists, that was Shanghai. In the distance, far off to the west, Margaret could see the mountains cut sharp against the sky, snow-capped peaks tracing a brilliant white profile on the deepest of blues. She sat back in her taxi and let the city wash over her. If someone had told her two years ago that she would one day feel at home in Beijing, she would have told them they were insane. But after the pain of her father's funeral, the sense of dislocation she had felt in Chicago, and the strangeness of Shanghai, it really did feel like coming home.

For the first time since rushing to catch a taxi out to Hongqiao Airport early that morning, she took the time to reflect on the previous night. She remembered the reading of the horoscopes, and wondered in the cold light of day if five thousand years of civilisation had given the Chinese insights into people and their compatibilities that Western society could not even guess at. Could Margaret and Li's conflicting birth years really explain the stormy nature of their relationship? Was she fighting a losing battle against the fates in even trying to hold on to him? She thought about Li's lucky number three, and Mei-Ling's dark and foreboding unlucky nine, her trigram the colour of dried blood. And for the first time, perhaps, Margaret began to see that there was a kind of desperation in Mei-Ling in her endeavours to win Li's affections and shut Margaret out. A *yang orphan* her aunt had said she was. And there had been a clue in her brother's description of her fight to succeed in a man's world. A compensation for something lacking in her life. Margaret realised that she really knew nothing about Mei-Ling, and wondered if perhaps there had been some tragedy in her life that had made her the way she was. Or maybe, as her stars suggested, that tragedy was still to come, a dark shadow hanging over her future. Margaret shivered, as if someone had walked over her grave, and felt a disquiet in the thought that disturbed her.

As her taxi turned off the expressway on to the third ring road, huge new structures rose all around into a sky crowded with neon advertisements for Japanese and American consumer goods. Margaret turned her thoughts to Li, and she remembered him making love to her in the semi-darkness of her hotel room. And then, through a fog of memories made hazier by alcohol, she recalled something else, something she had buried away in the depths of her subconscious. For even in her drunken state, she had been aware of a desperation in their lovemaking, that same quality she had seen in Mei-Ling. Something that owed more to fear than fulfilment. And now it came bubbling back to the surface and clouded her day with depression. She was, she knew, losing him, and perhaps the desperation she saw in Mei-Ling was merely a reflection of the hopelessness she felt in herself.

The taxi had negotiated its way on to the second ring road, and now turned south at the Yong Hegong Lamasery into a

labyrinth of *hutongs*, narrow lanes bounded by *siheyuan* courtyards that owed their origins to the Mongol conquerors who
swept down from the north centuries before. The Beijing
Municipal Police Department of Forensic Pathology was buried away in an anonymous white building in Pau Jü Hutong.
Margaret's taxi pulled up beside the concrete ramp that ran up
to gates leading into the basement of the building. She paid the
driver and stepped out into the midday chill. The brown, brittle
leaves of autumn rattled along the cobbles in the breeze. Margaret remembered a moment at this spot when she and Li had
almost kissed for the first time, pulling back only at the last
moment when they became aware of an armed guard watching them from the gate. There was still an armed guard at the
gate, but the world had moved on since then. She thought of
Li's whispered farewell in the early hours of last night. He had
to get back to his hotel, he had said. Mei-Ling was picking him
up in the morning. He had left Margaret's airplane ticket on
the bedside table and ordered an alarm call for her from the
telephone in her room. She had still been drunk, but not so
drunk that it hadn't occurred to her that the only reason Li
wanted to go back to his hotel was so that Mei-Ling would not
find out he had spent the night with Margaret. The faintest
traces of a lingering headache reminded her of her excesses
in toasting Mei-Ling to oblivion. It hadn't taken much. Which
was just as well, because Margaret had had a considerable head
start in the consumption of alcohol. She wondered how Mei-
Ling felt today.

The mutilated remains of what had once been a young woman
lay assembled on the autopsy table. Decompositional juices
trickled into the drainage channels and the smell of decay
hung thick in the air. When they found her body in February,

she had already been in the ground for about a week. Now the original carnage inflicted on her, followed by an autopsy and eight months in the freezer, and then four days of slow defrosting, had all taken their toll. The face of the severed head had been virtually obliterated by decay. The white crusting of freezer burn on the skin was being destroyed in turn by the formation of slimy dark green blisters filled with the collected fluids of decomposition.

"I am glad I never ask *her* out on date," Dr. Wang said and he grinned across the table at Margaret.

"Just as well. She'd probably have turned you down," Margaret said dryly. Wang made a little snort through his mask that indicated he was not amused. "Did you do the original on this girl?" Margaret asked.

Wang shook his head. "No. That was Dr. Ma Runqi. He is gone now."

"That's convenient."

Wang looked at her and asked guardedly, "Why?"

"Well, it means there's nobody to answer for this . . ." she turned and picked up the translation of the autopsy report, "this shambles." Wang did not respond. "Have you read it?" Margaret asked.

He nodded. "Sure."

"And?"

Wang shrugged noncommittally. He was reluctant to criticise a colleague, even one now departed. "It is not what I would have done," he said.

"No." And Margaret knew that Wang would have done a much better job. She had worked with him the previous year on the city's first serial killings, and developed a healthy respect for his work, if not for his sense of humour. She dropped the report on to the worktop and turned back to the body.

She scraped gently around the edge of the "Y"-shaped entry wound. The yellow-brown colouring of the betadine that Ma Runqi had noted in his report was no longer discernible, but there were still traces of mud clinging to the skin and clogging the open edge of the wound. "He didn't even clean off the body properly. And he missed the bits of black gritty material here in the areas of haemorrhage along the incision edges." She picked at them with the point of the scalpel. "You know what they are?"

Wang said, "Sure. Someone used electrocautery device to heat-seal small bleeders."

"Which would kind of lead you to think that maybe this person was still alive when they were cut open, wouldn't it? That and the iodine tincture applied to the skin before the incision was made." Wang nodded mutely. Margaret pressed on, "I mean, Dr. Ma notes the tincture, but draws no conclusions, and misses the cauterisation completely. No wonder Section One weren't making any progress with the investigation. This is a shoddy piece of work, Doctor. What else do you suppose we're going to find?"

Dr. Wang's silence spoke volumes. And for the moment, at least, his sense of humour appeared to have deserted him.

It was less than ten minutes later that Margaret came across her next "find." It was a tiny suture, half buried in the retroperitoneal fat behind the spleen, tying off one of the renal arteries. Margaret removed the blue polypropylene thread, still tied in its distinctive knot, and held it up for Wang to see. "I don't think it's any coincidence," she said, "that I found the same suture, tied with the same blue thread, in most of the victims in Shanghai. It seems that Dr. Ma didn't like getting his hands greasy." She took some paper towels to wipe the worst of the fat off her latex gloves to prevent her scalpel from slipping.

"So this one is same as bodies in Shanghai?" Wang asked.

Margaret shook her head. "No, it's quite different in a number of ways." She had not completed the re-examination, but already there were obvious differences. Wang looked at her for elucidation. She said, "Although it is clear that the subject was still alive when the procedure began, as with the Shanghai victims, the lungs and one of the kidneys are still present. As are the eyes. In Shanghai all these organs had been removed. Also, it is quite clear from the examination of the amputation wounds, that the bones have been sawn through, rather than chopped, as again they were in Shanghai."

"Then the girl was killed by different person?"

"No, I think it was probably just the circumstances that were different. I believe this girl was murdered by the same hand."

"How can you tell?"

"Well, there's plenty of circumstantial evidence. The iodine tincture, the 'Y' entry cut, the cauterisation of the incision edges. Then there's the toxicology. The succinic acid and the benzodiazepine in the urine." And with her tweezers, she picked up again the blue polypropylene suture knot. "And this."

Wang shrugged. "It is just suture knot."

"It's a one-handed tie. I remember practising this one for hours when I was at med school. The difference is, I'm right-handed. The way this one loops through, it could only have been tied by a left-hander, as were all the others in Shanghai. And it would be some coincidence if different surgeons hundreds of miles apart used exactly the same blue plastic thread, don't you think?" Wang nodded, and Margaret said, "I'll want to take a sample of the twine used to sew up the body back to Shanghai. Forensics will be able to determine if it's the same stuff."

"So why you think some organs and eyes are left?" Wang's curiosity was aroused, and Margaret guessed that he was jealous of her involvement in the Shanghai murders.

"I don't know," she said. "It's almost as if they were interrupted, or . . ." she lifted the original autopsy report again and scanned it thoughtfully, "or something made them give up." Something caught her attention and she frowned. "I see Dr. Ma notes that the right side of the heart was thickened and enlarged when he performed the original autopsy. So he didn't miss quite everything."

The heart, which had been found in a separate bag with the liver, one of the kidneys and the pancreas, had been cut open and was seriously deformed by decomposition. It was impossible now to see the gross evidence of inflammation that Dr. Ma had noted eight months earlier. Margaret stood staring at it for a long time. "I wonder . . . ?" she murmured, and she turned the heart over, carefully leaning in to ease open the stump of the aorta to get a look at the aortic valve. She scrutinised it carefully for several minutes before turning her attention to the pulmonary artery and the pulmonic valve. She let out a small gasp of satisfaction and glanced up at Wang. "You want to take a look?"

Perplexed, he leaned over the heart and repeated her examination. "What do you see?" she asked.

He said, "Tiny vegetations on the leaflets of the valves." He looked up. "I am not familiar with this."

"They're little crumbly chunks of bacteria, often collected from the skin at dirty injection sites," she said. "It's quite common for them to combine with fibrin and white blood cells on the flaps of the valves that separate the chambers of the heart. Probably not a phenomenon that's all that common yet in China. But it'll come."

Wang frowned. "She was junkie?"

"Heroin probably. And if Ma Runqi had been doing his job properly he would have seen those and gone on to look for injection sites, maybe in the foot or the inside crook of the arm." She sighed. "In all likelihood, that's exactly what the surgeon who killed her did. When he removed the heart he would have seen the telltale evidence of swelling on the right side and checked out the valve flaps. This guy knew his stuff, knew that the little vegetations gathered there meant that the girl was a user. He probably went on to do what Dr. Ma didn't – check for injection sites."

Wang was puzzled now. "But what difference would it make to them if this girl was junkie?"

Margaret had a sick, sinking feeling in her stomach. "I don't know. Unless . . ." she was reluctant even to entertain the thought, because it simply didn't make sense, "unless they were after her organs. In which case they'd have been useless because of the high risk of infectious disease."

Wang was watching her carefully. "You don't think they were?"

"Well, you tell me," Margaret said. "If you were going to murder someone for their organs, would you keep them alive while you removed them?"

Wang laughed. "Of course not. This would be insane." And she heard an exact echo of the words she had used with Li and Mei-Ling.

"My point exactly," Margaret said.

"So why would discovery that she is drug addict make them cut short procedure?"

Margaret shook her head, totally mystified. "If they weren't after the organs, then I have no idea."

They spent the next twenty minutes further retracing Dr. Ma Runqi's erratic steps, leading eventually to the bivalved womb which Dr. Wang laid out carefully on the table. In spite of further deterioration, Margaret saw that the endometrium bore the same distinctive adhesive scarring she had noted in several of the women in Shanghai. Wang let out a derisive snort. "Hmmmph! How often have I seen this?"

Margaret looked at him curiously. "You have?"

"Sure. These cowboy doctors. They don't give shit about the poor women when they scrape them out."

"Of course," Margaret realised. "She's had an abortion." And immediately she felt an empathy with the poor dead girl.

"Too many like this," Wang said. And he glanced around and lowered his voice, as if he might be overheard. "One Child Policy."

Margaret nodded. "I'd have thought maybe you guys would have got good at this by now, after all the practice you've had."

Wang shook his head. "Not this guy." He grinned. "Use condom, then no need abortion."

When they had stripped off their gowns and gloves and masks, and showered away the stench of death, Margaret and Wang met up again in his office to review their findings. Margaret was still browsing thoughtfully through Ma Runqi's original report. She looked up suddenly and found Wang watching her appraisingly. He was momentarily discomposed at being caught gaping so openly. She said, "These gold foil restorations she'd had done to her teeth . . . In the States, if you saw dental work like this on a Jane Doe, you'd think either she was very rich or very poor. Rich because she could afford to have it done. Or poor because she went to the dental school for free treatment and let the students practise on her with the gold foil." She paused. "Work like that would be expensive in China, right?"

"Ve-ery expensive," he said. "Only rich people and foreigner can pay for that."

"Yet here's this Chinese girl, a junkie, who no one seems to have missed, and she can afford to have work like this done on her teeth? I guess treatment's not free at the dental schools here?"

Wang shook his head. "No. And we check out all the clinics in Beijing that can do this."

Margaret frowned. "But what if she wasn't from Beijing? What if she was from Shanghai? I guess they've got places there capable of doing this kind of work?"

"Sure."

"So did anyone check out the clinics there?"

Wang shook his head. "Why should we think she come from Shanghai?"

"No reason. Until now, maybe." Margaret ran her hands thoughtfully back through her damp hair. "I'll take the x-rays down to Shanghai with me, and someone can check that out." And then, almost thinking out loud, "But if she *was* from Shanghai, then why would they follow her to Beijing just to kill her?" It suggested to her that the victims were not simply picked at random. Margaret lifted the report again. "Blood type O. The most common blood type on earth." She paused and thought about it. "Which would also make her a universal donor."

"But they no need to come to Beijing for blood type O," Wang said.

"No . . ." Margaret shook her head slowly. There was no clear understanding for her in any of this. She lifted Ma Runqi's report again. A thought wrinkled her brow. "I don't suppose anyone thought to DNA-match the body parts?"

Wang shook his head decisively. "Why would we, Doctah Cambo? Visual matching was only requirement. All the pieces were found together."

"According to the report the arms, legs and head were separately wrapped, even though they were found in the same bag as the torso. Dr. Ma notes that the severed pieces were slightly better preserved." She reflected on this for a moment. "Would it be possible for you to DNA-match all the parts now? I mean, do you have that facility here?"

"Not here," Wang said. "At Centre of Material Evidence Determination. At University of Public Security. It take a couple of days, maybe." He paused. "You think maybe the parts come from different bodies?"

Margaret took a long, deep inhalation of breath and shook her head. "I have not the faintest idea, Doctor. As we say in America, I'm flying a kite here."

Wang frowned. "You want to fly kite in Beijing, you should go to Tiananmen Square."

IV

Nine chairs, tipped to an angle of forty-five degrees, were balanced one on top of the other in an upward arc, counterbalanced by six upside down teenage girls in yellow and green costumes, stacked up like steps on a stairway to heaven. They appeared to be defying gravity and breaking all the laws of physics at the same time. A pale blue spotlight cast their shadows on a screen at the back of the stage. It was not until, with a small shriek, one of the girls overbalanced and all the chairs went tumbling across the stage, that Li saw the girls were supported on wires. They went spinning through the air, crashing into each other like demented birds.

Immediately, a middle-aged woman sitting in the front stalls got stiffly to her feet and began screaming imprecations at them for their clumsiness. Several boys came running on to the stage to retrieve the chairs, and the girls began slowly descending, faces pink with exertion, embarrassment and, perhaps, fear.

"I'm so sorry, Ma'am," the youngest of them whimpered. "It was my fault."

"You are all to blame!" the woman yelled. "You are supposed to be a team. Each one relies on the other. You all depend on everyone else making those little adjustments, all the time. What kind of fools are you going to look if you do that in front of an audience tonight?"

The younger ones hung their heads. One or two of the older girls, who were maybe seventeen or eighteen, thrust their chins forward defiantly. The boys had reassembled the chairs and were preparing to set up the stunt all over again.

"This time," the woman bellowed, "I want you to hold your positions for *two* minutes!"

There were audible groans from the girls. Li turned to Mei-Ling and whispered, "Do you think they're still attached to those wires during the real show."

"I hope so," Mei-Ling said. "There could be a lot of cracked skulls if they're not." She smiled wryly. "The trouble is, there are nine chairs. Lucky for some, unlucky for others. I should know."

The woman at the front, who had heard the voices from the back, turned round and glared at them. "This is a rehearsal," she shouted. "Members of the public are not allowed."

Mei-Ling followed Li down the right-hand aisle. "Police," Li said, and flashed his ID.

The woman glared from one to the other, and Li saw that she was only, perhaps, forty. But her face was set in a permanent scowl that made her look older, and she was supporting herself on a stout walking stick. "What do you want?"

"We're looking for Sun Jie," Mei-Ling said.

The woman's eyes narrowed. "Is he in trouble?"

Mei-Ling shook her head. "It's about his wife, Wu Liyao."

"You've found her?"

"Perhaps. That's what we'd like to discuss with Sun Jie."

"Well, maybe you'd like to discuss it with me first," the woman said. "The little bitch owes me. Disappeared right before we were supposed to go on tour. And then Sun Jie was no damned good to us. What did she do? Run off with some fat cat?"

"Actually," Li said, "we believe she might have been murdered."

Which took the wind right out of the woman's sails. She sat down very suddenly, leaning heavily on her stick, and waved her hand in the direction of the stage. "Take a break, girls," she called. Her eyes were strangely glazed for a moment before she turned them up to Li. "What happened?"

"We need to confirm identity first," Mei-Ling said. "Was she an important member of the troupe?"

"Oh," the woman said dismissively, "she no longer performed. She was too old for that. She and Sun Jie trained the young ones. And, anyway, she damaged one of her feet in a fall. She was no longer capable of producing the level of performance required."

Li and Mei-Ling exchanged looks. Li said, "Do you know the sort of people she mixed with, if anyone might have borne her a grudge?"

"The people she mixed with were all acrobats," the woman snapped. "This is not just a job, it is a way of life. And she had no life outside of the circus."

"What about her husband?" Mei-Ling asked.

"They both used to be stars of the show. But age takes its toll, you know." The woman smiled sourly. "I used to be a star of the show myself, and look what it did for me."

Li knew that it was neither time nor wear and tear that had imprinted the ugly scowl so deeply in the woman's face. That came from inside. A reflection of the soul. The stick was another matter. He said, "So where can we find Sun Jie?"

"Huh!" the woman was scornful. "He's a waste of space, that one. He was beside himself when Liyao went missing. Eventually, when they couldn't find her, he rejoined the tour. But he's never been the same man since." She sneered, "He's found *religion* now, you know. He's a *Buddhist*." She couldn't keep the contempt out of her voice. "He spends his afternoons at the Jing'an Temple." She checked her watch. "If you hurry you'll catch him there now."

A pall of sweet smoke hung in the still air over the temple like a protective cloud. Here was a bizarre anachronism, a corner of ancient China lurking behind brick walls and surrounded on all sides by towers of glass and concrete and steel. The entrance courtyard, behind high gates, was crowded with people burning paper offerings and incense in large smouldering metal boats. Yellow and red flags hung from covered balconies where monks roomed beneath crumbling black-tiled roofs. Covered passageways, supported on rust red pillars, provided shelter for elaborate gold-leaf altars presided over by giant Buddhas.

Li looked around in wonder. He had never been in any kind of temple before. Religion was a mystery to him, intriguing, perplexing, even a little frightening, and beyond all comprehension. He stared in amazement as young women knelt on crimson altar cushions, hands clasped in prayer, incense sticks smoking between pressed palms. Men and women of all ages and backgrounds sat sociably around tables lining the courtyards and passageways, folding sheets of gold and silver paper into tiny origami shapes with which they filled red paper carrier bags and old shoe boxes before burning them. He had no idea why.

He was surprised when Mei-Ling took his arm and leaned in confidentially. "This place was a hotbed of corruption in the twenties and thirties, you know. Legend has it that it was run by a six-foot, four-inch abbot. Apart from being married to a very rich woman, he had seven concubines. He conducted business with the gangsters of the day, and wouldn't go anywhere without his White Russian bodyguards."

They wandered through an inner chamber where people were pasting thousands of gold-coloured strips of paper to the walls. Some of them bore small photographs. Perhaps, Li thought, pictures of dead relatives. Through another courtyard, eyes stinging in the smoke, they saw saffron-robed monks gathered around a huge jade Buddha, chanting incantations from open prayer books.

"There is a much grander temple up the road," Mei-Ling said. "The one the tourists all go to. Filled with treasures from the past. It only survived the Cultural Revolution because the monks cleverly pasted giant posters of Mao Zedong over the gates, and the Red Guards would not defile the likeness of their hero to gain entry. So it survived intact."

From here, Li and Mei-Ling turned south, through a circular opening in a yellow wall and into a narrow passageway, with prayer rooms leading off to left and right. Shrubs and miniature trees grew everywhere in terracotta pots. The eerie mumblings, and chants and cants of small gatherings of monks, drifted out of open doorways. They heard the steady clapping of hands, the deep, sonorous and monotonously regular beat of a drum. They followed the directions given them by the crippled manageress of the acrobatic circus and found themselves in a room at the end of the passage where half a dozen monks sat around a long table reading in silence. A solitary figure in a shabby blue suit sat alone at one end of a row of seats at the back of the room. He leaned forward, his elbows on his knees, his hands clasped in front of him, his head bowed. Long strips of red cloth hung from the ceiling, embroidered with black characters. A red velvet cloth was draped across the prayer table, and candles burned around a small Buddha at one end of it. Several of the monks glanced curiously at Li and Mei-Ling as they entered and approached the man in the blue suit. It wasn't until Li asked him if he was Sun Jie, and he looked up, that Li realised he was still a young man, perhaps under thirty, even younger than his lost wife.

Several shaven heads turned now from the table and glared at them for having had the audacity to break the silence of the room. *Their* silence. Li produced his Ministry ID and said to the man in the blue suit, "We want to talk to you about your wife."

Li saw a moment of hope light in Sun Jie's eyes, then cloud again almost as quickly with fear. He glanced nervously towards the monks. "Not here," he said, and he stood up and hurried out into the passageway. Li and Mei-Ling followed.

Sun Jie led them quickly away from the main courtyard, passing through two circular openings, until finally they found themselves in a deserted square beneath the rising balconies of the monks' living quarters. It was a tight, claustrophobic space, several levels of roof plunging downwards in a dramatic sweep overhead, only to turn up at the last moment, rising to narrow points at the corners. The chanting and the smoke and the beat of the drum seemed a long way away from here. The monks' daily washing, draped across plastic lines on the balconies above, stirred slightly in the breeze. Sun Jie stopped and turned to face them suddenly, as if he had been steeling himself to confront the truth. "Is she dead?"

Li saw no point in offering false hope. "We have recovered the body of a woman who may be your wife. Unfortunately her features are – " He hesitated. "She has suffered a certain amount of decomposition. We would like you to make an identification."

There was no perceptible change in Sun Jie's expression. But he was silent for a very long time before he said, "What makes you think it is Wu Liyao?"

Mei-Ling said, "She had stress fractures in one of her feet. The pathologist thought it might have been a sports injury."

"Which foot?"

"The right."

Sun Jie's head sank. "When do you want me to look at the body?"

"Today, if possible."

He nodded, and Li said, "Is there anything at all you can tell us about your wife's disappearance that might help shed light on what happened to her?"

Sun Jie lifted his head to gaze hopelessly at the heavens. Then he looked at Li. "She went out shopping one Saturday morning and she never came back."

"Do you think she planned it?" Mei-Ling asked.

He looked at her with dead eyes. "She left a pot of soup simmering on the stove, and she was halfway through writing a letter to her mother. She had just put in a washing to pack clean clothes for a tour." He paused. "So I think she meant to come back."

Mei-Ling pressed him, "There was no chance she was seeing someone else?"

"None."

"How can you be sure?"

His smile was a sad one. "Because the demands of the troupe were such we barely had time for one another, never mind anyone else." He shook his head, eyes laden with regret. "The things you think are important . . ." He turned his gaze on Li. "So you never found the man who was following her?"

"What?" Li was startled. There was no mention in the report of a man following her. He looked at Mei-Ling and she shrugged.

"I knew they didn't believe me at the time," Sun Jie said. "A distraught husband trying to find excuses for a wife who'd left him. But she saw him several times. She told me. She was really spooked."

Li felt his scalp tighten. It was the first break they'd had, the first hint that any of these women might have been watched, that they might have been stalked and snatched. "What exactly did she tell you?"

Sun Jie fumbled in his pockets for a cigarette and Li lit it for him. "The first time she saw him, she told me, she was coming home from the theatre one night after a performance. I had the flu and was in bed. She'd seen him in the atrium outside the theatre, and then again on the bus. She hadn't thought much about it until she saw him again a few days later standing across the road from the bus stop, outside the exhibition hall, smoking a cigarette and watching her as she got on the bus. She still wasn't particularly concerned. But a couple of days after that she saw him in our street, standing just inside the entrance to an alleyway. And she knew he was watching her. She got really scared then. And that's when she told me."

"What did he look like, this guy?" Li asked. He was almost certain Sun Jie was going to describe someone very like Jiang Baofu.

Sun Jie drew on his cigarette and blew smoke at the sky. "Well, that's the thing. That's why she noticed him at all. I mean, a face like that you wouldn't forget. Liyao said he had long, greasy hair. He wasn't very tall, kind of squat and thick-set. She said he looked like a Mongolian, and he had a real ugly scar on his upper lip. She thought it could have been a hare-lip."

V

The miniature house of tin and glass mounted on the rear of Mei Yuan's tricycle was looking a little battered and the worse for wear. The pink tin roof was dented and discoloured, and the searing heat of the hotplate inside had scorched the cream-painted sides. Mei Yuan, too, was showing signs of age. Wrapped in a thick padded jacket and scarf, a woollen hat, with a turned up peak, pulled down over greying hair, her face was red raw with the cold. Her lips were cracked, and her brow furrowed in a concentrated frown against the icy wind. She wore thick gloves and stood stamping her feet on the sidewalk beneath the trees at the corner of Dongzhimennei Street and Chaoyangmen. She gave the appearance of being crushed by the onset of winter.

But the moment she saw Margaret her eyes lit up, and the familiar dimples appeared in her cheeks, like deep scars in her round face. She was almost overcome by excitement. "*Ni hau, ni hau, ni hau,*" she babbled excitedly, and threw her arms around Margaret in a very un-Chinese expression of affection. Margaret held on to her tightly. It felt as if Mei Yuan was about the closest thing left in the world to someone who cared about her. Then Mei Yuan held her at arm's length and inspected her. "*Ni chi guo le ma?*" she asked – the traditional Beijinger's greeting – *Have you eaten?*

"Yes, I have eaten," Margaret lied. It was the traditional response. But, in truth, she was ravenous. She had not eaten all day.

"I will make you a *jian bing,*" Mei Yuan said, astutely. "I need the practice. I have hardly sold one since midday."

And Margaret watched as Mei Yuan poured a ladleful of her pancake mix on to the sizzling hotplate behind the glass screens of the miniature house. When she flipped it over, she spread it with chilli sauce and hoisin and then broke an egg on to it, before sprinkling it with chopped spring onion and pressing down a square of deep-fried egg white. The whole thing was folded over twice and wrapped in brown paper. Mei Yuan handed it to Margaret, her face gleaming with pleasure. "So," she said, "how is my Li Yan? I am missing him."

Margaret bit into the soft savoury pancake and tried to seem natural. "He's fine," she replied. But Mei Yuan had an unerring instinct for the truth, and for the obfuscation of it. Her smile vanished immediately.

She said, "What is wrong?"

"Nothing is wrong," Margaret responded.

"And I ride home each night on a dragon's back," Mei Yuan said.

Margaret chewed reflectively for a moment on her *jian bing* before she said, "He has found someone in Shanghai who I think maybe he likes better."

Mei Yuan snorted her derision. "How can he know he likes her better when he cannot know her as well as he knows you?"

Margaret shrugged. "Perhaps he has gotten to know me too well and doesn't like what he sees. Anyway, she is Chinese. I am not."

Mei Yuan waved a hand dismissively. "Culture and colour do not count. It is only the heart that matters. Here . . ." She started rummaging in the bag hanging from her trike, and pulled out a dog-eared paperback book. "I have been keeping this for you." It was a volume of Chinese love poetry, translated into English. "You'll see," she said. "Chinese are no different. We all feel and express the same things." She paused, and with a twinkle added, "You should give this to Li Yan."

And Margaret thought what an extraordinary person Mei Yuan was. A well-read and educated woman, torn down by the ravages of the Cultural Revolution, content now to sell *jian bing* on the street corner and indulge her passion for reading. She had lost her son during those terrible years, as Li Yan had lost his mother. And by some strange quirk of fate they had found each other on a street corner, and somehow managed to fill the missing parts of each other's lives. "Thank you," Margaret said, and she gave Mei Yuan a hug. "When do we collect little Xinxin?"

Kites filled the sky like birds, and the children cast shadows several times longer than themselves. The vast expanse of Tiananmen Square meant nothing to them, other than limitless open space and empty skies in which to fly their simple structures of wire and plastic. None of them had been born when the tanks rolled in, leaving the blood and hopes of a generation to stain the paving stones. A century of bloody change had been played out here, and now it was just a place to fly a kite.

Mei Yuan said the kindergarten often brought the children here to fly their kites in the late afternoon when the sky was clear and the cold winds blew down from the north. Now the sun was very low in the west, and the strong shadows it cast somehow charred all colour from the scene, except for the red walls of the Forbidden City, and the orange-tiled roof of the Gate of Heavenly Peace. A troupe of armed police in long green coats and peaked caps marched past them in rigid formation, eyes fixed and unblinking. A woman with a thick scarf wrapped around her mouth tried to sell the two women a kite shaped like an eagle. The square was busy with tourists up from the country. There was barely a Western face in sight, and so Margaret was an object of great curiosity. Several groups of peasants followed them for some way before hurrying off excitedly to tell their friends about the blue-eyed, fair-haired foreign devil.

When Xinxin saw Margaret she squealed with excitement, but was caught in a quandary. She wanted to run and jump into her arms, but she was flying a kite and could not let go. Her little face was a picture of conflicting emotions. Mei Yuan resolved the problem by taking the line from her, and freeing her up to give Margaret the biggest of hugs. Margaret crouched and held the child to her, and felt her warmth and her love through the thick layers of clothes. Although only six, Xinxin had already picked up a few words of English. And so she stood back and said solemnly, "How do you do? So nice to see you."

Margaret grinned and said, "*Ni chi guo le ma?*" Which sent Xinxin and her classmates into a fit of hysterical giggles. Xinxin's pink coat was buttoned up to the neck, and her face was the same colour of crimson as her woollen tights. Mei Yuan had tied her hair in bunches high on each side of her head, and Margaret thought she looked good enough to eat. Fleetingly she wondered what her own child would have been like. Much older than Xinxin now, and no doubt she would have taken all her worst features from her father. She shook the thought aside and asked if she could have a go at flying the kite. Mei Yuan translated for her, and Xinxin nodded vigorously, and all the children and their teachers gathered round as Margaret took the line and pulled and tweaked until she had Xinxin's box-kite soaring into the deepening blue. Applause broke around her and she found herself laughing. She had forgotten what a wonderful release it was to fly a kite. She had not grown up in the Windy City for nothing.

In the taxi out to the airport, Margaret read to Xinxin in English from a big, coloured picture-book. Xinxin loved to have Margaret read for her, even if she did not immediately understand all the words. And it was amazing just how many words she had picked up in the last year. Conversation through the medium of English alone was limited, but just possible.

Margaret looked up to find Mei Yuan watching them fondly. The older woman said, "I have a riddle for you to take to Li Yan." Margaret smiled. It was a game Li and Mei Yuan had played for years during encounters at Mei Yuan's *jian bing* stall.

"What if I guess it first?" Margaret said.

"You usually do," Mei Yuan grinned.

"Okay, try me."

Mei Yuan said, "Imagine you are a bus driver on the number one route through Beijing. When the bus stops at the Friendship Store it is empty, but six passengers get on. At Wangfujing, three get off and another eight get on. At the Forbidden City five get off and fifteen get on. It is getting busier now. At Xidan, eight passengers get off, but ten get on." She paused. "Are you still with me?"

Margaret nodded. She had been furiously doing her arithmetic and trying to keep up with the constantly changing calculation.

"Okay," Mei Yuan said. "So what height is the driver?"

Which stopped Margaret in her tracks. It was the last question she had been expecting. She had a figure of twenty-three in her head, and was wondering where the trick was. But the driver's height . . . ? She blinked uncomprehendingly at Mei Yuan, and Mei Yuan laughed and raised her hands.

"Don't try and work it out now. Think about it," she said. "But do not ask Li Yan until you have the answer yourself. For you will see then how important it is that you ask this question correctly."

"What are you talking about?" Xinxin demanded to know. "Speak Chinese, speak Chinese!"

Mei Yuan laughed. "I was just giving Margaret a message for your uncle. When you are older, perhaps, Margaret will pass it on to you, too."

Xinxin was almost beside herself with excitement when they got on to the main concourse in the new departure hall at the Capital Airport. She had never been anywhere so big, with so many people and so many lights mirrored in so many shiny surfaces. It was dazzling. She had never flown before, either, and with the fearlessness of the young could not wait to get aboard the airplane.

Margaret asked Mei Yuan to stay with Xinxin while she checked them in at the airline desk. Xinxin's little case was small enough to travel as hand-luggage, and Margaret only had her briefcase. She stood in a long line waiting to check in, and then hurried away across the concourse to the shopping area to purchase a pack of mints for Xinxin to suck during take-off and landing. If she had never flown before, her ears might react badly to the change in pressure. There was a queue here, too, and Margaret stood letting her mind and her eyes wander.

Suddenly a face on the far side of the mall impinged on her consciousness, and a stab of fear shook her to the core. It was a face she had seen before. Flat Mongolian features, long greasy hair, a scarred lip stretched over yellow protruding teeth. And he was staring back at her. A tour group led by a guide wearing a silly yellow baseball cap and carrying a blue flag crossed her line of sight and the Mongolian disappeared for several moments. She craned to try to catch a glimpse of him through the heads, but when the group had passed he was gone, and for a moment she began to doubt that she had seen him at all.

She had forgotten all about the mints now, and left the line, rushing across the concourse, eyes darting left and right, trying to get a sight of him. But he was nowhere to be seen. Where could he have gone? How could he possibly have been here in Beijing? She remembered his face from that dark night on the Bund as clearly as she had ever remembered anything in her life. She could not possibly have mistaken him. Could she? She stopped and felt the bumping of her heart beneath her breast, like someone physically punching her. Her breathing was fast and shallow, her mouth dry.

"Magret, Magret, what wrong?" Xinxin's little voice crashed into her thoughts. And a little hand slipped into hers. She turned round to see Mei Yuan and the little girl staring at her curiously. What kind of sight must she have presented?

"Are you all right?" Mei Yuan asked, concerned.

"Sure," Margaret said, unconvincingly, trying to control her breathing. "I'm fine." But she wasn't.

CHAPTER NINE

I

What Li found hard to understand was the calm with which Sun Jie had identified the mutilated and decomposed body of his wife. He had stood staring at her for several minutes, unaffected apparently by the stench or by the sight of her. His eyes had closed briefly, then he had simply nodded and walked from the room. In the car park, where spots of rain had begun to fall again, Sun Jie had turned to Li and said, "So now I know she is at peace I can be at peace also and know that she has moved on to a better place. For she was a good person." And for a moment Li had found himself envying that simple faith, that the end of life on earth was not the end of life. It just all seemed too easy, somehow.

He stood now on the concourse at Hongqiao Airport and felt the warmth of Mei-Ling standing close to him. He was excited by the thought of seeing Xinxin, but apprehensive about Margaret's return. He knew she would not respond well to Mei-Ling being with him, but he was determined not to give in to her petty jealousies. He only wished that in some way it was possible for him to separate his private and professional lives. And then he remembered again those eighteen women who had been slaughtered in Shanghai, their husbands and children, fathers and mothers, and the thought put his own problems back into their proper perspective.

Xinxin saw Li immediately, standing among the waiting crowds on the other side of the Arrivals gate, and she went running to leap up into his arms. Margaret smiled at the sight of the two of them together. Li liked to present an image of himself as tough and unyielding, a hard man, with his flat-top crewcut and his square, jutting jaw. Margaret knew him, in reality, to be a big softie. But the smile on her face froze as Li turned, with Xinxin in his arms, to introduce her to the woman standing on his right. Mei-Ling was all smiles and sweetness, shaking Xinxin's hand and then delving into her purse for a pack of candy. Xinxin's initial shyness immediately evaporated and lights shone in her eyes. How easily the affections of a child could be bought. Margaret remembered that in her panic at seeing the man with the hare-lip in Beijing, she had forgotten to buy the mints for Xinxin.

Li put the child back down, and Mei-Ling spoke rapidly to her, eliciting an immediate smiling response. She held out her hand which Xinxin took without hesitation, and the two of them headed off towards the shops on the far side of the concourse. Li turned self-consciously to meet Margaret. Margaret thrust Xinxin's case into his chest. "Maybe Mei-Ling would like to carry her bag for her as well." Li's heart sank, but Margaret wasn't finished yet. "Did you have to bring her with you?"

Li sighed. "I do not have transport here. She offered me a lift. All right?"

"No, not really. But then, I don't suppose it matters what I feel."

"Look, I thought after last night all that jealousy stuff would be behind us."

A thousand angry responses ran through Margaret's mind. About Li's insensitivity in bringing Mei-Ling to the airport, about last night changing nothing as far as Mei-Ling was concerned – or Li, apparently. About how she'd just spent a gruelling day poking over the remains of a rotting corpse as a favour to Li, and how the least she could expect was some time alone with him and Xinxin. But all she said was, "It is." Then, "When do you want my report on the autopsy?"

He was surprised by the sudden change of subject. "In the morning," he said. "You can brief Mei-Ling and myself, and then we'll brief a full meeting of detectives at Section Two."

"Why can't I brief the meeting myself?" she asked.

"Because not enough of them speak English, and to have to translate everything would just be a distraction."

"So now I'm a distraction as well. I suppose that's another one to add to the list," Margaret said. She saw the annoyance in Li's eyes and knew that she was doing nothing to win back his affections. If anything, her continuing hostility was having exactly the opposite effect. But she couldn't help herself. It was a natural response to the constant hurt – the need to hurt back. She understood Li's reasoning for not involving her in the full briefing. It made absolute sense. But it only served to increase her sense of exclusion and underline the fact that being Chinese was like being part of a very exclusive club, a club of which she could never be a member. She glanced over to where Mei-Ling and Xinxin were sharing a joke at a toy stand at the shops, and felt her insecurity wrap itself around her like a blanket. No matter how well she and Xinxin got on together, they would always speak different languages. With Mei-Ling, communication would be easy for Xinxin, not an issue. For a moment Margaret caught Mei-Ling's eye as she glanced towards Margaret and Li, and Margaret knew that

Mei-Ling would try to take Xinxin from her as well. And that she would probably succeed. Margaret turned back to Li. "Shall I come back to the hotel to tuck Xinxin in?"

Li shook his head. "No, not tonight. I'm taking her to meet her babysitter. They'll be sharing a room next to mine."

Margaret tried again. "You said she'll be going to kindergarten here. I could take her there in the mornings and pick her up again in the afternoons."

Li shifted uncomfortably. "Actually, Mei-Ling will be running her to kindergarten in the mornings – or delegating another officer to do it if she can't."

"How very kind of her," Margaret said, and Li felt the sting of her tone. But Margaret was losing the will to fight. "Look, why don't I just get a taxi back to my hotel? Then I won't have to take you out of your way." And she pushed past Li and headed for the exit, forgetting that she had meant to speak to him about the man with the hare-lip.

II

"You look like someone who could do with a drink."

Margaret turned and found Geller standing at her side. She was perched on a stool in the bar of the Peace Hotel leaning over an empty glass. As usual the bar was deserted. She said, "I thought you'd never ask."

He slipped on to the stool beside her and signalled the waitress. She shimmied along the bar and he ordered a beer and another vodka tonic for Margaret. "You look tired."

"I am. I've been to Beijing and back today."

"Do you mind if I ask what for?" He lit a cigarette and ran a hand back through his mop of unruly hair.

"No."

He waited. "And . . . ?"

"And what?"

"What were you doing in Beijing?"

"I said I didn't mind if you asked. I didn't say I'd tell you."

He smiled wryly and rubbed a hand across his unshaven jaw. It made a soft rasping sound. "Guess I must be slipping."

Margaret looked at him. "Well, you're certainly not shaving."

"I hate shaving," he said. "If I use a razor I always cut myself. If I use an electric shaver it makes me break out in a rash."

"You're such a sensitive soul." She reached out and ran her fingers lightly over his silvery stubble. "Having sex with you must be like making love to a sheet of sandpaper."

"Hey," he said, "did you say *having sex with me*? I mean, is that a thought that even crossed your mind?" She laughed and he said, "Listen, lend me your razor and I'll shave right now."

She laughed again, and somewhere at the back of her mind she wondered what it would be like making love to Jack Geller. Less intense, she thought, than with Li Yan. But more fun, perhaps. At least she and Jack could share a joke, have a laugh without stopping to choose their words and wonder if they were the right ones. "Sorry," she said. "All my blades are blunt."

He said, "You could always use your tongue. It's pretty sharp."

"Too sharp for my own good," she said. "People get too close to me I cut them." It was difficult to keep the bitterness out of her voice.

He looked at her for a moment. "You're not a very happy lady."

"Is it that obvious?"

He shrugged. "You do a pretty good job of hiding it. Most of the time."

"But not, of course, to a seasoned student of human nature like yourself."

"Naturally." He paused and took a long pull at his beer, then studied her for a moment or two as she sipped at her vodka.

"Have you had dinner?"

"I did last night," she said.

He stubbed out his cigarette, slipped off his stool and drained the last of his beer. "Come on, then."

"Where?"

"To a place that's got the best view of Shanghai in the whole city."

Shanghai opened up below them. The Huangpu River, reflecting lights from both sides, snaked through the heart of it, the Bund glowing along one side of its length like a bejewelled glow-worm, the lights of Pudong on the other, reaching into a sky crisscrossed with coloured searchlights dissecting and bisecting the night. Immediately beneath them a Japanese cruise ship, from here no bigger than a model boat, was docked at the International Passenger Terminal, its lights blazing out across the water, its passengers returning from an exploration of the city's commercial pleasures. From the twenty-eighth floor of the Shanghai Bund International Tower at number ninety-nine Huangpu Road, the semi-circular sweep of floor-to-ceiling window in the bar of the American Club gave on to an unparalleled view of the city. The bar curved around the central sweep of the window, and Margaret and Geller sat at it in comfortably upholstered bar chairs which looked past what appeared to be two very small barmen to the view beyond.

"Why," Margaret said, "are all the barmen here so vertically challenged?"

Geller frowned, for a moment not understanding, then he burst out laughing. "Dwarf barmen," he said choking on his cigarette, and both barmen glared at him, not amused. "They're not really midgets," Geller said. "It's a sunken bar."

"Why would anyone want to sink a bar?" Margaret asked.

"I dunno. I guess so that when you're sitting at it the bartender's looking straight into your eyes. Anyway, listen, vertically challenged or not, these guys make great vodka martinis, and they got olives here the size of apples."

"Is that an offer?"

"You bet."

They ordered two vodka martinis which each came with three enormous olives on cocktail sticks. Margaret took a sip and nodded approvingly. "You're right, they *are* good." On top of her vodka tonics, she felt the alcohol soothe away her tension and began to wonder vaguely if she was heading for a drink problem. She cast an eye distractedly over a large menu handed to her by the maître d' from the restaurant next door, and realised with some pleasure that the food was very definitely not Chinese. "I'll just have the roast salmon and some salad," she said. Geller ordered a steak and a bottle of Californian Zinfandel.

When the waiter had taken their order, Geller looked at Margaret thoughtfully for some moments. "So," he said, "what progress in the battle of American girl versus Chinese girl for the favours of Chinese guy?"

She smiled and sucked in more vodka martini. "No competition," she said. "The Chinese girl's winning hands down. In fact, it looks like she'll even get the kid as well."

"The kid?" Geller frowned. "You two have a kid?"

Margaret laughed. "I entertained thoughts of children once. But I got talked out of that quickly enough." She hesitated, then explained to Geller about Li's niece and the fact that she had instantly become a new battleground in the fight for affections. She shook her head. "The thing is, I'm not sure I care any more. If he doesn't want me, if he wants her, then she can have him. Kid and all."

"Only it's not true," Geller said. She turned to find him looking at her earnestly.

"What isn't?"

"That you don't care."

"And you'd know."

He shrugged. "Like you said, I'm a seasoned student of human nature."

"Which of course makes you an expert on fucked-up pathologists with a predilection for self-pity and alcohol."

He let her bitterness wash over him and added a dash of his own. "No," he said. "But when it comes to fucked-up *people* with a predilection for self-pity and alcohol, I'm the world's foremost authority." He paused and smiled sadly, adding, in case she had missed the point, "Being one myself."

She looked at him curiously, and for a moment that curiosity made her forget about herself. "What are you doing here, Jack?" she said. "What are you running away from?"

He laughed. "Oh, I'm not running away from anything. I wish I could, but I wouldn't know where to run to."

"What about home?"

"This is it. Shanghai. That's home. I don't have another one."

She frowned. "How come?"

"I guess, like Springsteen says, I was born in the USA." He chuckled. "But I never spent much time there. My folks moved around the world. Africa, Middle-East, South-East Asia. My old man was in the ball-bearing business. You'd be amazed

how much money there is in ball-bearings. Anyway, I managed to see the inside of just about every American school on
every continent you can think of. Just long enough to get to
know the name of the kid at the next desk, and then off again.
And then my dad goes and dies on us. In Thailand. And my
mom gets offered this job in Shanghai. So she flies him back
to the US, puts him in the ground in Connecticut somewhere,
and then heads for Shanghai. I've spent more of my life here
than anywhere else in the world."

"How did you get into journalism?"

"Oh, that was an accident. Amazing really how little of our
lives we plan for ourselves." He lit a cigarette. Down below
them, at the International Passenger Terminal, the Japanese
cruise liner was pulling out into the deep navigation channel, mid-stream. It looked like a floating Christmas tree as it
headed slowly downriver towards the estuary. Geller's eyes
seemed fixed on it for several moments before he said, "My
mom met this Chinese guy here. Got married again. I'm in
my mid-teens and probably a bit difficult, so they send me off
to the States to go to college." He shook his head, lost in some
distant memory. "I hated it. What was I supposed to do there?
I didn't know anyone. Didn't have any friends. No family – at
least, not any that I knew. And then, when I finish college, I
see this one-year course in journalism advertised in Boston.
I sail through it. For the first time in my life somebody actually
thought I might be good at something. I spoke fluent Chinese.
So after a couple of years as a cub on the *Globe*, it wasn't hard
to get a job stringing back here for a whole bunch of US pub-
lications. It was like coming home. I've been here ever since."

"What about your mom. Is she still here?"

The brightness in his eyes dulled and he lowered his head.
"She's dead," he said. "So's my stepdad. Just little ol' me left."

He looked up and forced a smile. "Goddamn it," he said. "I could've wished for better company."

"Oh, I don't know," Margaret said. "I'm quite enjoying it."

He looked at her very seriously for a moment. "I come with a lot of baggage," he said.

"Don't we all." She raised her glass. "To misfits the world over," she said.

He grinned and chinked her glass, and they both sipped from the large conical glasses. "So listen," he said. "You want to give the kid a treat? Put one over on the Chinese chick?"

Margaret grinned and shook her head. "I'd be happy just to make Xinxin happy."

"Then take her to Tiantan Traffic Park."

"What the hell's that?"

He leaned forward, demonstrating with his hands, a boyish enthusiasm about him. "It's a great place. Out on the west side. You'd never know it was there if you didn't know it was there – if you know what I mean?"

She smiled. "I think so."

"It's just a small park, but it's laid out with miniature roads and sidewalks and replicas of famous buildings in Shanghai. There are traffic lights at the intersections, and little overhead bridges. Folks take their kids there to teach them the rules of the road from an early age. They rent little battery-powered automobiles, and the kids drive them around, with mom or dad sitting in. I tell you, the kids love it. They just love it."

"Sounds neat," Margaret said, and it never occurred to her to ask him how he knew about it.

The maître d' came to tell them that their table was ready, and they followed him through to a large dining room with windows down one side and an elaborate buffet down the other. He seated them at a table by the window, and they saw the Japanese cruise liner just before it disappeared round the curve in the river beyond the Yangpu Bridge. Margaret put her hand over his. "Thank you for this," she said. "You don't know how much I needed it."

He shrugged, and was suddenly self-conscious. After a moment's hesitation, he said, "Just don't ever forget why, Margaret."

She frowned. "What do you mean?"

"You said it yourself the other day. You're just work to me."

Margaret felt unaccountably disappointed. "I thought maybe I'd become a little more than that."

Geller said, "Even if you had, I couldn't allow that to get in the way." And she saw that he was absolutely serious, and felt the first stirrings of anger with him.

"So it's all right for you to bring your work to the dinner table." She snorted. "You wouldn't be very happy if I did."

"That's exactly what I want you to do, Margaret," he said. He took a deep breath. "I want to know what's happening, what progress you're making with your investigation. You know that."

She wondered why she should feel such a sense of betrayal. After all, he had made it clear from the start it was what he wanted. But she really did think they had moved on from there. "And you think you can buy my confidence with dinner and a vodka martini?"

He made the smallest of shrugs. Perhaps it was an apology. "It's important to me, Margaret." And there was a strange intensity about him.

A waiter was endeavouring to spread a starched white napkin in Margaret's lap. She took it from him and folded it on the table. She sighed and said, "Well, I'm sorry, Jack, I don't come that cheap." She stood up. "But thanks for the offer." And she turned and made her way back through to the bar and out

to the elevators, leaving Geller sitting on his own, a forlorn figure with a medium rare steak in front of him, a piece of roast
salmon on the plate opposite, and a very empty feeling inside.

III

"Jiang Baofu? The medical student?" Margaret was taken
aback. "You don't really believe *he* did it?"

Nine small tables had been pushed together to make one
long one in the centre of the room. Margaret sat at one side
of it facing Li and Mei-Ling on the other. The skulls of murder
and suicide victims watched them from behind the glass doors
of a display cabinet at one end of the room. At the opposite
end, pieces of human organs hung suspended in jars of preser-
vative: a section of stomach showing the hole where a knife
had entered; a bullet hole in a lung. Along the wall facing the
window hung a profusion of velvet banners, awards made for
police bravery and success in criminal detection.

Li said, "Do you not think he would be capable of performing these procedures?" Jiang had arrived back at his apartment
the previous night, as forensics were completing their search
of the place. He had been arrested and spent the night in custody and was now sitting in an interview room downstairs
awaiting interrogation.

"Fifth year at med school? Specialising in surgery? He would
certainly have the skills. What's his motive?"

"Ah . . ." Mei-Ling said, "the American obsession with
motive."

"Okay," Margaret said levelly, determined not to be ruffled,
"what evidence do you have against him? Other than the fact
that he's a bit creepy and was the night watchman at the building site."

"Everything we have learned about him would lead us to believe that Jiang may be . . . mmm . . ." Mei-Ling searched for the right word, "unbalanced. You said yourself we should be looking for a *psycho surgeon*." She said the words with a tone.

Margaret raised a sceptical eyebrow. "The fact that he might be a little odd hardly constitutes evidence. And, I mean, the collection of evidence, that's the Chinese way, isn't it? The painstaking piecing together of the facts, bit by bit. Surely you must have some if you've arrested him?"

Li said, "His medical background, the testimony of his tutors, his unique access to the site where the bodies were found – all of these things justify our bringing him in for questioning."

"Ah, yes," Margaret said. "'Helping the police with their inquiries.' That's what the British police say when they're struggling for evidence, isn't it?" She clasped her hands in front of her on the table. "So what now? Beat a confession out of him? That how it goes? I mean, why bother with the autopsies? Why bother trying to identify the victims when you can just pull someone off the street and pin a confession on their chest?" She knew she was being unreasonable, but she was enjoying herself. Enjoying their discomfort. "That's what the Chinese police are always being accused of, isn't it?" She paused for effect. "So is it true?"

Li kept his anger buttoned down and, after a very long moment of tense silence, said coldly, "Perhaps you would like to tell us what you discovered in Beijing."

"Ah, so now back to the evidence," Margaret said brightly, opening the file in front of her. "Good. Makes me think there might be some point in my being here after all."

"And you have given us so very much to go on so far," Mei-Ling said, her voice heavy with sarcasm.

Margaret looked at her steadily. "I can only tell you what's there, Miss Nien," she said. "I can't make it up for your convenience. Although I *have* been able to provide you with sufficient evidence to identify two of the victims."

"Three," Li said. Margaret looked at him for elucidation. "The girl with the stress fractures in her foot turned out to be an acrobat. She went missing three months ago."

"Well, that's progress. And, of course, there was also the identification made through fingerprints," Margaret said, and she turned back to her notes. "I'll give you a full report in due course, but you can take it as read that the girl in Beijing was murdered by the same person who killed the girls in Shanghai. The evidence is overwhelming, from the entry cut to the toxicology."

"But there are still major differences," Li said.

Margaret said, "Yes, there are. Not all of the organs were removed, and those that were, were found with the body."

"Can you explain that?" Mei-Ling asked.

Margaret shook her head. "No. I can only give you the facts, and you can draw your own conclusions." She paused. "The girl was a junkie, a heroin addict. One of several things your pathologist missed. I believe the killer only discovered this after he had removed the heart. And it was at that point that he appears to have abandoned the procedure."

Li frowned, forgetting for the moment the animosity around the table. "Why would discovering she was a junkie change anything?"

"Risk of infection," Mei-Ling said suddenly. "She could have been infected with anything from hepatitis to AIDS." She thought about it for a moment. "Which would make her organs unusable as well."

Margaret nodded acquiescence. "If you chose to believe that organ theft was the purpose of the exercise, yes."

Li said, "Tell me why it would *not* make sense to keep these girls alive to remove their organs. I mean, the organs would be fresher that way, would they not?"

"Not if you killed the victims and removed the organs immediately," Margaret said. "Keeping them alive would be a completely unnecessary complication." She shook her head. "And, anyway, why would they only take the organs of women?"

None of them had an answer to that. As the evidence accumulated, it made no more sense to them than when they had started collecting it. Mei-Ling said, "And no clues to her identity?"

Margaret pulled the x-rays of the victim's jaw from a large brown envelope. "Only her teeth," she said, "and some pretty expensive gold foil restoration."

"We checked those out in Beijing," Li said.

"But not in Shanghai," Margaret said. "Now we know the murders are connected, it's quite possible the girl you found in Beijing came from here." She slipped the x-rays back in the envelope and pushed it across the table to Mei-Ling. "Worth checking out?"

Mei-Ling gave a curt nod, then glanced at Li. "I will put Dai on to it." And she got up and left the room.

In the silence that followed her departure, Li lit a cigarette and blew smoke at the ceiling. Neither Li nor Margaret knew what to say. Margaret was already beginning to regret her petulance. She was driving herself remorselessly and uncontrollably on the road to self-destruction. Li had finally lost patience. And anger with Margaret was a good way of ameliorating his own sense of guilt. But still there were no words. It seemed to both of them then, sitting alone at that large table under the glare of naked fluorescent lamps and the sightless gaze of the yellowing skulls in the cabinet, that their relationship was finally over. And there was something inestimably sad about that, about the loss of the warmth and friendship and humour they had shared, the deep well of emotions that had sustained them for so long. Margaret wondered where these things went. How they could be, and then not be? Had she and Li just thrown them away? Or was it Margaret who had done the damage all on her own, with her petty jealousy and her fiery temper? She picked at a corner of her folder and could not bring herself to meet his eyes. It was extraordinary how articulate the silence between them was. Finally she said, "It looks like my involvement here is just about done. It'll take me a couple of days to write up my reports, then . . ." Then what? She had no idea. She looked up, finally. "I'd like to spend some time with Xinxin." Why? she wondered. To say goodbye?

Li nodded. "Sure."

"I'll pick her up from kindergarten then."

Li said, "I will let Mei-Ling know."

And Margaret felt a brief flare of anger. Why did everything need that woman's approval? But she said nothing, and let the anger seep out of her. What was the point?

"And maybe we should talk," Li said.

"About what?"

He shrugged. "Things." A pause. "Us."

Margaret wondered if there was any point in that either. "Let's meet for a drink at my hotel, then. Around eight?" He nodded, and she said, "I'll try and stay awake this time."

Jiang Baofu sat back in his chair, legs crossed and stretched out in front of him, picking bits of food from between his teeth with an old matchstick. He did not appear unduly concerned at his predicament. And when Li and Mei-Ling came in he made no effort to move. "Hey," he said lazily. "What's happening? Why am I here?"

The two detectives drew up chairs on the opposite side of the table. Mei-Ling said with unexpected aggression, "We want some answers from you, you little shit!" Both Li and Jiang were taken aback. Jiang sat up abruptly.

"What!"

"And if we don't get them," Mei-Ling said, "then we'll send you along for interrogation by the professionals." She paused. "And you wouldn't like that much."

"Hey," Jiang protested, "all I did was go and spend a couple of nights at a friend's place. So I didn't tell Public Security. It's not a crime, is it?"

"Actually, yes," Li said. "But we hadn't thought of that one."

Jiang looked as if he wanted to rip his tongue from his mouth. Mei-Ling said, "You told the caretaker at your apartment block that you were going to visit a cousin."

"You don't have a cousin," Li said.

"So?" Jiang was getting defensive. "It's none of her fucking business where I go."

"So why tell her anything at all?" This from Li.

Mei-Ling followed up without waiting for an answer. "Why did you kill them, Jiang? Kicks? Profit? Practice?"

For a moment there was panic in Jiang's rabbit eyes. "Me? I didn't kill them! I didn't kill anybody. I swear on the grave of my ancestors. Hey, you can't seriously believe I did it?" And even as he said it, it seemed to strike him as ridiculous, and he laughed. "Come on, guys. This is crazy. You can't have any evidence against me, 'cos there isn't any."

Which was true. A preliminary report from forensics had turned up nothing out of the ordinary in Jiang's apartment.

In fact, the chief forensics officer had been moved to comment on how abnormally clean, almost sterile, the place had been. Margaret's words came back to haunt Li. *The fact that he might be a little odd hardly constitutes evidence.* And the words of his uncle came back to him, too. *The answer always lies in the detail, Li Yan.* The trouble was, they had virtually no detail to work with. They had established the identity of only four of the victims. The autopsies had revealed how the women had been murdered, but not why or when. There was nothing to link them, no common factor other than their sex. And beyond the disquieting coincidence of Jiang Baofu being the night watchman at the building site where the bodies were uncovered, there was absolutely nothing to link him to the murders. It didn't matter that people thought he was weird, or that he was obsessed with the surgeon's knife. There was no evidence.

A lack of any response from the detectives seemed to give Jiang confidence. "So, are you going to let me go or what? I mean, I'm still happy to help. If you need to draft in any extra assistants at the mortuary, I'm your man."

Li felt almost as if he was laughing at them. There was something not right here, something about Jiang Baofu that didn't quite figure. Li searched his mind furiously. He had already ordered bank records to be seized, employment and payment records to be obtained from Jiang's various employers. He was convinced they would never account for Jiang's apparent affluence. But the lumbering bureaucracy of state enterprises, and the reluctance of foreign companies to release records, meant that the process would take time. In the meantime there had to be something else, something they were missing. He ran back through the details in his head, and almost immediately tripped over a thought which he had tucked away for later scrutiny and then forgotten. He said suddenly, "What did you do last Spring Festival?"

Jiang was caught by surprise. "What?"

So was Mei-Ling. Li was aware of her glancing at him. But he pressed on. "I mean, what did you do during the holiday? Were you working?"

Jiang made a great show of thinking about this for a bit. "No . . ." he said at last. "No . . . last Spring Festival I went home for the holidays. Yeah, I'm sure that was last winter."

"So the Medical University would be closed for what – a month?" Li looked to Mei-Ling for confirmation.

She nodded. "Usually a month."

He turned back to Jiang. "So you were at your grandparents' home at Yanqing through most of February." The body of the girl Margaret had just re-examined in Beijing had been found mid-February, and had only been in the ground for about a week.

Jiang nodded hesitantly. "Yeah, I guess."

"And that's how far from Beijing? Under an hour by rail?"

"It's pretty close."

"So you could go into town after breakfast to do a bit of shopping, have some Beijing duck at lunchtime and be home in time for dinner?"

Jiang laughed. "You could. If you were mad."

"Or even stay overnight at your sister's."

Jiang's smile faded. "I haven't seen my sister in years."

"So you didn't go visit her last Spring Festival?"

"No, I didn't."

"How often did you go into Beijing?"

"Never."

"Never?" Li was incredulous. "You were home for a whole month and you never went into the city once?"

"What would I go into Beijing for? I don't know anyone there except for my sister, and she and I don't get on."

"So you stayed at home the whole time?"

"Didn't I just say that? Hey, do I get a prize? You know, like one of these quiz shows on TV, if I answer all your questions?"

"There are no prizes for fulfilling your obligations as a citizen," Mei-Ling said. "It is your duty to co-operate."

"Well, that's what I'm doing, isn't it?" Jiang held his hands out, appealing for sympathy. "And, hey, listen, I don't hold it against you guys. I know you've got a job to do."

But Li was not going to be deflected. "What did you do at home that month?" he asked.

Jiang shrugged. "I studied, watched TV, saw some friends . . ."

"And your grandparents would be able to verify that?"

"Sure. But, listen, don't go bothering them. They'll just get worried about me."

Li sat back and looked at the young man thoughtfully. Apparently he had all the answers, his confidence unshakeable. For a brief moment Li had thought he had made a connection. But if Jiang's story checked out, they would be no further forward. He began to feel a sense of despondency creeping over him.

Li's sense of despondency increased at the detectives' meeting. The room was packed and hot and filled with smoke, and not much else. The proceedings were all conducted under the brooding eye of the sullen Section Chief Huang who sat in his accustomed seat with his back to the window so that Li could not see his face clearly. The investigation was not going well and everyone knew it. The atmosphere in the room was tense.

Li had just started briefing the detectives on the results of Margaret's re-examination of the body in Beijing when there was a sharp rap at the door, and it opened to reveal the tall, uniformed figure of Procurator General Yue. There was an almost audible intake of breath. It was unheard of for a Procurator General to attend a detectives' briefing meeting. "As you were, Detectives," he said, and he closed the door behind him and pulled up a chair beside Huang. He sat down and crossed his arms, and in the silence that followed his eyes found Li's. His expression was grim. "Carry on, Deputy Section Chief," he said. Li took a moment or two to collect himself and then continued.

He led them through all the evidence to date: the conclusions of the autopsies, the four victims so far identified, Margaret's re-examination of the body in Beijing and the possibility that x-rays of her teeth might lead to her identification. He went over the interviews he and Mei-Ling had conducted with Jiang Baofu's course tutors, the interview with the caretaker at his apartment block, the search of his apartment. Everyone around the table agreed that there were more than sufficient grounds to regard Jiang Baofu with great suspicion, but no evidence whatsoever that tied him to the killings. "The best hope we have," Li said, "of connecting him in any way is by establishing that he was in Beijing at the time the girl we found there was murdered. We know he was at home at Yanqing at that time. He claims he never went into the capital. If his grandparents confirm that, then we've reached another dead end. If not, then we've got every reason to lean hard on him."

The most exciting development, he told them, was the description given them by the husband of the murdered acrobat, of a man who she had told him was following her. Li repeated the description for them of the long, greasy hair, the

Mongolian features, the protruding teeth and the scarred hare-lip. "She saw this man on several occasions, in different locations, in the days before she disappeared. She was concerned enough to tell her husband about it and describe the man for him. There is a very strong possibility that this is the man who seized her. That he had been watching and waiting for his opportunity. And if this is the case, then others might have seen him, too, before they disappeared."

Mei-Ling said, "We need to distribute this description among the families of all the missing women whose files we've pulled so far. Some of them might just have reported seeing him. Another couple of confirmations would start to establish a pattern, and might also help us identify more of the victims. It certainly doesn't sound like he trained as a surgeon, but he might be the grab man."

The meeting broke up in slightly more optimistic mood than it had begun, but it was clear that morale was beginning to suffer at the lack of any real progress. As Li gathered his papers together he watched Huang and the Procurator General exchange a few words, then Huang hurried out, his head down. Mei-Ling said to Li, "I'll catch you later," and dashed out after him.

The room emptied and the smoke began to clear, drawn out into the corridor, as if it, too, were anxious to escape the impending storm. Li and the Procurator General faced each other across the width of the table. The Procurator General stood up, very slowly and deliberately, and closed the door. He remained standing by it. Li lit a cigarette and waited while the older man chose his words with care. "Four identifications. A sketchy description of a man with a hare-lip. A medical student who cannot be connected to the crime." Very succinctly he had summed up the limited extent of the investigation so far. "Not much to show for five days' work and the entire resources of Section Two at your disposal," he said.

"These things take time, Procurator General Yue," Li said.

"Time," Yue said, "is not on your side, Deputy Section Chief." He raised one eyebrow as if to underline his point. "In fact, time is very much your enemy. The Mayor requested that you lead this investigation in the hope that you could bring it to a speedy conclusion. You chose to embarrass his administration by contradicting the press statement issued the day after the discovery of the bodies. And you have since failed to come up with a credible alternative. Our silence is becoming the subject of much speculation in the American media. The Mayor is not happy."

If he had not realised it before, Li knew then that he had been handed a poisoned chalice. "Perhaps, Procurator General, in such a high-profile case as this, it would be more appropriate for the investigation to be taken over by your department." Li saw the Procurator General's expression harden. It was not without precedent for the investigation of sensitive cases to be handled by the Procurator General's office. But the last thing that Procurator General Yue would want was to have the poisoned chalice passed on to him. He understood immediately that Li was, in effect, telling him to back off – unless he wished to have the investigation landed on his own desk. And he realised he had underestimated Li's political acumen, something that might also have surprised Margaret. This was not someone who would be easily intimidated.

The Procurator General glared at Li. Now he would have to find an exit line that would allow him to leave without loss of face. Li had just made an enemy. "If the Mayor had thought that appropriate, then I have no doubt that is the course he would have followed," he said. "However, he and his policy adviser have chosen to put faith in you, Deputy Section Chief, and the reputation which precedes you. I am quite certain they would not like to be proven wrong in that choice." He forced his lips into a smile that found no echo in his eyes. "I look forward to hearing that real progress has been made in the very near future." He made his exit then, dignity intact and leaving Li with a sick, sinking feeling in his gut.

Other officers avoided Li's eye as he walked down the corridor. They knew that he had been involved in some kind of confrontation with the Procurator General, and they did not want any part of it. Li stopped outside the door of Section Chief Huang's office. It stood half open, and he could see Huang standing grim-faced by his desk, Mei-Ling next to him talking earnestly. Li could not hear what they were saying. Mei-Ling touched her boss's hand lightly, and put her other hand on his arm. There was something so strangely and casually intimate in this that Li immediately felt a restriction in his throat, and his heart quickened. He realised that what he felt was jealousy. The same feeling, although he did not know it, that Margaret had experienced when she saw Mei-Ling touch his hand in almost the same way.

Mei-Ling turned towards the door, and Li started guiltily along the corridor, as if he had been caught in some illicit act of voyeurism. He heard Mei-Ling exiting from Huang's office behind him and then her footsteps hurrying in pursuit. "Li Yan," she called, and he half-turned, trying to appear natural. She fell into step beside him and lowered her voice. "Huang Tsuo's just had word from the hospital. They're sending his wife home. Reading between the lines, I think they're expecting her to die there."

Li felt an odd sense of relief. It was sympathy he had witnessed, not intimacy. And then he immediately felt guilt at the thought that news of a woman's approaching death had prompted him only to feel relief. "Will that put you in charge during his absence?" he asked.

Mei-Ling shook her head. "He won't take time off. Not while this investigation's on-going. Apparently he's employing a nurse to look after her."

Li wondered briefly why Huang felt it necessary to remain in situ while his wife was dying. After all, he was only nominally heading the investigation. In truth, while he may have had a watching brief, he had had virtually no involvement in it.

They turned into Li's office and found the young forensics officer who had attended the autopsies waiting by the window. He was cleaning his gold-rimmed spectacles with a white handkerchief, and staring blindly out at the apartment blocks opposite. He turned as they entered, hurriedly pushing his spectacles back on his nose. His green uniform looked faintly rumpled, and the ubiquitous stubble still clung to his jaw. He pulled a folder from under his arm and thrust it towards Li. "That's my final report on the search of Jiang Baofu's apartment," he said. Li still remembered the look on the officer's face when Margaret had asked him to slip his hand inside the degloved skin of the seamstress's hand to take her fingerprints. "I don't think you'll find it any more helpful than my initial verbal," he said.

Li took it and dropped it on his desk. "Thanks," he said listlessly. More bad news was not what he needed right now.

"But you might be interested in this." The officer took a clear plastic evidence bag from his pocket and handed it to Li.

"What is it?"

"It's a girl's bracelet. We found it at the back of a drawer in the apartment."

Li held it up for Mei-Ling to see and they looked at it closely. It comprised a fine gold chain about six inches in length, with four tiny carved jade Buddhas dangling from it at half-inch intervals either side of a jade nameplate engraved with the character for the word *Moon*. Li looked at the forensics officer. "What's the significance?"

The young man shrugged. "Maybe none. I just thought, you know, you said he was a loner. No friends. So probably no girlfriends. And it doesn't look like something he'd wear himself."

Li dropped the bracelet, still in its evidence bag, on to the table. "You want to tell me about this?" he said.

Jiang sat forward to look at it and immediately blushed to the roots of his hair.

"Don't tell me we've discovered your little secret," Mei-Ling said. Jiang looked at her with something like panic in his eyes. "You're a cross-dresser." He frowned, not understanding. "Oh, never mind," she said. "I take it you don't wear this yourself – secretly or otherwise?"

He shook his head.

"You recognise it, though," Li said. At last, he felt, they might have caught him out on something.

"Of course."

"So . . . ?"

"So what?"

"So what is it?"

"It's a bracelet."

Li bristled. It felt as if Jiang was playing for time. "I can see that. *Whose* is it?" he snapped.

"It's mine."

Li leaned his elbows on the table and clasped his hands slowly in front of him. He said very quietly. "Don't fuck with me, son. Tell me about the bracelet. Who is *Moon*?"

"She was a girlfriend I had back in Yanqing. Years ago."

"You had a girlfriend?" Mei-Ling said incredulously.

Jiang blushed again. "Well, she wasn't exactly my girlfriend. She was . . . well, you know, I kind of hoped she would be. So I bought her the bracelet. Cost me a small fortune." He glanced from one to the other and then shrugged. "But she wouldn't take it. Said she wasn't interested in me."

"Surprise, surprise," Mei-Ling said.

"And she could corroborate this?" Li asked.

Jiang shook his head vaguely. "I don't know. If you could find her. Her family moved away years ago. I can't remember what the family name was."

"Well, try," Li said dangerously.

Jiang met his eyes briefly but couldn't hold them. "She probably wouldn't even remember," he said.

"The name," Li said.

Jiang scratched his head then picked up the bracelet to look at it again, and Li saw that his hands were shaking. "Zhang," he said eventually, uncertainly. "Zhang. I think that was the family name. They lived near the middle school."

Li took the bracelet from him and stood up. "Go home," he said.

Jiang looked at him, surprised. So did Mei-Ling. Jiang said, "What!"

Li said, "You're free to go. Just don't even think about leaving Shanghai without asking this office first."

Jiang stood up quickly, all smiles, relief written all over his face. "Hey, thanks. You know, I'm still happy to help. Any time. Just give me a call."

"Go home," Li said, and the boy nodded and hurried from the room.

Mei-Ling looked at Li. "What did you do that for?"

Li shrugged. "We've no reason to hold him. We know where he is if we need to find him."

"What about the bracelet?"

"It's a feasible story. We should find the girl and see if she remembers. Even if she doesn't, that's not proof of anything." He handed the bag to Mei-Ling. "But let's get it photographed and circulate a description round the team."

For the first time, Li sensed that Mei-Ling did not agree with him, and she appeared to think long and hard about whether or not to express that disagreement. Then she gave him a curt nod. "Sure," she said, and she turned and left the interview room. Li was beginning to feel a little embattled, and very much on his own.

IV

Xinxin's kindergarten was in a large international hotel on the west side of the city, in a suite of rooms off the first-floor mezzanine. There was a large play area, and several classrooms. The children were aged between three and six, and as Margaret waited in the hall, she could hear the tuneless screeching of children playing violins in a music class. From other rooms the sound of laughter, the imperious voices of children raised in inquisitorial clamour, demonstrating in a thousand questions that earliest of human passions, the hunger for knowledge. Parents, mostly mothers, were gathering in the hall overlooking the reception area below, waiting for the big doors to open and the children to come flooding out. These were wealthy Shanghainese who could afford to send their children to kindergarten in a place like this, but wealth did not necessarily equate with sophistication, and they stared as curiously at Margaret as if they had been peasants at a market.

When, eventually, a bell was rung by hand somewhere that sounded very far away, the children did not come out in the expected rush, but in twos and threes, chattering excitedly, being gathered up by parents finished work for the day and heading home for family meals. Margaret felt out of place here in more ways than one.

Finally she saw Xinxin heading out on her own, but before she could greet her, a uniformed policewoman stepped forward to take her hand. Margaret pushed through the waiting mothers and called out the child's name. Xinxin turned, and as soon as she saw her let out a yelp of delight. She broke free of the policewoman's grasp and ran to Margaret for a hug.

Almost immediately the policewoman was there, pulling Xinxin away and shouting at Margaret, her face contorted in anger and indignation.

"What the hell do you think you're doing?" Margaret shouted back, and she reached for Xinxin's hand.

But the policewoman yanked the child away and stabbed a finger in Margaret's chest, her voice raised in anger. Xinxin started to cry. Mothers drew their children to them for safety and looked on in amazement. The Chinese are born spectators. Any spectacle or argument will do. One of the teachers came hurrying out from the kindergarten and there was an exchange between her and the policewoman. The teacher looked at Margaret. "You speak English?" she asked.

"You bet," Margaret said.

"What you want?"

"I'm here to pick up Xinxin. She's the niece of my colleague, Deputy Section Chief Li Yan of the Beijing Municipal Police."

The teacher looked uncertain for a moment. There was a further exchange between her and the policewoman, and then she spoke to Xinxin who responded rapidly and eagerly, glancing up several times at Margaret.

"Well?" Margaret said. "Did she tell you who I am?"

The policewoman spoke again, still full of aggression, and the teacher translated. "She say it no matter. You are foreigner. You need special permission for visit kindergarten. This policewoman say she have instruction to collect girl. You go away now."

"Jesus Christ!" Margaret's frustrations bubbled over. There was no doubt in her mind that this was Mei-Ling's doing. Li had said he would tell her that she was going to collect Xinxin. She stabbed a finger at the policewoman. "You're in big fucking trouble, lady," she shouted, and turned to the teacher. "Tell her that. Tell her she's in big fucking trouble."

The policewoman pushed Margaret's hand aside, took Xinxin firmly by the arm and headed for the stairs, Xinxin pulling against her the whole way and calling back for Margaret. Margaret stood rooted to the spot, anger welling up inside. She knew there was nothing she could do. She had neither the language nor the power to make a difference here, and all she could do was listen to Xinxin's cries all the way down the stairs. It was breaking her heart.

CHAPTER TEN

I

Li sat in the dark and contemplated the mess that his life was in. He could hear the distant roar of traffic on the elevated ring road. People on their way home from work. People with a home to go to. People, he thought, who probably had just as many problems as he did. Probably worse. Death was worse, wasn't it? And he thought of Huang, and of his poor wife being sent home from the hospital to die. But Huang had never shown him any warmth, and it was difficult to sympathise with people you did not know. And however great other people's problems might be, knowing that did nothing to diminish your own. And so Li sat and brooded in the dark and felt sorry for himself.

A knock on the door, and the light that came in from the corridor as it opened, flooded into his thoughts. He blinked in the sudden light, and the figure in the doorway was just a silhouette. But he recognised Dai's voice. "You really like the dark, huh, Chief?"

Li leaned forward and switched on his desk lamp. "What do you want?"

Dai stepped forward and dropped a large manila envelope triumphantly on Li's desk. "Got an ID on that girl's teeth,

Chief. Straight from the horse's mouth, so to speak." And he laughed at his own wit. Li quickly opened the envelope, slid out the large sheet of x-ray and found a report clipped to it in English. Dai said, "Sino-Canadian joint venture dental clinic at the World Medical Centre downtown. They did the gold foil work about eighteen months ago. Had her records on file. A twenty-two-year-old called Chai Rui, but she liked to be called *Cherry*. They even had that noted on her file."

Li scanned the address. "Xujiahui," he said. "Where's that?"

"Big new futuristic development down the south-west of the city, Chief. Fancy apartment blocks and upscale shopping centres. Not a cheap place to live." He paused. "Just a spit away from the Medical University. I don't know if that's significant." Li glanced up at him. "Anyway, I had a long chat with the dental assistant. A young guy. He remembered her well. Said she was a real looker, flirted with him apparently. Boasted that she was a hostess at the Black Rain Club."

"Where's that?"

"It's off Huaihai Road, up in the old French Concession. Little more than a high-class brothel and strip joint."

Li frowned. "So why haven't you closed it down?"

Dai shrugged. "They say it's owned by the Taiwanese Mafia. These guys have bought up a lot of property in this town. Got a lot of influence here."

Li shook his head. It seemed incredible to him that people like that should be allowed to operate anywhere in China. It would not happen in Beijing.

"Anyway," Dai continued, "she paid cash. No problem. And work like that didn't come cheap."

Li felt his spirits lifting. It was another step forward. Another victim identified. "You passed this on to Deputy Section Chief Nien?"

Dai shook his head. "I would have. But I don't know where she is, Chief. Doesn't seem to be in the building." He hesitated for a moment. "So, anyway, now do you want the bad news?"

Li felt his newly uplifted spirits sink again. "What is it?"

"Jiang's family up in Yanqing confirm what he told you, Chief. He didn't go into Beijing once when he was home for the holidays last Spring Festival. They say he never goes into the city." Again he paused. "But he did lie about one thing." Li waited patiently. "He didn't see any friends when he was up there. He doesn't have any." Dai grinned.

Li slipped the x-ray back into the envelope. In a way the news about Jiang was no more than he expected. He was more interested in the identification of the Beijing girl. "That's good work, Detective," he said. "I take it there have been no developments in tracking down this Zhang girl that Jiang said he bought the bracelet for?"

"Not that I've heard, Chief. Qiu's been working on that." He headed for the door.

Li said, "Hang on a moment . . ." He thought for a bit and then said, "You got the photograph and description of that bracelet?"

"This afternoon."

"I know this is a pain in the ass, Dai, but how would you like to check it out with the families of all the missing girls we've pulled from the file so far?" Dai groaned. "And if you can't find a match in the first twelve months, go back another twelve."

Dai stood glaring at him. "This is my reward for tracking down the owner of those teeth? Hey, Chief, you really know how to build team spirit." And he closed the door none too gently behind him.

Li stood up and lifted his jacket from the coat stand. Then he remembered that he had arranged to meet Margaret at the

Peace Hotel at eight. He checked his watch. It was after seven already. He picked up the phone and asked the operator to get him the reception desk at the Peace Hotel and left a message for Margaret that he would be late.

The shrill whistles of the traffic wardens cut above the roar of the traffic in Huaihai Road, but no one paid them any attention. The street was choked with cars and trolley buses and cyclists jostling for space in the blaze of lights from shop fronts and neon hoardings. The reflections they cast in the rain were like daubs of wet paint. Cyclists peered out from beneath the hoods of dripping capes, cursing the spray thrown up from the road. The sidewalks were jammed with coloured umbrellas bumping and squeaking against each other like balloons above the heads of desperate citizens in search of a night life.

As Li's taxi fought to reach the kerb, an irate cyclist banged on the roof with his fist, and the driver leapt from his cab to grab the other man in the rain, threatening him with physical abuse if he laid another finger on his vehicle. They jostled and shouted and pushed, and people gathered on the pavement to watch, traffic grinding to a standstill, other cyclists trying now to separate the two. Li sighed and dropped a note on the driver's seat and slipped out on to the sidewalk. A young girl in a red *qipao* beneath a red and gold-braided jacket, stood under a canvas awning outside one of Shanghai's two Beijing Duck restaurants, trying to attract customers. But all she was attracting were the leering taunts of a drunken old man who kept trying to paw her. Li grabbed him and pulled him away from her. He turned angrily, taking a wild swing at his assailant, but Li caught his fist and showed him his ID. "Go home," he said firmly and pushed him away. The girl flicked him a frightened look, unsure whether to be grateful or afraid. Li pulled the collar of his leather jacket up against the rain, and hurried on down the street, checking the numbers.

A young man clutched at his arm as he passed. "Hey," he said. "What's the hurry? Where are you from?"

Li glared at him. "Beijing."

The young man grinned. "I know a good Beijing bar in Shanghai," he said. "Plenty of girls who like Beijing men. You wanna massage?"

Li was shocked. Was this what China was becoming? Was this the future? He thrust his Ministry badge in the young man's face and said, "You want to come with me to police headquarters and discuss the sentence for pimping?"

The young man shrank away immediately, his face a picture of fear. "Sorry, sorry," he said. "I made a mistake." And he disappeared into the crowds as quickly as he had appeared. Li felt the rain trickling down the back of his neck.

The entrance to the Black Rain Club was in a lane that ran north off Huaihai Road. A black canopy over the entrance dripped rainwater on to a red carpet. Glass doors were set in a polished brass frame, and a burly attendant wearing a dinner suit and bow-tie stood in the doorway. He looked Li up and down. "You a member?"

"No."

"Piss off, then." Li felt his hackles rising. He opened his ID for the third time in as many minutes. But the man wasn't impressed. He took a moment to scrutinise it and said, "From out of town, huh? So I guess you don't know any better. We got protection here."

"Not from me," Li said.

"Like I told you," the man said, "piss off." And he reached out to grab Li's arm to turn him away. But Li had seized the hand before it even reached him, finding the nerve in the fleshy part between the thumb and forefinger, and pressing hard. The pain, he knew, was disabling. The big man gasped and immediately dropped to his knees, unable to offer resistance or even try to pull his hand from Li's grip. Li turned him around and banged his face up against the glass of the door. He could hear the squeak of greasy flesh on shiny glass, and through the door he could see a staircase winding up to a first-floor landing. The banister was polished brass on wrought iron. The stairs were carpeted in thick-piled red wool. At intervals on the staircase, beautiful girls stood glittering in slinky evening dresses, sipping champagne and chattering like birds on mobile phones. There was a constant traffic on the stairs of what Li presumed to be "members," dressed in designer suits and button-down shirts. They all turned now to look down at the fracas in the doorway.

Li had the doorman's arm twisted up his back, and saw the glass bend as he pushed the man's face harder into it. "Now listen," he said quietly. "It'll take me all of five seconds to put scum like you behind bars. So you'd better show me the respect that an officer of the law deserves, and go and tell your boss that I'd like to speak to him."

When Li let him go, the doorman got back to his feet, mustering as much dignity as he could, straightening his jacket and heading stiffly off up the stairs to find his boss. He left behind him his distorted faceprint on the glass of the door. Li heard one or two giggles from the girls on the stairs. Perhaps they didn't like him very much.

Li walked into the lobby and saw, through enormous double doors away to his left, a large dance floor surrounded by tables. There was a bar at the far side, and as he wandered in he saw that there was a small stage at one end and a tiny orchestra pit. Coloured lights danced and sparkled in the affected subterranean gloom. The tables were busy, but no one was dancing. The nine-piece orchestra finished some jazzy Western dance number, to be replaced immediately by a deep, hammering disco beat that thundered out from speakers around the room. Spotlights snapped on, and bikini-clad dancers with high white boots rose up on small round podia, contorting themselves in some bizarre parody of nineteen-sixties America.

He felt a tap on his shoulder and turned to find himself facing the doorman and a clone flanking a smaller man wearing a white dinner jacket. "What do you want?" the Dinner Jacket shouted above the noise.

Li nodded towards the lobby. "Outside," he shouted back, and they moved through into the comparative quiet of the entrance hall.

"Well?" The Dinner Jacket was impatient.

Li said, "You employed a girl here called Chai Rui."

The Dinner Jacket frowned and shook his head. "Don't know her."

"About eighteen months ago," Li said.

Still the Dinner Jacket shook his head. "Girls come and go. So, if that's all . . ." He started to turn away and Li caught his shoulder. The man pulled free and turned, eyes blazing. "Don't fucking touch me! Do you know who I am?"

Li said quietly, "I don't care who you are. And I don't care what friends you think you have in this town. The only thing that matters here is who I am. I represent the law of the People's Republic of China, and I am investigating a murder. And if you fuck with me you could end up in a football stadium somewhere picking lead out of your brains. And that's after I've closed down your club, put your whores in prison and confiscated your assets."

Conversation on the stairs had come to a halt, mobile phones slipped back into purses. The Dinner Jacket stared long and hard at Li. This was a supreme loss of face in front of his employees and his customers, but there was no doubting that Li was serious. It was not how the owner of the Black Rain was used to being dealt with by the authorities. His two henchmen shifted uncomfortably on either side of him.

"Her nickname was Cherry," Li said, helping him out.

Now the Dinner Jacket nodded slowly. "Yeah," he said. "I remember her. Good-looking girl. She didn't work here long. Couple of months at the most. I fired her."

"Why?"

"She was a user. Heroin." He shook his head. "No good. I like my girls clean."

"How very fastidious of you," Li said. "Where did she go after you fired her?"

"Don't know. Don't care. If I sack a girl I don't expect to see her again. This is not a social club." He took a beat. "Is that it?"

Li was reluctant to let it go at that. But there was no point in pursuing it. If the girl had only worked at the Black Rain for a couple of months and left sixteen months before, it was unlikely he would learn much here. He gave a small nod, and the Dinner Jacket immediately turned and hurried up the stairs with the second henchman in his wake. The doorman who'd left his faceprint on the glass resumed his position at the door. Li pulled up his collar again and hurried out into the rain.

He had only got a couple of hundred metres down Huaihai Road when he felt a tugging on his sleeve. He turned to find himself looking into the upturned face of a very pretty girl under a bright green umbrella. She had a white trench coat gathered around a sequined dress, and Li could see tiny flashes of light from beneath it as she brushed the hair out of her eyes. She glanced behind her nervously. "What happened to Cherry?" she asked.

"Someone took a surgeon's knife and cut her open," Li said, and he immediately regretted the brutality of his words when he saw the girl's face go pale, and the anguish in her eyes. She nearly buckled at the knees, and he held her elbow to steady her. "You knew her?"

"She was a friend. Only one I ever made at the club. She was really beautiful."

"Where did she go after she was fired?"

"She couldn't get any work. You know, in this game word gets around pretty fast if you're a user. The only way is down. She tried to kick it, she really did. But she still couldn't get any work. She heard of an opening in Beijing about a year ago and went up there to try her luck. I never saw her again."

The rain from her umbrella was dripping on to Li's shirt. But it didn't matter. He was soaked to the skin anyway. He said, "Do you know anything about her? Her family, any other friends?"

She flicked another nervous glance behind her then shook her head. "She was pretty tight about all that kind of stuff. A very private person, you know? She lived in a really expensive apartment on Zhaojiabang Road. I don't know how she could afford it, or the girl she had in to look after the kid."

"She had a kid?" Li was surprised.

"Yeah, it was just a couple of years old. A little girl. She paid some peasant girl to babysit while she was working."

"So where's the kid now? Did she take her with her to Beijing?"

"I don't know." Another nervous glance behind her. "Look, I got to go. They'll dump me for sure if they know I talked to you. They think I ran out for cigarettes." She turned and hurried back through the crowds, tiny steps in quick succession, heels clicking on the sidewalk. Li watched her go, and still the rain fell.

At the end of Hengshan Road, Li wiped away the condensation on the window of the taxi and smeared the lights of Xujiahui junction across the glass. Floodlit towers and giant globes, and flashing neon; Toto, Hitachi, American Standard; a bronze statue of a young woman clinging to the arm of a young man speaking animatedly into a cell phone. The rain that still drummed on the roof of the Volkswagen appeared to be having no deterrent effect on the night life of the city. The streets were still congested with people and traffic. The taxi took a left and dropped him at steps leading up to a pedestrian footbridge that spanned the six lanes of Zhaojiabang Road. Li dashed across the bridge, getting soaked all over again. Steps on the other side took him down to the bright lights of a multiplex cinema beneath a cluster of six tower blocks of private apartments. The main movie house was showing the latest Bond film.

The manager of Chai Rui's apartment block remembered her well. He had had a crush on her, he confided in Li, and then begged him not to tell his wife. She had paid for the apartment monthly with a direct debit from her bank account, he said. It had continued to pay out for a couple of months after she went to Beijing, and then suddenly stopped. When the next payment came due and was not forthcoming, he had emptied the apartment and re-let it. He led Li down a long corridor to a locked room at the end. "The majority of the apartments are furnished," he said, "and she'd taken most of her clothes with her, so there wasn't much to clear out." He unlocked the door and switched on the light in a small storeroom with metal racked shelves around the walls. He lifted down a cardboard box. "This is all there was. Just a few personal things. I kept them in case she ever came back." He grinned. "You can live in hope." He paused. "What's she done?"

"She hasn't done anything," Li said. "Someone murdered her."

The manager went very pale. "Oh, no," he said. "Poor Cherry."

"Do you know anything about her family?" Li asked.

The manager shook his head. "She never said anything about family."

"What about her kid? Did she take the little girl to Beijing with her?"

"I've no idea. She wasn't in the habit of discussing her plans with me. Sadly." He shook his head again. "Poor, poor Cherry."

Li took the box from under his arm. "I'll take that now."

II

It was nearly nine when Li walked into the Peace Hotel. Margaret was sitting on her own at the bar. She was on her second vodka tonic. The anger she had been nursing, first towards Mei-Ling over the Xinxin fiasco and then towards Li for standing her up, had begun to dissipate. Li had dropped off the box of Chai Rui's possessions at 803 and taken a taxi straight there. He was still soaking wet. Margaret took one look at him and couldn't resist a smile.

"So now I know why you're late," she said. "You just had to have a shower before you came out. Pity you forgot to take your clothes off first."

He grinned sheepishly. "It stops them from shrinking."

She laughed. "You want a beer?" He nodded and she called the waitress over and ordered him one. "And I also know why they put you in that other hotel – you can't afford the prices here on your salary." She chuckled. "Trouble is, on what they pay me at the University of Public Security, neither can I. I'm having to take out a mortgage to pay my bar bill."

Their mood was easier and more relaxed than it had been for some time. In some strange way, accepting that their relationship might be at an end, albeit unspoken, had removed the tension between them. Li picked up the drinks menu and looked at the prices. He whistled softly. "In the name of the sky, a hundred *kwai* for a beer? Some people don't earn that much in a week! I'll have to be careful not to spill any." He took a drink and rolled the beer around his mouth. "Funny," he said, "it tastes just the same as it does out of a five *kwai* can."

Margaret looked at him thoughtfully for a moment, and then decided to broach the subject she had been brooding over for the last few hours. "Listen, I don't want to spoil good relations or anything, but that little shit really screwed me over this afternoon."

Li frowned. "What are you talking about?"

"Mei-Ling. When I went to pick up Xinxin, there was this uniformed female cop there. Wouldn't let me near Xinxin and dragged the poor kid screaming down the stairs. Clearly on instructions from a higher authority."

"Oh, shit," Li said, and his face flushed pink. "I am so sorry, Margaret. I forgot to tell Mei-Ling that you were going to collect Xinxin."

Margaret felt unaccountably disappointed. "Oh. So, I can't blame *her*, then. Pity. It makes me feel better if I think everything around here is her fault." She took a stiff draught of vodka. "Tell you what, though, you need to do something about that female cop. That is no way to treat poor little Xinxin. The kid was really distressed."

Li nodded grimly. "I'll sort it."

She hesitated for a few moments, then, "I thought I might take her out tomorrow," she said. "Seeing that it's Saturday. I figured she wouldn't have kindergarten."

"Sure," Li said.

Margaret smiled. "There won't be any big, dikey police-woman there trying to stop me, will there?"

Li laughed. "You have my word on that. Where are you going to take her?"

"There's this park I heard about over on the west side of the city where kids get to drive little electric cars around minia-ture streets. I figured she'd probably like that."

Li laughed. "You will probably not get her to leave." He paused. "Where did you hear about it?"

He did not notice the slight clouding of Margaret's eyes, or how the brightness of her smile became a little too fixed. "I can't remember. Read about it somewhere, I think." She hated lying to Li, but she didn't think this was the moment to discuss Jack Geller. Margaret looked at Li and thought how attractive he was for an ugly man. She decided to change the subject. "So," she said, "are you going to tell me the real reason you kept me waiting for an hour?"

"We identified the girl from Beijing. From those dental records that you brought down."

Reality returned, and Margaret felt her lighter mood slip away. "And?"

"She was just a kid. Chai Rui was her name, but everyone called her Cherry. She was twenty-two. Probably making a liv-ing as a hooker. She had been working as a hostess at a club, but they fired her when they found out she was using." He told her about the upscale apartment, about the little girl and how nobody knew what had become of her, about the box of belongings that were all that remained of a tragic life.

Margaret thought of the putrefying remains she had examined on the autopsy table the day before. She shook her head sadly. "You know, it's easier somehow if you don't know anything about them. When they don't have a name and you don't know about their husband or their lover. Or their child." She tried to blink away the tears that had suddenly filled her eyes. "Shit," she said, "I'm getting soft in my old age." But she couldn't throw off the image of the body-bags lined up in the mortuary, all those women whose lives and loves, and hopes and fears, had been cut so brutally short, butchered without thought for the people they loved, or who loved them. And then a thought formed, coming out of nowhere, drawing on a hundred different subconscious sources, a revelation that had been secretly brewing somewhere deep in her mind without her even being aware of it. And suddenly all the emotional baggage of the last few days fell away and she was thinking with great clarity. "Wait a minute," she said. "You're telling me this girl had a kid."

"Sure. So what? You'd have been able to tell that from autopsy, wouldn't you? What was it you said, the cervix got stretched in childbirth and ended up looking like fish lips?"

"It's a good indication," Margaret said, "but it's not a guarantee." She held a hand up. "Just . . . just give me a minute." She tried to think. How many of the women that she had autopsied had given the appearance of having had kids? But then, hadn't she just told Li that you couldn't tell for sure? And she didn't know about the others, the ones she hadn't autopsied herself, and it wasn't an area to which she had paid much attention. She switched tack. "Of the five women we've identified, how many had kids?"

Li frowned. He couldn't see where this was going. "All of them, I think." Then, "No, wait a minute . . ." He ran through them all in his mind. The seamstress who took it in turns with her husband to take their son to kindergarten; the opera singer whose mother looked after her little girl; the fingerprint girl whose parents had been given custody of her baby; the night club hostess whose baby girl had disappeared when she did. That left the acrobat and her husband, Sun Jie. Li could not remember him making any reference to a child. "Four of them," he said. "I don't think the acrobat had a kid."

"Are you sure?"

"No, I'm not. I mean, we can find out, but what difference does it make? It's not unusual for women of that age to have kids, is it?"

Margaret said, "I don't know." She was still in a state of excitement. Something was trying to work its way through from subconscious fog to conscious clarity. "But if all these women had borne children – I mean, all of them – then it would be something they had in common, wouldn't it? Something to link them."

Li shrugged. "I guess." He still couldn't see any great relevance.

"Could we find out now?" she asked.

"Find out what?"

"If the acrobat had a kid. Is there any way we can find out right now?"

Li looked at his watch. It was nearly nine-thirty. The evening performance at the Shanghai Centre Theatre would just be coming to a close. "If we're quick we could probably catch the husband after the show."

Margaret abandoned her vodka and jumped down off her stool. "Let's do it."

Escalators ran them up into the atrium from the Long Bar above the car park in the Shanghai Centre. The acrobatic show was over and most of the audience had dispersed. Li wondered if the girls with the nine chairs had managed to perform their stunt without falling. Half a dozen tiny clusters of people stood smoking and talking in the vastness of the atrium, their smoke and voices rising into the huge void that lifted over their heads and glassed out the night. Backstage, young acrobats were running back and forth gathering props and costumes, shouting and laughing and tangling playfully half-naked in open-doored dressing rooms. Nobody gave Li a second glance, but Margaret was an object of considerable interest. The manageress limped into the corridor on her sticks. She took one look at Li and then nodded to a room further down.

Sun Jie was pulling his coat on, ready to leave, when Li knocked and he and Margaret entered. His expression hardened when he saw Li. He appeared not even to notice Margaret. "What do you want?" he said wearily. "She's dead, I need to put this behind me now."

"I'll not bother you again," Li promised. "I just wanted to know if you and Liyao ever had any children."

Sun Jie's eyes narrowed and he looked at Li almost accusingly. "Why do you want to know that?"

Margaret watched, feeling very excluded, as the two men spoke in Chinese. And yet, not understanding the words seemed to give her a greater insight. Sun Jie, initially hostile and laconic, started pouring out his heart. Margaret could see the pain in his eyes, and then the tears that formed there.

Finally he sat down and began talking, apparently to no one in particular. Big silent tears rolled down his cheeks as he shook his head at some unbearable memory. He and Li spoke for several minutes before Li turned and took Margaret's arm. "Come on," he said softly. "Let's go." And they left Sun Jie sitting weeping on his own in the dressing room. Tears he had not spilled at the mortuary when he identified his wife ran freely now. Li pulled the door shut behind them.

In the atrium Margaret could contain her curiosity no longer. "What did he say? Why was he in tears?"

Li looked tired, weighed down by the other man's grief. "He has an eight-year-old daughter. His mother used to look after her when he and Liyao were performing or away on tour. Now she looks after her full-time." *I hardly know her*, Sun Jie had told him. *And she hardly knows she has a father.*

"Why the tears?"

"Apparently she got pregnant again a couple of years ago. He suspects she was trying to. She was desperate to have a boy. He flew into a rage and told her they would be heavily penalised under the One Child Policy if she had it. They had terrible fights about it. In the end he won and she agreed to have an abortion. He says he bullied her into it."

Margaret knew that this was painful for Li, too. It almost replicated his sister's story. She supposed that it was a universal story in China, a tragedy that got played out in nearly every family.

Li said, "He reckoned their relationship was never quite the same after that. They'd had a furious row once and she had called him a murderer, the killer of their unborn child." Li shook his head. "I think that's left a scar on him that will never heal. Poor bastard." He looked at Margaret, but he knew immediately that she was somewhere else. There was a strange burning quality in her eyes, and the colour had risen high on her cheeks. "What is it?"

She looked at him now, with something like pain in her expression. "I fucked up, Li," she said. "It's been there in front of me the whole time and I never saw it."

He was perplexed. "What do you mean?"

Her hands were shaking as she clutched his arm. "I want to get the bodies out of the refrigerator and back on to the table – now," she said.

"What?" Li was incredulous. "At this time of night!"

"Right now," she said.

III

The sweat beaded across her forehead and was instantly chilled by the low working temperature of the autopsy room. It felt cold and clammy on her hot skin. Her eyes were burning with fatigue, dry and gritty. She wondered what time it was. She had been in here, it seemed, for hours, ignoring the simmering resentment of tired mortuary assistants called from their beds to move the bodies around. On the table in front of her lay the uterus and pelvic organs of the last of the victims, the remaining body parts still in their bag laid out on a gurney. The womb was the same familiar pink-tan in colour. At the bottom end, where it opened into the vagina, Margaret saw the tell-tale scarring of the endometrium. Something made her look up, and she caught Li leaning against the door watching her.

"What's the time?" she asked.

"Four a.m."

"Jesus." She had been in there for almost five hours.

"Are you nearly done?"

She nodded. "Where have you been?"

"Having a stand-up row with Dr. Lan. He takes exception to me opening up *his* mortuary and calling out *his* staff in the middle of the night without reference to *him*. I do not know who called him, but someone did. He does not like getting out of his bed at four in the morning. He is pretty pissed."

"I'm pretty pissed, too," Margaret said. "And I haven't even been to bed."

Li smiled weakly. He was also tired. "Who are you pissed at this time?"

"Myself," she said bitterly. "For not seeing this before, for not even thinking of it." She looked at him. "You know, it's that thing of too much information obscuring the obvious." She laughed, but it was an empty laugh. "I'm sorry. It's my fault. I wasn't even looking in the right place."

He crossed to the table, eaten up by curiosity. "Are you going to tell me now what it is you have found?"

She smiled. "The answer to a riddle."

He frowned. "What riddle?"

"A riddle that Mei Yuan asked me to pass on to you. Only I didn't, because she said not to tell you until I had worked it out for myself. Then I would realise the importance of how the question is framed."

"So when did you figure it out?"

"In the atrium outside the theatre. I could have kicked myself for being stupid enough not to see it before."

"I thought it was this case you were having some revelation about."

"It was both. They're one and the same thing, really."

Li scowled. He could not get his mind around this, especially at four in the morning. "Do you want to tell me what the riddle was?"

"Okay," she said, "imagine you're a bus driver in Beijing . . ." And she took him through the whole trip from the Friendship Store, past Wangfujing Street and Tiananmen Square to Xidan, picking up and dropping off passengers en route. She changed the numbers, made them up as she went along. She knew it didn't matter. But she watched him doing the mental arithmetic. "All right? You follow all that?" He nodded. "Okay, so what height was the bus driver?"

She could see that his reaction had been the same as hers, and for the life of her could not imagine how she had been so easily fooled. He shook his head. "You cannot know the height of the driver."

She laughed. Of course you can. And she repeated the question. "Imagine *you're* a bus driver in Beijing . . ."

He groaned. "I always fall for these. It is typical of Mei Yuan."

"But the point is," Margaret said, "the answer was there all along, staring you in the face." She laughed. "But you're too busy doing the arithmetic, getting distracted by all the numbers, and the names of the stops. So you don't see what's obvious."

Li looked at the bivalved womb on the autopsy table. "So what's obvious here that you didn't see?"

"The thing that connects them, that ties them all together beyond any possible coincidence, that I never even thought to look for. Until now."

"Better late than never. Do you want to tell me?"

She folded the uterus over, as it would have been before bisection. "I have this little trick," she said, "when I'm doing an autopsy." She took a pair of forceps and demonstrated how she would slip them up through the cervix into the body of the womb. "I can then use the forceps as a guide for my knife so that I can draw it up through the womb and cut it easily in half.

Of course, it only works if the subject is female." She grinned, but got no response from Li and shrugged. "Anyway, with these ladies, in a couple of cases I couldn't get the forceps in, and when I finally got the uterus open I found that there were adhesions on the inner lining that scarred the uterus closed."

"I remember," Li said. "You thought maybe the damage had been done in childbirth."

"That's right. But there's something else that can cause this kind of scarring." And with her right index finger she traced the adhesions on the endometrium in front of her. "It was you telling me about the acrobat having the abortion that made me think of it. And then I remembered Dr. Wang in Beijing commenting on similar scarring in the womb of the body found there. He said he'd seen it frequently as a result of careless abortion."

"And that's what caused the scarring that you found?"

Margaret nodded. "Suction curettage is probably the commonest form of abortion. And that's what's been employed here. A kind of freshwater weed called *Laminaria* is usually inserted into the cervix to soften or ripen it, and allow passage of the suction tool." She glanced up and saw the look of disgust on Li's face. She said, "You guys don't know the half of what we women have to go through." And although her delivery was light, there was something deeper there that caused Li to look at her for a moment.

"I'm not sure I want to," Li said.

"Well, in this case you have no choice," Margaret said. "And neither did this poor girl. Whoever performed her abortion was too vigorous with the suction tool, and instead of sucking out just the foetus along with the placenta and the superficial lining, they removed a whole portion of the lining of the womb, causing it to scar closed. She probably couldn't have had another baby even if she'd wanted."

Li looked thoughtful. "How many of the victims had scars like this?"

Margaret looked sheepish. "Nearly half of them." She shrugged. "The only excuse I can offer is that I didn't perform all the autopsies, and the womb was pretty far from the focus of attention. Also, it *would* have been possible for complications in childbirth to have resulted in scarring like this."

Li brushed aside her guilty apologies. "Only half of them? You said you'd found something that connected them all."

"I have," she said. "You'll have to come through to the other room."

On the tables in the room next door, Margaret had laid out the wombs and the other pelvic organs – the urinary bladder, ovaries and Fallopian tubes – of another two victims. It looked to Li like a bizarre collection of human pieces. The bodies from which they had been taken were laid out inside their open body-bags on gurneys beside each table.

Margaret moved to the nearest table. She said, "Another abortion technique is called D & C. Dilation and curettage. The cervix is softened in the same way, but then the foetus and the uterus are literally scraped out using a long-handled sharp spoon, a little like an ice-cream scoop, but smaller than an old fancy sugar-cube spoon."

She heard Li exhale through his teeth. "Do I really need this detail?" he asked.

"Yup. It's important." She was not prepared to make any allowances. "The trouble with this procedure is that it has a much higher complication rate. There's a greater danger of perforation and haemorrhage at the time it is carried out, and as a result, more infections afterwards." She held open one of the tubes leading from the womb. "This is one of the uterine, or fallopian tubes," she said. "Sometimes, if the womb is infected after the D & C, the infection can travel up the uterine tubes and scar them closed. That's what's happened here."

Li leaned forward and saw the distinctive pattern of scarring in the bisected tube.

Margaret said, "The pathologist who did the autopsy on this woman would have had no reason to consider it significant. And, anyway, this kind of scarring is more commonly caused by a number of venereal diseases." She moved away to the other table. "Now this poor woman," she said, "suffered at the hands of the Japanese." Li's frown caused her to smile. "They invented the process," she said. "Yet another crude, and quite brutal, way of ending a life. You'd think in this high-tech age we'd have evolved more sophisticated techniques. But then, since it's usually men who invent these things, it's probably not very high on their list of priorities." She flattened out the bivalved uterus and ran her finger along an irregularly healed scar on the cervix. "One of the tell-tale signs," she said. "And you can see up here on the inside of the uterine wall this thinned, tough, pale area. That's another." She sighed. "What's happened here is that the fluid has been drawn out of the bag of water around the foetus and replaced by a concentrated salt solution. That has caused the foetus and placenta to spontaneously deliver about forty-eight hours after the infusion."

"What's caused the scarring?"

Margaret shrugged. "There are various complications that can cause the cervix to be scarred like this, but this pale area inside the body of the uterus . . . that's a result of some of the salt solution escaping into the muscular uterine wall, effectively killing it. *Myometrial necrosis*, it's called."

She pushed her head back and then stretched it left and right to try to take some of the tension out of her neck. She slipped off her mask and shower cap and moved away to the sink, removing her gown and her gloves. Li followed her and leaned back against the stainless steel worktop. "So how many of our victims showed scarring like this?"

Margaret said flatly, "All the remaining women had either one or other of these procedures performed on them."

Li thought about it for a long time. "A lot of women have abortions in China, Margaret," he said.

She turned to look at him. "About three hundred thousand a year in Shanghai," she said. "That's the figure that guy at Director Hu's banquet came up with the other night, wasn't it?"

"Cui Feng." Li nodded. "That's right."

"And there are what, maybe six million women in Shanghai?"

Li shrugged. "About that, I guess."

"So on a very crude calculation, over a ten-year period, fifty per cent of the women in this city will have had abortions. So out of, say, twenty women picked at random you'd expect half of them to have had an abortion. Of course, that's just an average. In some groups there would be seven or eight. In others there might be thirteen, even fourteen." She paused to let her arithmetic sink in. "Here we have nineteen women, if we include the girl in Beijing, and every single one of them has had an abortion. Li Yan, that's statistically impossible."

CHAPTER ELEVEN

I

"You do *not* run this department, Deputy Section Chief. *I* do!" Section Chief Huang's anger showed itself in the tiny flecks of spittle that gathered around his lips. He stood glaring at Li from behind his desk.

Li closed the door and said quietly, "I was put in charge of this investigation."

"That does not give you the authority to go pulling *my* people out of their beds in the middle of the night and embarking on a course of investigation that has not even been discussed with me."

Li felt his patience waning. He said, "I can't win, can I? Yesterday the Procurator General tells me if I don't speed up the investigation it's my neck on the block. I make a breakthrough during the night and you want me to wait till you've had breakfast before I follow it up." He took out a cigarette.

"Don't light that in here," Huang said.

Reluctantly, Li slipped the cigarette back in its packet. His eyes were stinging from lack of sleep, and he had a bad taste in his mouth. He glared back at Huang. "If you don't get out of my face, Huang, I'm taking this to Director Hu, and I'm going to tell him I can't pursue his investigation because you're obstructing me."

Huang snorted his derision. "You think the Mayor's policy adviser will see you at *your* request? Director Hu sees you when *he* wants to see you. And in the meantime you'll deal with me and Procurator General Yue, like it or not." He searched on his desk for a sheet of paper. He found it and waved it at Li. It had scribbled notes on it. "I had a call last night from the Chief of Section One. It seems you went and ruffled a few feathers at the Black Rain Club." He breathed stertorously through his nose. "That is not how we deal with these people here?"

"Oh, really?" Li said. "So what do you do, roll over and let them shit on you?"

Huang's eyes burned with anger and dislike. "You are walking on seriously thin ice here, Li. In Shanghai, insubordination and abuse towards a senior officer are usually rewarded with instant demotion, if not dismissal."

"So fire me," Li said, and he locked eyes with Huang and wouldn't look away. His position as head of the investigation was an issue he was determined to force. Director Hu had appointed him over Huang's head, and he was not about to let the Section Chief undermine his authority because of petty jealousy and internal politics.

Huang was spared having to respond by a knock at the door. It opened and Mei-Ling entered. She was immediately aware of the charged atmosphere that filled the room and closed the door quickly behind her. She looked at Huang. "What's up, Chief?"

Huang still held Li's gaze. "Not only does our friend from Beijing drag half the pathology department out of their beds in the middle of the night, but then he calls in the entire detective shift two hours early and embarks on an investigation of a personal friend of Director Hu."

This was all news to Mei-Ling. She looked at Li in amazement. "What's going on? Why didn't you call me?"

"I needed foot soldiers, not generals," Li said.

She was clearly not pleased. "Do you want to tell me what it was that was so important you had to get everyone else out of their beds but me?"

Li sighed. He did not need hostility on two fronts. "Margaret made a breakthrough last night. She found something that linked all the victims."

Mei-Ling frowned. "What?"

"Every single one of them had had an abortion."

"Oh, had they?" she said. And she digested the information for a moment. Then, "So how come this 'breakthrough' wasn't made at autopsy?"

But Li was determined not to be deflected. "That's not important right now. What matters is that these women could not have been picked at random. And if the thing they have in common is that they've all had abortions, then that puts the investigation on a whole different footing."

Mei-Ling was still struggling to keep up. "How's that?"

"I had the guys check with the relatives of four of the five girls we've identified so far. All four had their abortions done at clinics belonging to Cui Feng. Remember him? We met him at Director Hu's banquet."

Huang cut in, "So now he wants to go harassing a personal friend of the Mayor's policy adviser." He turned on Li again. "There is *nothing* unusual about these women having had abortions carried out at Cui's clinics. His organisation performs most of the abortions in Shanghai."

"In the name of the sky!" Li let his exasperation escape through clenched teeth. "I am not suggesting there is anything sinister in that. I want to ask Cui if he will give us access to his files. We can then check them against the missing persons files and find out which of them had had abortions. That way there's a good chance we can narrow down the identities of the other dead girls."

Mei-Ling drew a deep breath and looked at Huang. "It does make sense, Chief."

But Li was wound up now and didn't want to let it go. "I mean, what is this guy anyway, untouchable? Just because he's a pal of Director Hu?"

Huang turned a very dangerous look on Li. His voice was low. "Cui Feng is a Party member and a very influential member of this community," he said. "I will not have his reputation impugned in any way by this department. Is that understood?"

There was a tense silence, broken finally by Mei-Ling. "But we can ask him to let us see his files, can't we, Chief?"

Huang held Li's eyes for several more seconds before tearing them away to focus on Mei-Ling. There was almost a sense of hurt in them, a feeling perhaps of betrayal that she had taken Li's side rather than his. "Yes," he said finally. "You can ask to see his files."

The traffic was backing up along Fuxing Road from roadworks outside the Music Conservatory. Li and Mei-Ling had sat nursing their own thoughts in the car all the way south and west from 803. The tension between Li and Huang had transferred itself to Mei-Ling. She was brooding darkly behind the wheel of the car. She glanced at Li as they sat idling in the traffic, fumes rising all about them in the rain, only the sound of windscreen wipers scraping back and forth breaking their silence. "So where is she now?" she said at last.

Li dragged himself from his private thoughts. "Who?"

"Margaret."

"She's gone back to her hotel to try and get some sleep. She was up most of the night."

"Oh, what a shame," Mei-Ling said in a tone that dripped with sarcasm. "Maybe if she'd spotted these abortions in the first place she wouldn't have needed to go catching up on her beauty sleep."

For Li it was the last straw. He turned his aggression full on Mei-Ling. "Look," he said, "I don't know what the hell you and Margaret have got against each other, but I'm fed up being caught between two women eating vinegar. I want this jealousy to stop. And I want it to stop now! We've got nineteen women here hacked to death by some maniac with a blade, I think we owe it to them to keep ourselves focused on catching their killer. Don't you?"

Mei-Ling was shocked, both by his anger and by his more than implied criticism. She reacted coldly. "Of course," she said.

But Li was tired, his resistance low, and there were other things he wanted to get off his chest. "And that policewoman you sent to pick up Xinxin . . . ? I don't want her going near the kid again."

Mei-Ling flashed him an angry look. "Why?"

"Because she refused to let Margaret near her, and scared Xinxin half to death. In future I'll make my own arrangements to have her collected. All right?"

Mei-Ling's cheeks reddened. Anger was mixed now with hurt, and she retreated into herself like a wounded animal. She nodded and kept her eyes fixed firmly on the traffic in the road ahead. They did not speak again until she turned the car into the car park outside the red-roofed villa that housed Cui Feng's central clinic.

The clinic was set behind a high gated wall and a profusion of densely leafed trees in a quiet residential street on the edge of the consular district. This had once been the heart of the old French Concession. Elegant villas sat brooding in discreet isolation behind walls and fences. Private cars were parked along secluded, tree-lined avenues, with only the odd cyclist whirring past on a rickety bicycle. What had once been the garden of the villa was paved, and half a dozen cars sat backed up against the wall. A small private ambulance was parked under a canopy supported by two pillars above the main entrance. The windows had all been double-glazed, and the view into their interior was obscured by cream-coloured vertical blinds. A brass plaque on the gate revealed in Chinese and English that this was the SHANGHAI WORLD CLINIC.

A nurse in a white, starched uniform led them up thickly carpeted stairs and along a passageway hung with original scroll paintings by famous Chinese artists. It felt more like an opulent private residence than a medical clinic. They passed an oriental gentleman in a wheelchair being pushed by a male nurse, and then were shown into a large study with a sofa and two armchairs gathered around an original fireplace. There was a huge, leather-tooled desk in the bay window, stripes of watery daylight falling in through the blinds and lying across the contours of the captain's chair that sat behind it. Cui Feng came around the desk as they entered. He wore an expensively cut dark suit and had the same gentle bedside manner of the family doctor that Li remembered from their first meeting at Director Hu's banquet. Soft spoken and smiling, he shook their hands warmly, inviting them each to take an armchair. "It is

a great pleasure to meet you again, Deputy Section Chiefs."
He gave a small laugh at his plural abbreviation. "It is a great
relief that you share a rank," he said, "or we could be here all
day just addressing each other." He sat down on the edge of
the settee and leaned forward, his elbows on his knees, and
placed his hands together almost as if in prayer. "Now what
can I do for you?" he asked. "I understand that some of those
poor women you dug up had abortions done at some of my
clinics." And Li realised that Huang had already been on the
phone to Cui to smooth the way for their arrival.

"That's right," Li said. "In fact all the victims have had
abortions performed on them." He hesitated for the briefest
of moments before adding, "Not very expertly, according to
our pathologist. Otherwise it would have been very difficult
to tell."

But Cui was not ruffled. He said, "In that case, perhaps they
were not all performed at my clinics. We operate to very high
procedural standards."

"I don't doubt it," Li said. "But since you perform most of
the abortions in Shanghai, this seemed like a good place to
start."

"Start what, exactly?" Cui appeared uncomfortable for the
first time.

Mei-Ling stepped in quickly to prevent Li from discomfiting
him any further. "We were wondering, Mr. Cui, if you would
allow us access to your files so that we could cross-check them
with the women on our missing persons file."

He frowned. "What good would that do?"

"It might help us narrow down the identities of the remaining victims," Li said.

Cui pursed his lips and turned this over briefly in his mind.
Then, "All right," he said. "I can see no harm in it. But since

our files are normally confidential, perhaps I could appoint one of my staff to liaise with your people and do the actual comparisons. That way we could continue to maintain the confidentiality of our patients."

Li was not happy with this proposal. He wanted direct access to the files and was about to say so. But he glanced at Mei-Ling and picked up her almost imperceptible shake of the head, Huang's words of warning about Cui's membership of the Party and his influential friends still ringing in his ears. So he forced a reluctant nod of agreement instead. "That would be acceptable," he said.

"Good." Cui relaxed and sat back in the settee. "You will have some tea." It was not so much a question as a statement. Li and Mei-Ling had no time to respond before there was a knock at the door and a young woman carried in a tray with a pot of jasmine tea and three cups of the most delicate bone china. She set it on a low table in front of the fireplace and filled the cups before making a small bow and hurrying out.

"So do you actually perform abortions here at this clinic?" Li asked.

"Good Heavens, no," Cui said smiling at Li's apparent naïvety. "The Shanghai World Clinic is exclusively for the use of foreign residents living in Shanghai." He laughed. "Generally very wealthy people whose companies provide comprehensive medical insurance. We Chinese might as well make the most of any ill-health that befalls them while they're here, don't you think?"

Li did not think that anyone should profit from ill-health, but he knew better than to say so. Instead he said, "And what kind of medical care do you provide, exactly?"

"Oh," Cui said airily, "we can deal with anything from a broken toe to open heart surgery. We have a highly qualified and very experienced international team of doctors and nurses here. And if we don't have the expertise in-house, we bring in consultants on a freelance basis."

"So the bulk of your patients are American, or European," Mei-Ling said.

Cui smiled and shook his head. "Actually no, Miss Nien. There are a number of North American or European joint-venture clinics in Shanghai which the Westerners seem to prefer. Perhaps they think that Chinese medicine only deals in acupuncture and tiger's blood." There was the merest hint of a bitter edge to his voice. "Surprisingly, perhaps, most of our customers are Japanese." Li noticed his use of the word "customers" rather than "patients." It was clear that to Cui medicine was a business and illness an opportunity to make money. Cui said, "Would you like to see our facilities?"

Li had no desire to inspect the facilities. He disliked all things medical and had a morbid fear of hospitals, which perhaps owed more than a little to all the autopsies he had attended. But before he had a chance to decline the offer, Mei-Ling said, "Yes, we'd like that very much." Li had forgotten that she had studied medicine for four years, but he was still a little surprised by her apparent interest.

The clinic was on four floors, including a suite of rooms built into the roof, and a large basement which housed two operating theatres, as well as preparation and recovery rooms. A large elevator had been installed to take patients from operation in the basement to recovery in the attic, and all stops in between. There was a four-bed intensive care ward on the ground floor, as well as several luxurious single-bed rooms that made Li think more of a four-star hotel than a hospital. Each room had en-suite toilet facilities and satellite TV. Office and administration was on the first floor, with another four single-bed rooms. There were a further six bedrooms in the attic. "At any one time," Cui said, "we can accommodate fourteen patients as well as our four intensive care beds." But on their tour, Li had seen only a handful of patients. The clinic was far from full.

"You don't appear to be very busy," he said. For some reason he had begun to take a singular dislike to Mr. Cui. He was altogether too smooth, too possessed.

Cui laughed. "Good health is bad for business, I'm afraid."

No doubt, Li thought, the hundreds of thousands of abortions Cui carried out each year would subsidise any slump in business at his Shanghai World Clinic. He stretched out a hand to shake Cui's. "Thank you very much, Mr. Cui, for your help. We'll send an officer over to liaise with your staff."

Cui smiled beneficently, shaking both their hands. "Not at all, not at all. Anything I can do to help, please don't hesitate to ask."

In the car, Mei-Ling looked at Li and said, "You don't like our Mr. Cui very much, do you?"

Li looked at her, surprised, then conceded, "No, I don't. Access to health care used to be everyone's right in this country, not just a privilege afforded to the wealthy." He paused. "Was it that obvious?"

"To me. But, then, I don't like him that much either."

"Why's that?"

She shrugged. "I hate to find myself agreeing with Margaret Campbell." She glanced at Li. "But much as I support the principle of the One Child Policy, it doesn't feel right that someone should make money out of other people's unhappiness."

And Li remembered Margaret's bold words to Cui's face, accusing him of profiting from other people's misery. He had been shocked at the time, and angry. Now he remembered her bluntness almost fondly. Margaret had no sense of tact or diplomacy, but at least whatever she presented to the world came from the heart.

Almost as if she had read his mind, Mei-Ling said, "If I were to make an educated guess, I'd say that at some time your Miss Campbell has had an abortion herself."

II

Margaret was standing by the window in Li's office when he and Mei-Ling got back to 803. Li stopped in the doorway, surprised for a moment to see her there. Her hair tumbled freely over her shoulders, catching the late morning sunshine that was squeezing in appearances between banks of dark, wallowing, low cloud. She was wearing khaki cargo pants over brown suede boots, and a yellow tee-shirt under a green waterproof jacket that was drawn in at the waist. There was a touch of red about her lips, and brown-pink around her eyes. She had a radiance about her that Li had not seen in a long time, and the sight of her kick-started a fluttering sensation in his stomach, and the faintest stirring in his loins. With the icy cold presence of Mei-Ling at his side he felt himself flush with embarrassment, as if she or Margaret could somehow read his feelings.

"Hi," Margaret said brightly. And she cocked her head, frowning slightly and giving Li an odd look. "You look like shit," she said. "You couldn't have had much sleep."

"I have not had any," he said.

"Poor thing," Margaret smiled, although her tone suggested anything but sincerity. She rounded the desk. "Look, I know you two are busy . . ." She let that hang for a moment. "So I'll not get under your feet. I just dropped by on my way to pick up Xinxin. I thought you might be interested to see this." She lifted a sheet of paper off the desk and held it out to Li.

He took it. "What is it?"

"A fax from Dr. Wang in Beijing. He sent it to my hotel. I asked him to DNA-match the body parts of the girl in Beijing, just in case the pathologist who did the original autopsy got the visual matching wrong and we were really looking at pieces of two victims."

Li looked up at her, horrified by the thought that they could have got it so wrong. "Are you telling me they do not match?"

"No, they match perfectly."

Li frowned. "So, what's the problem?"

"There's no problem," Margaret said. "It's the girl's HLA type that the DNA-matching threw up . . ."

Mei-Ling took the sheet from Li and examined it. "DQ-alpha allele '1.3'?" She shook her head, nonplussed. "What is special about that?"

"Wait a minute," Li said. "What is DQ-alpha allele?"

Mei-Ling said, "The HLA DQ-alpha gene is one of the markers on the DNA panel used to match body parts. Right?" She looked to Margaret for confirmation.

"Something like that," Margaret conceded. And then to Li, "An allele is a variant of any particular gene on a chromosome in your DNA. Some of them show statistical differences between races."

He said, "So what is significant about this '1.3' allele?"

"I don't know about its significance," Margaret said, "but it's certainly unusual. In fact the HLA DQ-alpha allele '1.3' is *never* found in the DNA of a Chinese."

Li was being very slow on the uptake. "I don't understand. What does that mean?"

Mei-Ling had the answer. "It means that your little hostess at the Black Rain Club was, in the doctrine of American political correctness, of mixed parentage. Or, as people used to say, a half-caste." She looked at Margaret. "European? American?"

"Impossible to say. But on the statistical balance of probability, it's unlikely."

"Why?" Li asked.

Margaret said, "I did a little checking on the Internet. That's where I discovered that the '1.3' is never found in Chinese – or South-East Asians for that matter. Hispanics have a pretty low incidence of it. Only about four-and-a-half per cent of blacks have it. Caucasians have the second highest frequency. But that's still only eight-and-a-half per cent. So it's pretty rare in any racial group. Strangely, the highest incidence – about twenty-two per cent – is found in Japanese. So the chances are her mom or her dad came from the Land of the Rising Sun."

Li started searching through the untidy piles of papers that were strewn across his desk.

"What are you looking for?" Mei-Ling asked.

Li said, "I asked Dai to dig out as much background on the Chai Rui girl as we had available from public records." Fatigue was fraying his temper and his patience now. "Where the hell is it?"

Mei-Ling said, "You've kept the guys pretty busy all morning, Li Yan." She sighed. "I'll speak to him." And she picked up the phone.

Margaret smiled at Li and put a hand lightly on his arm. "Try and get a break if you can," she said, and this time he saw she meant it. "I'll see you later."

Li had a very powerful desire, then, to kiss her and close his eyes and just hold her there. But all he said was, "Sure."

Margaret hesitated briefly, as if perhaps she had felt the same impulse, but then she turned and went out. He lit a cigarette and rubbed his eyes with the heels of his hands, but only succeeded in making them burn. He blinked at Mei-Ling as she hung up the phone. "Well?"

"Dai's got the stuff on his desk. But you've got an appointment first." He scowled, and she said, "The Commissioner of Police wants to see you in his office straight away."

The Commissioner of Police sat behind his desk, the crossed flags of the Republic on the wall behind him. There was nothing on the desk except for a telephone and a lamp. Not a pen or a pencil, not even so much as a scrap of paper. Its surface was polished to such a high shine that the Commissioner was almost perfectly reflected in it. He wore his official dark green uniform with two gold stripes at the bottom of each sleeve, and the gold, red and blue badge of the Ministry of Public Security on his left arm. His carefully trimmed receding hair, was brushed back from a round, heavy-jowled face. His hands were folded in front of him on the desk. He did not ask Li to sit, and Li stood uncomfortably to attention in the middle of the room. The Procurator General stood by the window, peering at Li over his round steel-rimmed reading glasses. He held a swatch of papers in his hand, but never once referred to them. He remained a mute witness to the proceedings.

Even before the Commissioner opened his mouth, Li knew that he was going to talk about his Uncle Yifu. "I met your uncle on several occasions," the Commissioner said, and Li sighed inwardly. "He was a very unusual man."

"Unusual?" This was unexpected.

"He possessed the twin virtues of great intelligence and great humility." He paused. "I understand that you were abusive to Section Chief Huang this morning and that you threatened to resign from this investigation."

Li said stiffly, "That is a matter of interpretation, Commissioner."

"And no doubt your interpretation is superior to that of Section Chief Huang?" There could be no doubting the sarcasm in the Commissioner's tone.

Li stayed cool. "No, Commissioner. Not superior, just different."

The Commissioner bristled. "The use of semantics as a means of deception is self-deluding," he said sharply.

"Should I pass that on to the Section Chief?" Li asked. In the silence that followed, the tension was thick enough to cut with a cleaver.

Eventually the Commissioner, the tremble of anger in his voice, said, "It is a pity you did not inherit your uncle's gift for humility."

"My uncle always said that the cock who hides his feathers will not win the hen," Li said. And before the Commissioner could respond he looked at him very directly and said, "People are always telling me, Commissioner, what my uncle was and wasn't. People who had met him 'on several occasions.' I lived with him for ten years. I think I know what my uncle was."

The Commissioner glowered at him. It was a defining moment. Li knew he had overstepped the mark, but he was determined to stand his ground. Then the Commissioner smiled. But it was a condescending smile, his way of saving face in the presence of the Procurator General. "At least, I see, you have inherited his native cunning." Perhaps a truer insight into the Commissioner's real view of Yifu's humble origins. Li made no comment and waited patiently for the Commissioner to get to the point. Eventually he said, "Section Chief Huang advised you against the harassment of citizen Cui Feng. And yet you chose to ignore that advice."

"No, Commissioner. I sought Mr. Cui's co-operation in gaining access to medical files that might help us throw light on the identity of the remaining victims."

"Not according to Mr. Cui."

This was a turn for which Li was caught entirely unprepared. "I . . . I don't understand, Commissioner. Mr. Cui was very co-operative."

The Commissioner lifted his hands from the desk, and Li saw the patch of damp they had left on its polished surface. "Mr. Cui is a very influential figure in this city, Deputy Section Chief. Take your investigation along another track."

Li glanced from the Commissioner to the Procurator General and back again in disbelief. "Access to Cui's files is vital to identifying those girls," he said.

"Find another way," the Commissioner said. And before Li could reply, added, "That is not a request, Deputy Section Chief. That is an order."

Li dropped heavily into his chair and lit a cigarette. He breathed smoke like fire through his nostrils and looked at Mei-Ling, anger burning in his eyes. "I don't fucking believe it? Do you believe it? We were as nice as nine *kwai* to Mr. I-have-powerful-friends Cui. And he goes accusing us of harassment!"

"Not necessarily," Mei-Ling said.

Li frowned. "What do you mean?"

"I mean there is a very thin dividing line between police, politics and power in this city. It might just be that someone up there's worried that you go ruffling the wrong feathers."

"Huang?"

"Well, you certainly ruffled his, and that won't have helped. But I think it probably goes higher than that." She put her hands on her hips and took a deep breath. "What you're forgetting, Li Yan, is that this is a highly sensitive case. Money, politics, international investment, high-powered reputations. We have to steer a very careful course through them all. But you're charging around taking on people you can't hope to beat. People we need on side if we're going to get through this." She shook her head. "And when you first arrived, I thought you were smart. Don't you know you should never fight a war you're not sure of winning? Sunzi knew it two-and-a-half thousand years ago. You've still got a lot to learn." She dropped a file on his desk. "That's the stuff Dai dug up on the Black Rain girl. I'd better go and see if I can achieve a little damage limitation here so that we can get this investigation back on track." Her superiority made Li feel like he had been petulant and immature.

She left him sitting pulling contemplatively on his cigarette and feeling homesick for the icy winds from the Gobi Desert that would be blowing now through the streets of Beijing. Outside, the rain had started again. He hated this city, he decided. He did not feel like he was in China. It was some strange hybrid that owed more to the influence of the West than the East. He was uncertain of his footsteps here, for he did not know where it was safe to walk. And he hated the rain. He missed the bright, sharp, cold winter days in Beijing. He missed the sun, even when you couldn't feel its warmth.

Slowly a sense of defeat began to descend upon him. Gentle at first, but increasing in weight, until it was crushing. All the conflicting facts and contradictory evidence filled his thoughts. Nineteen women, cut open by a skilled surgeon who had gone to great lengths to keep them alive, only to kill them by cutting out their still-beating hearts. Nineteen women who had all had the beginnings of life scraped from their wombs. Was that why they had been selected? Was it some kind of twisted revenge exacted by an avenging surgeon on women who had killed their unborn children? And what had he done with their organs? Sold them as recompense, as an atonement for their sins?

He thought of the creepy medical student who cut people up for fun, who had worked part-time on the building site and had more than ample opportunity to bury the bodies there.

He thought of Cui Feng in whose clinics most of the victims had probably had their abortions. He thought about the man's mercenary views on health care, of his status and influence in the upper echelons of power, of the fact that he had been put "off-limits" by Li's own bosses.

He thought of Director Hu and his concern for the impact of the murders on inward investment to the city.

And he wondered how many people really cared about all those poor women whose lives had been so clinically taken. And, of course, he knew exactly who cared. He remembered the thin-faced tailor at his table in a back alley, and his anguish in identifying his dead wife. He remembered the sullen boy-friend of the opera singer, and his silent, surprising tears. He remembered Sun Jie seeking solace in the arms of Buddha in a smoky temple, and the tears he had spilled in a dressing room, remembering the fight he had had with his wife over the decision to abort their second child. And all those others out there who did not yet know that their lover, or their daughter, or their mother, had been butchered and dumped in a hole in the ground.

Worse than all that, Li felt the force of his own ineffectiveness. For all the evidence accumulated, there had not been a single step forward. In almost a week he had discovered nothing that gave him a clue as to the identity of the killer, or the motive for the slaughter. He had made enemies of his superiors, and had singularly failed to achieve the one thing Director Hu had asked him to do – bring the investigation to a quick conclusion. And there was nothing on the horizon that led him to believe that the end was anywhere in sight.

He had also failed himself. He had allowed personal feelings, conflicting emotions about Mei-Ling and Margaret, to distract him from his professional obligations. And he had failed to do the only thing he had ever sought to do – to make a difference. It was why he had wanted to join the police all those years ago. He had seen it as a means of reinforcing his own very powerful sense of right and wrong, of fairness and justice. He knew he could never bring fairness to the lives of those poor dead women, but now he was failing to deliver them justice as well.

He stubbed out his cigarette and lit another, feeling himself sliding into the slough of despond. He let his eyes wander across the mess of papers on his desk, until they came to rest on a cardboard box sitting on the floor against the wall. It was the box the caretaker at the Xujiahui apartments had given him of Chai Rui's belongings. He had dumped it in his office the night before and not yet had a chance to go through it. He leaned over and lifted it on to the desk, sifting idly through its meagre contents. Some cheap jewellery, a diary without a single entry, bottles of perfume and nail varnish remover, the miscellaneous contents of a bathroom cabinet, a hairbrush with strands of her hair still caught in it. He teased the hair out through his fingers and smelled her perfume on it. For family, friends, perhaps lovers, that scent would spark memories, half-remembered moments from a life cut so short. Twenty-two years old. Li looked at the contents of the box and thought how little they were to show for a life.

Face down at the bottom of the box was a dog-eared photograph. He lifted it out. Chai Rui was grinning gauchely at the camera. It was a cheap print, and the colours were too strong. He remembered the body parts laid out on the autopsy table ten months earlier. All life and animation long gone. Standing beside her, an arm around her shoulder, was a Western man, considerably older. He had a head of thick dark hair starting to go grey, and there was a warmth in his smile. Li wondered briefly if he might have been a customer. But there was something more intimate in the body language. Had he been a lover? He stared at the picture for a long time, held by the eyes that gazed out at him from the cracked glaze of the print, and felt terribly sad. If he could not make a difference, what was the point?

He dropped the photograph back in the box and pushed it away. He wondered what had happened to Chai Rui's little girl. If she hadn't taken her with her to Beijing, then someone, somewhere, must surely still be looking after her. He remembered the file on her that Mei-Ling had retrieved from Dai, and he lifted it towards him and opened it up. Immediately he was disappointed. There was very little in here. Some official records, copies of birth certificates, death certificates, school documents, a medical report. Chai Rui had been the only child of Chau Ye and Elizabeth Rawley, an American who had lived in Shanghai since the early eighties. So Margaret had been wrong about the Japanese genetic heritage. Statistics did not always lead you to the right conclusion. He shuffled through the remaining documents. Just about the time she had left school her parents had been killed in a car crash, and she had simply vanished off the official record, swallowed up into the anonymity of what the authorities called the "floating population." This ever-expanding section of Chinese society, created by growing unemployment and the collapse of the state-owned enterprises, was a breeding ground for crime and corruption, where drug abuse and prostitution flourished and festered. It was, inevitably, where Chai Rui had slipped into addiction and sexual abuse.

And yet here was another contradiction. She had lived in an expensive apartment, paid cash for costly dental work, been able to afford a babysitter for her child. It did not fit with everything else they knew about her. Li wondered again what had happened to the child, and the thought led him to his own problem of Xinxin and her future. It was no life for her, stuck in a hotel room with a babysitter, moved around from one kindergarten to another, never knowing where to call home or who would come through the door at night. It was a problem he knew he would have to deal with as soon as this case was over. If this case would ever be over.

III

Xinxin's shrieks of pleasure split the air and echoed around the park. Her knuckles glowed white as she gripped the tiny steering wheel on the little red, plastic car and pressed the accelerator pedal to the floor. The car sailed through a red light at a cross junction, narrowly missing a small boy on a blue motorbike and sidecar. Margaret, almost helpless with laughter, tried to explain to Xinxin that running red lights was not the object of the exercise. But communication that sophisticated was not possible. And, anyway, there was no real danger. Margaret could have climbed out of the car and walked faster. Xinxin was in seventh heaven, her bunches bouncing around on either side of her head, her face a picture of concentration and happiness. She flew round a roundabout the wrong way and her laughter pealed out again in the misty afternoon. She stole a glance at Margaret, and something about the mischief in those dark eyes led Margaret to believe that Xinxin knew only too well which way she was supposed to go round the roundabout, and that you were meant to stop at red lights.

They passed under a bridge, and an elderly couple sitting on a bench at the side of the miniature road waved, laughing at the sight of the little Chinese girl shrieking like a banshee and the blue-eyed foreign devil with the blonde hair squeezed into the tiny car beside her. They passed a yellow car coming in the opposite direction, a proud father smiling fondly as his son took evasive action to avoid a head-on collision with Xinxin.

The streets were bordered by narrow, paved sidewalks, and cut through large grassy areas planted with trees and neatly manicured shrubs and hedges. At intervals, there were five- and six-foot replicas of landmark buildings in Shanghai including, Margaret noticed as they whizzed past it, a model of the Peace Hotel, with its distinctive green copper roof rising to a point. In one corner of the park children played on chutes and swings under the watchful eyes of adoring parents. In another, dads and sons, and moms and daughters, pedalled tiny carriages around an overhead monorail. Beyond the fence that marked the boundary of the Tiantan Traffic Park, skyscrapers and tower blocks rose pale and colourless into a burned out sky. Somewhere above the mist, the sun was trying to push its way through, and it was sticky warm.

They swung around again past the entrance gate, where three-foot models of Goofy and Mickey Mouse and Donald

Duck and Pinocchio caused Xinxin no end of amusement. She gazed at them in delight as they passed, and Margaret had to grab the wheel to prevent them from mounting the sidewalk. They passed stone statues of a boy reclining and a girl dancing, and Xinxin swung them back into the main drag that bisected the park. She showed remarkable control of the tiny vehicle, and Margaret thought she would have no trouble getting a job as a taxi-driver in Beijing. They took a left, heading towards the open shed where the toy cars and motorbikes were collected and returned, then right again, past an area under construction. A workmen's grey van was parked there beside a mechanical digger. Xinxin made another round of the park, and Margaret just sat back and enjoyed the ride. She had not felt this relaxed or this happy in a long time. She felt nothing but warmth and affection for little Xinxin. The only cloud on her happiness was a distant ache somewhere inside for a child of her own, and a sense of loss over the child she might once have borne.

They went around for a fourth time, and as they turned right at the gate and along the top end, Margaret made Xinxin stop outside the toilet block. She made it clear to the child that she was to wait there with the car. Margaret would only be a moment. Xinxin nodded vigorously and watched as Margaret hurried up the path and into the ladies' washroom. She could have been no more than two minutes, but when she came out Xinxin was gone. Margaret cursed. She was sure the child had understood that she was not to move. She looked left and right and saw a green car and a yellow one, and a blue three-wheeled motorbike negotiating the roundabout at the far end of the main street. Several of the green benches along the sidewalks were occupied by elderly people, or students with their heads buried in books. She could hear the shriek and laughter of children and a babble of adult voices from the play area at the far side of the park. Margaret could not have said what it was exactly, but there was something in the absolute normality of everything that started pushing panic buttons in her head. Everything was normal, except for the fact that Xinxin was nowhere to be seen.

Margaret called out her name. Once, twice. And then she positively yelled it. Heads turned in her direction, and she started running along the main street, looking left and right for the little red car and Xinxin with her familiar pink dress and hair in bunches. She stopped at the first roundabout as the workers' grey van she had seen earlier cruised slowly past her towards the exit. And then she saw the car. It was sitting at an angle in the middle of a parallel street about fifty metres away, next to the area under development. Margaret sprinted towards it, calling Xinxin's name again. The car was empty. It had about it a sense of abandonment, the wheels turned hard left to full lock. The elderly couple she had noticed before were still sitting on their bench about twenty metres further down the road. She ran towards them. "What happened to the little girl? Did you see where the little girl went?" she called breathlessly. They looked at her, a little alarmed, as if they thought she might be insane. "For God's sake, can't you speak English!" The panic was rising now in her throat, constricting her breathing. The couple looked at her blankly. Margaret pointed back along the street to the abandoned car. They looked and then shook their heads, uncomprehending.

She gave up and ran back towards the collect and return point where they had picked up the car half an hour before. There was a small group of parents and children gathered around the office window paying for cars. And then Margaret saw Xinxin at the far side of the lot sitting on a yellow motor-bike.

Her knees nearly folded under her with relief. "Xinxin!" she shouted and ran towards the child. But Xinxin wasn't paying her any attention, and as Margaret got close and called again the child turned, startled, and Margaret saw that it was not Xinxin after all. She had the same high-gathered bunches, but her dress was pale green. The little girl looked alarmed and began crying. The adults at the office window turned and glared in Margaret's direction, and in her heart Margaret knew then that Xinxin was gone. "Oh, God," she wailed. "Oh, God, help me, please. Someone please help me."

Rain wept from the sky like the tears that ran down Margaret's cheeks. She sat stock still, staring into an abyss, a black hole that was her own personal hell. She was numb from the shock of it, choked still by disbelief. In two short minutes a child had vanished and her world had come to an end.

Police radios crackled somewhere nearby. Uniformed officers combed the park for clues. A line of mothers and fathers and children stood outside the gatehouse waiting to be interviewed. Shock and fear stole among the adults who knew that a child had gone and that it could so easily have been one of theirs. The comfort and security of their lives had been shattered. The Disney characters that stood clustered on the grassy bank just inside the gate seemed only to mock them now. In the street outside, a huge crowd was gathering as news spread through the shops and apartments in the surrounding streets. More than a dozen police vehicles were drawn up at the sidewalk, and already the traffic cops were arriving to take over crowd control. A fast food store on the other side of the tree-lined Zunyi Road, which advertised "Metro Sandwiches New York Style," was doing brisk business.

There was a slightly hysterical pitch to Li's voice as he barked commands at uniformed officers. He had been on the scene within twenty minutes of Margaret's call. It was now an hour since Xinxin had gone missing. With the exception of a few terse questions, he had barely spoken to Margaret. She knew he blamed her. She blamed herself. You cannot leave a six-year-old child on its own anywhere, at any time.

And yet it had felt so safe here.

She reflected on how, finally, in near hysterics, she had found a middle-aged man who spoke a little English. The alarm had been raised, the police called, and word spread through the park that a child had vanished. Everyone, then, had started to search for Xinxin. The women at the gate had not seen her leave. They would have seen her for sure, they said. And yet she was nowhere to be found within the park.

A red-faced uniformed officer approached Li at a run. "There's been a development, Boss, you'd better come to the gatehouse." Li followed him quickly to the small concrete building at the gate, green canopies shading door and windows. They passed the line of parents and kids, and ducked inside. Three undernourished-looking men stood smoking in the tiny office, engaged in animated discussion with another two uniformed officers. They were dressed in blue workmen's overalls. They had dirty faces and big, callused workers' hands. One of them was older, with thinning hair. The other two had thick untidy mops speckled with plaster dust. The older man spoke for them.

"We just got here, Chief," he said nervously. "We didn't know."

"Didn't know what?" The dark fear that lurked in Li's heart was making him aggressive.

"That the van was missing. The boss just sent us to get it."

"Hold on." Li put up a hand to stop him. "Start from the beginning. Who are you?"

"We work for the parks department. On contract from the street committee. You know, sometimes they got work for us, sometimes they don't. Anyway, we was here this morning, demolishing that old building on the far side of the park. We loaded up the lorry with the debris and drove it down to an in-fill site way over in Pudong. Two of us had come in the van, but we had to leave it here when we took the crap away. The boss just told us half an hour ago that we better go get it." He hawked a gob of phlegm into his throat and was about to spit it on the floor when he thought better of it and reluctantly swallowed instead. He dragged his sleeve across his brow to wipe away the sweat. "Anyway, we get here and the place is crawling with cops. Takes us ages to persuade that bossy big bastard out there to let us in to get the van. Eventually they let Mao Jun here in to fetch it." He nodded towards one of the younger men. "Only it's not there."

"You mean someone's taken it?" Li asked.

The man shrugged exaggeratedly. "Well, I don't figure it drove off all by itself."

Li glanced quickly at the other uniforms in the office. "Anyone see it leave?"

One of them nodded. "The woman at the ticket desk said it went out not long before the alarm got raised about the kid." He pulled a face. "But she didn't see who was driving it."

Li turned back to the workers. "It couldn't have been one of your people?"

"Shit, no. There's only us and the boss in our unit."

"What about keys?"

"What about them?"

"Well, was it locked?"

"Naw, the keys was in the ignition," the man said. He shrugged again. "We didn't figure there was any danger of the kids taking off in it."

Li drew in a deep breath to steady himself as he tried to take in the implications of all this. A grim-faced Dai rapped sharply on the door and squeezed into the overcrowded office. "We're getting reports of some foreign guy seen sprinting down Ziyun Road towards the Yan'an flyover a little over an hour ago, Chief. Several people saw him."

"Foreign?" Li frowned. "What do you mean by foreign?"

Dai shrugged. "A Westerner. Dark-haired, wearing jeans and a pale-coloured jacket. That's the best description we've got. He was running south down the middle of Ziyun Road. It was kind of unusual, you know, so people noticed. Apparently he was chasing after a light-grey van and actually caught up with it briefly at the junction, banging on the side of it, before it sped off up on to the overhead road. People said he stood for a long time in the middle of the street just breathing real hard. Then he stopped a taxi and got in, and it went off in the same direction as the van."

Li put his hand to his forehead and pressed middle-finger and thumb into his pounding temples to try to alleviate the pain there so that he could think clearly. None of this was making much sense. If the van had been stolen at around the time Xinxin disappeared, did that mean someone had snatched her? And why? What possible reason could there be? He could barely address the thought for the fear it conjured in his mind. But what about the Westerner running down the middle of the road chasing the van? Was it connected? Was it even the same van? He turned to Dai. "See if we can match up the description of the van with the one that's missing."

He waved a hand at the workmen. "These guys might be able to tell us if there was something, anything, distinctive about it. And let's see if we can find the taxi-driver who picked this guy up." He could see the despair etch itself on Dai's face at the thought. There were more than a hundred and seventy-five thousand privately licensed taxis in Shanghai. He added, "Let's get an appeal out on radio and television. Anyone who was in the area who might have seen anything, we want to talk to them."

He found it no easier to breathe outside, and compounded his distress by lighting a cigarette with trembling fingers. His legs were like jelly, his stomach had turned to water, and as the full realisation sank in that Xinxin had not just wandered off, that she might have been kidnapped, he felt fear, like bile, rising in his throat. The sign on the gate read: SPARETIME SCHOOL OF TRAFFIC REGULATIONS FOR CHILDREN. TRAFFIC OFFICE, SHANGHAI POLICE BUREAU. And even as he read it, the characters were blurred by his tears. He was not, he knew, the best person to lead this operation. Every thought, every judgement, was coloured by emotion.

He turned to see Margaret being led to a car by a police-woman. Her face was streaked black with mascara, her eyes red-rimmed and bloodshot. She moved like an automaton, no emotion visible in her expression. Before she stooped to get into the car she turned and saw Li watching her. At that moment he felt something more than anger. It felt like hate. Somewhere, buried so deep inside him as not to make a difference, he knew perhaps that it wasn't really her fault. But every conscious part of him blamed her. Every muscle and sinew strained to scream abuse and blame, to punch and slap and hurt her. She recoiled slightly, as if from a blow, almost as though his darkest thoughts had taken physical form. He made no move towards her, no sign. She got into the car with her misery, and he turned away as it drove off.

IV

Japanese warlords in period costume strutted about a stylised set gesturing wildly at each other, eyes staring and burning with a kind of madness. Chinese subtitles flashed on and off the screen, lines of tiny characters that could not possibly be read in the allotted time. The sound on the television was switched to mute, and its flickering luminescence was the only light in the room.

Margaret sat on the edge of the bed, close to a phone which had resolutely refused to ring all evening. In her hand she clutched a tumbler of whisky. She had worked her way through all the miniatures in the mini-bar, and was now on to the Scotch. But it didn't seem to matter how much she drank, she couldn't get drunk. Oblivion was all she sought, and yet it remained elusive, despite her best efforts.

Her mouth was dry, and the pain thumped in her head with every beat of her heart, each pulse a reminder of her guilt, of her shame, of her failure. Responsibility for a young life had been placed in her hands today and she had not lived up to her obligations. She was not fit to be a mother. She was not fit to live. She remembered once, during her time as an intern, losing a patient in the emergency room. A young woman, the victim of a knife attack. Margaret had been incapable of stopping the internal bleeding. It wasn't her fault, but it had been a turning point in her life, a moment when she realised that no matter how well trained, no matter how experienced, control of that moment which ultimately decided between life and death was never really in your hands.

But today, Xinxin's life had been in her hands. She had had absolute control and failed to exercise it. As a young doctor she had turned from the futility of trying to save the living, to the predictability of dissecting the dead. Now all she wanted to do was to give up life completely, her own life, and find some escape in the final embrace of death, her own death. But she was, she knew, too big a coward for that. And, besides, death would be too lenient a punishment.

She emptied her glass and stood up, crossing unsteadily to the window and drawing back the curtains. Saturday night. Nanjing Road was filled with people and traffic. She looked down at the crowd below her and wished that she were one of them, freed from the burden of guilt and fear for a child she had failed. But, then, who knew what pain other people carried in their heads, what private grief, what personal hell. She would not be the only person suffering in the world tonight. But that knowledge did nothing to take away the pain.

She was haunted by the look in Li's eyes as she got into the car outside the park. She had never felt such a searing look, so filled with hurt and darkness and hate. It had reached inside her and burned itself into her soul, and it was smouldering there still.

Now she turned away from the window and the thought, fumbling in the dark to the mini-bar. But she had finished all the little bottles, and they rattled emptily away from her clutching fingers. She wondered if maybe Jack would be in the bar looking for her. He must have heard the news by now. There had been appeals on radio and television all night. He was, perhaps, the only person in Shanghai who might not blame her for what had happened. But she was not sure she deserved that. She caught a glimpse of herself in a mirror and thought for a moment she was looking at an apparition. There was a deathly pallor in her face, eyes sunken and ringed with dark smudges, and for the first time in her life she saw herself looking like her grandmother. Her father's mother. She had never before seen the resemblance, and for one brief alcoholic moment she had actually believed she was her grandmother's ghost. She let out a tiny, involuntary cry and looked quickly away. She lifted her key card and hurried out into the brightly lit hall.

Jack was not in the bar. As usual it was deserted. Margaret slipped stiffly on to a barstool and ordered a vodka tonic. And she knew there would be no sympathy or redemption for her tonight as Xinxin's face swam up with the bubbles through the tonic to feed her worst fears of what had become of the child.

The yellow light of the streetlamps on the overhead road fell into Li's bedroom through nicotine-stained net curtains. The headlamps of vehicles on the road raked the window at irregular intervals, and a blue neon light flashed intermittently somewhere close by. He had placed the phone on the table next to his chair. It was nearly midnight. He had not slept for nearly forty hours. His eyes were on fire, and there was a dull ache behind them. The room was full of smoke, and his ashtray filled to overflowing. All the radio and television appeals had turned up nothing new, and he had finally left 803 an hour ago at the insistence of the detectives on night shift. They promised to call the moment they had anything fresh.

In the hours after Xinxin had vanished, he had played out every nightmare scenario in his mind until he had become so numbed that nothing seemed to affect him any more. He had been over and over every last detail, examined and re-examined the statements of everyone questioned at the park. None of it had brought him any closer to an understanding of what had happened or why. Someone, clearly, had grabbed the child and made off with her in the stolen workmen's van. Minutes later, a Westerner had been seen chasing that same van down a nearby street, banging on its side. They had neither found the van nor made any progress in identifying the Westerner. And Li was simply no longer able to think clearly.

He sat in the silence smoking cigarette after cigarette, concentrating hard on trying to keep the nightmares at bay.

A knock at the door startled him. He jumped up and hurried across the room to open it. Mei-Ling was in the hall, holding a carrier bag with steam rising from it, the smell of food carried in the vapour. "My dad got them to prepare you some stuff at the restaurant."

"I'm not hungry."

"You've got to eat, Li Yan." She pushed gently past him and closed the door. She laid the bag on the table and started taking out dishes of food in cardboard cartons, and placed two cans of beer beside them. She paused then and looked at his swollen eyes as he stood, hangdog, in the middle of the room, like a man in a trance. "I'm so sorry," she said. His eyes were glazed and gazing off into some unimaginable middle-distance. But he acknowledged her with the slightest nod of his head. "The food's there if you want it. You know where I am if you need to call me."

She stopped to squeeze his hand, and then turned towards the door, but he grabbed her arm and held her fast. He was still unable to meet her eyes. "Don't go," he said, and she turned back, and after only a moment's hesitation slipped her arms about his waist and pushed her head into his chest so that he could rest his head on hers. His arms enveloped her, and she felt rather than heard his sobs.

They were standing in a building site, not unlike the one in Lujiazui where they had found the bodies of the eighteen women. The broken stumps of an abandoned concrete foundation stuck out of the ground like bad teeth. The whole site was awash with mud. Only, the mud was frozen solid. Every attempt to break it with shovel and pick had failed. Now a big man with a yellow hard hat was wielding a pneumatic drill, and freeing chunks of frozen mud from around a central post with a plank of wood strapped across it like a Christian cross. The letter had said she would be here, under the mud, a temporary grave beneath the sign of a foreign religion.

From between the splintering wedges of mud, a little arm flopped out, pink and cold, the hand open, palm up. And as the man in the hard hat began to drill afresh, Li screamed at him to stop. One of the fingers had moved. But the workman couldn't hear him, and he drilled on. Long piercing bursts of vibrating metal on ice, right into the heart of the little girl beneath the mud.

Li woke, still yelling, and with the sound of the phone filling the room. He was lying on top of the bed, fully dressed, sunlight streaming in through the open window along with the roar of the traffic on Yan'an Viaduct Road. Mei-Ling was crossing the room to answer the phone. He was immediately aware of the warm impression she had left in the bed beside him. So she had stayed all night. He took a deep breath and felt the phlegm of too many cigarettes crackle in his chest. He could not believe he had slept. Last night it had felt possible that he might never sleep again.

He became aware of Mei-Ling's voice. "When was this?" she was saying into the phone. "And have they recovered the van?" A moment as she listened, then, "Well, I hope the

uniforms didn't touch anything before forensics got there . . .
Good. We'll be straight over." She hung up and turned to Li,
clearly energised. "They found the van." He sat up, rubbing
his face and trying to clear the sleep from his mind. She said,
"But even better . . . the guy who took it? They think they've
got him on video tape."

The flashing red light on the dash on Mei-Ling's Santana created a strobing effect in the car. Her siren wailed through
the early morning quiet of this Shanghai Sunday. The streets
were almost deserted. The city was just waking up. Margaret
sat dazed in the back of the car, her head thick and sore, a
foul taste in her mouth after several bouts of vomiting during
the night. She hoped she was not going to be sick again. The
strobe effect of the red light was not helping.

She had been shocked by Li's appearance when he turned
up at her hotel. His eyes red and puffy, his cheeks pale and
blotched. And he had been taken aback by her appearance,
too. But she had not had the courage to look in a mirror. There
had been developments, he had said. She was needed, in case
she could make an identification. He had not told her anything
further, except that they were going to the Police Command
Centre to view video tapes. And now she sat in the silence of
the car, afraid to ask what the developments were. Mei-Ling
had not even acknowledged her, and Li had not spoken since
they left the hotel.

The Command Centre was in a fourteen-storey tower block
on the corner of Jianguo Road and Ruijin Road next to Ruijin
Hospital. Mei-Ling showed her pass at the gatehouse, and the
gates swung open to admit them to a car park bounded by
palm trees and potted plants. They ran up steps to the main

entrance and took the elevator to the third floor. The Deputy
Commander was waiting to meet them in the hall. They shook
hands and he led them through glass doors to the operations
room. Rows of desks lined with computer terminals faced fifteen giant projection video screens on the far wall. They were
flanked on each side by eight smaller television screens which
flickered at regular intervals from street scene to street scene,
fed by cameras mounted at key vantage points all over Shanghai. Beneath the screens, facing back into the room, were
eight uniformed officers sitting at terminals taking one-one-oh
police emergency calls. At another desk running the full width
of the room, banks of coloured phones were linked to rows of
fax machines that chattered and printed out screeds of information coming in from police stations around the city. At the
back of the room sat the controllers, who evaluated all incoming information and determined what pictures were relayed
on to the big screens.

The Deputy Commander introduced them to a grim-faced
middle-aged man in a green uniform buttoned up to the neck
who sat at the centre of the back row, a bank of knobs and
switches and sliders in front of him, a microphone on a flex-
ible gooseneck projecting towards him from his console. "Officer Su is the senior duty controller," he said. And to Su, "Do
you want to take them through it?"

Su nodded and addressed himself to Li. "Mid-afternoon yesterday we had a serious road accident at the Zhongshan-Wuyi
intersection, just where the slip road feeds down to the Hu Xi
Stadium. A lorry swerved to avoid a cyclist, hit the kerb and
overturned, spilling its load of timber all over the roadway.
Several private vehicles were unable to stop and there was a
multiple pile-up."

Margaret had no idea what he was saying, and Li seemed none the wiser. He said, "What's this got to do with the little girl being snatched at the traffic park?"

Su said, "We have a camera on that intersection. Normally we only record from these cameras in the event of an incident. So in this case we have more than an hour of recorded tape of the intersection following the accident." He reached for a pack of cigarettes on the desk and offered them around. When no one took him up on his offer, he lit up himself. "One of my people was monitoring all incoming information following events at the Tiantan Traffic Park yesterday. In the early hours of this morning he had an idea. It was quiet, and he had nothing much else to do. So he ran the tape of the Zhongshan–Wuyi intersection. It's less than half a mile from the park, and eyewitnesses had reported seeing the grey van heading north, in the direction of the stadium. That was about half an hour after the accident. He figured there was a good chance we might have caught the van on tape." He took a long pull on his cigarette. "Turned out we caught a lot more than that."

He leaned forward and threw some switches. Nine of the fifteen projection screens, which had been displaying a map detail of a northern city suburb, switched to one giant black-and-white projection of the tape of the Zhongshan–Wuyi intersection which Su had set to play. The lorry was lying at an angle on one side. Timber was still strewn all over the road. Four private cars with varying degrees of damage had been abandoned in the middle of the carriageway while their owners shouted and gesticulated, clearly attempting to deflect or apportion blame. Traffic cops were already coning off the slip road and a couple of recovery vehicles were parked half on the hard shoulder, hazard lights flashing.

The little group at the back of the control room stood watching the screen expectantly. The picture, blown up to that size, was blurred. Su leaned forward and said, "Watch the screen at the top right." The portion of the picture it carried showed the Wuyi Road intersection, with the stadium rising in the background, almost in the shadow of the overhead road. There were vehicles parked all along one side of it, and traffic was backing up from the slip road. "There," Su said suddenly, pointing. "You see it?" And they saw a light-coloured workmen's van pull out of the stream of traffic going in the opposite direction, and draw into the side of the road. Su stopped the tape then, flicked another couple of switches, and the picture from the top right screen filled the others. The definition was very poor, but they could clearly see the figure of a man jump down from the driver's seat and slide open the side door. He leaned in quickly and lifted out a small limp bundle wrapped in some kind of blanket or tarpaulin. As he carried it to the car parked behind, a little arm fell free, momentarily hanging in the air, just as in Li's nightmare. The man quickly covered it, and dumped the bundle into the trunk of the car.

A slight moan escaped Li's lips in a breath. "It's Xinxin," he whispered.

Until that moment, the man had always had his back to camera. Now, as he turned to get into the driver's door, they saw his face for the first time. The picture was indistinct and very grainy, but it was still possible to make out his flat, high-cheekboned Mongolian features, his long, straggly hair, and the distortion about his mouth that might have been a scar.

Margaret let out a cry that sounded like pain, and they all turned to look at her. Her face was a mask of fear. Her breathing was so rapid and shallow that she could hardly speak.

"What is it?" Li said urgently. "Do you recognise him? Was he in the park?"

"I know him," she gasped. "But not from the park. Oh, my God. Oh, my God, if only I'd known."

Li grabbed her shoulders and almost shook her. "Where have you seen him, Margaret?"

She forced herself to meet his eyes. "The night we were going to have dinner and I fell asleep in my room . . . After I phoned you, it must have been three in the morning or later, I went out to get some air. I went for a walk along the promenade on the Bund." She pointed towards the screen. The controller had frozen the picture on the face. "He was following me. He was close enough to touch me at one point, near the underpass. I saw his face clearly in the light. I got such a fright, I just ran."

"You never said anything? Why didn't you tell me?"

She shrugged hopelessly. "I don't know. I didn't think it was important. A stupid woman getting freaked because she saw a man with a hare-lip in the middle of the night." She closed her eyes and shook her head in despair. "But I saw him again. At the time I thought it wasn't possible, that I must have imagined it. It was only a fleeting glimpse."

"Where, Margaret? Where did you see him?" Li's voice was insistent and commanding.

"In Beijing," she said. "At the airport. When I was coming back with Xinxin."

There was a moment of stunned disbelief, and then Mei-Ling said, "Did you say he had a hare-lip?" Margaret nodded. Mei-Ling turned to Li. "Li Yan, you remember the description Sun Jie gave us of the man his wife said was following her?" And Li remembered every detail of that moment, from the sadness on Sun Jie's face to the very words he had used to recall his wife's description. *She said he looked like a Mongolian, and he had a real ugly scar on his upper lip,* he had said. *She thought it could have been a hare-lip.*

V

Margaret had spent more than an hour with the police artist at 803. A computer-enhanced print of the Mongolian's face had been taken from the video. But it was still blurred and lacking definition. Margaret had provided the detail for the artist to give it the definition required to make it recognisable. She looked now at the finished graphic on the sheet of paper that trembled in her hand. It was eerily like the face that had confronted her that night on the Bund. There was something in the eyes that was as chilling now as it had been then. The fact that this was the man who had snatched Xinxin did not even bear thinking about.

"Is it okay?" Mei-Ling asked. Margaret looked up at her and nodded. Mei-Ling took the sheet from her. "I'll get it copied and circulated." She left the office, and Li and Margaret were alone for the first time since Xinxin had been kidnapped.

Li could hardly bring himself to look at her. He remembered, with a sense of shame now, the hatred and blame that had consumed him yesterday afternoon and through the night. "I'm sorry," he said at length.

She looked surprised. "What for?"

"For blaming you."

She shook her head. "It was my fault."

"No." He moved around the desk towards her. "I don't understand it all," he said, "but this was no random kidnapping. The hare-lip guy was following you. All the way to Beijing. Just like he followed the acrobat, just like he probably followed all the others. If he hadn't got Xinxin in the park, he would have got her some other place, some other time." He clenched his fists and let out a howl of frustration. "Why? Why Xinxin? What could they possibly want with her?" And he immediately flinched from the answer that came to him.

Margaret took his hand. "We'll find her, Li Yan. We will."

He looked at her, dry eyes all cried out, and they embraced, holding tight for comfort, for hope. Somehow everything was linked. There had to be an answer, and there had to be a way to find it.

The door opened, and Mei-Ling stopped briefly in the doorway as Li and Margaret broke apart, then she stepped into the room. Her face gave no clue as to her feelings. She said in Chinese, "Forensics have found several hairs in the back of the van. We need some of Xinxin's for comparison so that we can confirm it really was her we saw on the tape."

Li thought for a moment. "Her hair brush," he said. "There's bound to be some caught in it. It's in her hotel room." Mei-Ling nodded and went without another word.

"What was that about?" Margaret asked.

"Checking samples of Xinxin's hair against hair found in the van."

It was routine. It was the kind of thing they had both been involved in many times as a matter of course. But this was Xinxin's hair, and the picture it conjured up of her tiny prone body wrapped in a blanket and lying on the floor of a battered old van, was almost too painful to contemplate. Margaret wondered briefly how she had been sedated. Something quick. Chloroform on a handkerchief? Whatever it was, if the Mongolian had really snatched all these other women, he would be well practised in its use.

Li lit a cigarette. Not because he had any desire for one – he had smoked till he was sick of smoking – but simply for something to do, a mechanical act, a routine to cling to. Margaret went to open a window. The air in the office was already sour with stale smoke. She turned back from the window and saw the box of Chai Rui's possessions sitting on Li's desk. The photograph which Li had dug out from the bottom of it was lying on top. For a moment it seemed to Margaret that her heart had stopped. In a very small voice she asked, "Who's that in the photograph?"

Li, distracted by other thoughts, glanced at the box. "Chai Rui," he said. "She's the one whose body you re-examined in Beijing. That's the stuff that was left in her apartment in Shanghai."

"Oh, my God," she whispered, and Li looked at her, suddenly alarmed.

"What is it?"

"The guy in the picture with her . . ."

Li frowned. "You know him?"

"His name's Jack Geller." Her thoughts were awash with confusion.

"Who the hell is Jack Geller?" Li asked, incredulous that Margaret should know him.

"He's an American journalist," she said. "He's been haunting me since I arrived in Shanghai, looking for an inside line on this story."

"In the name of the sky, Margaret, why didn't you tell me?" Li's voice was filled with accusation.

"It didn't seem important," she said. "I never told him anything." And she gave Li a look. "And anyway, you were busy with Mei-Ling." The words were barely out of her mouth before she was hit by a sudden realisation. "Oh, Jesus . . ." She looked at Li, horrified by the implications. "It was Jack who told me about the Tiantan Traffic Park."

Li glared at Margaret in disbelief for some seconds. "Then he's got to be involved," he said finally. "Have you any idea where we can find him?"

"No, I . . ." She paused. She had been going to say she had no idea. He had always sought *her* out. But she remembered then that first meeting in the airport. It felt like a very long time ago. He had handed her a dog-eared business card. At first she had refused to take it, but he had insisted. *You never know when you might want to give me a call*, he had said. And Margaret had told him she couldn't imagine a single circumstance when she would. Never in her wildest dreams could she have imagined this. She searched quickly in her purse, and there it was. JACK GELLER *Freelance Journalist*. It listed his address, and home and mobile numbers. Li snatched it from her.

Geller's apartment was on the eighteenth floor of a modern tower block in Xinzha Road, a few minutes north of the Shanghai Centre. Dozens of other blocks sprang out of the squat, two-storey workers' housing that spread in every direction around them in narrow, treeless streets. The uniformed security officer in Geller's block took a long time examining the search warrant Li handed him. The ink from the Municipal Procuratorate was barely dry on it. He glanced uneasily at Margaret, and then at Dai and Mei-Ling and the two detectives who accompanied them. Weapons, signed out from the armoury at 803 only fifteen minutes earlier by Section Chief Huang, bulged visibly in their holsters beneath loose-fitting jackets. Only Li and Margaret were unarmed. "Okay," he said at length. "I'll let you in."

They rode up in the elevator to the eighteenth floor in tense silence. On the landing a curved panorama of windows gave out on to a spectacular view of the city below. A little sunshine was forcing its way through the mist, cutting sharp shadows down the sides of buildings. Cranes rising along the river bank were just visible in the far distance. At the door of Geller's apartment, the detectives drew their pistols and stood either side of it ready to enter. Li and Margaret stood a little further down the hall. The security guard, now very nervous, quickly unlocked the door and stepped back. The detectives were also nervous. Mei-Ling nodded, and they burst in, the first two fanning off to the sides, the second two covering the middle. They yelled at the tops of their voices as they entered. Margaret had no idea what they were shouting. But the screaming didn't stop as they moved from room to room in a rehearsed pattern. Doors banged and feet slammed down on polished wooden floors.

Margaret followed Li into an entrance hall. They could hear the armed detectives in a room further along it. A door opened into an L-shaped living room. It was very spartan. Two patterned settees sat in the middle of the floor. A large coffee table strewn with papers and empty coffee mugs stood between them. A single dining chair was pushed against a naked white wall next to an electric point, a coffee maker sitting at an angle on the woven seat. Some framed pictures leaned against the far wall waiting to be hung. There was an antique dresser on the opposite wall, but its shelves were bare. Beige curtains hung from floor to ceiling on either side of sliding glass doors that led to a balcony. It felt like a house that someone was either moving out of or moving into.

Margaret suddenly became aware that a silence had descended on the apartment. Then a single voice called out.

It was Mei-Ling. Li grabbed Margaret's arm. "Come on," he said, and they hurried down the hall, past a door that lay open to reveal a study with a cluttered desk and a desktop computer on a tubular stand. A glass door gave on to a modern kitchen that looked pristine and unused, except for a bucket full of empty beer bottles in the middle of the floor. The detectives had left the bathroom door lying open. A damp towel hung over the shower cabinet, a pair of pyjamas hung from hooks on the tiled wall above the toilet. Dirty underwear lay strewn on the floor. Everywhere the white walls were naked, undressed. And although the air was warm, the apartment felt cold. It did not seem to fit with the Jack Geller that Margaret knew. And she realised that, of course, she really knew nothing about him at all. There was an impermanence about the place that made her think he had not so much been living here as camping out. She felt sick. It was beyond both imagination and comprehension to think that he might have had something to do either with the kidnapping of Xinxin or the murder of all those women. Or both.

At the end of the hall they entered the bedroom. There was an outer dressing room with a settee and a television set on a table. In the main part of the bedroom the bed was unmade beneath a large wall tapestry. Mei-Ling and the other three detectives stood in the archway between the two rooms, blocking out the view of the window. Li and Margaret pushed through and stopped dead. Margaret gasped in horror. Geller was kneeling in front of the sliding glass doors that gave out on to the balcony, facing back into the room. His arms were raised above his head in grotesque parody of a crucified man, pulled to each side by cord tied to either end of the curtain rod. Although he was silhouetted against the city spread out below, she saw immediately that he was naked. There was a ten-inch wound drawn horizontally across his belly from which his small intestine hung in a shiny mass of pale tan distended loops. There was a large pool of sticky blood on the floor at his knees. It was still dripping from his crotch and trickling slowly down his thighs. His head was tipped forward. Margaret knew he was alive because he was still bleeding, but he appeared to be unconscious.

"For Chrissake, will someone call an ambulance," she said. And she moved quickly to the window to try to untie the cord that held him. But it was knotted tight, his weight dragging against it. She heard one of the detectives talking rapidly on his mobile. "Someone got a knife? We've got to cut him down." The desperation she felt was compounded by the knowledge that he was almost certainly going to die. He had lost a huge amount of blood, and his system was probably already fevered by bacterial infection from the intestine.

She was almost shocked when he lifted his head, and she found herself looking into his glassy eyes. "No," he whispered. "Leave me."

"Jack, we've got to get you to a hospital."

An almost imperceptible shake of the head. "Too late."

She knelt on the floor in front of him and felt his blood soaking into her jeans. She put her arms around his chest and strained to lift him slightly to take the weight off his arms. Li cut the cord, and then helped her lay him on the floor. "Something for his head," she said sharply. And Mei-Ling hurried to get a cushion from the settee in the dressing room. Margaret slipped it under his neck to support his head.

"There's an ambulance on the way," Dai said.

Geller was shivering now, a cold sweat gathering in the creases of a forehead furrowed by pain. "Who did this to you, Jack?" Margaret asked softly.

He gazed up at her like a mournful dog desperate for for-giveness from an angry master. "I've been following you," he said. He swallowed with difficulty. "I was there at the park . . . Other side of the fence." He swallowed again. "I saw him grab her, but I couldn't . . . couldn't . . ." His breathing was becoming laboured. "Chased the van. Nearly got him."

Margaret held his hand. It was as cold as ice. "Did he do this to you?"

Geller nodded. "Saw me."

And Margaret realised that if the Mongolian had been fol-lowing her, he must have known who Jack was. She could have wept then. Jack had nothing to do with the kidnapping of Xinxin. He had tried to save her. But, still, none of it made sense. "Why were you following me, Jack?"

He tried to smile. "You wouldn't help me . . . Had to know."

"Know what?" She glanced at Li for some help in under-standing this. But he just shook his head helplessly. She turned back to Geller and wiped the perspiration from his forehead with the back of her hand. "We found a photograph of you with one of the dead girls." And whatever agony he had suf-fered up until then intensified. He screwed up his eyes and let out a small cry of pain. After a moment he opened them again and she saw that they were wet with tears.

"Chai Rui?" he said. Margaret nodded. He swallowed hard. "She was my little sister." And he started sobbing. "Mom and my stepdad were in a . . . a road accident . . . He died straight off . . . she lasted a few days. That's when I came back from the States . . ." He was fighting now for his breath. "Last thing she made me promise . . . was to look after Cherry." He shook his head. "Really fucked up, didn't I?"

Li said, "Ask him what happened to her little girl."

Geller's eyes flicked up towards him. "With friends," he managed to say.

"Oh, Jack," Margaret said, "why didn't you just tell me all this?"

"Scared," he said. "Thought she might be one of them . . . Missing all that time." The tears ran from the corners of his eyes down each side of his head. "Didn't want it to be true." And his body was racked by sobbing. "Poor Cherry." And he stopped suddenly and opened his eyes and stared straight into Margaret's. "You get them," he said. "Whoever it was . . . you get them."

Margaret's own tears dragged like hot wires down her cheeks. "I'll get them," she said. And she looked up at Li. "We'll get them." Li nodded grimly, and by the time she looked back at Jack he was dead.

And she knelt there in his blood and wept for him. Poor Jack. She remembered their first encounter at the airport, his story about the racecourse, his juvenile amusement at the LONG DONG GARDEN. She remembered their drinks at the bar in the Peace Hotel. He had been amusing, attractive. *Did anyone ever tell you you're very attractive for someone who cuts up people for a living?* he had asked her. And now he lay dead on the floor, disembowelled because he had tried to save a little girl's life, because he had wanted to know what had become of his little sister. And he had died with grief in his heart, and guilt for having failed his mother.

In the distance Margaret heard the siren of the ambulance, and Li helped her gently to her feet.

CHAPTER TWELVE

I

They had their meeting in the room with the skulls. Sightless eyes watched them from glass shelves, and their eternal silence contributed to the hush that filled the room. Almost the entire department was squeezed in. Standing-room only. Huang stood by the door, his face the colour of the yellowed remains in the display cabinets. Mei-Ling had whispered to Li as they entered that his wife was not expected to see out the day. Smoke from dozens of cigarettes hung over the table like a shroud. All eyes were on Li. He saw in them curiosity, sympathy, pity, and it was all he could do to keep his voice from cracking.

In slow, measured sentences, he described the discovery of Jack Geller in the apartment in Jingan District, and Geller's dying identification of Xinxin's kidnapper as his killer. Eyes flickered down to the dozens of images of the Mongolian that were scattered around the table. The Mongolian, Li said, was also suspected of stalking, and perhaps abducting, one of the eighteen women found in the mass grave at Lujiazui. He had also been stalking the American pathologist, Margaret Campbell.

He took another moment to collect himself. "There is no doubt in my mind," he said, "that the murders of the eighteen women in Shanghai, the one in Beijing, and the abduction of my niece, are inextricably linked." The implications of Li's simple statement went through the mind of every detective in the room, and their silence so filled it that it seemed to expel all oxygen. Someone at the back opened a window. "So," Li said, "does anyone have any ideas?"

Dai cleared his throat and everyone looked at him expectantly. He blushed. "I got a confession, Chief," he said. "Remember you asked me to check through all those files of missing girls to see if any of them had a nickname that matched the one on that bracelet we found at Jiang's place?"

Li inclined his head slightly. "I remember."

"Well, I delegated. You know, we all had so much on our plates, I was still tracking down the Zhang family from Jiang's home town . . . I didn't think you'd mind."

"What's your point, Dai?" Li asked impatiently.

Dai glanced at another, younger officer across the table. "You want to tell him, Qian?"

The young detective remained composed. He nodded and looked at Li. "I found a match this morning," he said. He opened up a file on the table in front of him. "A girl called Ji Li Rong. She was a second-year student at Jiaotong University. Disappeared about nine months ago. Everyone called her *Moon*. I spoke to her parents. It was her father who first called her that because when she was a baby her face was round like the moon."

"Did you show him the bracelet?" Li asked.

Qian nodded. "It was hers all right."

It was the smallest chink of light in a dark place, but to Li, after so long in that place, it was blinding. However, his face betrayed no emotion. He said, "Can we find out if this girl ever had an abortion?"

Dai said, "We thought of that. I got Qian to go back and check."

"She had an abortion halfway through her first year," Qian said. "Didn't want an unwanted pregnancy to get in the way of her education." And yet in some way that Li still did not understand, that abortion had cost the girl her life.

He said, "We need to get them to look at the bodies. Identify her, if they can."

Dai said, "They're on their way to the mortuary right now."

And Li felt his stomach lurch. He thought of the fourteen corpses still unidentified, the horrors that awaited these poor people as they tried to discern the features of their little girl from the pulp of decaying human flesh that would be wheeled out by men in white coats and rubber gloves. But if they were able to make that identification, the investigation would have come full circle, ending where it had begun, with a medical student working as a night watchman on a building site. Li shook his head at the irony.

Dai cleared his throat again. "There's one other thing, Chief," he said. "I'm not sure how important it is. And I guess I should have spotted it before now." He made a face. "But, then, probably we all should have." And in this there was a hint of accusation to deflect guilt. "It was right there all the time on the goddamn kid's résumé."

Li frowned. "What are you talking about?"

"The medical student," Dai said. "Jiang Baofu. You know, all those vacation jobs he had, working in various hospitals and clinics?" He paused. "One of them was the Shanghai World Clinic." Li glanced immediately at Huang standing by the door. The Section Chief was impassive. Dai said unnecessarily, "You know, Cui Feng's place."

Margaret sat alone in Li's office. She had showered off all the blood, scrubbed and scrubbed, and watched it wash away down the drainer. But like Lady Macbeth, she still felt its taint. Only, this was no dream. Her face was pale and without even a trace of make-up, her hair still damp and scraped back. She had on the khaki cargoes she had worn the day she lost Xinxin, and another pair of trainers. Her black tee-shirt contrasted sharply with the whiteness of her skin. She looked at her hands and saw the first lines of age there, a prominence of the knuckles as the full flesh of youth thinned and became sinewy and tough. There was a thickening of her neatly trimmed nails, and the half-moons beneath her cuticles appeared paler than usual. Even as she looked at them, her hands started to shake, and she pressed them palm down on the table to make them stop.

But she could no longer focus on her hands, or the shadows on the wall where once posters and papers had been pinned, or the sound of the rain as it fell again from the heavens and battered on the window. Pictures that she had fought so hard to displace kept forcing their way into her mind. Pictures of Jack in his final moments as he lay in his own blood on the floor. Pictures of Xinxin laughing with joy as she manoeuvred her little red car around the miniature roads in the park. Pictures of a dark-skinned Mongolian face with an ugly hare-lip stretched across protruding brown teeth. An endless procession of half-decayed faces on autopsy tables. And closing her eyes could not shut these pictures out.

She was startled when the door burst open and Li strode in. His expression told her immediately that something had happened. Mei-Ling followed closely in his wake. Margaret stood up quickly. "What is it?"

But all Li's attention was focused on the telephone, and as he reached his hand towards it, it began to ring, almost as though he had willed it to do so. He snatched it from its cradle. He listened intently for several seconds, then there was a brief, staccato exchange before he hung up. Margaret could see that he was drawing quick, shallow breaths. "Jiang Baofu," he said.

"The medical student?"

Li nodded grimly. "A bracelet belonging to one of the dead girls was found in his apartment." He turned to Mei-Ling. "The parents just identified her," he said in Chinese. And to Margaret, "He also spent two summer vacations working at a clinic belonging to Cui Feng."

Margaret was still attempting to take all this in. "An abortion clinic?"

Li shook his head. "No. Cui has a clinic that deals exclusively in the treatment of foreigners. Insurance work."

Margaret's confusion deepened. "I don't understand. What's the connection?"

"That's what we're about to ask him," Li said.

Jiang Baofu's hair was gelled and spiky. Li could smell the perfume of the gel. He was wearing his long coat, shoulders peppered with dark spots of rain. He had on the same high leather boots he had been wearing the night they first interviewed him in the hut on the building site, his jeans tucked into them at calf height. Li imagined that Jiang thought he looked pretty cool, modelled on one of those Hong Kong rock singers he watched on Channel "V." He did not appear quite as composed as he had during previous interviews. He was leaning back in his chair, trying to convey the same careless attitude of relaxed indifference. But there were lights in his eyes, and they were wide and cautious.

Mei-Ling sat down opposite him, and Li took his time closing the door before approaching the table and pulling up a chair. He made no attempt to switch on the recorder. Instead, he held the boy in a gaze of icy intensity. Jiang shifted uncomfortably. Li said, "My niece was kidnapped yesterday. She is six years old."

There was a long silence before Jiang decided to respond. "Why are you telling me?"

"I want you to know," Li said slowly, "so that you will understand that I mean it when I say if one hair on her head has been harmed, I will tear out your heart and stuff it down your throat." His almost conversational tone gave his words a chilling, believable edge.

Jiang's eyes widened and he sat himself more upright. "I don't know what you mean?"

Li nodded to Mei-Ling and she switched on the cassette recorder. "November twenty-sixth," she said. "Eleven-fifty a.m. Interview with suspect Jiang Baofu. Present Deputy Section Chief Nien Mei-Ling, Section Two, Shanghai Municipal Police, and Deputy Section Chief Li Yan, Section One, Beijing Municipal Police, Criminal Investigation Department."

Jiang's rabbit eyes flickered from one to the other. "Suspect?" His face cracked into a frightened smile. "Hey, you don't really think I did this shit?"

"We have reason to believe," Li said calmly, "that you murdered at least nineteen young women by cutting them open while they were still alive, and then removing vital organs, thereby killing them."

Jiang stared at him for a moment in patent disbelief. And then a sort of calm visibly descended on him. "No," he said. "You're trying it on." His confidence was returning. "Like I said before, you can't think I did it. There's no evidence."

"How can you know that?" Mei-Ling asked.

"Because I didn't do it." This directed at Mei-Ling as if she were an idiot.

Li saw her bridle and stepped in quickly. "We traced the Zhang family from Yanqing," he said. And a hint of concern reappeared in Jiang's eyes.

"And?"

"The daughter doesn't remember you trying to give her a bracelet. In fact she doesn't remember you at all."

Jiang shrugged. "I didn't have much confidence then. You know, it was kind of worship from afar. Not surprising really that she doesn't remember me."

Li placed his forearms very carefully on the table in front of him and leaned forward. "And her nickname isn't *Moon*."

Jiang said, "That's just what I called her. Because she was beautiful, you know, like the moon. She had this lovely, round face . . ."

"Bullshit!" Li's voice reverberated around the walls, and Jiang nearly jumped out of his seat. Li produced the bracelet from his pocket and laid it on the table. "It belonged to a girl called Ji Li Rong. She was a student at Jiaotong University. Her father nicknamed her *Moon* when she was a baby. She was one of the girls we dug out of the mud at Lujiazui. Her parents just identified her at the mortuary."

Jiang stared at the bracelet for a long time. He showed a distinct reluctance to meet Li's eyes again. "It's . . . it's similar," he mumbled, almost to himself. "Maybe I . . . you know, it's possible I picked it up at the site. I just confused it with the other one, you know, for the Zhang girl . . ."

Li said, "I'm going to bring this interview to a close now and have you formally charged with murder."

Jiang's eyes shot up from the bracelet. "No!" he nearly shouted. "You can't. I didn't do it."

"I figure it'll go to trial pretty quickly, given the high-profile nature of the case. That means it'll only be a matter of weeks, Jiang, before they're putting a bullet in the back of your head. Of course, I'll be there to watch. But, really, execution's too good for you. Personally, I'd rather see you rot in a stinking prison cell somewhere for the rest of your unnatural life." He turned to Mei-Ling. "You can switch the recorder off now."

"No," Jiang shouted again, and he quickly held out a hand to prevent her from reaching the recorder. She stopped and waited. There was a long moment of silence. Jiang screwed up his eyes and then, as if angry at having to admit defeat, hissed, "What do you want to know?"

Li said, "I want to know where you got the bracelet. I want to know where you got the money to buy all the fancy clothes and electrical goods and pay for an expensive apartment. I want to know exactly what work you were involved in during two summers at the Shanghai World Clinic."

Jiang went limp, and slumped forward on the table, his head in his hands. Li could see his scalp between the clumped spikes of gelled hair. Then Jiang made himself sit upright. "As long as you understand," he said, "I had nothing to do with killing these women. They wouldn't let me near the theatre. I was never in there once when they were . . . you know, when they had someone in." Finally he dragged his eyes up to meet Li's, making some sort of appeal to be believed. "I didn't even know anything about it until I found all the body parts in the freezer. I mean, hell, there were a lot of bits in there."

"When did you discover this?"

"About a year-and-a-half ago. First summer I was there. I was just an orderly. I mean, I didn't know what they were up to, didn't want to know. Some kind of research or something. I just thought, you know, if they needed space in the freezer I could get rid of the bits for a little extra cash."

"You blackmailed them," Li said.

"No." Jiang was quick to deny it. "It was a . . . business arrangement. I had a night job as a watchman on a building site out west. I knew it would be easy to dump the bodies, and in a few weeks a few thousand tons of concrete would bury them forever."

"How many?" Mei-Ling asked.

"How many what?" Some of Jiang's cockiness was returning.

"Bodies."

He shrugged. "I think there were eleven that first time."

Li felt his stomach turning over. That brought the body count to thirty. "How many times were there, Jiang?"

The boy shrugged vaguely. "Three . . . I guess, four, including the ones you found at Lujiazui."

Both Li and Mei-Ling were shocked into a momentary silence. Finally Li asked in a husky voice, "And how many bodies were there the other two times?"

Now that Jiang had decided to talk, he actually appeared to be enjoying it. He was on a roll. "I think there were fifteen up at Zhabei, and either eight or nine at Zhou Jia Dou over in Pudong again." He scratched his head. "No, I think it was nine there."

They were up to fifty-four now, and had ventured into territory that Li could never have imagined. He glanced at Mei-Ling. She was very pale. He turned back to Jiang. "And all women?"

"Sure."

"Why?"

"I've no idea. Like I said, they kept me at arm's length, you know? Even though I was trained." He smiled ruefully. Then, "But they did let me cut them up afterwards. I offered, you know, for a bit of extra cash. And I was good at it. I would have jointed them, but they didn't want that. Just cut them up, they said." He laughed. "With a goddamn cleaver! Can you imagine? Someone with my skills and they give me a cleaver. But I was good at it. Accurate. Third cervical vertebra. Upper third of the humerus. Mid femur. But your pathologist must know that. What's her name . . . Margaret Campbell? She did all the autopsies, didn't she?"

"Who did you deal with at the clinic?"

"A couple of people."

"Who?"

"I don't know their names. They weren't exactly chatty, know what I mean? And there was this woman from upstairs who always gave me the money. You know, in a big white envelope. Big bucks." He grinned again. "I thought I'd died and gone to heaven."

"It's not heaven you'll be going to," Mei-Ling said grimly.

"What about Cui Feng?" Li asked. "Ever deal with him?"

Jiang looked blank. "Who is he?"

"The boss."

"Oh, him. Naw. He never even spoke to me. He'd walk past you in the corridor, and it was like you weren't even there."

Li said, "Tell me about the bracelet?"

Jiang's smile faded, and for the first time he looked genuinely sad. "She was beautiful," he said. "Of all of them, she was really the most beautiful. Perfect. I don't know how they missed the bracelet. I mean, usually there wasn't as much as a stud earring. But there it was dangling from her wrist when they brought her out." He shook his head. "Broke my heart to see her like that, all cut open. She was so beautiful." He looked from one to the other, appealing for their understanding. "I fell in love with her, you know? Hardest thing I ever had to do was cut her up. But she was dead. Nothing I could do. So I kept the bracelet." He picked it up now and ran it lovingly between his thumb and forefinger, recalling with sadness some scene of unimaginable horror. A young girl murdered, cut open, hacked up. And he had somehow found love in it.

Li looked at him with undisguised disgust. The kid was sick. Crazy. Beyond redemption. He slipped a copy of the graphic of the Mongolian from his folder and pushed it across the table. Jiang drew his attention away from the bracelet to look at it.

"Ugly bastard, isn't he?"

"Do you know him?"

"Never set eyes on him."

And much as he hated to admit it, Li thought the boy was probably telling the truth.

Li's anger at Procurator General Yue hummed across Huang's office. He was exhausted. After more than three hours of detailed interrogation, emotional stress and lack of sleep were crushing down on him, and his patience was at its end. "I don't care who Cui's pals are," he said through clenched teeth, "or how long he's been in the Party, or whether he dresses to the left or to the right. I want that search warrant."

Yue remained calm. He exchanged looks with Section Chief Huang and said, "I understand that the kidnapping of your niece has placed you under extreme stress, Deputy Section Chief Li, and so I am prepared to overlook your behaviour on this occasion."

Li gasped his exasperation. "Don't bloody patronise me!"

Yue continued, unruffled. "You have absolutely no evidence against Comrade Cui, or any of his employees. I can't justify issuing a warrant to search his premises. All you have are the ramblings of a demented medical student who *admits* to hacking up the bodies and burying them at Lujiazui." He stood up, animated for the first time, and gestured to the heavens. "I mean, even if we are to believe him, in an organisation the size of Cui's it is perfectly conceivable that these procedures could have been conducted without Cui's knowledge."

Li would have laughed were it not so tragic. "Have you *been* to the Shanghai World Clinic?" he asked. And without waiting for an answer, "It is a converted villa from the days of the Concession. There are two small operating theatres and a handful of special care beds. It is where Cui has his office." And, echoing Yue's choice of words, "It is *in*conceivable that more than forty women could have been surgically murdered right under his nose without him knowing about it."

Yue waved a hand dismissively. "*If* we are to believe your . . . medical student," he said. "And I see no reason why we should." He took a deep breath. "I don't know what more you need, Li. You have your man right there. It doesn't take much of a leap in imagination to conclude that this young man abducted these women and cut them open for his own perverse pleasures. Probably in the operating room at the Medical University when everyone else had gone for the day."

Li knew that, by addressing Cui as "Comrade," Yue was letting him know that he, too, was a Party member. But it made no difference to Li. He shook his head. "The sample of twine we took from the university didn't match the twine that was used to sew up the women from Lujiazui."

"So?" Yue said. "It was a different ball of twine. The point is, there is nothing to connect Cui to any of this except for the extravagant claims of this lunatic you have in the cells downstairs."

"What about the abortions?"

"We've been over this before," Yue sighed wearily.

"And the Mongolian?"

"Who knows?" The Procurator General shrugged theatrically. "A friend of Jiang's. An accomplice."

"We have nothing that connects the Mongolian to Jiang."

"Or to Cui!"

There was a tense stand-off between the two, and a long silence broken only, in the end, by the ringing of Huang's phone. The Section Chief, who had been sitting listening impassively, answered it quickly. After a short exchange, he hung up and got to his feet. He looked like a man carrying the weight of the world on his shoulders. He said, "I have to go. My wife is dying."

That simple statement of fact was shocking somehow in the context of what had preceded it. Both Li and Yue were chastened by it. "Of course," Yue said. "I'm sorry, Huang."

Huang nodded, lifted his coat from the stand, and hurried out. But somehow he left behind him the ghost of his not yet dead wife, a presence in the room that stood between Li and Yue. For fully a minute neither man spoke. Li crossed to the window and stood staring out at the rain, hands plunged deep in his pockets. For Li, Huang's dying wife was not an issue. For reasons beyond him, but somehow connected to this case, Xinxin had been kidnapped. His first, and most pressing, loyalty had to be to her, and the hope that he could find her kidnappers before they harmed her – if they had not already done so. He turned to face the Procurator General, grimly determined.

He said, "I am taking a team of detectives and forensics officers to the Shanghai World Clinic. I can go either with or without a warrant. If I have to go without, then you will leave me no choice but to charge you with attempting to pervert the course of justice, and I will begin corruption investigations against you."

The Procurator General visibly paled. He was not used to being threatened by a junior law officer. But he was in no doubt that the threat was a real one. He opened his mouth to respond, but Li held up a finger to stop him.

"Don't," Li said, "interrupt me until I am finished." He drew a deep breath. "If I have to, I will take this to the highest authorities in Beijing, and let me assure you that your friendship with some adviser to the Mayor of Shanghai will not afford you the least protection. You may recall that in the last few years a Deputy Mayor of the city of Beijing, a Minister of Agriculture and a Deputy Procurator General have all been executed after being found guilty of corruption charges. I can't claim credit for all three, but I brought the charges against two of them."

Procurator General Yue glared at Li, a deep simmering anger smouldering in his eyes. Li returned the stare, unwavering. Finally Yue said, "Let me assure *you*, Deputy Section Chief Li, that if you fail to find any evidence against Comrade Cui, this is the last time you will ever threaten anyone."

"Does that mean I get the warrant?" Li asked.

Margaret sat at a table in the corner of the canteen watching officers come and go. She had been there for over an hour, ever since Li had insisted on getting an officer to take her there. She knew very little about what was happening except that the medical student had confessed to burying the bodies, and that the women were suspected of being murdered at Cui Feng's foreign residents' clinic. But she was aware that there were politics involved here that she neither knew nor wanted to know anything about.

She was still in a state of shock after the discovery of Geller's body, and as the day slipped away like sand through their fingers she was becoming increasingly despondent about finding Xinxin alive. She had seen first-hand what the Mongolian had done to poor Jack.

Only a handful of the thirty tables in the canteen were occupied, plain-clothed and uniformed officers glancing curiously in her direction, whispered conversations that she could not have understood, even if she had overheard them. The kitchens, behind sliding glass shutters at one end of the room, were no longer serving anything but tea. A bowl of noodles sat almost untouched on the table in front of her, faintly coloured by some indeterminate sauce. She had told Li that she had no appetite, but suspected that he had simply wanted her out of the way for a while.

She looked up as one of a line of glass-panelled doors leading out to the car park opened, and her heart sank as Mei-Ling walked in. The Deputy Section Chief responded vaguely to greetings from her fellow officers, but ran her eyes around the canteen until they alighted on Margaret. She headed for her table and sat down. "Hi," she said.

Margaret nodded cautiously.

Mei-Ling looked at the bowl of noodles. "Not hungry?"

"Not much."

And they sat without speaking for what seemed like a very long time before Mei-Ling said, "I guess you do not like me much."

"About as much as you like me." Margaret faced her down more boldly than she felt.

"We got off on the wrong foot."

"We didn't get off on any kind of foot."

"No . . ." Mei-Ling forced a sad smile. She sighed. "Anyway, I just wanted to say . . . I am sorry."

Margaret was surprised by this, but determined not to show it. "What, sorry that I'm still here?"

Mei-Ling smiled. "Sorry that I ever came between you and Li Yan."

Margaret shrugged. "Li Yan came between me and Li Yan. And so did I. We've never had the easiest of relationships."

"And I did not make things any easier."

"So why the change of heart?"

Mei-Ling said, "He is a nice man."

"Damned by faint praise."

Mei-Ling laughed, that braying laugh that had irritated Margaret so much when they first met. A laugh that she had not heard for some days. "No," Mei-Ling said. "I mean he is too nice for me."

Margaret frowned. "How's that?"

Mei-Ling shrugged, a sense of resignation in her eyes. "I would never make him happy. Seeing him with Xinxin . . . with all the instincts and concerns of a father. Seeing what losing her is doing to him." And she looked very directly at Margaret. "Seeing your shared pain." She shook her head. "I could never give him that. Sure, I can amuse a kid for an hour or two, but then I would be bored. I do not think I have a maternal bone in my body."

"And you think I have?" Margaret asked.

"Xinxin adores you. You were all she talked about that night when I drove her and Li Yan back to the hotel. About how

Magret came to get her at Tiananmen Square, about how great *Magret* was at flying a kite, about the hours *Magret* spends reading to her at bedtime." She smiled ruefully. "I could never be those things to her. So I could never be those things for Li Yan." She looked down at her hands, and Margaret was almost shocked to see that her eyes were moist. "The men in my life always seem to have other priorities. I'm just getting to recognise it a bit earlier now."

Margaret didn't know what to say. She thought about Xinxin babbling on to Mei-Ling about *Magret* this and *Magret* that. She thought about all those hours spent reading and re-reading the big picture books, the jigsaws that they pieced together time and again. She thought about how Xinxin would slip into the big double bed with Li and Margaret on a Sunday morning when Margaret would stay over on a Saturday night, her warm, soft little body insinuating its way between them, snuggling in for comfort. And suddenly all her fears and anxieties spilled over in big salty tears that ran silently down her face. She wiped them quickly away with the back of her hand. "I just hope we find her before . . . before that bastard does anything to hurt her."

Mei-Ling looked up and saw the wet streaks on Margaret's face. She nodded grimly. "We have that in common at least."

Neither of them had been aware of the door to the canteen opening, and they were not aware of Li until his shadow fell across the table. A momentary frown flitted across his face. Something, he knew, had passed between Margaret and Mei-Ling. But none of that mattered any more. "I have a warrant," he said, "to search *Comrade* Cui's clinic."

II

Darkness fell as the convoy of police and forensic vehicles headed west on Yan'an Viaduct Road. The last daylight glowed faintly under the pewter-coloured clouds that were gathered on the far horizon. The haloed lights of another Shanghai night pricked the darkness around them, dragged in liquid smears back and forth across rain-battered windscreens.

Margaret sat in the back of Mei-Ling's Santana. She saw her own reflection in the side window switched off and on like a TV screen image as she reflected the light from the overhead street lamps at regular intervals. She looked haunted, like the ghost of her grandmother that she had seen in herself the night before.

Everything now was moving so quickly it was difficult to maintain a grasp of it all. The only constant was the fear that gnawed like a hungry animal trapped inside her. Fear of finding Xinxin and realising a nightmare. Fear of not finding her. Fear of *never* finding her, which would be worse, almost, than anything.

She caught Mei-Ling watching her in the rear-view mirror and wondered what had brought about her change of heart. Had it really been seeing Li with Xinxin, hearing Xinxin babble on about Margaret? *The men in my life always seem to have other priorities*, she had said, and her words had been laden with the bitterness of experience. A *Yang Orphan* was how her aunt had described her. And Margaret remembered Aunt Teng's grave interpretation of Mei-Ling's Heavenly Element of water – meaning danger, something hidden, anxiety.

The convoy, lights flashing, eased its way between the parked cars in the street leading to the clinic. Cyclists, huddled in dripping capes, swerved aside to let them by. But even from here Li could see that the clinic was in darkness. When they drew up outside it, he saw also that the gates were closed, and secured with a chain and padlock. His first reaction was anger. He jumped out of the car and ran to the gates, and stood impotently in the rain, clutching the black-painted wrought iron, peering between the spiked uprights for any sign of life beyond. There were no vehicles, no lights, just puddles forming in the pitted tarmac between clumps of weeds that had not been apparent when the car park was full. He rattled the gates in frustration and turned to find Mei-Ling and Margaret sheltering under a large black umbrella. Officers were gathering behind them on the sidewalk. The rain ran down Li's face. "They knew we were coming," he said through clenched teeth. "Someone told them we were coming." And he felt as if he knew exactly who that someone was. "Somebody get some cutters and get this fucking gate open," he shouted.

It was nearly ten minutes before an officer arrived with a large pair of cutters that sliced through the metal chain like a hot knife through butter. He opened the gates and all the vehicles crowded into the forecourt. Under the shelter of the canopy over the main entrance, the detectives and forensic officers who were to enter the clinic stripped off wet outer clothing and pulled on white gloves and plastic shoe covers. Margaret did the same. She saw that Li's white tee-shirt had been soaked, even through his jacket. It was almost translucent, and she could clearly see the firm, muscular shape of him underneath. Margaret looked round to find Mei-Ling watching her again. Mei-Ling drew her brows together, made a moue with her mouth and drew a short sharp breath in through her lips. In spite of everything, it made Margaret smile. In other circumstances, perhaps she and Mei-Ling might have found something more in common than a shared lust for Li.

Detective Dai forced the double doors into the clinic. A splintering of wood. Then silence, except for the crackle of a dozen or more police radios. And then a loud creaking as the doors swung open into the darkness beyond. Several flashlights snapped on, and a small group led by Li pushed open internal glass doors and entered the reception hall, beams of light criss-crossing in the dark. The floor here was tiled. A reception desk facing them was empty. The drawers of two large filing cabinets behind the desk stood open, picked out by several flashlights. Whatever records they might once have contained were gone. There was not so much as a single scrap of paper in the reception area. Only a half-drunk mug of tea on the desk gave any clue as to the hurried evacuation of people and files.

None of the light switches was working, and an officer was dispatched to find where the electricity supply came into the building and restore the power. Li said, "There must be some state record of who was employed here. I want names. And I want arrest warrants out on all of them."

"You got it, Chief," Dai said, and he unhooked the radio mike from his belt.

"Including Cui Feng," Li added. Which silenced everyone. Dai glanced at Mei-Ling.

She said, "Be careful, Li Yan. We can't go arresting someone like Cui Feng without evidence."

"Then let's find some!" Li's raised voice startled everyone. "I want every employee brought in for questioning."

"Sure," Dai said, and he turned away into the dark to bark instructions into his radio.

"Where's the operating theatre?" Margaret asked.

"In the basement," Mei-Ling told her.

Margaret looked at Li. "Can I take a look at it?"

He nodded. Mei-Ling said, "I'll take you."

The two women followed the beams of their flashlights through double doors and down a narrow staircase to the suite of rooms in the basement where all the clinic's operations took place. Upstairs they heard other officers moving around, systematically working their way through the building, calling to each other in the dark. Down here it was deathly quiet. Across the hall, through double swing doors, were the preparation and recovery rooms. Facing them were the doors to the theatre suite. Above the door, Margaret's flashlight picked out the normally illuminated box sign in Chinese and English warning that they were about to enter the surgical area. On the wall to the left was a square push-button about the size of a postcard, that could be punched or hit with the elbow to let in any one of the surgical team, or the patient's gurney. Only in this case, Margaret thought, if Jiang Baofu was to be believed, it was not a patient on the gurney, but a victim.

Suddenly the overhead lights came on, startling them both. The boxlight over the door buzzed and flickered and then illuminated its warning. Margaret glanced at Mei-Ling before hitting the square button with the flat of her hand. The doors opened electronically into a small reception area with a desk. A white board on the wall was smeared blue and red and green where the names of patients and operating schedules, written up with coloured marker pens, had been wiped off. To their right, the doors to the changing rooms stood open, and doors at the far end, beyond the lockers, opened on to walk-in cupboards lined with shelves piled with hair- and shoe-covers and neatly folded smocks. Ahead of them were the doors to two operating rooms. Floors and walls were tiled, and stainless-steel washbasins were mounted on the wall outside each theatre. In normal circumstances no one would be

allowed beyond this area without wearing scrubs, and the hair-
and shoe-covers they would have donned in the locker rooms.

Margaret had been through the procedure many times early
in her career, when the living rather than the dead were her
concern. She would have tied on her surgical mask before
scrubbing her hands and forearms in the stainless-steel basin
for at least ten minutes, a prescribed number of scrubs per finger and hand, scraping under the fingernails with little plastic
sticks. Then, hands held up above her elbows, pushing through
the door to the theatre with her backside so as not to contami-
nate the freshly scrubbed hands. Inside, a nurse would pass
her a sterile towel to dry her hands and then help her into a
surgical gown before holding open latex surgical gloves into
which she would plunge her hands.

Now, the concern was not bacterial contamination so much
as the danger of disturbing evidence. With her gloved hands,
Margaret pushed open the door to operating room number
one, and Mei-Ling followed her in.

A strange chill fell upon Margaret as she entered the theatre. The air was warm, but still the hair rose up on her neck
and her forearms, goose bumps on her back and shoulders.
And she saw in her mind's eye a succession of women wheeled
in here to be butchered. A conveyor belt of them. Fifty-four at
least, since Jiang had become involved. She almost felt their
presence, and knew instinctively that this was the place. That
this was the killing room.

It was only dimly lit by pale yellow lamps set in the ceiling,
casting deep shadows beneath the sheets that were draped
over all the equipment like shrouds. Two walls were lined with
glass and stainless-steel storage cupboards filled with various
sizes of gloves and types of suture. Carefully Margaret and
Mei-Ling lifted the sheets, uncovering the lamps that hung on

jointed arms from the ceiling and would so brightly illuminate the surgeon's table when lit; the large, wheeled, steel table where the surgical nurse would set out all the sterilised tools on a sterile sheet; an electrocautery machine, light blue, with a couple of knobs on the front for adjusting the temperature of the cautery, and a couple of indicator lights. A power cable led from the box to a wall socket, and a wire connected it to the cautery pen that the surgeon would use to cauterise the small bleeding veins along the edge of the wound he would make with his scalpel. Margaret remembered the black gritty material she had found in the areas of haemorrhage along the incision edges of the entry wounds in the women from Lujiazui – charring made by the cauterisation.

Set on the surgical nurse's table alongside the toolbox were a stainless-steel bowl, a couple of empty litre jugs and several plastic "turkey basters," like giant eye-droppers. On a shelf stood two blue and white plastic cool boxes, the kind you might pack with ice to keep beer cold on a picnic. Margaret looked at them for a very long time and became aware that her breathing was starting to become rapid and shallow.

Her thoughts were interrupted by Mei-Ling crossing to where a CD player sat on the shelf of one of the cabinets against the far wall. It was wired into speakers hanging from all four corners of the operating room. The surgeon whose theatre this was, liked to listen to music while he worked. Mei-Ling switched it on and hit the play button. The room was immediately filled by the deep, sonorous tones of a church organ, stepping down in time to a slow, rhythmic descending bass note that was suddenly given relief by a surge of violins. Every hair on Margaret's body stood on end. She knew this music. It was one of her favourite pieces. Albinoni's Adagio in G Minor. But the pictures it conjured for her now were almost too horrific to contemplate. Of a surgeon delicately wielding his scalpel to murder and butcher a succession of young women to the strains of one of the most beautiful pieces of music ever written.

She reached back and switched on the big surgical lamps, and suddenly the room was thrown into an almost blinding blaze of light burning out on white tiles. A solo violin swooped and screeched to a pitch, like the scream of every dead girl who had passed through this hellish place. Margaret's legs nearly gave way under her, and she reached for the surgical nurse's trolley to steady herself. One of the litre jugs toppled over.

"Are you all right," Mei-Ling said, and she switched off the music. The silence that replaced it was almost worse.

"I'm okay," Margaret said, and she looked at Mei-Ling. "You know this is where it was done," she said. There could be no equivocation. There was nothing scientific about it, but she knew it with an absolute certainty.

Mei-Ling nodded grimly. She felt it, too. Margaret could see from her pallor that the blood had drained from her face. "Do you know this music?" Mei-Ling asked.

"Attributed by some to an Italian called Albinoni," Margaret said. "Probably composed in the early eighteenth century." She paused. "I used to love it." And now she shook her head. "But I don't think I'll ever be able to listen to it again. It sounds to me now like music straight from hell." She thought for a moment. "It would make me think that the surgeon was not Chinese. And if we take the 'Y' cut into consideration, probably not European either. I'd say there was a good chance this monster is an American."

The radio on Mei-Ling's belt crackled, and Margaret made out Li's voice talking rapidly in Chinese. Mei-Ling responded, and then said to Margaret, "He wants us up in the administration office."

Now that the power had been restored, they were able to ride up to the second floor in the elevator. A number of detectives and forensics people were standing in the corridor outside the main office. Inside, Li was going through the files on the hard disk of the office computer. It was a Macintosh PowerPC G4 with a twenty-one-inch flatscreen monitor. Nothing but the best and latest in technology for Cui Feng, Margaret thought. Li looked up as they came in.

"Anything down there?" he asked.

Margaret said, "That's where they did it."

Li froze. His eyes widened. "How do you know?"

"I just know," Margaret said. "Everything about it. And more. But I doubt if you'll find much in the way of forensic evidence. It's a sterile environment."

"We found the freezer," Li said. "Big walk-in cabinet. Could probably hold anything up to twenty bodies in there. In bits." He shrugged. "It was empty. We will defrost it, and see what forensics find in the melt water."

"I wouldn't hold your breath," Margaret said. "These people have been very careful."

"Yes, I know," Li said. "Everything's gone. All the files, patient records . . . All the bedrooms are empty, the beds all made up with clean sheets. They did not just do this in a couple of hours. Cui must have figured we would be back after our visit yesterday." He stood up. "I wanted you to have a look at this thing, Margaret. You probably know more about computers than most of our people."

"I'm no expert," Margaret said.

"We will get experts in," Li said. "But I need you to have a look at it now. From what I can tell, all the files have been erased."

Margaret slipped behind the desk and took in the computer screen. It was empty, apart from a few system pull-down menus along the top, the time display, and the hard disk and trash icons. She opened up the hard disk. There were only two folders in it. The system folder and an applications folder. Inside the applications folder were coloured icons representing various programs. Accounting, database, word processing, an internet browser. She looked up. "You're right. They've erased all the files. Probably backed them up on Zip disk and taken them where we'll never find them, or even destroyed them."

Li said, "Shit!"

Margaret forced a smiled. "It might not be as bad as you think. The operating system and all the software have been left untouched. Which means they didn't erase the hard disk. Just the files. And when you erase files, they're usually still there until they've been written over. You just can't see them. But with the right kind of software you can pull them back on-screen."

"Can *you* do that?" Li asked, suddenly re-energised.

She shook her head. "You'll need one of those experts," she said.

Li turned immediately to discuss with Dai and Mei-Ling how soon they could get a computer expert on site. Margaret turned back to the computer. She stared at the screen for several moments, remembering that dark afternoon in Chicago after her father's funeral when she started up his computer and in a moment of idle curiosity discovered things about him she wished she hadn't. Using the mouse, she guided the on-screen arrow to the Internet Explorer icon and double-clicked on it. The internet browser immediately opened up on-screen, and she heard the familiar series of beeps in rapid succession which indicated that the internal modem was dialling up to connect her to the Internet. It was followed by a short burst of white noise and a sequence of chirruping as her computer talked to another computer, extending some kind of digital handshake across the ether.

Li and the others turned around. "What's happening?" he asked.

"I'm going on-line," Margaret said. "I discovered recently that people leave trails and traces on their computers that they sometimes forget are there." She remembered the *Aphrodite Home Page*, and *SAMANTHA — Click me to watch live*, and *JULI — I like women*. And she remembered, too, the shock of discovering that her father was paying for pornography on the Internet.

It was one of the wonders of the new global technology, Margaret reflected, that she could sit here in China and open up the same computer software that was on her father's computer thousands of miles away in Chicago. This was a Chinese version, and so in Chinese characters rather than English. But the graphics were the same, and Margaret had no difficulty finding her way around. The modem had connected the computer to the Internet and downloaded the home page of some Chinese medical institute. Down the left side of the screen were the same four tabs as those on her father's computer, name tabs on folders in an electronic filing cabinet. Margaret pointed the arrow to the HISTORY tab and the file slid out across the screen. And there they were. The last five hundred Internet sites visited by this computer, all neatly packaged in dated folders. Margaret opened up the top folder, which was dated two days before. The address of the last Internet site visited was *www.tol.com*. It meant nothing to Margaret. She clicked on it and waited while the computer delivered the address into cyberspace and received the website in return. It came back in fragments, strips of colour, little logos indicating that graphics or photographs would fill their spaces. And then the screen wiped blank and the *tol* home page appeared in full.

Margaret sat staring at it, the skin tightening all across her scalp. She heard the murmur of voices as Li and the group of officers standing in the doorway engaged in some muted discussion. She heard the rain pattering on the glass of the window and dripping on the ledge. She could hear her own heart pumping blood through ventricles and arteries and tiny capillary veins. She heard the silent scream inside her head.

And then the voices had stopped, and Li was saying, "Margaret? Are you all right?"

She forced herself to look up and meet his eye. Everything she did and said felt as if it were in slow motion. "I was wrong," she said. "When I saw those cool boxes in the operating theatre, I think I knew it then. I just didn't want to believe it."

Li frowned. "What are you talking about?" He moved round the desk to look at the screen. A logo was blazed in red across the top of it. TRANSPLANTS ONLINE. Underneath it, on the left, was a photograph of a serious-looking man with grey hair and a white coat. He had a stethoscope around his neck. The caption beneath it revealed him to be Dr. Al Gardner. Li's heart felt as if it were beating in his throat as he quickly scanned the short biography below it. Dr. Gardner was the Chief Executive of the New York Transplant Co-ordination Clinic. He described himself as a "transplant co-ordinator," *working*, it said, *to bring donors and recipients together across the globe in a miraculous fusion of life.* Down the right-hand side of the page was a long list of organs: kidneys, hearts, lungs, livers . . . each underlined, a small blue "GO" button beside each one. Li said, "I do not understand."

"We've got access straight into the site because the computer's pulled this page up out of its memory," Margaret said trying to stay controlled, to think clearly. "I guess normally they would have to enter a password of some kind." She moved the mouse to the right side of the screen and clicked the "GO" button beside *Kidneys*. Almost immediately another page appeared on screen. There was a column of code numbers beside a list of recipient requirements: age, sex, blood type, HLA . . . Mei-Ling had squeezed in beside Li and was looking at the screen.

"What is all this stuff?" Li asked.

"All the information you need to know to match a kidney to a potential recipient," Mei-Ling said. Margaret glanced up at her and saw that she was ghostly pale.

Li said, "Are you saying that is what they have been doing here? Killing these girls for their organs?"

Margaret nodded reluctantly. "I guess."

"But you ruled it out. You *and* Dr. Lan."

Margaret said, "Because it never made sense that they would keep them alive during the procedure. It still doesn't. I mean, it takes several minutes for the heart to stop after you kill someone. If you removed the organs immediately, they would still be perfectly fresh and undamaged. But these bastards went to a lot of trouble keeping these poor women alive, riding on the very edge of consciousness."

"But now you're saying it *was* the organs they were after?"

Margaret looked back at the screen. "I don't know how else to explain it." She glanced at Mei-Ling. "And everything we saw downstairs would be in keeping with the removal of organs. The stainless-steel bowl that they would probably have kept filled with crushed ice for packing around the organs in the cool boxes. The litre jugs that would have been filled, probably with a saline solution, for flushing and irrigating the organs to cool them first – using those big turkey basters we saw . . ." She turned back to the screen. "And this." She shook her head. "I mean, I've heard of this guy."

Li looked incredulous. "Really?"

"He was in the news in the States a couple of years ago when he was investigated by the FBI on suspicion of trading in organs. He insisted he was just an honest broker, taking a small commission for bringing together needy US recipients and legally available organs around the world. They couldn't find any evidence to the contrary."

Mei-Ling said, "But you think he has been trading with Cui Feng?"

Margaret said bleakly, "If we accept that Cui Feng's people have been murdering girls here for their organs, the only reason they would have a direct link to Al Gardner's website would be to sell them."

"How would that work?" Li asked.

Margaret shrugged. "They'd have organs from a girl with a specific blood type and HLA tissue type, they'd go on to Gardner's website and look for specific matches on the recipient list. Once they'd found the matches, presumably they'd contact Gardner and he'd bring organ and recipient together."

"Here?"

"I guess. Though possibly also in some third, neutral country. India, maybe, or somewhere in the Middle East."

Li was frowning. "There is something I am missing here," he said. "These recipients . . . who would they be?"

"I guess, people who're going to die without a transplant and have the money to pay for an organ, no questions asked."

"Americans?" Li said.

Margaret was puzzled by the question. "I suppose most of them would be. If not all."

Li glanced at Mei-Ling. "But Cui's clinic was full of Japanese."

"Japanese?" Margaret was caught completely off balance.

"That is what Cui told us," Mei-Ling said.

Tiny electrical charges went sparking off between nerve endings in Margaret's brain. She could almost feel them, seeking to build bridges between deeply buried memory and conscious recollection. Fragments emerging from the deep started locking together in partially assembled pieces of a sub-conscious puzzle. And as she began to recognise and catalogue some of these pieces, her brain told her heart that it needed more oxygen, and her heart started beating faster. Finally, it all found expression in a whispered oath. "Jesus Christ!" she said under her breath.

Li was startled. "What!"

She remembered reading something a couple of years ago. Some report on international traffic in organs. A task force who had found no proof of anything. And then there was David. That night in the *sushi* restaurant in Chicago. What was it he'd said? *They got this weird religion in Japan. Shinto. They have a pretty strange view of the sanctity of the dead body.* And something else . . . She fought to remember, and then suddenly it came to her. Because, of course, he was a cardiac consultant. *Last time a doctor over there performed a heart transplant was in nineteen sixty-eight, and he got charged with murder.* Then the name she'd been searching for came to her. "The Bellagio Task Force," she said. "That's what they were called."

"Margaret, what are you talking about?" The frustration in Li's voice was clear.

"Bear with me," she said, and she turned back to the computer and called up an Internet search engine to try to find what it was she was looking for. It only took a couple of minutes before she had the report up on the screen. THE BELLAGIO

TASK FORCE REPORT ON TRANSPLANTATION, BODILY INTEG-RITY, AND THE INTERNATIONAL TRAFFIC IN ORGANS. She scrolled quickly through the pages, and then stopped suddenly. There it was. "Listen to this." And she read, "*Asian concepts of bodily integrity, the respect due elders, and objections to a standard of brain death, practically eliminate cadaveric organ donation in such countries as Japan. Despite an embrace of most medical technologies and deeply ingrained habits of gift-giving, transplantation from cadaveric sources is rare. Heart transplantation is not performed at all and the limited number of kidneys donated come from living related persons.*" She turned to Li and Mei-Ling, wide-eyed, almost exultant. "You see? If you're Japanese and you need a heart transplant or a new liver, or a kidney, the chances are you're not going to get it in Japan. Even if you have all the money in the world. And you're not going to get it in the States either, because there's more than sixty thousand people in the queue ahead of you." She paused, considering for herself the implications of what she was saying. "So you're going to die."

Li was still toiling to take all this on board. "But why can they not get organs in Japan?" he said. "Are they not one of the most technologically advanced nations in the world?"

"And one of the most religious and superstitious," Margaret said. David's words came back to her again. "Shinto," she said, and she turned and entered the words *Shinto* plus *Transplants* into the search engine. Within twenty seconds she was spoiled for choice. Dozens of documents came up. She picked one at random. *In Shinto, the dead body is considered to be impure and dangerous, and thus quite powerful.* She clicked on another. *In folk belief context, injuring a dead body is a serious crime.* And another. *It is difficult to obtain consent from bereaved families for organ donation, or dissection for medical education, or pathological anatomy . . . the Japanese regard them all in the sense of injuring a dead body.*

And in a moment of absolute clarity, she knew exactly what had happened, and why these women had become unwitting donors.

"Oh, my God," she said. "The man is a monster." She turned to Li. "These women weren't picked at random to have their organs stolen. They were exact matches for specific Japanese recipients with the money to pay for them."

"How would he know these women were exact matches?" Li asked, puzzled by this sudden leap.

"Because they'd all had abortions at his clinics," Margaret said. "Three hundred thousand women a year pass through his clinics. That's one-and-a-half million since he started. And nothing would be easier than to tissue-type them when they came in for the procedure. He must have the most comprehensive list of organ donor matches in the world. Only, these women were never donors, they had their organs taken without consent. As soon as Cui had a client, some wealthy Japanese facing certain death, he could consult his files and find an exact match. They'd snatch the girl and take the organ." She stopped, as another revelation struck her. "That's why they went after the girl in Beijing. Jack's sister. Because her HLA DQ-alpha gene was almost unique in China. She must have been a rare, but perfect match for some Japanese. Only, she turned out to be a junkie and they killed her for nothing."

She stood up and walked towards the window, hands clutching her head. Every nerve-end was tingling, every fibre of her straining to come to terms with her revelation. She saw her reflection in the window and thought she was staring at a mad woman. She spun round to face the others.

"And do you know what's really sick? The thing that I could never understand? They were keeping them alive to meet the needs of some Japanese religious or superstitious fear of violating the integrity of a dead body. It didn't matter that they were killing a living person in the process." She threw back her head and stared up at the ceiling. "Jesus, life's always so much cheaper, isn't it?" She lowered her head again and stared wild-eyed at Li and Mei-Ling. "Cui Feng was offering a unique service. Life-saving organs from a living body. Maybe one could be charitable and suggest that perhaps the recipients didn't know that the donors were ultimately paying with their lives. But, then, you don't take someone's heart and expect that they'll still be alive. Do you? Jesus . . ." She leaned forward on the desk and shook her head, blinking back tears of shock.

There was a long silence. Li glanced towards the officers standing in the doorway. He was not sure how much they had understood, but they knew for sure that something dramatic was unfolding here. Mei-Ling sat down in the seat vacated by Margaret. She was a dreadful colour, and Li saw that her hands were trembling. He looked at Margaret again. "So why did Cui need to sell organs through the Internet if he had ready-made customers in Japan?"

Margaret looked up from the desk. She had been focusing very hard on the grain of the wood, trying not to think about what it was she knew. If she had been unhappy to know about her father's predilection for pornography, she would never have wished to know this, could never have imagined it. She said, "Waste not, want not. Once Cui had fulfilled his contract to his Japanese customer, there was still a lot of money to be made by selling on the other organs." And having said it out loud, she realised just what a cold-blooded and mercenary operation Cui had been running here. If it was possible to conjure up an image of hell, this would be it. They might never know just how many poor women had been butchered in operating theatre number one, while some wealthy Japanese recipient lay anaesthetised on the table in the operating theatre through the wall waiting for one of their organs. A life for a life.

There was a loud beep from the computer and Margaret looked at the screen to see a message informing them that the connection had been terminated due to lack of network activity.

"Of course," she said. "There is no proof of any of this. Unless you can find the back-up copies of whatever files they kept on the computer."

"Or retrieve them from the hard disk," Li said.

Margaret nodded distractedly. She was thinking of Chai Rui and how she had died so completely in vain, and how that had led, ultimately, to Jack Geller's murder. And she let her mind drift to the hundreds of thousands of people around the world who were dying needlessly because organs for transplant were so difficult to obtain, and how the fears and superstitions of potential donors had led to the appalling trade that had been conducted from this clinic. It all seemed like such a waste. She looked sadly at Li. "And it doesn't bring us any closer to finding Xinxin," she said, and the pain in the pit of her stomach intensified with the thought.

Mei-Ling spoke for the first time in a long while. She still looked unwell, and stood up shakily as she spoke. "You said you thought the surgeon might be an American," she said to Margaret.

"It's a guess," Margaret said. "He might be Chinese, trained in America."

Mei-Ling said to Li, "We should put checks on all points of departure. As soon as we get a list of employees we should know who we are looking for." Li nodded, and she said, "I'll go back now and put things in motion."

She hurried out, past the bemused officers standing in the corridor who had only the vaguest idea of what had gone on inside. In the silence of the administration office, all that could be heard were the hum of the fluorescent lights and the computer, and the rain on the window. Margaret looked into Li's eyes and saw in them his fear for Xinxin, bleak and full of hopelessness.

III

Painted on three of the white panels of the high blue wall were toucans in flight, each one balancing two pint glasses of Guinness on its yellow beak. A haphazard jumble of bicycles was parked along the wall under the dripping trees. By the gate, a painted ship in a bottle stood over a sign for *O'Malley's*. Margaret and Li huddled together under their umbrella, splashing through the gutters. They had left the investigating team to de-construct the clinic piece by piece. Dai had offered to drive them back to 803, but Li had said they would get a taxi. In Shanghai it was not possible to walk ten paces along any street without a taxi cruising by. But they were well off the beaten track, and on this wet Sunday night they had walked the length of two streets and seen only one sodden cyclist shrouded in a glistening cape. Li cursed himself for not having telephoned a taxi from the clinic.

Margaret said, "Let's go in here."

Li looked at the bizarre sight of the Guinness-balancing toucans and asked, "What is it?"

"It says it's an Irish pub," Margaret said. "Improbable though that might be. But they're bound to have a phone."

As Li pushed open the high blue gate, Margaret felt like Alice stepping through the looking glass into Wonderland. What greeted them on the other side of the wall could not have been imagined from the street. Here lay a beautifully kept garden, with manicured lawns and a crazy-paved path lined by trees. White-painted wrought-iron garden furniture stood dripping in the rain. Concealed lighting led them down the path past an old-fashioned road sign mounted on a black and white striped pole. In Gaelic and English, signs pointed in three different directions to Cork, Galway and Dublin. Apparently they were only nine miles from Dublin. Under a pitched roof raised on pale blue pillars there were more tables and chairs sheltering beneath redundant sun umbrellas splashed with the Irish harp of the Guinness logo. Above the entrance to a large, white-washed house, a painted blue and gold sign incongruously announced O'MALLEY'S IRISH PUB. The covered courtyard was lit by coach lamps.

Margaret almost whispered, "What the hell is this place? Are we still in China?"

Li shook his head in amazement. He had never seen anything like it. "You would not think so," he said. After the revelations of the last hour, neither of them was prepared for dealing with this.

They walked inside to a gloomy interior hung with fishing nets and glass buoys. There was an open stone fireplace, old sea trunks, ancient glassed bookshelves lined with anti-quarian books leaning at crazy angles. Above the bar a musket and a pair of ancient pistols flanked a sign that read: IRISH GOODS SOLD HERE. Around the central bar area, a railed gallery looked down upon them. Margaret felt as though she had either strayed through some kind of time warp, or walked on to a film set. The place was empty. It was still early. Not yet six o'clock. "Hello," Margaret called out.

A tall girl with long red hair and green eyes stepped out from a back room to greet them from behind the bar. To Margaret, after a week of blue-black hair and Asian faces, the girl seemed absurdly out of place. She smiled at them. "Hello there, folks, yer early tonight," she said in a lilting Southern Irish brogue.

"Is there a telephone I can use?" Li asked.

"Sure. Just through the back there," she said, pointing. Li went off to phone, and the girl turned back to Margaret. "I'm Siobhan," she said. "You look like you might have a bit of Celtic blood in you."

"On my father's side," Margaret said, and she thought how bizarre it was that the part of her father that she carried in her genes should somehow connect with an Irish girl in Shanghai.

"American," the girl said. "You been here long?" Margaret shook her head. She didn't feel like indulging in idle conversation. The girl said, "I been here a month. It's great. This is where all the ex-pats hang out, you know? Three hours from now the place'll be jumpin'. It's great crack." She paused, perhaps realising that Margaret was not interested in small talk. "You want a drink? Sure, yer man there looks like he could do with one."

It wasn't the girl's fault. She was just trying to be friendly. She had no idea that just a couple of streets away dozens of women had been slaughtered for their organs, hacked to pieces and stuffed in a freezer. She was just here for a good time, a six-month adventure in exotic Shanghai, serving drinks to wealthy ex-pats in a quasi-Irish bar. Home from home. Just don't ever get an abortion, Margaret wanted to tell her. Instead, she said, "No, thanks. He's just calling a taxi."

The girl shrugged. "Oh, well, if you need me for anything, just holler." And she disappeared into the back room again.

Li came back from the phone. "There'll be one here in a few minutes."

They stood in silence in this strange place, uncertain what to say, how to pass the time as they waited. Margaret perched on the edge of a bench seat, and Li stood with his hands thrust in his pockets staring into space.

After a very long minute he said, "I should never have brought her here."

Margaret looked up, full of sympathy, sharing his pain. She wanted to hold him and tell him it would be all right. But it wasn't. And she didn't know that it would be. "You had no choice," she said.

"I do now," he said. "At least, I will if . . . *when* . . . we find her. She deserves better than this."

"What will you do?"

"I will quit the police."

Margaret was shocked. "You can't do that, Li Yan, it's your life."

He shook his head. "It is not *my* life that is important." He took a deep breath and tried to hold back the emotion that was building up inside him. "Besides," he said, "I am sick of this. Death, murder, brutality. If that is all we ever know, all we ever see, what does it turn us into, what does it make us?"

"It grinds us down and makes us tired and cynical when our resistance is low. And that's no time to be making decisions about anything." She paused. "You told me once, Li Yan, that you believed in fairness and justice. That's why you joined the police."

He snorted his derision. "Justice! I cannot even bring Cui Feng in for questioning."

"You will," Margaret said. "When you get the evidence, you'll get the warrant. Don't lose sight of that, Li Yan. That's what's important now. Getting the evidence."

"What is important now is getting little Xinxin back," Li said fiercely. "If he has hurt that little girl . . ."

Margaret stood up and took both his hands and squeezed them. "Li Yan," she said softly, with a confidence she did not feel, "we will get her back. We will." She felt the tension straining in him.

"I am scared, Margaret. I am so scared for her."

And they heard their taxi peeping its horn outside the gate.

CHAPTER THIRTEEN

I

Lights blazed from the windows of 803 into a black Shanghai night. And still the rain fell. Li and Margaret ran the twenty metres from the gate to the main entrance, but got soaked all over again. On the eighth floor, the detectives' room in Section Two was in chaos. Phones rang, keyboards chattered, cigarettes burned in ashtrays creating the impression that the place was on fire. Condensation misted the windows. Shirt-sleeved detectives talked into phones, shouted to one another across the room. Uniformed secretaries hurried in and out with faxes and files. Margaret headed on down the corridor to Li's office, and Li pushed his way through the chaos looking for Mei-Ling. Someone grabbed his arm. He turned. It was Detective Qian. He was clutching a sheaf of papers.

"We've got that list you were after, Chief. All the employees at the Shanghai World Clinic. We're trying to get the warrants processed now to bring them in."

He nodded, but Li was distracted. "Where's Deputy Section Chief Nien?"

"Don't know, Chief. Around somewhere." Li was about to move off, but Qian snatched at his sleeve again. "You'll like this bit, though." Li stopped. "For the last five years Cui has been employing the services of an ex-pat American surgeon who's been in Shanghai since the early nineties." Qian looked triumphant. "One Daniel F. Stein. He's fifty-eight, married to a Chinese girl half his age, and he's not at home."

"Have we checked the airport and the docks?"

"Doing that right now."

"Good." Li paused. "Do we know where Cui is?"

Qian looked at his watch. "He's due to attend one of Director Hu's banquets at the Xiaoshaoxing Hotel in about an hour and a half."

A spike of anger stabbed at Li's chest at the thought of Cui eating and drinking with the wealthy and powerful, breathing in the rarefied air of Director Hu's banquet, untouched and untouchable, while Xinxin was held captive somewhere or, even worse, lay dead in some cold, dark place. He wondered what the celebration was. Escape from justice? "Let me know if there are any developments," he said.

Qian nodded and Li pushed off through the hubbub in search of the night duty officer. He found him sitting in his small, cluttered office two along from Li's. The duty officer was wearing a pair of half-moon reading glasses and was wading through copies of the warrant requests that had been sent to the procurator's office for processing. He looked up as Li came in and nodded acknowledgment. "Deputy Section Chief," he said.

Li said, "Have you seen Mei-Ling?"

"Sure," the duty officer nodded. "About half an hour ago." He glanced beyond Li to the corridor and got up to close the door. He lowered his voice, as if he thought they might be overheard. "I spoke to her about a rather . . ." he searched for the right word, "delicate matter." He offered Li a cigarette, and when he accepted lit it, then lit one for himself and returned to his desk to sit down again. "Section Chief Huang signed out four firearms to the detectives who accompanied you to the American's apartment this morning. Only three have been returned."

Li frowned. This was totally unexpected. Almost a distraction. "Well, you must know which officer it was that didn't return theirs."

"That's just the trouble," the duty officer said, and he did indeed look troubled. He peered up at Li over his glasses. "They all claim to have returned their weapons to the Section Chief."

"What does Section Chief Huang say?"

The older man shook his head. "I haven't been able to contact him."

"And you told all this to Mei-Ling?" The duty officer nodded. "And what did she say?"

"She was very agitated, Deputy Section Chief. She looked like shit when she came in, and she looked even worse after I'd spoken to her. She said to leave it with her."

"And you don't know where she is now?"

The duty officer held out his hands, palms up. "I haven't seen her since I spoke to her."

Li was tempted for a moment simply to dismiss the whole thing. An irksome oversight by the Chief, or by one of his detectives. But there was something in the duty officer's description of Mei-Ling's reaction that gave him pause for thought. "Well, have you tried Huang at home?" he asked. "He left to go there this afternoon. Apparently his wife was fading fast."

The duty officer nodded. "I know. I've telephoned several times, but there's no reply."

Li went back down the corridor. Mei-Ling's office was empty. He tried the detectives' room again, and Huang's office. But there was no sign of her. He went into his own office and found

Margaret sitting brooding at the desk. She looked up hopefully as he entered. "Have you seen Mei-Ling?" he asked. She shook her head and he went straight back out.

The duty officer looked up, eyes full of interest and caution, when Li returned. "Did you find her?"

Li said, "She's not in the building." He hesitated for only a moment. "I want Huang's address and a car."

Huang's apartment block was an older building in a quiet residential area in Ni Cheng Qiao District, north of People's Square, a private rental paid for by the Municipal Police. The block was in a compound behind a high wall, affording it some privacy from the road. There were streetlamps and trees, a few cars parked near the entrance, and dozens of rickety bicycles jammed cheek by jowl under a corrugated plastic canopy that shed copious amounts of rainwater on to the forecourt below. Lights shining from uncurtained windows peppered the east face of the twelve-storey building like moth-holes in a lamp shade. Huang's apartment was on the second floor.

Li drew his car at an angle into the sidewalk beside Mei-Ling's Santana. He looked at it for a moment, saw the little bell that chimed so sweetly hanging motionless from the rear-view mirror. He had a bad feeling about all this. He started to get out of the car. "You stay here," he told Margaret.

"I will not," she said fiercely. "I'm not sitting out here on my own." And she got out the passenger side.

The door of the elevator stood open in the lobby, throwing a cold yellow light out into the dark. Inside, a middle-aged woman wrapped in a padded blue jacket sat on a stool, her face buried in a book, a jar of cold green tea at her feet. There was a smell of stale cigarette smoke and urine. She did not even look up as they entered. "Second floor," Li said.

The woman kept her eyes on her book, reached out and felt for the second button up on the tarnished steel panel and pressed it. The elevator jerked, as if it had made a little cough, and the doors juddered shut. The steel box started a slow ascent. At the second floor the doors jerked open again and Li and Margaret stepped out into a gloomy corridor. As the doors shut behind them they heard the woman pulling a crackle of phlegm into her mouth and spitting it out on the floor.

They found Huang's apartment at the end of the passageway. The light bulb here had burned out and not been replaced, and it was even gloomier. The steel gate in front of the door stood ajar, half opened into the corridor. Beyond it, the main door stood wide open. Inside, the apartment appeared to be in complete darkness.

Li pulled the gate fully open. "Stay here," he said to Margaret. "And this time I mean it." She nodded mutely. She had no idea what was going on, but she sensed Li's tension and it scared her.

Li felt almost smothered by the deep silence of the apartment. In the distant, reflected light from the landing, he felt his way gingerly along a narrow hallway. He passed an open door into a tiny kitchen. The next along was half-glazed, limp curtains providing a small measure of privacy for an equally small bathroom. As he got further down the passage, and his eyes became accustomed to the dark, he saw a faint glow falling out across the hallway from an open door at the end. The apartment seemed infused with an all-pervading smell of antiseptic and disinfectant, like a hospital. It reminded Li of Jiang Baofu's place. His own tremulous breathing sounded inordinately loud. "Hello," he called, to make some louder sound, and his voice cracked feebly. He cleared his throat and tried again, louder. "Hello?"

He was greeted only by silence. He turned into the frame of the open door and was bathed in the soft warm glow of a nightlight on a bedside table. The smell of antiseptic was almost suffocating in the warm air of the room. The gaunt figure of a woman lay on the bed, a single sheet draped across her lifeless, wasted body. Her eyes were open and staring at the ceiling, her jaw hanging slack, her mouth gaping. A tiny noise somewhere behind him made Li spin round. The door opposite was also open, the room unlit. But in the blackness, Li saw a small movement of light, and in a moment of choking fear realised that it was the reflected light in the movement of an eye.

A lamp snapped on and he was, for a moment, blinded and startled. He raised an arm, almost defensively, to shield his eyes, and saw Section Chief Huang sitting in a chair at the far side of the room across the hall. He was drawing one of his hands away from a small lamp on a table at the side of his chair. The other pointed a gun directly at Li. In that same moment, Huang realised who Li was, and he lowered the gun slowly into his lap. The two men stared at each other, unmoving for an immeasurable period of time, before gradually Li became aware that a shadow on the floor just inside the door opposite was cast by the leg and foot of someone lying just out of his line of vision. A sick feeling rose in his stomach. There was something horribly familiar about the faded denim and the scuffed white trainer. He stepped slowly forward, crossing the hall and entering the living room where Huang still sat motionless, watching Li with unblinking eyes.

Careful not to make any sudden movement, Li raised a hand and pushed the door wide. Mei-Ling was lying face down on the floor, a large pool of blood soaking into the carpet around her. Li could see her face in profile, long black hair lying untidily across it, her mouth open a little, lips pursed where a small amount of blood had oozed out. "Oh, God," he whispered, without knowing which God he was appealing to. Any one would do. He knelt quickly at her side, and with trembling fingers felt for a pulse in her neck. But she was already quite cold, and he almost recoiled as the shock of it gripped him. He looked up at Huang, full of incomprehension and confusion. Huang looked back at him like a dead man from his grave. The lamp beside him cast an orange glow on one side of his bloodless face, the other was striped white by the light of the streetlamps that fell in narrow wedges through the Venetian blinds.

"I swear on the graves of all my ancestors," Huang said, his voice barely a whisper, "I never intended to kill her."

Slowly, with legs like jelly, Li got back to his feet. "Then why did you? In the name of the sky, Huang, why?"

"She was going to arrest me. I couldn't let her do that. I had paid enough. I had to be my own executioner."

Li felt like a man sleepwalking through a nightmare. None of this seemed possible, none of it made sense. "Why would she want to arrest you?"

"From the moment you found out what had been going on at Cui's clinic, she knew that I was involved. I guess she probably suspected for a long time." He shook his head. There was pain for him in remembering. "She couldn't understand why I was so hostile to the idea of bringing you in on the investigation. You never knew it, but she was fighting your battles for you behind closed doors. Why was I being so obstructive over approaching Cui Feng? Why wouldn't I support your request for a search warrant?"

Li looked at the small, frail body of Mei-Ling lying on the floor. He remembered her smile, her twinkling eyes, that braying laugh of hers, her jealousy of Margaret. How easily all that

life and vitality had been taken from her. He turned his tearful
gaze back on Huang. For the first time, the Section Chief could
not meet it. He looked away and took a long, deep breath.

"It must have been so clear to her. She knew, of course, that
it was only a liver transplant three years ago that saved the life
of my wife." He shook his head and forced himself to meet Li's
eyes again. "She knew that only too well, because up until then
she and I had been lovers." His eyes flickered to the body on
the floor. "I don't know now whether it was love, or lust. But
it was full of passion. I was going to leave my wife." He paused.
"Until she was diagnosed with terminal liver disease." And he
looked quickly at Li, an appeal for understanding in his voice
and his eyes. "I couldn't leave her then. I couldn't just aban-
don her. I don't know whether it was guilt, or whether somewhere deep inside I still loved her, but I simply couldn't bring
myself to walk away. I had to choose between them. But I *had*
no choice." His appeal for understanding, even sympathy, fell
on stony ground, and he retreated back into himself. "I don't
think Mei-Ling ever really got over it." His voice had retreated,
too, almost to a whisper.

Li stood, unable to move, the silence singing in his ears,
before he became aware of the slow tick, tick, of a clock somewhere in the room. Even as it invaded his consciousness it
grew louder, until Huang's voice suddenly snuffed it out again.

"I don't even know how Cui found out about my wife, but
when he approached me with the offer of a transplant, how
could I refuse? I could never have afforded it. But Cui waived all
the fees. He told me I should regard it as a favour. A gift. A gift
of life." He shook his head. "I should have known, of course,
that he was simply investing in a little *guanxi*, in the knowledge that what was a small thing for him, was incalculable for
me. That I would be forever in his debt. But I could never have

known just how much. It was not the gift of life he promised
it would be. It was a gift of death."

Li said, "So he told you just how he had acquired the liver
that saved your wife's life." The mechanics of Huang's entrap-
ment had become suddenly very clear to him.

Huang nodded. "What could I do? I was appalled. But it was
done, and I couldn't undo it. And the treatment didn't stop
there. My wife continued to need constant care and expensive
medication against possible rejection of her new liver. If I took
any action at all it would kill her." His anger and frustration
raised the pitch of his voice now. "He *had* me. Held my very
soul in his hand, and there was not one damned thing I could
do about it."

"So you traded the life of a woman you had been about to
leave for the lives of all those poor girls."

Anger and guilt flashed at once in Huang's eyes. "What
would *you* have done?"

Li had no idea. He could not begin to imagine the circumstance. But he knew that what Huang had done was wrong.
He said, "So what did he want you to do? Apart from turning
a blind eye?"

Huang shrunk from the withering accusation in Li's voice.
It sparked his own guilt, and living with that was worse than
anything anyone else could do or say to him. "I provided him
with certification when he required it. Proof that the organs
he was selling abroad had been legitimately acquired from
the bodies of executed prisoners. They were little more than
official letterheads, but that was enough to satisfy his clients.
And, of course, everyone knows that the Chinese take organs
from executed prisoners. The dissidents have been screaming
about it in America for years. Only they claim it's done without

permission. Which is a nice scare story to feed the American fantasy of the Chinese bogey man." He shook his head. "As well as providing the perfect cover story for Cui Feng."

"And you never once thought about all those innocent women who were the real donors?" There was bile now in Li's voice. Angry and bitter.

"No," Huang almost shouted at him. "I didn't. I never knew the full extent of it until they found those bodies at Lujiazui. But I didn't want to know. I couldn't even contemplate it. How could I?" His eyes burned with the fire of his own futile defence. "And do you know the ultimate irony? The ultimate fucking irony?" His breath was coming in short gasps. He waved his hand helplessly towards the open door. "She died anyway. It was all for nothing." Tears, like acid, burned down his cheeks. "All the drugs, all the treatment, and in the end her body still rejected the damned thing. Three years on, and we were back where we started. She was slipping back into that same terminal decline, only this time there was nothing that could be done." He wept openly now, sobbing deeply, pressing his mouth into the palm of his hand to try to hold in the pain.

And as Huang descended into the hell of his own making, Li's anger ebbed away, leaving him washed up and spent on a bleak and barren shoreline. There was only one thing left on his mind, and he was almost afraid to pursue it. "Where's Xinxin?" His voice was hoarse.

Huang took a moment or two to bring himself back under control. "Wasn't my idea," he said eventually. "Cui thought if he had the kid snatched it would distract you from the investigation. At least long enough for him to cover his tracks."

Li felt his heart beat like a fist punching his ribs from the inside. "Where is she?" he asked again.

"I don't know." And there was something in Huang's tone that suggested he didn't much care. "If I was to guess," he said, "I'd figure they'd probably taken her to the safe house."

"What safe house?"

"Where they took the women after they'd been snatched. They were held there until the 'patient' had flown in and been prepared, then they were taken to the clinic for . . . well, for the operation."

"Where is it?" There was an imperative, dangerous quality in Li's voice now.

"Li Yan?" Margaret's voice calling from the other end of the hall crashed into the moment like a gunshot. Huang stiffened, his eyes suddenly shining and alert.

Li cursed inwardly, but ignored Margaret's call. "Where the fuck is it!" He was hanging on to his hope by a thread.

Huang looked at him and seemed to relax again for a moment. "Cui has a clinic at Suzhou," he said. "It's about sixty kilometres outside of Shanghai."

Li knew of Suzhou. It was famous in China for its beauty. The Venice of the East. And almost as if she were speaking to him from beyond the grave, he remembered Mei-Ling telling him that her family had come originally from Hangzhou. *We have a saying*, she had told him that night at the Green Wave restaurant. *Above there is Heaven, and on earth there is Hangzhou and Suzhou.* It was ironic, he thought, that all these women destined for death on the surgeon's table should have spent their last days and nights in a place that the Chinese believed was like Heaven on earth.

Huang said, "They kept the women in the basement. You can only get to it by canal from the rear of the building. It meant that at night they could take the women in and out by boat, and nobody would be any the wiser."

"Li Yan?" Margaret's voice was closer now, and softer. He heard her footfall in the hall. But still he kept his focus on Xinxin.

"Is she still alive?" His own voice sounded detached to him, distant, like an echo. He held his breath.

"I've no idea," Huang said. And it was like some last, petty revenge exacted on Li, as if somehow he were to be blamed for everything.

Li heard a gasp behind him, and he turned to see Margaret standing in the doorway. She was looking at Mei-Ling's prone and bloody form on the floor. She looked up at Li, and then beyond him to where Huang still sat in his chair.

Li turned quickly and took a step towards Huang. The Section Chief raised his gun and pointed it at Li's chest. "Don't even think about it," he said quietly. Li stopped, and Huang turned the barrel of the gun and placed it in his mouth. The shot rang out before Li could even shout for him to stop. It had a strange, muffled quality, and Li felt Huang's blood and brain tissue spatter hot across his face.

II

They had left the lights of Shanghai behind them some fifteen minutes earlier, and Li's foot kept the accelerator pressed to the floor so that their car maintained a steady one hundred and thirty kilometres an hour. Shortly after they crossed the Wusong River, known in the days of the International Settlement as Suzhou Creek, they passed out of the Shanghai administrative area and into Jiangsu Province. There was very little traffic on the Shanghai–Nanjing expressway. The odd truck rumbling west, the occasional bus, a few private cars. The windscreen wipers beat against the thrashing of the rain, and beyond the ring of their headlights the night was black and impenetrable.

Margaret sat in the passenger seat in a state of shock. The picture of Mei-Ling lying in her own blood was etched indelibly in her mind's eye and she could not rid herself of it. She saw, still, the small hand stretched out on the floor, delicate little fingers, crooked slightly as if attempting to grasp at something, perhaps a vain attempt to hold on to life. There was no way to give expression to the sadness Margaret felt, no way to take back all the things she had said and felt in anger and jealousy. *The men in my life always seem to have other priorities*, Mei-Ling had told her. Only a matter of hours later, the man in her life had killed her and then put a bullet in his own brain. Had she had some kind of premonition of what was to come? Her Heavenly Element signifying danger, her trigram, *K'an*, the colour of blood. Margaret glanced at Li. Huang's blood was still smeared on his face. Poor Mei-Ling, she thought. And she wondered what you ever really knew about other people's lives?

Occasionally the police radio crackled and interrupted her thoughts. Earlier, Li had spoken briefly to someone at headquarters as he had turned the car up a ramp on to the Zhongshan Xilu ring road. A few minutes later he had relayed to her the contents of a cryptic return call. They would be met in Suzhou by officers of the local public security bureau. And his request for an arrest warrant for Cui Feng had been turned down by the Procurator General, on grounds of lack of evidence. Neither had passed comment on this, and there had been no exchange between them since.

The journey felt interminable although, in truth, less than an hour had passed since they had left Huang's apartment building. An endless succession of broken white lines, illuminated by their headlamps, threw themselves at the wind-screen and vanished into history. But in spite of their hypnotic effect, the image of Mei-Ling still lingered. Closing her eyes, Margaret could not erase it. Only the dreadful spectre of what they might find when they reached Suzhou could compete for space in her burned-out imagination.

Shortly before they saw the lights of Suzhou in the distance, the rain stopped. Somewhere away to their right, the waters of Yang Cheng Lake lay brooding in the darkness. Li took a spur off the expressway and they turned south towards Lou-men Gate at the north-east corner of the old city wall. Beyond the gate, a convoy of five police vehicles was pulled in at the side of the road, red lights flashing. Li pulled up beside them and got out. Margaret remained in the car and watched as he walked forward to be met by the senior officer. There were about a dozen men in total, all in uniform. They spoke for several minutes before Li returned to the car. He said, "They have a small sampan waiting to take us to the basement at the rear of Cui's clinic. It is only approachable by river." He took several deep breaths. "There will be three officers with us. The officer in charge was afraid that a motor boat would alert any-one who might be on guard. Some of the others will remain at the landing stage and the rest will cover the building from the road at the front. Apparently there are no lights on there at the moment. The place appears to be locked and empty." His words had a focused professionalism. He was trying to be a police officer doing a job, rather than a man afraid of what he might find in Cui's basement.

They followed the convoy of police vehicles through the brightly lit modern streets of the new town, catching only glimpses to their right of the narrow streets that ran off into the old city, where hundreds of steeply arched bridges traversed the dozens of natural waterways on which the town had been built two-and-a-half thousand years before.

At an intersection, the convoy split up, and now they were following only two vehicles into the narrow streets of the ancient city, a jumble of whitewashed houses built one on top of the other. Beyond the steeply pitched grey-tiled roofs, Margaret saw the tiers of a pagoda rising into the night sky. They passed a tearoom perched on the edge of a narrow creek where old men would sit through the day, listening to the chirrup of their caged birds, and gaze on the tranquillity of life that drifted by.

In a dark, quiet square, they pulled into the kerb and got out of their vehicles. Several of the Suzhou officers stared curiously at Margaret. Their senior officer barked a command and Li steered Margaret gently by the elbow to follow him through an elaborate brick-carved arch, into a narrow lane that weaved its way between the crumbling whitewashed walls of ancient private dwellings. They crossed a number of humpbacked bridges over impossibly narrow waterways. Margaret saw covered corridors linking one house with another across deep, dark water. Finally, they reached a much wider river, and climbed down steep, uneven steps to where a sampan was bobbing gently on the swell, and the smell of raw sewage filled the damp air.

A fisherman in blue cotton pants and a white shirt held the boat steady as Li, Margaret and three uniformed officers climbed aboard. It was very dark. The houses on either side of the river rose straight out of the water, stones jutting out from the walls to form an arrangement of steps leading up to shadowed doorways. There were lights in only a few windows, and they cast pale, flickering reflections on the water. Margaret heard the steady slap, slap, of river water on the side of the boat and the breathing of the men who gathered around her in the belly of the small craft. The fisherman cast off and stood at the stern of the boat, grasping a long oar in both hands, working it easily backwards and forwards to propel them with surprising speed downriver. The old wooden vessel creaked and groaned against the resistance of the water, but the fisherman barely broke sweat. Margaret was wondering how on earth he managed to see in the dark, when suddenly, overhead, the clouds parted and an almost full moon poured a bright silvery light down upon them. It was a transformation. The whitewashed houses glowed like ghosts on either side of a river of mercury. Trees that overhung the water from between buildings, rustled gently in a breeze that had sprung from nowhere. It was immediately cooler, and Margaret shivered.

They passed under two bridges, before gradually slowing and drawing in towards the right bank. The helmsman looked back along the riverbank and appeared to be counting. Then, finally satisfied, he pulled up at a flight of stone steps that looked much like any other. At the top of them a stout, studded, wooden door stood firmly shut. The windows on the lower level were all barred. There were another two levels above that, accessible, Margaret assumed, from the street on the other side. A cloud scudded across the moon and they were plunged briefly into darkness before, in a moment, being flooded again with light.

Li jumped on to the bottom step and drew out the gun he had removed from Huang's dead hand. The blood had dried rust red on it. There was a brief, whispered exchange between him and the senior uniformed officer who was unarmed, before they proceeded up the steps. The fisherman helped Margaret out of the boat and she followed them. The other two officers climbed out after her, but remained on the bottom step.

At the top of the steps, Li tried the door. But it was securely locked. He put his shoulder to it twice, but could not move it. After another whispered exchange one of the other officers hurried up the steps with a long metal crowbar. Slowly, working it backwards and forwards, he managed to insinuate it between the door and the jamb until he achieved sufficient leverage to force it open. There was a splintering and cracking of wood that was deafening in the stillness of the night. The door swung open and they were met by a rush of damp, fetid air. Everyone stood stock still, but there was nothing to be heard. Li felt inside the wall for a light switch, but found nothing. The darkness beyond was inky black. The third officer climbed back aboard the boat and grabbed two flash lights. He jumped out again and ran up the steps to pass them to Li and his senior officer.

Li snapped on his light, and its strong beam penetrated the blackness to reveal a long, narrow corridor with a flagstone floor. Stone walls ran damp with condensation. Somewhere up ahead a small creature, probably a rat, scurried away from the light. Li froze for a moment, then began moving cautiously inside. The senior officer switched on his flashlight and followed. Margaret stepped gingerly after them, her hand recoiling from the cold, slimy touch of the wall.

There were half a dozen doors at regular intervals, on left and right. The first two they passed stood open. The doors had small, barred, unglazed openings in them. In the rooms beyond, there were cot beds freshly made up with sheets and blankets, small bedside cabinets, rush matting on the floor.

Halfway down, Li came to the first door that was shut. He tried the handle. It was locked. He shone his flashlight through the opening in the door and saw, huddled against the wall at the far side of a rumpled cot bed, a pale young woman in her early twenties. She was wearing only a thin cotton smock, and her legs were pulled up under her chin, arms folded around her shins, trying to make herself as small as possible. There was no colour in her face, and she cowered from the light like a trapped animal. She was making tiny whimpering noises.

"It's all right," Li said softly. "We're the police." He handed his flashlight to Margaret, braced himself against the opposite wall, and kicked the door several times with the flat of his foot. On the fourth kick the lock tore free and the door flew open. The girl screamed, curling herself into an even smaller ball. Li snatched his flashlight and hurried into the room. The girl pressed herself into the wall as if hoping somehow she might be absorbed into it. Li put his light on the bed and with warm, tender hands gently took her shoulders and pulled her into his chest. "It's okay, it's okay," he said softly. "You're safe. You're absolutely safe. I'm not going to let anyone hurt you."

Her response was immediate, as she uncurled herself and then clamped herself on to Li, sobbing uncontrollably. Margaret stood watching from the doorway. There was nothing that she could do or say; the girl would not understand her. Vaguely, she was aware of the officer who had come in with them making his way further down the corridor, his shadow growing long behind him from the reflected light of his electric torch.

The girl was icy to the touch, and Li held her tightly to him, rocking her slowly back and forth on the bed, whispering softly all the time. But nothing would stop her shivering.

Eventually he said to her, "Is there another girl here? A little girl? Do you know? Have you seen her? Have you heard her?" But if the girl understood she was incapable of answering.

Suddenly there was a cry from the far end of the corridor. A man's voice, the sound of a struggle. Margaret turned back into the corridor in time to see a flashlight tumbling across the floor. Before it smashed against the wall, she saw the figure of the uniformed police officer on his knees. A flash of blood, an expression of pain fixed on his face. And then darkness, and a sound like the wind, and Margaret felt, more than saw, the shape that flew at her. She screamed, and from somewhere a light flashed across a face made hideous by fear and anger. A face she knew from a moment of panic on a dark night on the Bund, a face with high, wide cheekbones and a hare-lip. She smelled his foul breath, felt it hot on her face, and saw his blade flashing in the light as it rose to plunge into her chest. A single, deafening sound roared in her head. And she wondered, momentarily, if this is what death felt like, a revelation, an explosion of light and sound. She fell backwards to the floor, with his weight on top of her, and immediately she was aware of her blood running warm across her chest and neck. There was no pain, but the chill of the stone flags beneath her felt like death, and she heard the screaming of the girl in the cell like a distant call from hell.

And then the weight, miraculously, was lifted from her and she was blinded by a light in her face. "Jesus . . ." She heard Li's voice, and for a moment was struck by the incongruity of a Christian oath in a Chinese mouth. "Margaret, are you all right?"

She sat up, breathing hard, and looked at the blood that soaked her tee-shirt, realising for the first time that it was not her own. And then, in the reflected light, she saw the

Mongolian lying on the floor, half his head blown away by the shot from Li's gun. "I'm fine," she heard herself saying, and then thought, no I'm not. The girl was still screaming.

She heard the calls of the other officers as they ran in from the steps. Li helped her to her feet. "She's got to be here," he said.

Margaret nodded, unable to speak. Li took her hand, and ran with her down to where the wounded policeman lay in a pool of his own blood. Margaret knelt at his side and turned him over. But the blade had severed the carotid artery on the left side of his neck, and the life that had pulsed through his veins only minutes earlier had already ebbed away. She heard Li shouting, and looked up to see him at the bottom end of the corridor kicking furiously at another locked door. She scrambled to her feet and ran after him as the door finally tore free of its lock and crashed open. She arrived in time to see Li falling to his knees at the side of a cot bed. On top of it lay the tiny, prone figure of little Xinxin. Her hands and feet were bound, and she was gagged and blindfolded. Margaret felt a surge of anger and fear robbing her of strength, and she staggered forward.

Li turned the child over, fingers working feverishly to untie the gag and tear away the blindfold. Her eyes were closed, her mouth gaping. He leaned over her, and Margaret heard the moan that escaped his lips involuntarily. He looked up at her. "She's not breathing," he said.

CHAPTER FOURTEEN

I

The car felt empty without Margaret or Mei-Ling. Li's eyes were fixed on the white line that seemed to reel him in like a fish. In the far distance the lights of the city lit the underside of dark clouds on the horizon. He felt everything now with a heightened sense of awareness: the vibration of the tyres on the tarmac, the air that blew in his face from the vents on the dash, the sweat that gathered in the creases of his palms where he gripped the wheel with a tension that verged on ferocity.

He was startled when the radio spluttered and he heard Dai's voice repeating his call sign. He unhooked the microphone and pressed the transmit button. "Li," he said, his voice flat, emotionless, like a dead man.

"Chief," Dai's voice came back to him. "The boys at the airport picked up that American surgeon. Daniel Stein. He was trying to board an Air India flight for Delhi. Had a briefcase full of computer disks that look like they might have some very interesting material on them . . ." There was no response, and Dai's voice crackled again around the interior of the car. "Chief . . . ? Did you get that . . . ?"

* * *

The elevator rose smoothly up the inside of one of the two green glass tubes that characterised the exterior of the Xiaoshaoxing Hotel. Li felt like a man floating. He looked down on the chaos of traffic and bicycles and pedestrians in Yunnan Nan Road below, red lanterns strung between buildings dancing in the night breeze, steam issuing from the open windows of dumpling takeaways. He couldn't hear any of it, locked away in his glass capsule. Only the distant hum of the electric motor that pulled the cables. None of it seemed real.

The elevator came to a halt on the eighth floor and the doors slid noiselessly open. Li stepped out and walked briskly down the carpeted hallway, following the footsteps he had taken with Margaret and Mei-Ling less than a week before. He looked left and then right into luxurious banqueting rooms. Several gatherings were in the process of breaking up. Others had already gone. Li felt each footstep jar through his body. He was aware of other feet following in his wake, but only vaguely. His focus was elsewhere. Waitresses scurrying between banqueting rooms and kitchen, laden with the detritus of spent meals, gaped in astonishment and fear at the wild-eyed man spattered with blood who stalked the corridor.

Li turned left and then right, unwavering in stride and determination. At the end of the corridor he turned into the last and biggest of the banqueting rooms, just as a loud laugh rang out around the table. The laughter died almost as soon as he entered. Chairs scraped on the floor as people turned to see him standing in the doorway. There was a collective intake of breath. Cui Feng was sitting on Director Hu's right, and his face flushed dark when he saw Li. The smile that had been upon it faded. Director Hu, close-cropped grey hair bristling on his bull head, glared at Li. "I do not recall inviting you, Deputy Section Chief," he said.

Li said nothing. He reached below his jacket and drew out Huang's gun from where it was tucked in his belt, and raised it to point at Cui. There was a ripple of panic among Director Hu's distinguished guests, and several jumped to their feet, sending chairs tipping over behind them. As Li moved slowly among them, keeping his gun trained on Cui's face, they shrank away like sea anemones from a diver's touch. The remains of two dozen Shanghai crabs were strewn across the table. It was less than an hour since Li had driven past the lake where they had been caught.

Cui remained seated until Li was no more than a metre away, his gun pointed directly at Cui's head.

Director Hu, too, refused to stand or be intimidated. "You're finished, Li," he hissed. "Your career is over." But for the second time that night his words fell on deaf ears. He was not used to being ignored. He banged his fist on the table. "Dammit, Detective, put that gun down!"

Li kept his eyes fixed on Cui. "Get up," he said.

Cui got slowly to his feet and stood staring back at Li with the arrogance of a man who believes he is above and beyond the law. He looked down and saw that Li's hand was trembling, and in that moment may have realised that the law might no longer be the issue here. Li was after justice, or maybe revenge. And law, justice and revenge did not sit easily together. He looked back into Li's eyes, and what he saw there drained all colour from his face. First doubt, then fear, then panic, set in. "Don't," he said, his voice almost a whisper.

But Li just continued to stare, as if in staring long enough he might be able to see reason somewhere beyond the blackness of the man's soul. He felt perspiration make his finger slippery on the trigger of the gun. With all of his heart he wanted to pull that trigger, to obliterate evil. It would be so easy. A gentle squeeze of his finger. An end to it all.

"Chief?" He heard Dai's voice coming from where he and Qian stood in the doorway behind him. There was, in that one word, that single question, asked softly and without prejudice, an appeal to reason. Li stood for a moment longer, undecided, and then he reached into his inside jacket pocket and pulled out a folded wad of official papers. He held it up in front of Cui's face.

He said, "Cui Feng, I have a warrant for your arrest on suspicion of murder. The count begins at fifty-four and will probably go higher." And a smile that verged on a sneer, flickered across Cui's face, almost as if he believed he had won, because Li had not pulled the trigger. He had opted for justice, not revenge. He had chosen the law, and maybe Cui figured he was still above it. Li was only vaguely aware of Dai and Qian and several uniformed officers pushing past him to handcuff Cui and lead him out of the room. They left behind them a stunned silence. Li tilted his head to look at the Mayor's policy adviser. He said bleakly, "Marry a dog, stay with a dog; marry a rooster, stay with a rooster. You should choose your friends more carefully, Director Hu."

II

There was that smell again, of antiseptic and disinfectant. Li ran down the corridor, past orderlies wheeling gurneys, nurses in starched white uniforms. Someone called after him, but he ignored them. The intensive care beds were at the far end of a hallway that felt interminably long. When he got there, breathing hard, he stopped in the open doorway.

Margaret was sitting in a chair at the side of the bed. She seemed crushed and small and inestimably sad. She looked up when she heard Li's footsteps. Her eyes were dark ringed and bloodshot and she wore a loosely tied hospital gown. Li looked beyond her to where the tiny figure of Xinxin lay under the sheets, attached by wires to a bewildering array of electronic equipment. A clear plastic tube fed a drip from an overhead bag into her right arm. But she was not moving.

Margaret stood up. "They were keeping her dosed up on an almost toxically high level of sedative," she said. "She was dehydrated, almost comatose. If we'd been another hour or two . . ."

Li was almost unable to take her words on board. "She's . . . is she . . . ?"

"She's going to be okay," Margaret said wearily. And then she shook her head. "But, Li Yan . . . she's going to need a lot of love."

Li closed his eyes, took a deep breath, and then reached out and drew Margaret towards him. He had no idea what the future might bring, what remained of the love that he and Margaret had once had. But it did not matter. Only now mattered. The life of a child. He felt Margaret's body mould itself to his, and he held her tight. "We all do," he said. "We all do."

ACKNOWLEDGEMENTS

There are many people whose help has been invaluable in researching *The Killing Room*. In particular, I'd like to express my heartfelt thanks to Steven C. Campman, MD, the Armed Forces Institute of Pathology, Washington, DC: Dr. Richard H. Ward, Professor of Criminology and Dean of the College of Criminal Justice, Sam Houston State University, Texas; Professor Dai Yisheng, former Director of the Fourth Chinese Institute for the Formulation of Police Policy, Beijing; Police Commissioner Wu He Ping, Ministry of Public Security, Beijing; Professor Yu Hongsheng, General Secretary of the Commission of Legality Literature, Beijing; Professor He Jiahong, Doctor of Juridical Science and Professor of Law, People's University of China School of Law; Professor Yijun Pi, Vice-Director of the Institute of Legal Sociology and Juvenile Delinquency, China University of Political Science and Law; Mr. Qiu and Mr. Lin, public relations department of the Shanghai Municipal Police; Dr. Yan Jian Jun, Vice Senior Forensic Medical Expert, Shanghai Municipal Police; Lily Li, whose work as an interpreter opened many doors for me in Shanghai; Jennifer Dawson of "Sources, Far East," Shanghai, for her kind help and hospitality; "Tommy" Jiang, for being my Sherpa in Shanghai; Peter

Roe and Ann Hall, consuls at the Shanghai American Consulate; Tony Hutchinson, Cultural Affairs Officer, American Consulate, Shanghai; Jeanne M. Ward, for her wonderful work in Chicago; and Mac MacGowan, of ChinaPic, Shanghai, for his photos and his friendship.

ABOUT THE TYPE

Typeset in Swift Neue, 10.5/15 pt.

Swift Neue is an enhanced version of the Swift typeface
which was introduced in 1985. Originally intended for
use in newspapers, its strong serifs enhance readability
across a wide variety of paper and printing processes.

Typeset by Scribe Inc.,
Philadelphia, Pennsylvania.

PETER MAY was born and raised in Scotland. He was an award-winning journalist at the age of twenty-one and a published novelist at twenty-six. When his first book was adapted as a major drama series for the BBC, he quit journalism and, during the high-octane fifteen years that followed, became one of Scotland's most successful television dramatists. He created three prime-time drama series, presided over two of the highest-rated serials in his homeland as script editor and producer, and worked on more than 1,000 episodes of ratings-topping drama before deciding to leave television to return to his first love, writing novels. He has won several literature awards in France; received the USA's Barry Award for *The Blackhouse*, the first in his internationally bestselling Lewis Trilogy; and in 2014 was awarded the ITV Specsavers Crime Thriller Book Club Best Read of the Year award for *Entry Island*. Peter now lives in southwest France with his wife, writer Janice Hally.